BROKEN VOWS

ROHAN WEST

Copyright © 2016 Rohan West
The moral right of the author has been asserted.

Matador
9 Priory Business Park,
Wistow Road, Kibworth Beauchamp,
Leicestershire. LE8 0RX
Tel: 0116 279 2299
Email: books@troubador.co.uk
Web: www.troubador.co.uk/matador
Twitter: @matadorbooks

ISBN 978 1785890 826

British Library Cataloguing in Publication Data.
A catalogue record for this book is available from the British Library.

Printed and bound in the UK by TJ International, Padstow, Cornwall
Typeset in 11pt Minion Pro by Troubador Publishing Ltd, Leicester, UK

Matador is an imprint of Troubador Publishing Ltd

To Alec and Anne

CHAPTER ONE

12th November 1935

Auckland, New Zealand

Abigail McCarthy wiped away tears as the air, thick with coal and diesel exhaust fumes from the funnels, stung her eyes. The commotion of Queens Wharf compounded her disorientation. A throng of people, vehicles and freight littered the quayside, with an accompanying din of voices, horns, public announcements and cranes moving goods onto the ships. All manner of craft bobbed and heaved in the harbour. A couple of ocean liners dominated the view, with a few freighters, multiple ferries and the occasional fishing boat fighting for space.

She picked her way through the multitude to the gangway of the *SS Aorangi*. Wharfies in denim dungarees, busy in their work hurried in and out of the lines of passengers, while the commuters pouring off the ferries from Auckland's outer suburbs were corralled down special ramps on the other side of the wharf to keep them separated from the people headed overseas. A wave of fedoras, trilbies and the occasional pillbox hat and beret surged out of the ships and headed out towards Queen Street, ebbing to small ripples as they moved towards their places of work.

Abby jumped at every blast of a ships' horn. She clutched her passenger documents close to her chest, her eyes darting around the wharf, her breathing short and shallow. Suddenly, for the first time in four days she had some clarity of thought; she could easily slip unnoticed into the crowd and melt away to start a new life in

1

Auckland and escape the exile to which she was headed. She had to report to the head of the Ministry of Health's advance party to Fiji before boarding, but as yet she couldn't find them among the mass of people.

Every step took her closer to the ship and away from the wharf gates. She looked back at the entrance, her grip tightened on the handle of her brown leather suitcase, her knuckles turned white and she felt a small line of perspiration run down her forehead and get trapped in the crown band of her hat. A clear route suddenly opened up between her and the wharf gates. The opportunity beckoned. Thoughts and visions swirled around her head: no job, no home, family shame; and devotion to her profession. Before she could clear her head and take a step toward freedom, a large flatbed truck crossed her path, blocking off her potential escape route as fast as it had appeared. She dropped her head and turned back to the ship and shuffled forward a couple more steps. As she looked among the passengers, a handful of dock workers scattered to reveal a small group of people standing around a woman with a clipboard. Some had small, black leather doctors' cases and most of the women had the distinctive star of the New Zealand Nursing Service badge pinned to the left lapel of their jackets. She put her right hand on her own badge, turned her head one last time back to the gates and bit down hard onto her lower lip.

* * *

She didn't even know how long the voyage was to Fiji. She asked one of the pursers, who told her it was the best part of three days, maybe four if the winds were against them; and another twelve days to the ships final stop in Vancouver. She had to share a cramped third class cabin with another Kiwi nurse. Given that her mind was elsewhere, Abby only remembered the woman's first name,

Shirley. Her last name got lost in the haze; Fleet, Flint, something like that. What did stick was that Shirley was from Auckland, tall, sporty with a bubbly personality; she had volunteered for the advance party and seemed genuinely surprised to learn that Abby had been seconded. Abby didn't share the specific details of her situation, as she wanted those to be on a need to know basis.

Shirley opened the door of their cabin to reveal two single beds on either side of the room, separated by a bedside table with a small porthole located above it. Against the corridor side wall, a small white three drawer cabinet sat at the end of each bed. They both placed their suitcases on the beds and simultaneously pressed down on the mattresses with their fingers. There was a door on the right of the cabin which Shirley opened up, then stopped suddenly.

'Bloody hell, Abby. I knew it'd be small, but there's not enough room to swing a cat in here. One at a time for ablutions.'

Abby poked her head around the corner of the bathroom. 'Hmm, we should just be able to squeeze in.' She looked down at the vanity unit and saw some bars of Lux soap and a bottle of Yardley talcum powder. 'That's nice. Didn't expect that in third class.' Abby returned to her bed, opened her suitcase and started unpacking. She placed a gold handled hairbrush and personal mirror on the bedside table.

'Come on girl, leave that for later. Let's head up on deck for the bon voyage,' said Shirley.

Abby hesitated momentarily at her invitation; who on earth would she wave to? Wouldn't it just remind her that she was on a forced departure?

Shirley's voice dropped to a reassuring tone, 'Look, you've told me you're here on secondment and your family is in Wanganui. I know there's probably no one on the wharf for you, but its part of the tradition. You can wave at my mad family. There'll be enough of them there. Come on.' She took Abby by the hand.

'I don't know. It'll be a bit awkward.' The protest was ignored by Shirley as she hauled Abby out of the cabin and up to the deck level. The crowd on the quayside were waving frantically up at the passengers; the men with their hats in hand, the women with handkerchiefs or scarves.

'There's my lot,' yelled Shirley, pointing to her family and waving back at them.

Abby gave a small wave then scoured the crowd for a familiar face, even though she knew this was a forlorn gesture as none of her friends or family would have been able to get to Auckland on such short notice. Near the edge of the crowd, Abby saw a face that made her drop her hand immediately. She grabbed the railing and pulled her upper body over the barrier. It couldn't be him. He doesn't even know I'm here, she thought to herself. But it looks just like him. She was now breathing short and fast. As quickly as her emotions rose, they dropped away again, as the man took off his hat to reveal a mop of blond hair, not the greying dark brown of her love. As her excitement ebbed away, her eyes caught a glimpse of a face that struck her cold as death. In the back row of the well-wishers she saw her cousin, Moira. A satisfied smirk was fixed on Moira's face and she gave a knowing nod to Abby. Pushing back from the rail, Abby slipped through the rows of fellow passengers to go back to her cabin. She dabbed her eyes with her sleeve as she walked through the corridors of the ship.

Looking out from the room's porthole, Abby could see the ship was clear of the inner harbour, so she ventured back up on deck and positioned herself on the railing at the stern. The land slipped by and slowly grew smaller. As the last glimpse of the dark green hills of Northland sank below the horizon, so did Abby's heart. She watched her homeland vanish from view and the realisation of the extent of her predicament became clear, as the Pacific grew to seemingly endless enormity. When would she again see his face, let alone feel his touch on her skin? She felt lightheaded and nauseous at the thought.

At the first night's dinner, the whole party sat together at a couple of adjacent tables. Abby struggled to find something to her liking on the menu. Among the potted meats, corned ox tongue (to which she'd never been partial) and the Auckland rock oysters, she settled on the roast turkey. She did her best at deflecting questions or gave generic answers on her background and reasons for coming on the advance party. Over the meal, Matron gave them a briefing on what to expect once they arrived in Suva, that being a two-day orientation going over the Fijian hospital system; a crash course in basic Fijian customs and language; and finally their assignment to the various hospitals across the islands. It was this final remark that sparked Abby's attention. There was a chance she wouldn't even stay in Suva? She asked Matron for some more details, but she couldn't be more specific than there were a couple of hospitals on outlying islands that had Australian nurses, from whom they would be taking over, so their party had to assign a nurse to each facility. Abby felt a cold sweat envelop her at the thought of being sent to a remote post.

Over the next couple of days she spent the voyage wandering the decks aimlessly while the other passengers enjoyed their contests of shuffleboard, various types of board and card games, or lying on the wicker sun loungers. Many of the men had cast aside their dark wool suits of departure day and were now in cotton or linen, dominant colours were cream or tan. Panamas or boaters were the headwear of choice. Ladies wore a wide range of patterned sundresses, some daring to go with lengths just on or above the knee.

She struck up the odd conversation with a few passengers. Most of them were on their way to Canada or the United States so they quickly settled into a comfortable routine that would help them get through the two weeks at sea that they faced. She met a family from New Plymouth who were heading to Canada. The man had an uncle with a timber business in Calgary who was nearing retirement, but his only child was killed in the war, so there was no one to take over the business. He admitted they knew nothing about Calgary, except that the winters were extreme, but it was a chance for a fresh start. Abby noticed the collar of his shirt was frayed, as were the cuffs on his jacket. The woman added they had sold everything save for the dinner and cutlery sets they got as wedding presents. Her sundress was slightly faded, with a repaired tear down the side that had been hand-stitched. All through the conversation, the woman bounced a toddler dressed in homemade clothes on her knee.

For Abby there was no comfort to be found on board, for unlike the holiday makers, businessmen and those heading for new lives, she was off to purgatory. In any one hour she could swing from seething anger and resentment, through doubt and uncertainty to acute heartache and yearning for her sweetheart. Happy, upbeat thoughts, so much her normal mode, were rarities. Mostly she was still stunned that in the space of ten days she had gone from a hazy Saturday among the apple trees with him, to crossing the South Pacific to start an unknown period of virtual servitude. She was grateful for Shirley's company, as she was able to raise a smile with a witty remark, or her observations when they were sitting on the deck chairs on what animal each passer-by reminded her of: the tall, gangly man with an elongated neck (giraffe); the plump woman with buck teeth and a shawl (sheep).

After the first night dining together, Matron allowed the group to socialise separately. Shirley insisted that the two of them have dinner in the grand dining room, and took the lead to get them on a different table every night and would instantly strike up conversations. Any single gentlemen on the tables were delighted with their company and were eager to get them chatting. Abby found herself talking freely when the topics were restricted to dry matters such as the economic crisis, the state of public health in New Zealand, or the latest literary releases. However, when things turned to anything personal, she would quickly go silent, allowing Shirley to take centre stage. Abby noted the gentlemen's attention always drifted to her cabin-mate, a situation that didn't concern her in the slightest. Nevertheless, this and the after-dinner entertainments made the evenings fly by, a small blessing eagerly accepted. Abby did, however, always sneak back to the cabin just as the dancing started. She knew she wasn't ready to be in the embrace of another man, regardless of how platonic the setting.

On the last evening before they were due into Suva, Abby left the ballroom just as the band started its first number and decided to do a lap of the ship before retiring. A warm breeze allowed her to walk the decks with her shawl draped across her forearms, rather than over her shoulders. It had become noticeably warmer than the previous evenings and the air had taken on a slightly sweet aroma. Abby took a deep breath, immersing herself in the new atmosphere. She stopped at her favourite spot near the stern. The moon was still large enough four days after being full to light up the surface of the sea. The odd note from the band drifted out into the night – she could just make out they had moved from waltzes to swing numbers. A sudden thought came into her head – she had never actually danced with him. She had no idea how good, or otherwise, a dancer he was. Funny what you take for granted then only discover something different by accident. She assumed that they must have danced at some stage, but now she realised they had never stepped out in a social setting where dancing was an option and for the first year after they met he had his bad back. She thought he would be pretty good, he's well balanced, sure footed and has a firm touch. Oh, yes, his touch. She trembled slightly as she imagined his right hand settling on her lower back. A voice jolted her out of the vision.

'There you are. I've been looking all over for you.' Shirley was halfway between the doorway and the railing where Abby was. With the lights of the ship behind her, Abby could only see the outline of Shirley's silver three-quarter length cocktail dress. Her hair was pinned back so the moonlight accentuated her angular face.

'Just getting some air before bed. Why aren't you dancing up a storm?' replied Abby.

'I just had four in a row and honestly, I want an early night myself. We're on schedule to be in Suva tomorrow, so I want to be fresh for the arrival. Also, I don't want to give Matron any ammunition against me. You know what the old ones can be like.'

'Oh, yes. I know first-hand about that.'

'It's gorgeous out here. Look at that moon. It's a beauty.' Shirley raised her voice as she saw the vista.

'Now you know why I spend so much time out here,' said Abby.

Shirley regarded Abby with a raised eyebrow. 'There's something bigger than a nice view and fresh air. Isn't there?'

'No, there's nothing. I just like a bit of quiet time.'

'I might have been tearing around, getting into everything for the last couple of days, but I'm not blind,' Shirley took Abby's hand as she spoke. 'Either you're running away from something, someone, or you've been sent away. From a man, I suspect. Right?'

Abby exhaled heavily and looked down to the deck, 'I can't talk,' she stopped herself mid-sentence. 'You're right, but I just can't go into it. I hope you understand.'

Shirley put her arms around Abby 'It'll be alright. We're only here for six months. You'll see him again sooner than you think.'

Abby leant on Shirley; but knew her optimism was ill-placed. The likelihood of seeing him again was slim to none. A tear ran down her cheek.

CHAPTER TWO

Taveuni, Fiji

Just as the voyage had been her first time on the open seas, this was Abby's first time out of New Zealand. Even a month's worth of the steamiest summer days back home would have done nothing to prepare her for Fiji. Every breath was heavy; the heat seeped into her lungs. Her nurse's uniform clung to every part of her. She dabbed away the beads of perspiration that seemed to be now permanently attached to her forehead.

After a couple of days in Suva with the whole advance party, she had to say goodbye to Shirley when her fears were realised and she was posted to the remotest hospital available, in the village of Waiyevo, on the west coast of the island of Taveuni. It took nearly two days to get there from Suva, starting with an all-day ferry trip north to Savusavu on the second-largest island of Vanua Levu. There were two other nurses on board: one from Christchurch who was to be stationed in Savusavu itself and one from Invercargill heading to Labasa on the north side of Vanua Levu. Abby knew their names and faces from the trip up; but nothing else. The three of them grabbed seats near the stern of the ship and chatted continuously to pass the hours. Like Shirley, the other two had volunteered and were looking on this as an adventure of a lifetime, knowing they would be here for only six months, but the woman from Invercargill was already struggling with the humidity. Even Abby, who had lived in the warm climate of Napier, found it stifling here, so she knew that the other woman who came from the cold, deep south would find it particularly unpleasant. Both women had left boyfriends back in New Zealand; but didn't feel it would be too difficult to be away from them for a short time. When asked, Abby was economical with the truth, saying she didn't have someone waiting for her back home. Is this how her life was to be now? Being evasive and secretive to every new person she would meet? The strain of maintaining that veneer of ambiguity was against her nature and normal disposition. She added that to the list of things making her gloomy.

After an overnight stay in Savusavu, she faced the last leg of her passage, a six hour ferry to Taveuni, on an even smaller boat, barely bigger than the fishing boats that docked in Napier harbour. For the first time in over six days at sea, she finally succumbed to seasickness. Even on the calm waters between the two islands, the little boat bobbed and heaved. In the process of leaning over the rail at the stern, she was somewhat relieved to have her mind taken off the realisation that she was approaching the final stop in her exile. Her aching body overwhelmed the anxiety she had been feeling over the previous few days. She looked up when she heard the boat's engine ease off to see they were pulling alongside the jetty. An offer of help to get ashore by the crew was gratefully accepted. She leaned against a post and took half a dozen deep breaths. The usual sting of foreshore air wasn't as strong as she expected, mingled as it was with the sweet fragrance of tropical flowers. Although each breath was heavy and warm, the taste of the air agreed with her.

A thickset woman with ankles to match approached Abby. Sweat stains had discoloured her white nurse's uniform around the neck and armpits. 'You must be Abigail. Struth. You alright, dear? You're a bit pale.' Her strong Australian accent was coupled with a high pitch which didn't match her size.

'Just a little queasy. I'll be fine, thanks,' Abby replied as she moved away from her support post to greet the woman. 'Seasickness finally got the better of me.'

'Yeah, these little boats can knock ya around a bit. I'm Philippa Carmichael, but just call me Phil. Consider me the welcoming committee. It's great to have you here.'

'Pleased to be on dry land, I must say.' Abby couldn't bring herself to respond with the standard platitude about being pleased to be there.

'We'll get ya a nice cuppa once we're at the hospital. It's just ten minutes up the road,' Phil added, grabbing Abby's suitcase.

On the road to Waiyevo village, sights, sounds and smells fought for Abby's attention with every step. She had been to many Maori towns and villages around New Zealand, but there was a rawness here that she couldn't remember about those places back home. Men wore long, colourful, patterned skirts, with bare feet or sandals the footwear of choice. Children in shorts and no shirts. Grass-roofed huts with the odd pig and goat wandering among them. It was barely fifteen minutes before they arrived at the hospital, nothing more than a clinic to Abby's eyes. She wondered why the place was so quiet, thinking it was still the middle of the afternoon, but looked down at her watched to find it was twenty to six.

'No point looking around the place tonight. Everyone's done for the day and it'll be dark in a bit anyway,' said Phil.

'Dark soon? It's still quite light and not even quarter to,' said Abby. She hadn't noticed the early nights so far; but then she hadn't paid attention to so many things since leaving New Zealand.

'You bet. Bright sunshine to pitch black in less than an hour up here,' replied Phil. 'You get used to it soon enough. Come on, I'll give you the quick once over of the living quarters and get you set up in your digs.' Phil led Abby to the back of the hospital; where there was a rectangular building, twenty yards long by ten yards wide. They went in and Phil opened the second door on the right. 'This is your room, pretty sparse I know, but you have free reign over decorating it. No one's going to give a hoot what you do to it.'

Abby stepped into the tiny room and gave it the two second scan that its size called for. A single bed pushed up tight against the far wall, with a small bedside table next to it, a four drawer tallboy next to the door and a single wardrobe across from the bed.

'Thanks for taking the time to meet me and show me round. I think I'll just unpack and turn in. I'm shattered,' Abby said.

'No worries. It's brilliant to have you here. We'll rip into work things tomorrow, eh? I'll pop by at eight. Sleep well.' Phil closed the door behind her as she left.

Abby turned back to her room. Everything bar the bedside table was painted white, that little piece itself was a blond wood, probably pine, so it added no real colour to the room. Stark and antiseptic. Vacant and blank; to reflect the current state of her life. With Phil gone, she let her facade drop. She slammed the wardrobe door and kicked out at the furniture but lost her balance and fell onto the bed, too exhausted to cry yet her mind was running at a thousand miles and hour. Had Moira's warnings and prophecies now come to pass? Was the gamble now backfiring? She always knew it was fraught with danger – emotional, spiritual and now physical. Surely this wasn't God's punishment for loving, for loving one of his own? Her faith had always been questionable, especially to pious Moira, and she'd seen too much suffering to truly believe in a benevolent God. Was this His wrath? She wanted to believe it was petty, vindictive people protecting themselves and their precious institutions that were behind her predicament, not the hand of God, but many times over the past week, she had thought this was a biblical curse.

Eventually, she slipped into a deep sleep, her bags untouched by the door.

29th November 1935

By the end of the first week, Abby was comfortable with the relatively straightforward workings of the hospital. That afternoon she had to stitch and dress a wound inflicted by the misplaced blow of a machete on a young farmhand from one of the copra plantations. 'You're a lucky boy,' she told the teenager as she tied off the bandage, 'Any deeper and we would have had to send you to Savusavu to get fixed up.'

A voice came from behind her, 'Miss McCarthy – you have a visitor,' said the receptionist.

Abby looked around to the door, her face creased with confusion as to who it could possibly be. 'I'll be a couple of minutes.' Turning back to her patient, she continued. 'You'll be alright. Now, I know you won't stay off the leg, but can you at least promise me you'll keep it dry and as clean as possible?' The boy nodded vigorously. 'You're all done. You can hop down now.' She helped the boy to get off the vintage bed, which groaned and creaked as he shifted his weight to the edge. 'Come back to see me next week and I'll change the dressing for you. Be careful.'

Abby cleaned up, putting things in order, then stepped into the reception area but checked her stride as she saw a tall priest standing by the admissions desk. Thinking he would notice the surprise on her face, she quickly tried to take on a more natural look. He exemplified the very casual nature of life on Taveuni; he wore a short-sleeved black shirt, with a small Roman collar sitting loosely around his neck. His heavily tanned arms almost blended into his crisp dark shirt, and a layer of dust marked his black shoes and trouser cuffs. His 6ft 3 inch frame was topped off by a thick crop of dark brown hair. 'Hello, Father. How can I help you?' she asked.

'Abigail McCarthy?' The priest offered his hand. 'I'm Father McGuire. Welcome to Taveuni.' His smile was wide and his face was warm and natural.

'Thank you, Father.' She wasn't surprised he knew her name, but it still unsettled her. 'Appears news travels fast here.'

'Like lighting, but don't be too worried. I actually got official notification of your arrival just over a week ago; but wanted to give you a few days before I introduced myself.' His voice had an educated New Zealand accent with a reassuring low pitch. Abby estimated his age at early thirties, but given the slow pace and healthy lifestyle she had seen so far, he could easily be ten years older and aging very well. 'How's the first few days gone?' he continued.

'Still finding my feet. It's a big change from New Zealand.'

'Too right it is. I don't mean to take up too much of your time. You are most welcome to come to Mass at Holy Cross whenever you can make it. We are the only church on this side of the island. You are Catholic? I assume so with your surname.' McGuire queried with his eyebrows.

'Yes, Father. You've assumed correctly. That'd be nice. I'll try to come down soon enough.'

'Wonderful. You can't miss us. Just over a couple of miles straight down the road, heading south. Look forward to you joining us.' They shook hands again, he gave one more comforting smile then turned and stepped out of the building.

Abby stood staring at the door as it closed behind the priest, her hands on her hips and chewing on her lower lip, contemplating. So the Church knew I was coming, not surprising at all. So how long has he been waiting, watching, before today? Will I be under the eye for my whole time here? Surveillance heaped on top of heartbreak; could things sink any lower? She felt her ears getting hot, her saliva bitter and her jaw tighten. She spun around on her heel and stormed out the back door. The sound of the slamming door woke an old dog from its slumber and it gave her a quizzical look. Abby threw her head to the heavens and shouted, 'So you're all bloody in this together, eh? You and your minions spying on me.' The dog jumped up and ran off. 'I'll tell you now, you won't bloody break me. However long you conspire to keep me here, I'll take it and any other shit you throw at me. I will not deny my love, I'll take it with me forever. You hear me?'

* * *

The next week she was assigned to visit the island's villages and nursing stations. These expeditions actually helped to alleviate Abby's malaise. From Vuna on the south-west tip of the island, through Matei on the opposite extreme, to Bouma and Lavena on the east coast, the chance to meet and care for the villagers, especially the children, lifted her spirits. It was here she felt she was making an impact. The children were in very good health, a little underweight compared to similar aged Kiwi children, but she soon learnt this was down to their fundamental physical make-up and radically different diet. The main concerns were of European origin – flu and whooping cough. Philippa told her that the Fijians didn't have a great defence against flu, and her own memories of the epidemic of 1919 made her ultra-vigilant for any signs of it in the children. Abby hadn't lost anyone close, but two of her school friends had had deaths in their families. It was the fear and panic that Abby remembered most: having to go to school with face masks or handkerchiefs over their nose and mouth; the anxiety when any friend had even the smallest cough.

Holy Cross was the only Catholic Church on the island. In spite of her long standing ambivalence to the Church, which had slipped to even darker feelings in her current situation, Abby found herself walking south from Waiyevo for Sunday Mass. Why she was drawn to it, she couldn't definitively say, but some kind of force pulled her along with dozens of the locals, down the dirt track that acted as the main road between the villages. The phrase 'dressed in your Sunday best' might have been coined especially for the Fijians; bedecked virtually to the last man, woman and child in crisp white skirts, with shirts in every colour of the rainbow. As if like a magnet attracting shards of loose metal, the Church was still a constant force in her psyche, and once in its influence, the ability to break away seemed near impossible.

The church itself, at the centre of the Wairiki Mission, was positioned on a small rise about 100 yards from the shore. It held commanding views of the coastline and out towards Vanua Levu. Abby took in the structure; an exquisite example of colonial Romanesque church architecture. She could easily picture it in the Caribbean, or Latin America. An almost life-sized statue of the Virgin Mary welcomed the faithful in front of the church. She was dressed in a flowing white gown and bright, sky blue cape and scarf, her hands clasped in prayer, eyes to the heavens. The white stone building was glowing in the morning sun. It wasn't a large structure, maybe twenty yards wide by fifty long. It seemed to fit perfectly into its surroundings. The red corrugated iron roof and bell tower dome provided a strong contrast to the lush green vegetation that flanked it on three sides.

Even here there was the consistency of Mass. The same words, same ceremony, same prayers. With so many things being unusual and keeping her off balance, Mass provided a reassuring centre point, solid ground she could rely on.

After Mass, Father McGuire made a point of seeking out Abby. 'Miss McCarthy, I'm so glad you have been able to join us. You are very welcome to Holy Cross.'

'Thank you, Father. It was a nice Mass and it's a lovely little church. Very comforting,' said Abby, shaking McGuire's hand firmly.

'Isn't it? Built by French Missionaries about the turn of the century. How are you settling in? It's quite daunting at first. I remember my first few weeks were bewildering,' he said, picking up on Abby's tension. 'Don't worry, it gets easier rather quickly.'

'That's good to know. It has been a challenge, I won't deny that. Half my problem is that coming here happened so quickly, so I didn't have any time to prepare myself,' Abby cut herself off abruptly.

McGuire cocked his head slightly and narrowed his eyes, but didn't press the point. 'So where have you joined us from?'

'My family's from Fordell, near Wanganui, but I was working in Napier before I came up here.'

'Napier? Really?' McGuire's voice lifted as he spoke. 'I went to seminary at Mount Saint Mary's in Taradale.' Abby felt her heart quicken and her eyes widen. 'You know it?' he added.

'Yes, up on the hill. I helped out there for a couple of days in '31,' said Abby.

'A very sad time for them. That must have been difficult. The experience will help you here I think. Do you go to St. Patrick's? I went through seminary with Father Lynch.'

'Father Paddy,' Abby said warmly. 'Oh, he's wonderful. I really enjoy it when he takes Mass. You were at Mount Saint Mary's with Father Lynch? But he had his fortieth birthday this year, you don't seem– ...' she cut herself off quickly.

'Good heavens, no, I'm only thirty-three. Father Lynch was a late starter. Life is good here, but it isn't so good as to stop the aging process,' he replied with a broad smile. 'Wonderful to finally have you join us. See you next Sunday.'

She made a half turn to leave, checked herself then turned back. 'Father, can I ask you how you knew I was coming to Taveuni?'

'The Island's government superintendent showed me a cable he received from the head of your party the day after you all arrived in Suva.'

'So it wasn't a Church communique?'

'The Church? No, the arrival of a contingent of New Zealand nurses was big news right across all the islands.' He opened his arms and looked out toward the island of Vanua Levu.

'Thank you, Father. Silly question really. See you next Sunday,' she said, this time turning away and walking down the grass bank towards the road.

On her infrequent days off, Abby would walk the tracks around the base of Mount Uluiqalau, find a secluded spot with a good view and read her poetry books. Her favourite place, found during one of her village visits, was a waterfall between Bouma and Lavena, on the other side of the island; discovered whilst walking the coastal path between the two villages. It was a small track that headed inland; just wide enough for an adult, the path was lined with palm trees, giant tree ferns and dakua trees. After a couple of minutes, she heard the low, constant roar of the falls, but try as she did, couldn't see them through the foliage. Another hundred yards along, the track opened up and revealed the falls in all their grandeur. Seemingly coming from nowhere, water exploded out of the tropical forest, falling past what looked to be a cave behind the falls about three-quarters of the way down, then crashing into a deep pool some 70 ft below the falls' source, before meandering off into the forest. It reminded her of one of the swimming spots they'd gone to as children on those hazy summer days when school was off and farm chores were done. Days full of adventure down at the Whangaehu River, before the war, before this economic catastrophe, before the earth broke open. Innocent days.

Back then Abby would lead the group on the mile-long trek from her family's farmhouse to a big bend in the river with an inviting swimming hole. A large sweep of smooth stones provided the perfect place for picnics, fires and lying in the sun. In small pools of water could be found fresh water crays; the deeper, darker nooks and crannies were home to eels that the boys loved catching. They used gaff hooks they made themselves; the Maori boys from up river taught them how to snare them using traps. Her mother was expert at smoking the eels when they brought some home. She'd make a fish pie, topped with creamy mashed potato.

Abby sat down on a large, flat-topped stone close to the falls, closed her eyes and could almost taste it. She clung on hard to these memories and mementos of home. She opened her small satchel and took out her favourite poetry book, one by Rupert Brooke that her love had given to her last spring. Her mind drifted back to that day: stray shafts of sunlight flickered through the leaves of the apples trees. A zephyr out of the north made the branches dance lazily, causing a few blossoms to drift to the grass below. He leant against one of the trees, eyes closed, face turned up towards the sun. She lay on a blanket at right angles, her head on his lap, as she opened the book and started to read the poem, handwritten by her sweetheart on the inside cover:

> Who did save my world, She
> From weakened eye, an angel I did see
> Skin soft, her touch healing
> I, at the altar of her grace, kneeling
> The fragrance that surrounds her, lavender
> Heart warm, soul pure, no one kinder
> Untouchable, never to be as one, we
> Vows broken and exile, the price to be with She

The sound of voices and splashing water brought Abby back to her immediate surroundings. Some local children were diving from the cave into the waterhole at the base of the falls. Each child waved at her just before they jumped. She waved back, recognising them from her visits to the village. Somehow the air didn't feel so heavy, the sun on her face warmed her deep inside. The light breeze hit the back of her neck and sent a tingle down her spine, reminding her of the touch of his hands. A small smile came across her face. She wondered how he would be feeling now.

She had managed to send a short letter while she was in Suva, assuring him that she would be fine and not to worry for her, trying to hide her pain at being pulled away from him. A new and raw pain tore at her like a knife into soft flesh; nothing in her life had ever hurt so much. She hadn't loved this way before, so the pain was new and raw.

The nights were hardest. The heat, humidity and strange noises – exotic bird calls, pigs and goats left to wander and forage, waves hitting the shore; all conspired to keep her awake for hours. Time enough for her to run over the events of the past month. During the first couple of weeks in Fiji, she frequently cried herself to sleep. Recently she had chastised herself, demanding that she toughen up. This evening after returning from the falls was especially difficult. Something had disturbed the animals, the dogs howling in a canine chorus, which in turn caused the goats to bleat en masse. Lying on her bed wide awake some three hours after retiring, Abby's thoughts drifted back to New Zealand, to the day they met at the Palmerston North train station for their first rendezvous out of Napier. It was that day when her feelings changed from friendly affection to love. Seeing him on the platform waiting for her, his face almost exploding into a broad smile, replicated in his eyes, had started the turn. Such a handsome, dashing man, and so much the gentleman. Then his sweet conversation, delicately tiptoeing around his own feelings. She remembered how he couldn't take his eyes off her, almost mesmerised. It had made her a little uncomfortable at first, but she soon realised it was a mix of his nerves and affection for her. Despite her best efforts, tears came, but they helped her fall asleep.

Getting dressed the next morning, she realised she had been on Taveuni for one month. She grabbed her belt and went to do it up; she had to go in one extra hole. Even with the heat, a diet dominated by fish and vegetables, along with walking all over the island doing health checks at the villages, a notch in a month was a surprise. The crease in the leather that marked the previous resting place caused the belt to buckle. She patted it down a couple of times to no avail. The way she was dropping weight, it'd only be a matter of a few weeks before she'd have to go in another notch. She knew her appearance was changing quickly. Her 5ft 4 inch frame had always been healthy; with a hint of underlying strength and an early life on a remote farm with all the physical work that entailed ensured there wasn't much extra on her to begin with. In New Zealand, a country barely a quarter century out of its colonial adolescence, it was rare to see a double chin or spare tire on anyone under fifty. She now started to see lines and muscle definition that had been the preserve of the hockey and basketball girls she'd known at nursing school. Her light brown hair now had a definite blond tint and her skin a healthy tan. If this metamorphosis continued, would he even recognise her? She dabbed a couple of drops of lavender scent on her wrists and her neck. Not too much, as there was little chance of getting a new supply here.

Marooned on a small South Pacific island, working virtually every waking hour in a makeshift hospital amid heat, the archaic facilities, lack of supplies and medicines – how did it come to this? The parallels to five years ago weren't lost on her. Five years. Was it really that long ago? Some days it seemed only a few months since she went up to Mount Saint Mary's Seminary in those first few days after the quake. Many times since her arrival here, she had gone through the "what if's" – the earthquake hadn't happened; Moira wasn't so insistent that they go up to the Seminary; they'd chosen different patients to look after; she'd heeded the first warning and not written to him a couple of years ago. If any of those had gone another way, she wouldn't be here, maybe she'd be married with a family, but with who and would she have loved as deeply, as completely? But they did all happen, so was it fate?

Now it felt a lifetime ago. In the heat of Fiji, that life appeared to be lost forever. They said this posting was only for six months, but she suspected – no she knew – that it would be extended. For how long was the mystery. When she finally returned to New Zealand there would be no chance of a life together, or even a residual friendship. Eyes would be on them both for many years to come. For all her anger and frustration about her situation, Abby knew there had been a decision that the two of them had needed to make, but had been left unspoken. So someone else had forced their hand. Was that such a bad thing? She wanted to believe it was. She had better start planning how her life might be, whenever she got back home. At least she had her career. That could take her anywhere, get her a job in any town or city in the country. Wherever she ended up, she promised that she'd buy herself a nice little cottage, a place to call her own. She'd need to plan on making a life for herself into her seventies, but practicalities were the least of her worries. A life without love, making her way through the next forty years without the man who moved her, who had made her feel things no other man had. That's what she didn't know how to face.

Memories of school came flooding into Abby's mind, of sitting with her cousin Moira, joining their names with those of boys they liked, as if they were married: Robert and Abigail Thomas, Peter and Moira Osborne, Anthony and Abigail Smail (that combination ruled him out as a suitor), Roderick and Moira Southey. They'd spend hours talking about their future weddings, what they would wear, the type of flowers, who to invite (or not).

The daydreaming would naturally end up at babies and potential names. Moira would always revert to the Saints: Mary, Joseph, Francis, Agnes. For Abby rarer names appealed: Tabitha, Rupert, Tiffany, Nathaniel. Although she'd always liked the idea of having a family, she didn't have a burning maternal instinct. As the youngest of thirteen, she was mothered by her sisters and never got the chance to do the same. Yet the dawning that the decisions she'd made and the desire for the right man, rather than any man, and her advancing years (soon to be thirty-three), made her realise any chance of motherhood was quickly escaping her. What bothered her was that the option was being taken away from her, she wasn't in charge. She fully expected to be kept here till she was close to thirty-five and although maternity medicine wasn't her speciality, everything she'd learnt pointed toward that being a danger area for first-time childbirth. Her own mother was forty when she came along, but by then her mother was a seasoned veteran with a body well-versed and in tune with the rhythms of the process. Something that she had to prepare herself that she'd never experience.

* * *

She looked at her calendar – 22 January 1936. They'd be celebrating Wellington Anniversary Day back home. Her family would normally have a big dinner to mark the traditional end of the summer holiday period, back to school for the children and a number of milestones on the farm, such as the second cut of hay. Today was just another work day for Abby. As she was busy doing a stocktake in the clinic's dispensary, she concentrated on the task of ensuring all drugs, medicines and supplies were accounted for. It never took long as the clinic was chronically under-supplied. Upping the stock would be one of her first requests once the Kiwi management started in a couple of months. She didn't hear the door behind her open. A gentle hand on her shoulder startled her, but not as much as the familiar voice.

PART I

PART 1

CHAPTER 3

6th January 1931

Napier, New Zealand

Albert Robertson squinted as he scanned the quayside. The late afternoon sun was sharp as the ship berthed at Napier harbour. They had hit some rough seas coming out of Wellington, so the sparkling and calm waters of the bay came as a welcome relief. He crinkled his nose. The pungent, salty air of the wharf stung his nostrils. In the shelter of the inner harbour it was nearly ninety degrees. He pulled out a monogrammed handkerchief and mopped his brow and mouth. The cloth, a present from his last birthday, was embroidered with "AR – 23".

Away from the hot and dry climate of Hawke's Bay for three years, he had quickly adjusted to the cooler climes of Wellington some 200 miles to the south. He tugged at his collar to let some air in. The collar had always been too tight, even from his first day at the seminary, five years earlier. Maybe it was his large Adam's apple.

He scanned the hills in the distance. They were burnt brown but spotted with white dots. The resident sheep looked like woolly ants as they scavenged for grass. Gone were the vegetation and lush colours of Wellington. Movement on the dock pulled Al's focus down to the quayside. A group of twenty-odd men were milling around one of the sheds. Dishevelled, they were herded into lines by a couple of men in uniforms. Then in pairs or fours, they were dispatched to various parts of the docks to move cargo.

As he stepped off the gangway, a short, stocky man with a

ruddy face approached, his short gait interrupted by a limp. Dressed in a black suit and white Roman collar, it marked him as one of Al's brethren. At 6ft 1 inches, Al was a good four or five inches taller than his greeter. A meaty hand shot out in welcome.

'Brother Robertson? Welcome back to Napier. I'm Father Patrick Lynch, but please call me Father Paddy. No need for all that usual formality with me.' Al picked up a strong whiff of nicotine from Paddy's breath.

'Glad to be here, Father Paddy, and it's Brother Albert, or Al if you prefer. Very happy to be off the ship. Not much of seafarer, I'm afraid.'

'A bit green around the gills, eh? Ah, sure, we'll get you a nice cup of tea when we get settled in at St. Patrick's. Still it's better than the bus. A real kidney crusher, that road trip, especially the darned Rimutukas. You could'a taken the train. That all ya got?' Paddy asked at Al's two medium-sized suitcases and a canvas rucksack.

'They taught me to pack light at the seminary. I can always pick up any extra bits and pieces from Mount Saint Mary's over the next month if I need,' Al replied.

Paddy showed Al to an immaculate Model T, 'Compliments of a parishioner who kicked the bucket. Oops, sorry, passed away, a couple of years back. God rest his soul. It's getting a bit long in the tooth now, but I take good care of her. Old Henry Ford sure knew how to make them to last.'

As Al put his cases in the back seat, he noticed about half a dozen cigarette butts on the ground next to the car. They got in and headed away from the docks. Paddy gave a nod and a single finger wave to the men in uniforms who Al had noticed from the ship.

'Irish?' asked Al. Although there was only the slightest hint of an accent, the name and Paddy's use of "Ah, sure" sealed the question.

'Yes and no,' said Paddy. 'Born and bred here in the Shaky Isles, but Mammy and Pop came out in the 90's. From Garryowen in Limerick. Settled here in Napier straightaway. Can you imagine their shock at the difference in the weather? Mam still loves it when it rains. You?'

'Partly second generation. Mother was born here, but Grandfather and Grandmother Robertson and my father came out in the late 70's. They were from Antrim originally.'

'Antrim? Northern Catholics? Tough. Worse now, but no cakewalk back then. They must have been hardy types.' Paddy's lilt dropped and his voice deepened slightly as he spoke.

Al gave a slight nod, 'Yes, I suppose. Has it rained here lately?' stumbling over his reply.

'We usually get a bit in the winter and early spring, but it's been a bloody dry few months. They reckon it could be the driest spell for fifteen-odd years. The cockies are worried, especially the dairy boys,' replied Paddy.

As they pulled away from the Quays, Al saw another line of men, outside the gates sullenly looking in. Al could see them in closer detail. Weathered and sun baked faces, stark features etched with rapidly dwindling pride. Threadbare clothes at best, darned and patched up as well as possible. Boots and shoes scuffed and resoled with any and every material available. One man locked his gaze onto Al, yet there was nothing behind the stare. Al felt flushed and diverted his eyes.

As they turned off Marine Parade onto Hastings Street, Al marvelled that the old Model T was indeed in great nick; albeit slow-paced compared to the newer Model A's, Buicks, Studebakers and even the little Austin's. Sunlight danced off the chrome of the big American cars; the reflected light flashing across the Model T's windscreen. No sign of the new curvier cars that he'd recently seen in Wellington. Here they were older models, but in pristine condition.

They passed a large stone and brick church. 'That's not us,' chirped Paddy. 'St. Paul's Presbyterian Cathedral. Lovely church. Nice folk. Pity they're so uptight.'

Although air was flowing through the car, Al had to wipe his forehead and neck every few minutes. Paddy was waving and shouting greetings to every second or third person on the footpaths. 'G'day, Mr. Barker.' 'How are ya doing, Mr. Charleston?' 'Good afternoon, Mrs. O'Sullivan.'

Al soaked up the sights and sounds as they drove – ornate stonework on banks and government buildings, shops with their wares out on display, the rattle of the trams as they passed by. 'It's a pity,' he began then paused for thought. Paddy gave him a quizzical glance. 'In the two years I was at the seminary, I only came into Napier once or twice. I don't know the town at all.' Al's thoughts shot back to the standard day at Mount Saint Mary's, with its 5am rise, all-day classes, study, chores, mass, prayers and lights out at 9:30pm. Repeated six days out of seven, that seventh day being Sundays. No surprise he and his class mates rarely came into Napier.

'Well, we'll change that over the next month, eh,' replied Paddy.

As they neared the bottom of Hastings Street, a group of men and women were gathering close to the entrance of a building. 'St. Vinny De Paul's. Their soup kitchen and food parcels depot,' Paddy said. A couple of men started pushing each other. There was a muffled scream from one of the women. 'How's things in Wellington?' Paddy asked.

'Tough. No doubt about that,' Al said, deflated. 'At least we have the government and so many head offices. Insulates the city to a certain extent. But nowhere is immune.'

'We're hurting here. Been on a downer for close to five years now.' Paddy's almost permanent smile had left him. 'We were barely holding our own, but the last three or four months have been real tough yakka.' He fought the Model T's gear box, jerking the gear shift from first to second. 'I'm struggling to keep up with it all. Blokes losing their jobs by the dozen every week. The place is on a knife-edge. One little nudge could be bloody disastrous.' They made a couple of quick right turns, Paddy's chunky forearms strained against the heavy steering. 'I'm glad you're here to help tend the flock for a while. These people need us.' Paddy slowed down the old car at the side of the street. 'Righty-o, here we are.'

The words were barely out of his mouth when a woman came running up to the car. 'Father Lynch. It's the Simpsons.' Her raised voice had a degree of panic.

Paddy got out of the car and spoke gently to the woman. 'Slow down. What's going on?'

Al tried to listen, yet felt a spike of guilt for eavesdropping. 'Yes ..., I see... and Jerry... Right away. I'll be there in a few minutes.' Al thought he heard a softly spoken expletive as Paddy returned to the car. He looked pensive, rubbing his chin. 'Got a problem with one of the parishioners. Gotta go out for a while. I'll drop you off here at the cottage.'

'Can I help?'

'No. This is pretty serious. I want to take care of it myself,' replied Paddy.

'What's the story?' asked Al.

'It's a domestic. Mary and Jerry Simpson. They've been having problems lately. Jerry got canned a few months back and he's been hitting the bottle hard. He's come back from the boozer and given Mary a biff,' Paddy said as he held the steering wheel so tight his knuckles turned white.

'I can help. I'll look after the gentleman while you take care of Mrs. Simpson.'

'He's no bloody gentleman.' Paddy contemplated his options. Jerry Simpson could be a handful at the best of times, let alone when he was pissed up. He chewed on the inside of his bottom lip. 'Ah, bugger it. Let's go. Follow my lead though, lad. OK?'

31

'You are in charge,' said Al.

Paddy spoke as they drove. 'Jerry may be out cold. Drinks himself into a stupor. Becoming a habit by all accounts.' Al picked up disdain in Paddy's words. 'We need to be careful when we go in if he's still up and about. Let me do the talking, OK?'

'Is there a chance he'll lash out at us?' asked Al.

'A chance, but not likely. I know guys like him. They only have a go at people they have some control over, or know they can beat. Stronger people, or those in authority? Unlikely. Bloody cowards, the lot of them.'

Parking outside the tidy early-Edwardian brick bungalow, both men looked at the other with slight trepidation. Paddy led the way giving a light knock. 'It's Father ...' Before he could finish the door opened slowly, seemingly by itself. They stepped in to find Mary Simpson behind it. Her head was down and turned slightly away from the men. Her long black hair shielded her face. She closed the door very gently behind them. Paddy reached for her. Their hands met halfway between them.

'You alright, Mary?' Paddy's voice was soft and tender. Mary gave a quick nod and a barely audible sniffle. 'Come sit down.' Paddy led her into the lounge. They sat down close to each other on the sofa as Al stood in the doorway. The living room, in fact the whole house as far as he could see, was orderly, everything in its place. Most of the furniture looked quite new, no more than a year or two old, all the latest designs.

'Is Jerry about?' Paddy asked.

Mary shook her head slowly, 'He's in the bedroom. Dead to the world.'

Al motioned to Paddy that he'd to go check. 'Tell me what happened, Mary?' asked Paddy.

Down the dark hallway small shafts of the early twilight poked out from under closed doorways. He should have asked where Jerry's bedroom was. He gently opened the first door about six inches and looked in: spare room. Next door, the same routine; bathroom. Had to be the next one. Al figured the kitchen would be on the other side and at the back of the house. He placed his hand on the chrome handle, hesitated for a couple of seconds. Gingerly he pulled the handle down. The latch made a click loud enough to make Al wince. He didn't need to look in, as within a couple of inches of opening the door, Al was accosted by a wave of stale beer and sweat. He stuck his head through the gap and in the gloom made out Jerry Simpson in his bed, chest heaving, breathing laboured and nasal with the occasional snort. Al backed out of the bedroom and closed the door.

Al went to find the kitchen. Mary might like a glass of water. Walking in, he stopped quickly. Where the rest of the house was pristine, the kitchen was in disarray. The dining table was at an odd angle, one chair upturned, a large stain on a wall with a broken plate and spilled food on the floor below. The scene sent a chill down him. Violence was never a part of his family, not physical aggression, anyway. Al straightened the furniture, then went to the sink and filled a glass. He would clean up the mess after he got water to Mary.

Back into the lounge, he gave a nod and thumbs up to Paddy. He knelt down and offered the glass to Mary. For the first time Al saw her face as she looked up to take the water. His eyes widened and his jaw dropped slightly. Mary's left cheek was heavily swollen and already showing signs of discolouration. Dried blood ran in a line from the bottom of her nose to her chin. The top of her blouse was speckled with blood. He had never encountered a victim of wife beating, but his college boxing taught him that injury to the left side of the face would be caused by a punch by the right hand of the perpetrator. Paddy's words instantly came back to him "Bloody cowards." Conflicting emotions fought for his attention; compassion, anger. Thoughts raced through his mind, how could a man punch his wife? How could one lose control like that? He took in a couple of deep breaths to try to calm down.

'Mrs. Simpson, Father Paddy, I do have some first aid training. I would like to take a closer look. Is that alright?' asked Al.

Mary looked to Paddy for guidance. He nodded. 'It's fine, Mary,' said Paddy.

'Mrs. Simpson, I'm going to have to lightly touch your cheek and nose. It will be very tender and may hurt. Please let me know if the pain is extreme. Alright?' Al tried to be as reassuring as possible, yet firm. Looking at her this closely, he could see her skin was smooth but spotted with freckles. He guessed her to be early to mid-thirties. He placed his left hand behind her head for support and gently placed his fingers on her cheek. It was hot to the touch, blood was pouring into the damaged area. 'Have you put anything cold on your cheek yet?' Mary shook her head lightly. He knew her cheek was going to get big, to the point of closing up her eye. Al then moved his hand to her nose, index finger on the bridge, thumb on one side, middle finger on the other. He slowly applied some pressure and felt movement. Mary recoiled and gave a muffled yelp. She was well practised in not making enough noise to wake her husband.

'Mrs. Simpson, your nose is definitely broken. I think we need to take you to the hospital immediately,' he said, as much to Paddy as to Mary.

'No. I can't leave the house. Not when Jerry's home,' Mary said between sobs. Al raised his eyebrows at Paddy.

Paddy picked up the cue, taking both her hands in his. 'Mary, listen to me. This ain't going to be a discussion. You trust me don't ya?' Mary nodded. 'Well, trust me now like you never have before. If Brother Robertson says we need to go to the hospital, we have to. Don't worry about things up there. I'll take care of the paperwork. OK? Mary, OK?'

Tears streamed down Mary's cheeks, pooling at her jaw and dropping onto her outstretched forearms. She slowly nodded.

'Good. Nice and quietly, let's grab your shawl,' Paddy said. They all stood up and made their way to the front door. As Al fell in behind, Paddy grabbed his upper arm and gave him a smile and a nod. A degree of calm returned to Al.

With Mary in the back seat, so as to not draw too much attention to themselves, they drove through the streets to Napier Public Hospital. A stern-looking nurse at reception peered over her spectacles, tufts of grey hair weren't quite contained under her hat, 'Can I help you?'

'Yes. We've had a wee spill and just need to see a doctor,' Paddy said, taking the lead.

'What's happened then?' asked the nurse.

'Mary here slipped on the marble steps at the church and hit her face. Might have broken her nose,' Paddy continued.

Al took a small step forward and turned his head to look at Mary. She gave the slightest shake of her head and mouthed 'It's OK'. Al closed his mouth and stepped back.

'Really. Is that right, Ma'am?' the nurse replied as she pulled her glasses down a half inch and switched her eyes to Mary.

'Yes. That is right,' Paddy shot back.

'I was talking to the young lady. Never mind. Fill this out and bring it back to me. Seats are to your right.' Efficient and officious.

Form completed, Paddy dropped it back at the desk; and forced a smile. 'That marble can be treacherous. Thanks, Father,' the nurse said, putting extra emphasis on Father. About a half hour passed before a shortish, heavy-set doctor came up to them.

'Mary Simpson? Hello, Mrs. Simpson. I'm Doctor Peters. It is Mrs.?' His voice was deep and husky. Mary nodded. 'Wonderful. You've had a bit of a tumble? Let's take you into the back and have a look. Reverends, you'll be alright to stay out here?'

'That's Father and Brother. Can't we just hang around back there?' asked Paddy

'Sorry, Father. On both counts. Immediate family only. We shouldn't be long.'

Mary looked to Paddy. 'It's OK, Mary. The doctor will take good care of you.'

They watched Mary disappear through a set of double doors with Dr Peters. 'You've known Mary for a number of years?' Al asked.

'We go back a while, yeah.'

'Was it through school or just the Church?'

'Something like that,' Paddy said, still staring at the doors.

Al didn't need to be told. He sat quietly for the next few minutes.

Mary and Dr Peters finally returned to the waiting room. Mary looked calmer. Dr Peters gave them a quick debrief, 'Looks like Mrs. Simpson has a suspected broken nose. The cheek is just bruised, but we'll get her whole face X-rayed, just to make sure. Take these forms with you to the X-Ray Department down the hall, then come back here after they finish with you. Father, Brother, you're more than welcome to escort Mrs. Simpson.'

They took Mary through a maze of hallways. The X-Ray Department was such a recent addition to the hospital that even some of the orderlies couldn't direct them and there were few signs. They finally found it, near the back of the building and Mary was taken in by the nurse who asked the men to wait in the hallway.

'You alright to stay put?' Al asked, 'Need some air. Don't care for the smell of hospitals.'

'That's the polite way to put it,' Paddy responded.

'Never had to spend much time in hospitals, thankfully,' said Al.

'Not so lucky, me. I'm good as gold to stay. Will be out front if Mary comes out before you're back, eh?'

Al walked down the corridor and soon he found a bank of windows that gave a sweeping vista down the hill to the town below. The Norfolk Pines guarded Marine Parade like military sentries. The spire of St. Patrick's dominated the skyline. One of the windows was open, so he put his head out into the hot, still air of the early evening. At least it wasn't the antiseptic odour of the hallways. He felt invigorated, a tingle of excitement flowed through him. Real life. Real people. Yes, that's what he needed. Could be an interesting month at St. Patrick's.

After a few minutes of gazing upon the sights of Napier in the growing twilight, he pulled his head back in and turned back to the X-Ray Department. He sensed lavender. His favourite fragrance. He drew in deep breaths through his nose to soak up the aroma and quickly looked around for its source. All he saw was a nurse swiftly walking away from him, her voluminous caped hat flowing as she walked. She was short, maybe 5ft 4 inches and glided effortlessly over the floor. Al watched her until she turned down another corridor, taking the scent with her.

CHAPTER 4

Silence enveloped the car. They dropped Mary off at her house and she crept inside. Al wasn't so calm. Thoughts and emotions gnawed at him. His pursed lips twitched from side to side.

'Come on, lad. Spit it out,' said Paddy.

'I haven't got anything to say,' replied Al as he folded his arms and looked straight ahead.

'Suit yourself, but if we're going to be in each other's pockets for the next month, we'd better be as up front as possible,' said Paddy tapping the steering wheel with his thumbs.

Al sucked on his teeth for a couple of seconds. His eyes narrowed as he responded. 'Why did you lie at the hospital and why haven't you called the police?'

Paddy took a deep breath, 'You're going to have to learn a fair whack about this big bad world to be a good priest. First and foremost, when it comes to the parish, we look after our own. Always have, always will. There are things you let out in public and there are things you keep close to home. As far as Mary is concerned, the whole world doesn't need to know what's going on. None of their business. That nurse has a fair idea of what happened. She's seen a bit over the years, but it's better for all concerned that she and the hospital only know a certain version of events. As for the police, similar story.'

'But he beat her. It's a crime. He should be locked up.' Al almost yelled his reply.

'And what good would that do Mary, or him? He'd be a criminal, no chance of getting work when things come right.

38

Mary's got her own job, so she'd be OK money-wise, but she'd have to live with the shame and the gossip that goes with it. Don't worry, there are plans. He'll be taken aside for a chat in the next couple of days. If it happens again, she'll be looked after and he *will* be taken care of.' The emphasis on "*will*" hit Al like a punch. 'Like I said, we look after our own.' Paddy turned to Al as he said the last few words. Al was unable to hide his reaction.

'Don't look so shocked, lad. Come on. We're home now. Let's get that cuppa we've been after. Probably deserve something a bit stronger tonight.' Paddy gave Al a light tap on the shoulder.

They pulled into the driveway of a small cottage next to St. Patrick's. Digesting Paddy's reply, Al didn't notice he was out of the car.

'Oi. Come on, lad. Stop stewing and help me with your cases.' Paddy shouted to Al as he pulled the luggage from the back seat.

'Apologies, Father Paddy. I was a thousand miles away.' Al bent over and took the case he knew was the heavier and grabbed his rucksack.

'Meant to ask you about that. You a bit of a hiker?'

'Yes. Dead keen on the mountains and bush. I try to get out as much as I can.'

'We'll try to get up in the hills while you're here,' Paddy replied approaching the house.

The cottage was the standard Queen Anne, of the simple variety with no elaborate adornments. A shallow covered porch ran the entire width of the front of the house, single windows looked out to the world either side of a forest green painted front door. As soon as they entered the cottage, the temperature seemed to drop ten degrees.

'Bedroom's in the front. Yours is on the right, mine on the left. Drop your cases in here, eh?' Paddy opened the door to reveal a single bed (a little short, Al thought), a chest of drawers and a wardrobe. A wall hanging of the Blessed Virgin and a crucifix were the only decorations.

'Lounge is in the middle, with the kitchen and bathroom out the back. Loo is an outhouse. Haven't quite got around to building an attached one. Don't know about you lad, but I need a sit down.' Paddy eased himself down into a tan lounge chair, the arms of which were a little threadbare and the rug in front noticeably worn. He reached over to a radio on a side table. 'Let's see what's on the old wireless, eh?' The radio crackled and popped as it came to life. The glow from the light in the frequency dial grew brighter. They sat listening for a few minutes. Al could make out what he thought was a farming report. Every second or third word was clear through the interference "Sales ... lamb ... Britain ... falling. Drought ... worsening ... forecast ... extreme."

'She's not bad digs, eh. Father Murphy, the top brass of the parish, has the presbytery on the other side of the cathedral. Lowly me gets this cottage. But I have it to myself,' said Paddy.

'It's a nice little place. I'd say I'll be comfortable here. Do you cook for yourself?' asked Al.

'Strewth, no.' Paddy let out a hearty chortle. 'Grub-wise, the Ladies' Committee looks after me. I think Mrs. Bartholomew should be by anytime now with our tea. Speaking of which, time for a cuppa.' Paddy was up out of his chair and on his way to the kitchen before he had finished the sentence and Al followed him. 'I'll put the billy on, eh? I tell ya, lad, ye can't beat a good cuppa cha. Well, the odd drop of Jameson never goes astray. But ya know what I mean,' said Paddy as he grabbed the kettle, filled it with water and put it on the range.

Al gave a little smile. He'd better get used to being called 'Lad'. He sensed Paddy was using it in a friendly, almost brotherly way. As one may tease a younger sibling. He liked that. There was the unmistakable tinkle of steel on china as Al placed a couple of tea cups, saucers, spoons and sugar bowl on the bench. Paddy got the teapot out, nothing fancy, just a plain white china pot from some non-descript outfit in Stoke-on-Trent over in England. It had been white once; but now stained and off colour on the outside, its insides almost black with the staining of a thousand and one brews it had been called on to make in its lifetime. Two heaped teaspoons of tea went into the pot that would add its own layer to the dark lining. Over at the fridge Al grabbed a bottle of milk.

Suddenly the high pitched whistle of the kettle broke the calm. It screamed out that it was ready, like the tantrum of one of those tempestuous children that always interrupted Mass. Paddy rummaged around in a cupboard. 'Here we go. A couple of bikkies before tea. Won't spoil the appetite.' He gave Al a quick wink as he placed the packet of ginger biscuits on a plate.

Paddy gave the pot a couple of turns, holding it by the handle and twisting it around its base, allowing the leaves one last chance to release their flavour. Paddy poured out a strong golden brew into the cups, Al peeled the foil top off the milk bottle and added some to each cup, finally each man spooned in his personal preference of sugar. One small teaspoon for Paddy, two heaped spoons for Al. They both blew on their concoctions to try to cool the first sip.

Paddy started the conversation as they ambled back into the lounge, 'What's the story with you? All I know is that Father Connolly asked me to show you the ropes of parish life for a month.'

'I entered Mount Saint Mary's in 1926, did my first two years as a seminarian, took my temporary vows, and have my final profession ceremony in February,' said Al.

'Standard procedure. So how come you've been in Wellington for the past few years?'

'They gave me special dispensation to do my Bachelor's degree at Victoria. I'm going to be a science teacher once I finish at the seminary,' Al added.

'Science? Faith versus reason. Dogma versus fact. That's a bit of a conflict for ya,' said Paddy, breaking a biscuit in half.

'I don't think so. It's through science that we can understand the workings of God's great gifts, some of which are so amazing, so stunning, that it is almost impossible to believe anything but a divine power created them.'

'Interesting position. I can relate to that. So where do you want to get to?' Paddy slurped a large mouthful of tea.

'I want to be a deputy head of a college science department by the time I'm thirty-five,' replied Al.

'Ambitious. Good. Hopefully we can show you parish life, warts and all, before you set off on your upward trajectory,' said Paddy.

A knock on the front door and a female voice broke up the conversation, 'Yoo-hoo. Father Patrick, its Elizabeth.'

'Come in Mrs. B.' shouted Paddy.

Elizabeth Bartholomew came into the lounge, 'I popped by earlier, but you were out.'

'We had some parish business. Weren't too long. Sorry.' said Paddy.

Elizabeth nodded, 'I heard. No need to apologise.' She gave a quizzical glance at Al.

'Sorry. This is Brother Albert Robertson, from up the seminary. I think I asked you last week to start cooking for two. Didn't I?'

'Yes, Father Patrick. You certainly did. There's enough for the both of you,' she replied with a flick of her jet black hair and little smile as she stared at Al. 'You gents stay there while I go heat this up. I'll give you a shout when it's ready.'

'So, Brother Al, can I get you a wee drink before Mrs. B serves tea? I've a couple of bottles of stout, a bottle of red from the seminary's vineyard, gin and some Jameson.'

'Any sweet sherry?' asked Al.

'Good Lord. What are you doing drinking that? It's for old geezers.'

'Sorry. I just like the taste,' said Al, shrinking slightly.

'I'll have a look. Can't promise anything.' Paddy dug about in the drinks cabinet. Bottles clunked and tinkled as he moved them around. 'Well whadda-ya know? You're in luck. She's a bit dusty, but she'll do.' Paddy blew on the bottle and a plume of dust danced into the air. He pulled out a couple of tumblers and poured until they were about three-quarters full. Sherry for Al, whiskey for himself. Al raised his eyebrows at the measures.

'There ya go, Brother Al. Here's to the next month,' Paddy toasted.

'Cheers, Father Paddy.' They clinked their glasses. Al took a sip. When Paddy set his glass on the armrest, half his measure was gone.

Al took out his pipe and tobacco as each man went through his respective ritual of preparing his smoke. Al tapped his pipe on the sole of his shoe, catching the remnants of the charred tobacco in his hand. He pulled out a small wad of short cut tobacco and wedged it into the pipe, tapped it down with his middle finger. Paddy slipped out a single sheet from the packet of papers, and popped a corner onto his lip, the moisture held it in place. He then took a pinch of tobacco from his pouch, long cut for him, grabbed the paper from his lips and quickly and effortlessly rolled a thin tight cigarette. Almost simultaneously the men struck their matches and lit their particular smokes. A blue cloud rose quickly, engulfed them both for a couple of seconds before the slight breeze coming in the window took it off above them. They both inhaled, then exhaled deeply.

'Why a pipe?' asked Paddy.

'Suppose it's a bit of like father like son. Dad's always smoked a pipe as long as I can remember. I do like it, though. Every smoke is slightly different. Different smell. Different taste. I only started during my last year at school. Seemed like the mature thing to do for us seniors. I didn't bother with cigarettes. Went straight for the pipe, and rollies for you?'

'The war, plain and simple. There was actually a lot of sitting around in the trenches. When we weren't going over the top or shooting at Jerry, we were hunkered down listening to the artillery. Had to do something with our time. Smoking and cards were it. That and dodging the bloody rats. The size of cats or small dogs, they were. Cripes, gives me shivers just thinking about them,' Paddy said with a quick shake of his shoulders. 'When I took me shrapnel, there was even more sitting around, or in my case, lying around. More time, more smokes, so by the time I came home I was knocking off thirty or more a day.'

'Tea's ready,' Elizabeth shouted from the kitchen.

They took their drinks into the kitchen where Elizabeth had set the small dining table. They sat down to a couple of heaped plates of steaming food. Looked like a chicken casserole to Al.

'Just what ya need when the mercury's topped ninety,' quipped Paddy

'I can take it home if you don't want it, Father,' Elizabeth shot back.

'Steady on, Mrs. B. Just pulling your leg. I ever left food on my plate when you cook?'

'I'll leave you in peace. See you in a couple of days. Father Patrick, will you be bringing Brother Albert to the parish dance?' she asked.

'You fixing to fill up your dance card ahead of time, Mrs. B?' Paddy jibbed.

'Just keen to make sure Brother Albert enjoys himself while he's with us.' The same little smile as earlier lit up her face.

'You're incorrigible. Be gone. See you later,' Paddy replied, himself smiling.

Paddy said grace, with a special mention of Mary and a

welcome to Al to the cottage and parish. The two men ate in silence for a few minutes.

Paddy was first to speak. 'You're still angry about today, ain't ya?'

'I wouldn't say angry. More confused. I'm struggling to understand the whole situation.'

'And you think I'm wrong not to go to the police?' asked Paddy.

'Who am I to say what's right and wrong for your parishioners?'

'I have to look out for their long term interests. Not just what happens day-by-day. I gotta say I was bloody impressed how you handled yourself. Honestly, I thought the situation was going to be a bit out of your league.'

'Thanks, Father. It was quite daunting,' replied Al, yet also exhilarating, he thought.

'You have a way with people. Me? Hell, I'm like a bloody bull at a gate half the time. Put some folks noses out of joint. Oops. Not the best phrase in the circumstances,' said Paddy.

'I know what you mean. This is exactly what I need to be doing. A few hours ago you said you were delighted to have me to help tend to the flock. Looks like the flock needs some serious tending. I've been closeted away for the past five years, in either the seminary or at university. Totally removed from everyday life. I need this. I hope you don't expect me just to fill communal wine and count the collection money?'

'Based on today's effort? Not likely. We've got some serious work to do. Looks like you and me are gonna be busy boys. And it starts tomorrow. We'll spend most of the day at the St. Vincent's place we saw today,' said Paddy.

After washing up, Al decided he needed to call it a day. 'Father Paddy, it's been a big day, so I think I'll retire.'

'No worries, lad. I'll have another dram, a smoke and listen to the wireless a while longer.'

'Thank you again for everything today,' said Al.

Paddy offered his hand to Al and grabbed his shoulder as they shook 'No. Thank *you*.'

In his bedroom, Al unpacked his cases: the seminary issued six shirts, a spare cassock, a black suit, were hung up; underclothes, socks and handkerchiefs folded and placed in the chest of drawers; his rucksack in the corner of the wardrobe; a picture of him and his three brothers from a couple of years ago went on top of the drawers along with his fob watch, rosary and Bible. He sat on the edge of the bed and picked up the photo. He exhaled heavily, placed the frame back on the drawers and got ready for bed. During his prayers, he questioned the days events, 'Lord, help me understand the lessons Father Lynch tried to teach me. Yes, it is virtuous to protect Mary, but surely it is a sin to cover up the crimes of Jerry? Is it really for Mary's sake that he doesn't involve the police? I can't believe that your Church would condone such secrecy. Almighty God, guide me on the right path.'

After breakfast, Al and Paddy stepped out into the sharp morning light of another cloudless day, briefly stopping outside the front door of the cottage to take in St. Patrick's. It was an impressive church. Then again, Al hadn't seen too many Catholic churches that didn't impose themselves on their surroundings.

'Not as grand as St. Mary's in Wellington, but she's the largest on the east coast. Masterton, Hastings or Gisborne can't match it,' boasted Paddy.

Al nodded, 'It's quite stunning.'

St. Pat's Gothic spire was clearly visible from the seminary, five miles away. Al guessed it must be at least 150 feet tall, maybe even closer to 200. Four smaller spires guarded the base of the main spire, where it met the top of the bell tower. The wood cladding was almost glowing in the morning sun. Five large stained glass windows ran down the entire length of the church.

'The windows and the bell are all from Lyon, ya know, in

France, eh.' Paddy's chest puffed out slightly as he dropped the facts onto Al. 'Come on. Let's go in. I need to get cracking.'

They went in the back door, which lead to the sacristy and other rooms. The scent of incense was heavy in the air. They made their way through the darkened corridor until they came out into the public church, close to the altar. Shafts of sunlight burst through the windows and illuminated rows of pews. A handful of elderly ladies were dotted throughout. Once in front of the altar, the men knelt, crossed themselves and said a silent prayer.

Paddy rose first. 'Feel free to look around. Saturday morning confession is only an hour. Will see ya either in back or at the cottage.' He turned and quickly made his way to the confessional. One of the ladies rose and headed in the same direction.

Al started to walk around the edge of the church. Triggered by the incense, his mind went back to his childhood. He loved the smell. It was warm and comforting; always a stark contrast to the cool air inside St. Mary's in Wellington, where he would go as a boy with his family. He remembered the bells being so loud, almost deafening. Calling the devout, the faithful; and some not so faithful to worship. As a child he'd go around the church, studying all the Stations of the Cross. Hands in his pockets, smooth silver fob watch in one pocket, plain gold cross in the other. Dressed in his Sunday best. Mother wouldn't have it any other way. 'Don't show disrespect for the Lord by not wearing your best clothes to Mass,' was one of her mantras. Among many others.

'Excuse me, Father.' The words jolted Al back into the present.

'Sorry. I was a million miles away.' Al turned to look at his inquisitor. An elderly Maori gentleman stood in front of him with a ladder and toolbox in hand. Tall and strong looking, with soft, warm eyes. His silver hair picked up some of those shafts of sunlight.

'Sorry to bother ya, but I just need to get by.'

'Thanks for looking out for me. Brother Albert Robertson.' Al offered his hand.

'You're the young fella Father Paddy was on about. I'm Sonny Weepu. Janitor, come handyman for St. Pat's. Kia ora Brother Robertson. Welcome to the parish.' Sonny took Al's hand. Al felt a strong grip from his dark brown, wrinkled hand.

'Thank you very much. Only been here a day, but so far so good. I was just having my first look around the church. You couldn't give me a guided tour?'

'No worries, Brother.' Sonny showed Al around the rest of the church and into the back where he and Paddy had entered. 'I hear you had to go to the Simpsons last night.'

'News travels fast here,' said Al.

'Too right. It's a small town, eh. Not much happens that goes unnoticed.'

'Good to remember.'

'Anyways, that's the church and ya know the cottage. The presbytery is on the other side and the church hall is next to that. I looks after em all, eh. Anything ya need doin' round the church or cottage, just give us a yell, eh?'

'Thanks, Sonny. I will do. Very nice to meet you.'

'Likewise, Brother Robertson. Ka kite ano. Take care.'

The men shook hands again and Sonny gave Al a broad smile. Stepping outside, the sun quickly drained the colour from Al's vision as he walked back to the cottage. "Not much happens that goes unnoticed," Sonny's words lingered in Al's mind as he waited for Paddy. The small town bush telegraph; he hadn't had much exposure to that.

Once Paddy returned, the rest of the day was spent at St. Vincent De Paul's packing food parcels, helping to serve lunch, sorting donated clothes and talking to those who were willing to chat. Not many were, but of those who did confide there were recurring themes: worthlessness, embarrassment, despair. The tales were similar. The only significant difference was how long each person had been out of work. This was usually inversely proportional to the state of their clothes and their levels of despondence.

Al listened intently, gave words of consolation, but he felt shallow and inadequate. What comfort could he bring? He, a man not many years out of his teens. He, a man who's only known the cloistered world of Catholic education and training. He, a man who now had a vocation for life. In the Church, he'll never truly know want, hunger or desperation.

He began to question why he even bothered to come along when he felt a hand on his shoulder. 'That's us done for the day, lad,' Paddy whispered. They said their goodbyes and started back to the cottage. 'How'd ya find that?' Paddy asked.

'It was tough. No doubt about it. I really had no idea what people are going through. This slump is destroying people,' replied Al.

'Aye, she's brutal, alright.'

'Men trying to support a family on a couple of bob a day. That's if they are lucky enough to get some relief work. Virtually all the domestic work has also dried up, so the women can't contribute either.' Al looked at the ground as he spoke.

'Too many can't even cover their rent, so the soup kitchen is always busy.' Paddy added.

'Some of the men told me they need to wear big sugar bags over their clothes as they only have one pair of trousers that aren't already as good as rags. I can't imagine how they are coping.'

'Many aren't, lad. That's why what we and St. Vinny's do is so important.'

Dinner was waiting for them as Paddy continued the conversation, 'I was chatting to Sonny and I mentioned you like tramping. He's mad for the hills and bush himself. He reminded me of a track just off the Taupo Road. Me and him did part of it when he took me fishin."

'Do you know the track well? How long is it and what sort of terrain?' asked Al.

'I've only been up there once, but Sonny's a regular. He reckons it's a good track and would be a full day out. I didn't find it that tough to get to the fishin' spot.'

'When are you thinking we should go?' asked Al.

'How about next Saturday? I was looking at the parish diary and it's the only spare weekend day we have before you have to head back to the seminary,' said Paddy.

'That's good. We'll need to keep an eye on the weather,' said Al.

'Have you looked outside lately? Hasn't bloody rained in nearly a month and we're now in the driest part of the year. We'll be right. No worries there. So there we go, we have a plan.'

As they settled into an after-dinner drink, Paddy reassured Al, 'More good work from you, lad. Folks came to me after they chatted to you. They had great things to say. You definitely have a knack with people.'

'Thanks, Father Paddy. That's nice to hear. I felt next to useless, though. What can I tell them? What do I know?' replied Al.

'Sometimes it ain't what you know or your experiences but reassuring them that they aren't alone. That we and the Lord are with them. We won't abandon them like the economy or the government has. Ya do seem cut out for this. Was the cloth your first choice?' asked Paddy.

'The Church was always a big part of our lives. Mother is so devout. Still goes to Mass twice a day on Sundays. She was delighted I went to the seminary. Father wasn't so sure. He tried to persuade me to go into architecture or engineering. He said it's what a young country needs. Not more priests. He's a Clerk of Works. He helped build many public buildings. Even did a couple here in Napier. Mother, however, won out in the end.'

'Smart man, your father,' added Paddy.

'Probably, but this is definitely what I should be doing. It's starting to have real meaning now. After they left me at college and went to Wanganui, the Church was a safe haven for me.'

'You make it sound as if they aren't that supportive of you,' said Paddy.

'I'm sure they loved me, but I haven't seen much of them since I was twelve. Christmas holidays and the odd time through the year. They had my younger brothers to worry about, and the youngest was a very late addition to the family, so he's taken up their time and energy. So they just left me at college,' said Al.

'Loved? And they don't now?' quizzed Paddy.

'Sorry. I didn't mean to imply that. Just a loose turn of phrase. What about you? Did you go to the seminary straight after school?' asked Al, trying to deflect the conversation from himself.

'Oh, crikey, no. Worked on the wharves for a while. Jumped on the ex-servicemen's land grants. I got a couple hundred acres between Willow Flat and Putere. Turned out to be not much cop at being a farmer, though. Had a couple of bad years and sold my land to the Heays boys. The Church seemed like a safe punt.'

'You mentioned the war yesterday,' said Al.

'I enlisted and was shipped off to France pretty quick, then I caught some shrapnel in one of the first big battles. Patched up and shipped home again. I think it was less than eighteen months from start to finish for me.'

A rather uneasy silence enveloped the sitting room. Paddy looked at Al with a slightly narrowed gaze.

Al broke the silence 'It's been another big day. So I'll turn in. Goodnight, Father Paddy.'

'Night, lad. Early start tomorrow for Mass.' Paddy stroked his chin with his thumb and fore-finger. He didn't notice his cigarette was about smoulder down to the fingers of his other hand.

The pews for Mass were almost full. Napier's Catholic

community had turned out in large numbers on this steamy Sunday morning. The air was already thick with the heat of the morning and that of the assembled bodies. Many ladies were waving small fans vigorously in front of their faces, while the men were doing the same with their trilbies and fedoras.

Paddy led Mass. Al enjoyed his relaxed and warm approach to the service. Paddy's natural personality shone through the rituals. Just before he called on Father Murphy to give the days' sermon, Paddy quickly introduced Al, telling the congregation that he would be with them for the next month and for everyone to warmly welcome him to the parish.

Father Murphy ascended to the pulpit. 'Today's sermon doesn't come from the scriptures, rather from our Catholic theology. In these very testing times there is the very real opportunity for people to use the economic downturn as an excuse to prefer a life of inactivity, of choosing to be sedentary. Centuries of Catholic theologians from Pope Gregory I, St. Aquinas and even Dante, remind us that sloth, or inactivity, the failure to fully use all the talents God has bestowed upon each and every one of us, is a Cardinal or Mortal Sin. I see sloth seeping into the parish and with it the threat of damnation for the guilty.'

Al's eyes were transfixed on the pulpit, his mouth slightly ajar. He could scarcely believe what Farther Murphy was preaching. Aware that he wasn't doing a good job of hiding is astonishment, he closed his mouth and quickly looked at Paddy, who was staring intently at a spot on the floor a couple of yards in front of him. Pressure on his interlocked fingers had turned them white. Tension showed on his jawline.

After little more than one day in the parish Al knew that to pile guilt on top of despondence wasn't what the parish needed. Unseen and almost incomprehensible forces had thrown scores of the parish into the quicksand of despair. How could the threat of damnation inspire, or at least, comfort the victims of the invisible hand of worldwide economic destruction?

Farther Murphy continued his dispatch. 'The teachings of St. Jerome gives us a clear and stark lesson: *fac et aliquid operis, ut semper te diabolus inveniat occupatum.* Which has been amended through the centuries to tell us that the devil finds work for idle hands to do. The results of this idleness are in plain view for all of us to see. Abuse of intoxicating liquor, gambling and criminality of various guises are clearly visible throughout the country and here in the parish. So there is a direct link between the mortal sin of sloth, brought about by unemployment, and commitment of crime and the breakdown of civil society. I commend to all parishioners to shun inactivity, to seek out any opportunity for work. Only through dedication to action and industry and through confession can one overcome and expel this mortal sin.'

The last few sentences of the sermon drifted into the rafters of the church. The necessity to prepare for communion broke Al's attention away from Father Murphy. Al studied the faces of everyone who came up for the sacraments. There was the same emptiness that he saw at St. Vincent's yesterday. Shouldn't this be a place of enlightenment? A place where you could be uplifted, or removed from the troubles of the world? If only for the time during Mass?

After communion, Al and Paddy quickly made their way to the front doors and started talking to the parishioners, wishing them a good day. All who stopped to talk to him welcomed him warmly to the parish. Elizabeth Bartholomew sidestepped the line for Paddy and cut in to see Al.

'Lovely to see you again Brother Albert. Everything going well so far?' she asked Al as her hand shook his.

'Mrs. Bartholomew, delighted to have you here at Mass. Yes, thank you very much. It's been a busy couple of days, which helps the settling-in process.' Al tried to extricate his hand from Elizabeth's grip. 'And Mr. Bartholomew?'

'He only comes to Mass once a fortnight. Not his week. I think I'm to do dinner for you and Father Paddy on Tuesday...'

Her words started to blur into an indiscernible hum, as Al's attention was diverted. A soft hint of lavender reached him. He took a moment to remember where he knew it from. He searched for the source. Was it the nurse from Friday? He quickly readjusted his line of vision, for someone who matched his memory of the nurse. Nothing. No one fit the bill. Just before he returned to Elizabeth, he thought he saw her. The same walk, come glide. She made her way away from the church, with her back to Al. Almost the same view he had at the hospital. Yes, that was her.

'Brother Albert? St. Vincent's yesterday. How was it?' Elizabeth's voice was a little terse.

'Sorry Mrs. Bartholomew. St. Vincent's? Yes, very interesting. I mean tough. Difficult to see so much suffering.'

'Things seem to be getting worse by the day. I better get going. See you Tuesday.'

'Yes, yes. See you then. Have a nice day,' Al stuttered. His eyes shot back to the footpath. The woman had disappeared.

* * *

Day after day, the sun baked Napier. Every day was clear, without a hint of moisture. By Wednesday, faces and stories were becoming familiar to Al. Peter O'Callaghan, a thick set rugby player who'd lost his job at the stock and station agency a couple of months ago, he was still positive and looking forward to the new football season. Edward Waka had pulled his son out of Te Aute Maori Boys' College to cut costs and help earn some extra money for the family. Dot McAlpine who's supplementing her family's diet by sneaking into market gardens and orchards at night and picking up fallen fruit. Her deep-set eyes couldn't hide her sadness and shame. Arnold Jacobsen, the son of a Danish migrant from down Norsewood way. He's a carpenter, but hasn't worked on a building site for nearly a year, just odd-jobbing whenever he could. With every person Al saw, every life story he heard, he questioned his own capacity for compassion, and the words of Father Murphy. He marvelled at Paddy's bottomless reservoir of optimism. Never a harsh word nor disparaging comment, and no discernible note of negativity. His brightness was soaked up by those he talked with. Everyone seemed lifted by even the shortest chat with Paddy. To Al, he appeared deeply loved by the people of St. Patrick's. Now there's something to be emulated, thought Al.

Just after midday on Friday, Al and Paddy were on the road, covering the five miles to Taradale as fast as the old Ford was capable of. Mount Saint Mary's Seminary was just out in the country on the north-west corner of town, set up in the small hills that overlook the town. Down on the flats at the base of the hills were nearly ten acres of vines.

The seminary itself held an imposing position, perched up on the hill. An all wood two storey building some seventy yards wide with an impressive columned entrance. As Paddy pulled in around the back they were met by a priest in a flowing cassock. Small in stature, barely 5ft 7 inches, and slight in build, his sharp features gave him a slightly impish look. Narrow eyes were magnified behind wire rim glasses.

'Good afternoon, Father Lynch. Brother Robertson, welcome home. It really doesn't feel like three years that you've been away,' said Father Connolly, offering his hand to both men.

'Thank you, Father Connolly. I'm delighted to be back,' Al replied.

'How was your trip up from Wellington? Not too rough, I hope,' said Connolly.

'Yes, thank you Father. The voyage had its moments, but here safely. Thanks be to God.'

'He looks after his faithful servants. How are you settling into St. Patrick's? I think it will be a great enhancement to your education,' said Connolly.

'So far so good. Father Paddy is looking after me,' said Al.

'That's Father Lynch. Don't forget to respect those ahead of you. How was your time at university? Good reports have preceded your return. We're looking forward to your contributions to your final year here.'

'It was a great few years. I'm truly blessed to have been given the opportunity. I cannot thank you enough for allowing me to get my degree.' Al showed as much deference as he could.

'Wonderful. Father Lynch, make sure you don't lead Brother Robertson astray while he is in your care. Watch out for those parish dances, Brother Robertson. They are legend around here. I understand there is one scheduled soon.'

'Yes, Father. Friday the 30th actually,' Paddy replied. 'You are welcome to attend.'

'Thank you for the offer, but I'll be busy preparing for the return of the seminarians from camp, so I'll RSVP in the negative. Now, I'll organise someone to bring Father Gondringer and Brother Clairet up from the vineyard. You both know your way around. Brother Robertson, again, welcome back. We are all looking forward to the retreat in February and the final profession of your class.' With that Connolly was gone, down a corridor and into his office.

'Well now. Someone's very much in the good books. I haven't seen him that chatty or complimentary in quite a while,' said Paddy.

'That was a bit embarrassing. What do you say when he tells you he's expecting big things from you? Nothing like a bit of added pressure right off the bat,' said Al.

'No worries, Al. You'll be fine. He'll forget about you within a month or two of the start of classes. Come on, let's go find the others. I'll leave you three to talk vines and wine. I'm off to see what Matron McNeil's got brewing in the kitchen.'

Later that evening Al and Paddy relaxed in the living room of their cottage, Paddy with a cigarette and a whiskey, Al with his pipe and a sherry. Elizabeth had come and gone with the evening meal, although as a result of overindulging at lunch up at the Seminary, they hadn't eaten much, to Elizabeth's annoyance. A warm breeze ventured in through the open window, picking up the smoke and making it dance and swirl.

'What do you think?' Al quizzed Paddy as he looked out the window to inky blue late evening sky.

'We'll be fine. No worries at all. There's some rain coming but it ain't meant to arrive till Sunday. Besides, all our bad weather comes from the east, I reckon if we get any here at all it'll be light enough. Come on. You're itching to get up into the hills. This will be our last free day before you have to head back to seminary,' Paddy almost pleaded to Al.

'All right then. Let's get an early start though, to make the most of the daylight.'

Al spent the rest of the night preparing his pack for tomorrow's excursion. He pulled the battered rucksack out of the bottom of his wardrobe. The canvas felt coarse as he dusted it off. He eyed it affectionately, memories came back of hikes in the ranges around Wellington with his school mates. Al collected the supplies they'd need; knife, short length of rope, small tarpaulin, first aid supplies of bandages, cotton wool, a small bottle of iodine, a couple of dressings. They'd grab some food in the morning before they set off. He pulled out his tramping boots, still covered with mud. Thick woollen socks, undershirt, light cotton shirt and khaki trousers, and mountain jacket. He gave them a once over. All fine.

CHAPTER 5

The day dawned sunny and bright; a perfect day to head to the bush. Al got dressed into his hiking clothes. He fitted comfortably into his old faithful gear. It felt good to be out of the Roman collar, if only for one day. As normal, Paddy was up first, he was in the kitchen making breakfast. 'Morning, Brother Al. Scrambled eggs on toast with bacon alright?' he asked as Al walked in.

They tucked into breakfast; thick slabs of bread lightly toasted and lathered with quickly melting butter accompanied the bacon and eggs, then made their lunch and prepared to leave. Al grabbed two self-capping bottles, filled them with water and put them in his bag. Paddy went out to the garage and backed the Model T down the driveway. Al felt a slight breeze on his face, coming out of the south-west, as he waited on the driveway. He climbed onto the passenger seat, his pack landed with a thud on the back seat.

'All set?' asked Paddy.

'Raring to go,' replied Al. 'Where's your gear?'

'Right here,' said Paddy, tapping a small satchel on the floor of the car.

'Doesn't look like you have a lot in there.'

'Got me jacket and a couple of other supplies,' Paddy replied with a wry smile.

Heading north toward Eskdale, the sun streamed through the windscreen, bleaching colour from their vision. The Bay glistened in the mid-summer sun. They trundled past orchards and market gardens with locals selling their produce at roadside stalls. They turned left onto the Taupo Road, and the road started to climb.

Paddy struggled with the heavy steering wheel on the many twists and turns as they headed into the Maungaharuru Ranges. The Model T slowed considerably on the accent. The gradient caused the old car to cough and splutter. Just after Te Pohue, Paddy got off the main road, parking next to a small wooden sign marked with an arrow and "Mohaka River".

As Al got out of the car, he noticed the wind had picked up significantly. He grabbed his rucksack from the back seat and put it on his back. 'Want me to lead the way?' he asked Paddy.

'You're the expert in these things, lad. All yours.' Paddy deferred to Al.

The bush was thick, right up to the roadside. There was a small opening in the trees next to the sign. The bush swallowed them as soon as they stepped in. The bright sunlight and blue sky immediately disappeared. Thin shards of sunlight pierced the canopy like spotlights, illuminating small random patches of bush. The air felt cool and damp on their faces as they walked. Ferns of every shape and size lined the track. Virtually impenetrable stands of totora, matai and rimu dominated the forest on both sides. The odd punga poked its fern topped head through wherever there was space. Moss and creepers covered most surfaces. Dark and dank, yet full of life. Tui's serenaded them from the tree tops with their hypnotic verse. Fantail's darted and swooped around them, their bright white tails a stark contrast against the forest of almost every imaginable shade of green. Weka's foraged on the forest floor, barely noticing the human intruders to their world.

'I'd forgotten how different the air tastes in the bush,' said Paddy as he filled his lungs.

'It's thick with oxygen and plant decay. It's wonderful. I love it,' replied Al.

'Yeah, cheers for the biology lesson. Not sure I needed to know that much,' quipped Paddy.

The track, although narrow and uneven, only had a gradual

incline for the first couple of miles. 'You doing alright back there?' Al called to Paddy.

'May have almost ten years, a couple of stone and some shrapnel on you, but you ain't getting away from me. Right behind ya and feeling good.'

'Good man, Father Patrick. I wouldn't want you falling off the pace.'

'Watch it whipper-snapper. Built for endurance, me. Can go all day.'

Half an hour in and the track got noticeably steeper. They were now climbing quickly. Behind him, Al heard Paddy's breathing grow shorter and heavier. Al sensed the light had changed, it was dimmer, flatter. Ten minutes later the track started to go downhill into a gully. It opened up to reveal a creek, little more than ten yards from bank to bank.

'This is pretty much the start of the Mohaka River, eh,' Paddy said sucking air as he caught his breath. 'The Ripia and Taharua join a ways up stream. It's not much here, but by the time she gets to Willow Flat and Raupunga, she's a decent size.' Paddy told Al.

For the first time since they left the car Al could see the sky. Grey had replaced blue.

'Shall we have our first break?' Al asked.

'Blimey. Thought you'd never ask. I'm ready for a sit down,' Paddy replied, dabbing his brow with his sleeve.

They used a fallen tree by the bank for their rest spot. Al took off his pack and took out two apples and one of the bottles of water, gave an apple and the bottle to Paddy, who took a drink and handed it back to Al.

Al swallowed a couple of big mouthfuls. The water felt good. A calm quietness enveloped them for a few minutes as they rested. Although they were both educated men of the cloth, they were still New Zealand males. Sometimes silence was the most effective way to communicate.

Al stepped down the bank to the creek. The water chilled his hands as he filled the bottle. He saw neatly arranged stones in a line stretching from bank to bank. 'A few people must have come through here. There's a nice line of stepping stones,' Al said pointing out the stones to Paddy.

'Handy. Didn't much like the idea of getting me feet wet.'

'Ah. Getting wet and dirty is half the fun of tramping.'

'Maybe for you, me boy, but I prefer to stay dry,' said Paddy.

The creek and its stone covered shallows formed a grey gash in the blanket of greens as it snaked its way through the hills. It made for a dramatic contrast in colours and texture; harsh and metallic against the luxuriant softness of the bush.

Down at the riverbed, Al bounded across, two stones at a time. Paddy gingerly took each one in turn. On the opposite bank, Al gave Paddy a hand to get up from the creek bed. Al wasn't sure if it was a splash from the creek or a rain drop, but he felt water hit his hands as they turned away from the creek and back into the bush.

The terrain on this side was flatter than before. The easier going gave Al a chance to let his mind wander. He was delighted to be back in the bush. The closeness to raw nature, to God's creative hand, its tranquillity moved him. More than churches or cathedrals, this is where Al felt closest to the Lord. It was the balance, all components of plant and animal life seamlessly working together to achieve a symmetry. He loved the diversity, so utterly unique to this land.

Paddy also took advantage of the gentler ground. He slipped his hand into his satchel, unscrewed the top on the hip flask he'd put in the bag the night before. He took a quick gulp while Al wasn't looking and back into the satchel.

Ten minutes into the second leg of their hike, Al noticed the familiar, slap, slap of rain hitting the canopy high above them. So thick was the bush that no drops yet reached them on the ground.

He wanted a clearing so he could gauge how heavy the rain was. They had only packed for a short day tramp. The bad weather was supposed to be a day away, so Paddy had assured him.

Thirty minutes later Al got his wish. The bush suddenly stopped and there was a clear space, about half an acre in size. Tussock grass, flax and ferns covered the ground, but not a single outlying tree. Their appearance startled a group of Kereru wood pigeons. Their green and white bodies arched skyward. Al looked up as he followed their flight. They were enclosed on three sides by steep hills. The rain was light enough, but steady. The sky had darkened from when they were at the Mohaka River. There's more rain in them, Al thought to himself. It's only going to get heavier.

'What do you think?' Al asked of Paddy.

'I reckon its lunchtime. Whip out those sammies, Al.'

'No, Paddy. About the weather. Should we keep going?'

'Ah sure. It's only light. We ain't had a drop on us in the bush. She'll be right,' said Paddy.

'I don't know, Paddy. It looks pretty dark up there.'

'About two mile from here, we'll run into the Ripia. Why don't we use that as our turn around spot? That will be six, maybe seven miles in total on the way out. Go on, I'm feeling bonza, just getting into the swing.'

'Two miles?' Al asked.

'Absolutely, no more. The way we're trucking, we'll do that in less than half an hour.'

'Alright. Let's eat and have a drink and be moving again in ten minutes.'

'Excellent. Now get that food out, lad.'

They found a spot just on the edge of the clearing, still inside the bush, so they were out of the rain. 'Bloody good sammies. Even if I do say so myself,' Paddy said. 'So when did you start tramping? You must have been a young pup.'

'My mates and I were always tearing around the hills in

Wellington as kids, but it was a school camp up in the Akatarawa's in my Third Form year that got me hooked,' said Al.

'Hmm, so you were about thirteen. A very early start.'

'With the family up in Wanganui by that stage, my weekends were free to fill. I wasn't much of a winter sportsman, tennis is my main love, so a couple of mates and I would head up into the bush whenever we could. It's been in my blood ever since. You mentioned you were in the war. Do you mind chatting about it?' Al took the last bite of his sandwich as he finished talking.

'Not much to tell. I told you it was all over in about eighteen months for me. We shipped out in June of 15. Thank the Lord we missed that mess in Gallipoli. The voyage was the best part of being in the Army. We stopped off in Perth and Capetown. Hell, I'd never even been to Wellington before I joined up, and here we were in places we'd only just read about. Bloody amazing.'

'So how did you get the leg wound?' Al asked.

'Caught some shrapnel going over the top. Got no more than ten steps when a shell landed behind us. Next thing I know I'm face down in the mud, can't move me right leg. Mind numbing pain from me toes to my shoulder. Covered in mud and blood. One of the medics drags me back into the trench and carries me to the aid station. All got a bit hazy from then on. Next thing I remember was being in a field hospital. They shipped me back to England. Went to the Kiwi hospital at Brockenhurst. Bloody brilliant there. Went through recuperation, but I lost too much of the back of me leg to go back. I was home by Christmas in 16. That was my war. I was at sea and in hospitals longer than I was at the front.'

There was a flash of light and Paddy's face was consumed in the smoke of another cigarette, disguising the watery glaze across his eyes as his mind wandered again to memories he had tried to bury deep: mud so deep you couldn't see your ankles, sometimes up to your knees after a good rain. He couldn't even stand the smell of mud now. Smells? So many of them fought for attention then – gunpowder from your rifle and exploding artillery stung your nostrils, but at least it helped to swallow the stench of death and decay.

'Right, time to go?' asked Paddy.

'May as well,' but it didn't feel right to Al to keep going with the weather closing in. He knew it wasn't the rain on your face you needed to worry about. It's the rain up in the high country. What it does to creeks, streams and rivers in the blink of an eye. That's the real danger.

They crossed the clearing and headed back into the bush. The Kereru still skimmed the edges of the bush, as they tried to find a perfect roosting spot. Low cloud cascaded down the hills. Mist swirled through the tree tops like restless spirits released from their tombs.

By now the rain had accumulated enough to send large drops down onto them from the canopy. The ground was heavier, with pools of water in spots where the overhead cover cleared. The track went into a tight curve and Al disappeared from view. Paddy slowed his pace and managed to take another swig from his flask before he rounded the curve himself.

They came across a large fallen tree across the path. A grand old totora had succumbed to age and the elements. Its plunge to the forest floor had cleared a small swath in the overhead cover. Rain poured through the hole in the forest.

'Careful here, Paddy. Best way to handle one this size is to sit on it then swing your legs over to the other side. I'll go first and help you over.' Al made his way over the tree, the water logged moss left its damp print on the seat of his pants. He called Paddy to come across. 'That's the way, now just spin around so you're facing me. Perfect.'

Another few hundred yards down the track there was a much smaller log blocking the path. 'No need to sit on this one, Paddy.

Straight over it.' Al said as he took it in one stride. Al was already more than ten yards past the log when he heard a screech and a thump.

'Bugger me bloody days,' screamed Paddy back up the track.

Al turned to see Paddy on the ground clutching his ankle. He double timed it back to the log. He took off his pack and knelt down. 'What happened, Paddy?'

'Stepped on that stupid log. Slipped on the moss. Went over on me bloody ankle.'

'How bad is it?'

'Not bloody good. I felt a pop.' Paddy's face contorted in pain as he spoke.

'You'll be right. How's it feeling?' Al asked as he turned back to face Paddy.

'Bloody sore. Throbbing like crazy. And it's me good bloody leg, too. Shit.'

'Easy, Paddy. Just take a few deep breaths. OK?' Paddy nodded and winced. 'I'll just loosen your boot and give it a once over.'

Al thought he picked up a trace of whiskey on Paddy's breath. He put it out of his mind, thinking Paddy surely wouldn't be that stupid to drink while on a hike. Slowly and with as much care as he could, Al took off Paddy's boot and felt his ankle. He could feel a lot of heat around it and there were signs of swelling already. Al noticed some scaring and dry skin on Paddy's feet. Remnants of trench foot he assumed. He prodded the ankle in a couple of places.

'Hells bells, man. Steady on,' groaned Paddy.

'Sorry, Paddy. I'm trying to be a delicate as I can.'

'Try a bit harder, lad,' snorted Paddy, his breaths now short, shallow and rapid.

Al took out one of the water bottles and poured some water onto the ankle. 'I think it's a bad sprain, not broken, but it'll be difficult for you to walk out. I'll put on a bandage to try to contain the swelling as best we can.' He applied the bandage, gingerly slipped the boot back on Paddy's foot and tied up the laces. 'Up on your feet. We'll see if you can put any weight on it.'

Paddy cried out as his foot touched the ground. 'No good. Can't even straighten it.' Shards of excruciating pain shot up his leg with every heartbeat, like ten thousand pin pricks.

'Take it slowly. Nice and gentle,' Al encouraged.

He stumbled forward, losing his balance as he tried to take a step. Al caught his fall and eased him down onto the log.

'Nothing for it then. I'll carry you out,' said Al, patting Paddy on the shoulder as he spoke.

'No you bloody won't. Don't be silly. Just go out and get some help. There's got to be a farm close by the main road. You could be there and back in three to four hours. I'll be right.'

'Paddy, listen to me. I'm not going to leave you here. This weather is getting worse by the minute. We're close to that river. The way it's raining it could flood at any time. Certainly within four hours. Neither of us has wet weather gear and I only have a small tarp, which would give us minimal shelter at best. It may take a lot longer to get out, but we stand a better chance together than apart. Discussion over. Agreed?'

'Sounds like I have no choice.'

'Right. It took us just over an hour and a half of straight hiking time to get here. It'll be nearly three hours to get out, plus quite a few breathers.' Al put his ruck sack on his front and crouched down close to the log. 'Jump on, Paddy. Piggyback style.'

'Crikey. Haven't done this since I took that shrapnel at Ypres.'

Fifty minutes later they arrived back at the clearing where they stopped for lunch. 'You want to put your jacket on?' Al asked Paddy.

'Jacket? What?'

'The one you said you had in your satchel.'

'Oh, yeah, right. Um, sure,' Paddy stuttered in his reply.

Al lowered Paddy to the ground. 'You want me to help you?' Al offered as he reached for Paddy's small bag.

'No, no. I'm OK. It's me leg that's knackered. Arms are fine,' Paddy's reply was curt and clipped as he snatched the satchel from Al's grasp.

'Suit yourself. Was just trying to help.'

Rain lashed down at them on every step across the open space, soaking them quickly. Now there was no view of the hills. Dense angry clouds, five different shades of grey, swallowed the hills, viciously throwing their contents down to earth. A short break for a drink and then off again. Al could sense not only the elements, but time was against them. Every minute was critical now. After another hour and a half of leg burning slog through the bush they saw the Mohaka River.

'Bloody hell. It's a ruddy torrent,' shouted Paddy

'It must be really chucking it down back up in the hills,' Al replied.

The gentle creek they crossed a few hours ago had gone, replaced by a vicious cauldron of dirty, foam topped water. Spray spat at them on the bank, which itself had chunks carved out of it. Rocks clattered downstream at a bone breaking pace.

'Ya reckon we can make it across?'

'Not much option, Paddy.' Al raised his voice above the water's roar. 'Stay out in this with no tent or wet weather gear? I wouldn't like our chances.'

'You can't carry me across that though.'

'Too right. That'd be mad.' Al dug into his pack and pulled out a short length of rope. 'Here, we'll tether ourselves.' Al put one end around Paddy, looping it through his belt then tying it off with a strong knot. He did the same to himself. 'Alright. We need to stay close together. The length between us is about four feet, but you need to stay right behind me. With me?' Paddy nodded. 'Good. If one of us slips, the other will be close enough to lend a hand quickly. Down side is there's no slack. If someone takes a bad spill, likely they'll take the other with them. Ready?'

'No, but we're going, ain't we?' replied Paddy.

'Paddy, we're going to be fine. Let's go. Short, powerful steps, OK?'

'How about short powerful hops?'

'That'll do.' Al eyed the water in front of him. Where to cross? The stones they stepped across earlier were submerged, probably swept away. About seven yards downstream Al saw a potential. The creek widened by a few yards and it looked like it flattened out for a short stretch. 'Down there, Paddy. Looks like the flow is a little calmer. Jump on.'

Paddy clambered onto Al's back for the short trip down, then slid off. 'It's a little further across but the force of the water should be a bit less.'

'Yep. Looks bloody tranquil.'

Al looked for the right spot. He gave Paddy a quick nod and entered the water. Paddy's sarcasm wasn't far off the mark. The water pulled at his legs with the force of a horse. Al squatted slightly and leaned upstream. The rope went slack as Paddy followed Al into the creek. Paddy grabbed Al's pack to steady himself.

'What did I just say? Tranquil. It'll be a miracle if we make it.'

'We will, Paddy.' Ten, maybe twelve yards, probably fifteen steps to get across. We'll make it. We will make it, Al whispered to himself.

Gingerly they half stepped their way across. Water that had barely covered their boots on the outward crossing was now at the top of their thighs, at times rising to their waists. It tugged and clawed at them, sapping their dwindling energy. It was no more than three yards to the bank when Al heard the sound. The clunk, thud, clank of rock hitting rock. Al looked back upriver. He quickly scanned the water for movement. He saw it, partially submerged as it cascaded toward them.

'Paddy. Move.' He shouted and pulled the rope with all the force he could muster.

Just a little too late. The boulder clipped Paddy's right leg as he fell toward Al. The force took him away from Al's grasp. Paddy disappeared into the water. The rope went taught. Al knew he was also in trouble. He braced against the water behind him and Paddy's drag in front, but to no avail. He lost his foothold and was sucked into the water.

They careened downstream. 'Head up. Keep your head up.' Al barked, as much to himself as to Paddy. He tried to gain a foothold. Paddy rose and fell with the flow. It was too difficult to stand. Swim; or ride the flow into the bank where the only options.

Every fibre and sinew of his body was on fire. Nerves flashed conflicting and urgent messages from all parts of his body. The water clawed at him like the demons of a nightmarish Bosch vision, dragging him to certain doom. He had to stay sharp, look for an opening, any chance. The line suddenly went slack. Paddy was wedged on a large rock, its top above the waterline. Al kicked to make sure he made the rock. Miss it and he'd be gone, taking Paddy with him. Al stretched out his arms to grab the boulder. He hit it with a force that partially winded him, but he stuck. This was their chance.

'You alright, Paddy?'

'Bonza. Just having a wee rest,' Paddy shouted at Al.

'Get as high as you can,' said Al, as Paddy shuffled up the rock so just his calves were in the water. 'You got your breath back?' Al asked.

'Yeah, beauty. Feeling good, Al. Ready for another swim.'

'We've got about four yards to go. With a good push off, it'll be five decent steps.'

'No worries, Al. I'm sure not staying here.'

'Wrap your arms around my neck. Let your legs float. When I say the word, push off with your good leg.'

'Will give it a crack,' said Paddy.

'Slide down and grab a hold.'

Paddy slipped down the rock, draped his arms around Al's neck and shoulders. 'Ready, mate.'

'OK. One, two, three, push,' shouted Al.

They plunged into the water. The force hit them hard. They made a good yard or more. Al struggled to steady himself but managed to get a decent foothold. First step. Second step. Two more and he'd be able to reach the bank. A half pace. He steadied himself. 'Hold on, Paddy.'

He pushed off and up. They surged through the water. Al hit the bank waist high. He stretched out his arms and grabbed hold of some ferns. The foliage held.

'Paddy, slide around to my left. I'll shield you from the water.'

As quickly as he could, Paddy moved off Al's back. Al untied his end of the rope and wrapped it around his right hand. 'OK. On my count, jump up off your good leg. I'll give you a push up. Ready? One, two, three. Jump.' Paddy lifted off with what little energy he had left. Al gave him a hoist using Paddy's belt as a lever.

Paddy landed with a thud, his lower legs dangling over the bank. One last effort now. Al went into a shallow squat and pushed up, pulling forward with his arms. He landed, exhausted, next to Paddy. They both lay virtually motionless for a couple of minutes. Their upper bodies surged and sank as they drew in deep breaths. Adrenaline laced blood raced through them. 'How are you doing, Paddy?' The roar of the water forced Al to almost shout at his companion.

'Good as gold, Al, but it may have put me off swimming for life. That was a bloody close shave, eh?' Not quite an adequate description, Al thought.

They had ended up just over a hundred yards away from the track. To get back to the path would be the next challenge. No clear route, thick bush, right up to the bank in some places, with some fallen trees for good measure. The track will be the easy part.

'Let's take a couple of minutes. Then we'll make our way back to the track. You alright with that?' Al asked Paddy.

'Al, you're bleeding. Your head. It's running down your face.' Paddy said as he tapped the left side of his temple.

Al felt his head. Too wet to tell where the source was. No specific pain to pinpoint it either. He pulled his hand away and sure enough, blood on his palm. 'Bugger.'

'Swearing? It must serious.' A look of amazement drifted across Paddy's face. It was the first time he'd heard even mild profanity from Al.

'Paddy, for the love of God. Can you be serious for even a minute,' snapped Al, 'We could have died in there and all you're doing is cracking jokes.'

'Sorry, lad. I know you bloody well saved us there. I'm just trying to ease the tension.'

Al rummaged through his waterlogged pack for the cotton wool. He tore off a wedge and mopped up the blood on his face and dabbed the area where he thought the wound was. 'You ready to go? We haven't got much daylight left. It could take more than an hour to get out.'

'Aye, aye, captain. Ready when you are,' said Paddy.

'Jump up then.'

They picked their way through the bush to the track. They kept to the bank as much as they could as the vegetation was a little thinner there. After nearly ten minutes, which included a couple of rests, they found the track.

Al looked up at the incline facing them to get out of the gully. His heart sank a little. The steepest part of the track with energy levels near empty. Barely two hundred yards to cover, but Al knew it would tax him to the core. He tried to sound positive, 'Righty-o then. Let's make a start.'

Al's thighs shouted their anger at him with every step. His muscles were starting to spasm and cramp. For the first time during their trial, Al feared they may not make it. If his legs gave up or he lost his footing on this slope, he wouldn't have the strength to keep them from tumbling back to the river. He slowed his pace slightly, took extra care with every step.

Paddy picked up on the change 'You OK, Al?'

'Good as gold. Just making sure of my footing.'

'Take as many rests as you need. You must be bloody knackered.'

'We'll be…, at the top…, soon enough' Al's voice couldn't hide his exhaustion. It took just over half an hour to reach the crest.

'All down hill from here now, Al,' said Paddy.

'Easy to say from up there.'

'Touché,' said Paddy.

Although the last two miles where all on a decline, it still took nearly an hour. Any remaining light had almost gone as they cleared the bush. The last half mile was walked in virtual darkness as the bush soaked up the last light. Al fought to concentrate his last ounces of energy onto the track, now thick mud. His mouth was open, gulping in air, streams of saliva dribbled over his lower lip. Each step was laboured, his vision was blurred with rain, sweat, blood and exhaustion.

Out in the open the full power of the weather became apparent. The rain attacked them from a thick sullen sky. Wind whipped all around, from no given direction. Heavy rain drops stung their faces as they made their way to the car.

'Bad weather…, only comes…, from the east…, you say?' Al fought to get the words out.

'I might have got that one wrong, lad.'

Al squatted down and let Paddy off his back. Paddy leaned against the Model T. He opened up the passenger door and positioned himself inside. Al leaned against the wheel arch for a minute, his upper body heaving with every intake of air. He finally pulled himself to the driver's side and got in next to Paddy. He lowered his head on the steering wheel, as he tried to recover from the biggest physical challenge of his life. He gulped down huge breaths, his heart almost jumped out of his chest with every beat. His thighs still quivered and knotted every few seconds.

He didn't notice or feel Paddy's hand on his shoulder until Paddy gently tightened his grip. 'Bloody remarkable strength and courage, lad. That's the bravest thing I've seen since the War.'

Al turned his head slightly to face Paddy, his mouth still open. A small nod and mouthing thanks was all he could muster as fatigue swept over him and adrenaline levels started to plummet. It took Al a few minutes to be able to speak coherently. 'First stop, the hospital for both us.' Blood continued to trickle down Al's face.

'You sure you can handle the old girl?' asked Paddy.

'Not really, but we'll give it a crack.' Paddy had given Al a couple of lessons in how to drive the Model T and its peculiarities. But two or three laps around the block were different to nearly twenty miles in a storm with roads that resembled rivers.

'Treat her like a lady. Gently most of the time, but be firm when you have to.' Al gave Paddy a curious look at his instructions. 'Not that you'd know much about that. But you know what I mean,' added Paddy. 'I'll give her a crank to start her up.'

Al put the old car into first gear and pulled out onto the road. The little wiper blades were going as fast as they could; but made no impact on the water sheeting down the glass.

'Don't know which is scarier. The creek or this.' Al said as he squinted out at the road, his knuckles already turning white as he clenched the steering wheel a little harder.

'She's bloody rough. Take it easy, eh Al.'

'Absolutely,' Al almost shouted in reply.

'Enough dramas for one day. Let's have an uneventful

run into town.' Paddy said as much to nature and God as to Al.

The rain eased almost immediately as they came out of the hills. By the time they got to Napier it was barely drizzle.

'Right. Let's get you taken care of.' Al said as they parked by the entrance to the hospital.

They emerged a couple of hours later, slightly less bedraggled than when they went in. Al helped Paddy down onto a bench before he went to get the car. As he did, Al felt that odd sensation of being watched, almost as if fingers tapped your shoulder, yet no one close by you when you turned around. He definitely sensed eyes on him. To his left there was a small group of nurses. Some were smoking, some were talking, but one was looking straight at him. She was a little shorter than the others, but her mesmerising blue eyes were trained on him. Self-conscious and slightly embarrassed at his rough appearance, he wanted to look away, but those eyes, they rooted him to the spot and looked deep inside him. They locked on each other for only a couple of seconds yet it felt like time was suspended. She slowly returned her attention to her colleagues, yet her eyes never left him as her head turned. He felt those eyes had just pierced his soul.

CHAPTER 6

25ᵗʰ January 1931

A dust cloud exploded from the back of the Model T as they drove up the track to Mount Saint Mary's. It was their first visit to the seminary since their escapade in the hills the previous week. Al was eager to see Father Gondringer and Paddy was after some sympathy from Matron McNeil, and a roast lamb dinner.

They were about to go their separate ways when Father Connolly appeared from nowhere. His eyes narrowed to such an extent that Al thought he looked like a black clad Cyclops.

'If it isn't our very own Don Quixote and Sancho Panza. Didn't know there were any windmills up in the Maungaharuru's,' Connolly said with a sneer on his face. Paddy straightened, inhaled deeply, he knew what was coming next. 'We know all our actions reflect on the Church. Don't we?' Neither Paddy nor Al offered a reply. 'Wandering around the mountains isn't the type of activity we feel is best. Let alone almost getting yourselves killed.'

'We were never in any real danger, Father Connolly.' Al tried to defend them.

'Do not interrupt me, boy. This isn't a discussion. Father Lynch, I'd expected better from you. Then again, probably not. I won't be hearing about any further adventures from you two. Will I?' One final glare and he was gone.

Paddy huffed and walked quickly toward the kitchen and sanctuary, 'Fuck it.'

'Patrick.' There was genuine shock in Al's voice.

'Al, that was rubbish. We come close to buying the farm and all he thinks about is how it looks for the bloody Church. Only gives a shit about the Church's reputation. And his.'

'He does have a point. It was a little embarrassing,' added Al.

'Don't be a pup. There's bigger fish to fry than us tripping over in the bush. We're just an easy target and he likes his cheap shots,' said Paddy.

'Should we just go?' asked Al.

'Nah. You go see Father Gondringer and I'll get our dinner from Matron. We'll take it home. Don't think we'll be welcome up here tonight.'

30th January 1931

As she entered the living room, Abigail McCarthy did a twirl and threw a purple silk scarf over her shoulders. 'So, what do you think?' she asked her housemates.

'Sensational,' replied Patricia Murray, who was seated closest to the door.

'Fabulous. You look amazing,' said Jessica Tomlinson.

'A little short, isn't it?' said Abby's cousin, Moira.

'Short? It's a blimming inch and a half below the knee. It is summer, unless you've forgotten,' Abby said, turning to her with her hands on her hips.

'Don't listen to her, love. It's stunning,' Jessica interjected.

Abby did one more turn, then flattened down the light cotton floral print dress. 'Shoes OK?' she asked looking down at the cream suede thick heeled pumps.

'Top stuff. Is that the hat you're wearing? Then a perfect combo,' replied Patricia.

Abby held up her cream cloche style hat, with a purple ribbon and bow.

'Doctor Peters will have the most dashing partner at the dance,' said Jess.

'Just to mark your card, he lost his wife during the flu epidemic and that still comes up every so often,' Patricia said as she stood up and adjusted Abby's scarf.

'And be prepared to talk mainly about work,' added Jess.

Abby looked at them both with a quizzical stare.

'He has taken both of us out before, a couple of years ago now,' Jess replied to Abby's unasked question.

'Actually, a handful of the single nurses at the hospital, to be honest,' added Patricia.

'Wonderful. My cousin is being taken out by the biggest cad in town. That's it, you're not going anywhere tonight,' Moira interjected.

'He's not like that at all. He's a very sweet man, just a bit lonely. We think he's just desperate to get married again,' Jess responded.

'But, I'm not. I don't want to be someone's consolation prize, third choice, or worse. I'm not interested in stepping out with someone just because I'm the next best available,' Abby said.

'Sorry, that didn't come out right,' said Jess.

'He is very gentlemanly. We can't hold it against him that he does want to be married again. It's difficult to meet new people outside the hospital, you know the hours we all work, even more so for the doctors. Relax, you'll have a lovely time,' Patricia tried to defuse the tension by rubbing Abby's shoulders. 'If he's not your type, then so be it. He's not going to go down on one knee and propose tonight.'

Abby exhaled and gave a little nod, just as the sound from the front door knocker boomed through the house. Both Abby and Patricia jumped, they fell into an embrace, laughing loudly.

* * *

The parish dance was in full swing by the time Al and Paddy arrived. The hall was full to the gills, nearly 250 in attendance, according to Elizabeth Bartholomew, who was selling tickets. Al counted eight musicians in the band, pumping out the latest swing and big band numbers. He recognised a Gershwin song, followed by one by Duke Ellington. It didn't appear that many waltzes or Gay Gordon's would be getting an airing tonight. The hall was alive, it heaved and surged with energy, certainly not the staid and polite affairs he'd been used to back in Wellington. There was a rawness, an edge to this. A thin layer of smoke had built up already near the ceiling. Covert and not so covert drinking was going on. So much for Mrs. Bartholomew's fruit punch. It was being fortified by many an elixir. He didn't classify himself as a prude, and he certainly wasn't a fire and brimstone type, extoling damnation about the odd low level social vice. There were enough of them about already. Still, the vibrancy and intensity of the celebrations caught him by surprise.

They mingled for a few minutes, then made their way over to the bar. Al got his customary sweet sherry while Paddy opted for homemade lemonade. 'The hard stuff?' said Al.

'I think I'll take it handy for now. Maybe a glass too many up the seminary,' replied Paddy.

For the first time that evening Al noticed the large number of young women in the hall. Could well be the largest female crowd he'd been in since his college dances. For many years Al had been taught that women fell into two broad categories: Saints or harlots and jezebels. Quite how that squared with reality, Al couldn't see. It certainly didn't fit the women of St. Patrick's parish. He looked around the crowd: blondes, brunettes, the odd red head; tall, short, slim, some carrying a bit extra, but all dressed to the nines. A few outfits were a little threadbare and faded. Still, very eye catching. Suddenly Dorothy O'Sullivan was in front of him. She was neither young or tall, nor slim. That took care of his previous thoughts.

'Come, Brother Robertson. Up on the dance floor.' With one sharp tug of her meaty arm, she had Al up on his feet and twirling to the music.

'Good luck,' shouted Paddy with a chuckle.

'You're quite the dancer, Brother. So how do you like our little parish?' asked Dorothy.

'I'm really enjoying it. Napier's a nice place and everyone's been so friendly,' replied Al.

'Glad to hear it. I know Father Lynch is delighted to have you here.'

The band struck up another number before Al had a chance to reply. A couple of dances later Al managed to prise himself away from Mrs. O'Sullivan's vice like grip. Picking his way through the sea of gyrating limbs, Al looked for Paddy. Their glasses were there, but no sign of Paddy. A quick scan of the nearby area drew a blank.

He saw a familiar face, Mary Simpson. It had been two weeks since he'd seen her. He was glad to see her out and about. A layer of make-up was noticeable, but even this couldn't completely cover her bruises. Al stepped towards her, but Mary gave a quick shake of her head and pointed with her eyes to a man a few feet to her left. Al acknowledged the signal, presuming it was Jerry. She mouthed 'thank you' before she stepped to her husband. How can Mary stay with Jerry, and how could Paddy justify not going to the police? Maybe he was being naïve, but beating your wife was a crime. He wanted to tell her that he would support her if she wanted to break away, but knew it wouldn't happen and his intervention was likely only to cause more tension and stress for her. He would have to deal with his own internal conflict and try to reconcile it.

He turned back to face the dance floor and saw another

person he recognised, Doctor Peters, who treated Mary up at the hospital. He was dancing with a woman who looked familiar, but he couldn't definitely say he knew. She wore a cream hat pulled low so that he couldn't see her eyes. He watched them for a minute or two, he wasn't sure why these two captured his attention above the other couples, something about the woman pulled him in, he did feel some level of familiarity with her. She was doing her best with her dance partner, but Peters had all the grace and ease on the dance floor of a concrete block. His timing was half a beat off, his footwork heavy and clumsy. She appeared uncomfortable with his hand on the small of her back and her smile seemed forced. Al had an overpowering urge to go and cut in and save her from her obvious unease. She looked up and met Al's gaze; those eyes, he knew those eyes, but from where? The couple suddenly got swept up by a wave of other dancers and were sucked into the middle of the floor.

He caught a glimpse of Elizabeth Bartholomew standing on the other side of the hall and made his way over to her. 'Have you seen Father Patrick, Mrs. Bartholomew?' he asked.

'Don't worry about him. He's probably out front talking horses with the blokes. And when will you start calling me Beth?'

He made a half turn toward the doors, but Beth was too quick for him. She stepped to him, gently grabbing his arm. 'Brother, would you like another sherry? A cup of tea? Maybe some pudding? We have pav and fruit salad.'

'Thanks Mrs. sorry, Beth, I'm good. Plenty of trifle up at the seminary,' replied Al, his eyes darting around as he scanned for Paddy. He turned away, behind him Beth gave a sharp nod of her head. Halfway to the front doors Al was intercepted by Mrs. O'Sullivan. Not more dances with her, please, thought Al.

'Brother Robertson. This is my daughter Shelia. She'd love

a dance.' Shelia stepped behind her mother. Long red hair, that beautiful colour somewhere between strawberry blond and ginger, piercing brown eyes, yet Al sensed a sadness hidden behind those eyes and smile. She couldn't have been more than nineteen he thought.

Stumbling over his reply, Al's face couldn't hide his bemusement.

'Come now, Brother. Shelia won't bite. Well, I hope she doesn't,' Mrs. O'Sullivan added.

Guy Lombardo's "You're Driving Me Crazy" was being played. Good timing, thought Al. Shelia filled his senses. An aroma of lilac, soft skin, lightly tanned and freckled forearms, a small emerald broach on the right collar of her blouse.

'Are you still in school, Shelia?' Al stumbled over the sentence.

'Oh no, Brother. I've been at the Bank of New Zealand for almost two years' Shelia replied.

'At the main branch on Hastings Street?'

'That's it. Is it true you saved Father Lynch's life up by Te Pohue?' Her eyes grew wide with the question.

'That would be stretching the truth. He just turned his ankle, but we managed to get out OK. We were never in any real danger.' He felt a little lightheaded with the intoxicating mix of alcohol, tobacco, music, perfume and body contact. He sensed a rising sexual tension between them.

'That's not what I heard. They say you had to carry him for over five miles. Must have been scary, especially when you had to cross the river,' said Shelia.

'Some people talk too much. We missed the worst of the storm. We were lucky.'

'Brave, I'd say,' Shelia added with a seductive smile. Al felt her hands tighten their hold on him, pulling him closer to her. The heat of their bodies heightened his arousal as they continued to dance effortlessly without speaking for another minute.

'Speak of the Devil. There's Father Lynch now. If you'd excuse me, Shelia, I need to speak to him,' Al said, with a slight stammer in his voice.

Pulling away from her, Al exhaled, wiped his forehead. Sadness returned to her eyes.

'Bloody hell, Paddy. Where have you been?'

'Doesn't look like you needed me around.' Paddy replied with a raised eyebrow. 'You might need to be careful, young seminarian.'

'Don't be silly. Mrs. O'Sullivan forced Shelia on me.'

'Oh, the burdens we must endure for our calling. Still, she's an attractive young lady.'

'Patrick. That's enough. Anyway, where were you? It's been almost an hour.' Al queried.

'Didn't know you were now my keeper. Was out front, with some of the guys. Just chewing the fat. Any more questions? I'm off to the kitchen, if that's OK?'

Al eyed him wearily. Not for the first time, he picked up the smell of whiskey. He knew well that Paddy liked a dram or two, and he had made a discovery after their escapade in the hills. Al was no friend of the temperance movement, but he was beginning to think Paddy was too fond of the Jameson than was good for him. Especially with Father Connolly around, who definitely was a strict no alcohol man. He decided to leave it for now. Al headed back over to Mr. Bartholomew and got another sherry. The irony, if not the hypocrisy, wasn't lost on him. 'I'm not the one with a problem,' he muttered to himself, as he walked back to their seats.

A few more people quizzed him on what happened up in the Maungaharuru's. Seemed like this was becoming a local legend. He successfully dodged Mrs. O'Sullivan and Shelia for the rest of the evening. They retired to the cottage just before midnight, leaving the hall with the strains of "I Got Rhythm" in their ears.

'Patrick, can we talk about tonight?' Al stuttered over the question.

'What's on your mind?'

'Well, it's a bit delicate and I know it's not really my place to say anything, but I'm worried about your drinking. It's almost every night now, sometimes it's close to half a bottle at a time.'

'Too right, lad, it is none of your bloody business,' Paddy's voice was sharp and clipped.

'Paddy, come on. I know you were drinking that day up in the bush. I found a flask in your satchel when I cleaned the car a couple of days later.'

'So now you're blaming me for what happened? Next you'll accuse me of trying to kill us both.' Paddy's face flashed bright red.

'No, of course I'm not. That's not what I'm saying. That was just bad luck and bad timing. What if Connolly finds out? You know what's he's like if anything reflects badly on the Church.'

'Stuff him, he has no control over me, and stuff you. I need some air.' Paddy stormed out of the room, pushing Al out of his way.

Al called after him, but he was already halfway out the door.

'Lord, what have I done,' said Al. He knelt down in the lounge and prayed. 'Dear merciful Lord, your humble servant asks for forgiveness for what I've just done. I've been naive and disrespectful to Father Lynch. Lord, please provide your infinite wisdom and guidance to me to repair the damage I've done and show me how to let Father Lynch know of the genuine concern I have for him.' Al stayed kneeling in silent prayer until he lost all feeling in his lower legs.

* * *

Allan Peters parked his car, jumped out, rushed around to the passenger side and opened the door. An uncomfortable silence filled the air as they walked up to her front door. The light was on over the front door, illuminating the porch in a soft haze. Abby was the one to break the impasse, 'Thank you for a lovely evening, Allan.'

'I hope you enjoyed it. The dance wasn't too boisterous for you? I thought it got a bit too lively for a while,' replied Peters.

'No, not all. It was fun. The band was terrific.'

'Maybe we could go to the next one.'

Abby hesitated, looked down at her scuffed shoes. 'Um, yes, that would be nice.' Another pause enveloped them. Abby gave a quick glance to the front door. 'Best I go in. Thank you again. We'll see each other at work on Monday, I'm sure.'

'Yes, definitely. We could have afternoon tea during the week,' Peters said and taking her hand leaned in to kiss Abby on the cheek. His skin felt clammy and slightly uncomfortable on hers. They said their goodnights and Abby opened the door to find Moira leaning on the lounge doorway.

'So, how was it?' her cousin asked.

'Evening, Moira. Fine, thanks. It was a good time, the place was hopping,' Abby replied, taking off her shoes. 'He's not much of a dancer, that's for sure.'

'His dancing isn't going to put food on the table or a roof over your head. Is he nice enough? He's a doctor, has a car and owns a house.'

'You want to marry me off to him after one night? I'll be the final judge of who I settle down with. Now if you don't mind, I'm shattered. See you in the morning.' About to close her bedroom door, she turned back to Moira, 'Thank you for staying up and worrying about me.' She stood in front of her mirror as she took off her earrings and small gold crucifix necklace. Peters was pleasant enough, but there was no immediate spark and she didn't have that instinct he was right for her. That feeling of knowing someone makes an instant connection, touches you on a deeper level, wasn't there, but she would probably give it one or two more social engagements, just to be sure.

* * *

1ˢᵗ *February 1931*

Paddy hit the brakes heavily on the Model T, causing the car to shudder to an abrupt halt, jerking Al forward so he almost hit the windscreen.

'Sorry, lad, lead foot,' said Paddy.

'A broken nose on the first day back at the seminary would have interesting,' replied Al.

They got out of the car and grabbed Al's bags from the back seat. Al offered his hand, Paddy gave him a firm hand shake and a small smile.

'Thanks for everything you've done for me over the past month,' said Al.

'What? All I did was get you into a couple of scrapes, almost killed us both and subjected you to Saint Vinnie's soup kitchen almost daily. Not sure I should be thanked, lad.'

'Not so, Paddy. You've opened my eyes to the real world. A month in the parish has done more for me than five years in the seminary.'

'You might be overplaying it a bit, lad, but I reckon everyday life is the real school. Get yourself in there and catch up with ya mates. I'll be back next weekend for Matron's lamb roast.'

Before Al could reply, Paddy was back in the car, crunched the vehicle into first gear and was off. Al lingered for a few seconds as he watched the car go down the hill and disappear in a cloud of dust. He was frustrated as they hadn't talked about their argument of yesterday. He'd have to leave it for another time, another aspect of real life that Paddy had introduced him to. Real life, it certainly had more twists and turns than seminary life. The next ten months of five o'clock rises, classes, prayers and masses stretched out in front of him like a long, well-worn mountain track, extending over the horizon. He gave out a sigh, picked up his bags and turned to face the seminary.

The four friends sat in the dormitory lounge, smoking before dinner, Leo Spring and Al with their pipes, George Head and Iggy O'Boyle had rollies. An open window let the warm, late afternoon air waft around the room, causing the smoke to swirl and dance. They were all dressed identically in black full length cassocks, and sitting in four identical brown armchairs.

'So you have the reading tonight, Iggy. What have you got up your sleeve?' asked Leo, his almost permanent cheeky grin set off his bright teeth against his naturally olive skin, which was now deeply tanned at the height of summer. His complexion, his wavy, jet black hair and first name of Leonardo were thanks to an Italian mother.

'You have to wait to find out,' Iggy replied, with a smirk, raising his eyebrows three times in quick succession. He inhaled deeply, his meaty fingers tapped the end of the cigarette into the ashtray on the table that sat in the middle of the group. As he exhaled he blew a couple of smoke rings that moved slowly past his deep set, dark eyes. 'Don't worry, lads. You'll get a laugh out of it. Now, Brother Albert, a bit more about life as a varsity student. You've been a bit sheepish with us so far.' His fingers were tapping his hair where it was forming a distinctive widow's peak.

'Not much to tell. I stayed at Saint Patrick's College and went to Victoria every day for classes. I was still under a seminary timetable, so up at five-thirty, prayers, mass, breakfast, then up the hill to campus. Evening's as they are here,' replied Al.

'Come on, you must have a couple of stories,' asked George,

as he adjusted his wire rimmed spectacles, even though they were fine frames, they still looked slightly oversized on his thin, angular face. 'No high jinks at all?'

'I almost blew up the chemistry lab during an experiment,' said Al.

'That's a bit more like it. Details?' asked Leo.

'It all started innocently enough, with us testing potassium.' Al continued the story and a couple of other anecdotes of life at Victoria University that entertained the group. Afternoon gave way to evening and the room was bathed in the glow of approaching sunset. Shafts of sunlight were made visible as it hit the tobacco smoke. They all looked up together as the dinner bell rang out then joined the throng of seminarians as they made their way to the dining room. With the rule of silence inside the main seminary building, only the noise of footsteps and rustling clothes to be heard.

Between the main course and pudding, Father Connolly called Iggy up to the podium, to give the evenings reading.

'This is the Gospel according to John. Thanks be to God. Jesus is brought before Pilate. Early in the morning Jesus was taken from Caiaphas' house to the governor's palace. The Jewish authorities did not go inside the palace, for they wanted to keep themselves ritually clean, in order to be able to eat the Passover meal. So Prometheus went outside to them and asked, "What do you accuse this man of."

A wave of smirks and giggles rippled across the dining room, one of the Fathers wrapped his table with a knife. Al, Leo and George, turned to each other with a combination of shaking heads and raised eyebrows.

'What? Mixing Greek mythology with the Gospel of John?' whispered Leo.

'Iggy has surpassed himself this time,' said Al, trying hard to suppress a smile.

'What do you reckon he'll get? A week of kitchen duty?' said George.

'I'll take two weeks for a shilling,' said Al.

'Put me down for three weeks,' added Leo.

'Done. Let's see the colour of your money after tea,' said George.

Father Gondringer stepped up to their table and cleared his throat and gave them a look. The hushed conversation quickly ended.

After dinner Father Gondringer asked Al if they could talk. Al could feel his face tighten.

'No need to worry, Brother Robertson. This is nothing to do with breaking silence during dinner. Rather it's an opportunity for you. An invitation in fact, I forgot to ask you about this a couple of weeks ago when you came up with Father Lynch. I'm in the final throws of organising a small teaching mission to the Islands and wanted to gauge your interest in accompanying us.'

'The Islands? What is the mission? Who's going, Father?' Al's eyes grew wide as he listened to Gondringer.

'I have approval for a group of four to go to Fiji either next year or the year after. At the moment I have Brother O'Boyle and Brother Doogan coming with me. There's room for one more. With your propensity for science and mathematics, you would round our troupe very nicely. Brother Doogan will cover geography and social studies, while Brother O'Boyle will teach English and religious studies. Although after this evening's performance, we might need to reassess that.'

'It's a wonderful opportunity. What time of year will it be, Father? I'll be starting teaching next year, I don't suppose the college would allow me to go during term time,' said Al.

'It's planned for the summer recess period. I'll make sure you have all the clearances from the school hierarchy.'

'Fiji? Have you a place in mind?' asked Al.

'We have a mission in the village of Wairiki, on one of the out-lying islands called Taveuni. French missionaries founded it, but the Society of Mary took it over some years ago. One of our graduates is running things up there now. That's the connection. They don't have a great deal of resources or money, so we try to help them every few years. Have you ever been to the Islands?' Gondringer asked.

'No, Father. Never been out of New Zealand. Only been to the South Island once. It's a very exciting opportunity and it would be a privilege to join you and Brothers O'Boyle and Doogan.'

'Wonderful. Magnifique. I'll go to the P&O office at the harbour in the next few days to get you listed on our party's booking. Let's set aside some time later this week, towards the end of the retreat, when we can discuss the plans.'

'Thank you, Father. I'll talk to the Brothers about it later.' Al had a big smile as he turned away to go to look for Iggy and James.

* * *

Tuesday morning dawned the same as virtually every other day that summer: the sun bursting from the horizon, arched over the Pacific into a clear sky, the air calm and the mercury passing seventy degrees before they finished breakfast at six o'clock. Al looked out of his dormitory window, back over the tidal flats towards Napier, and gave a quick prayer of thanks that they'd be in the cool environs of the chapel on the first day of a week-long retreat that marked the start of the seminary's academic year. If the summer continued on this trajectory, surely the earth itself would start to boil, he thought. He found George, Leo and Iggy and they settled into the back row of pews of the chapel, a nod to their seniority as final year seminarians, as the first speaker got the retreat under way. Only a couple of minutes into the reading, Al's attention was pulled away by shafts of light coming through the stained glass windows to the right of the crucifix at the front of the chapel. On a fine summer's day, this was almost as regular as clockwork as the sun was at the perfect angle to shine through the glass. The red and blue refracted light seemed to dance across the left hand wall. Al was transfixed for a few seconds by its simple beauty.

The roar of thunder startled everyone. 'But there's not a cloud in...' Al couldn't finish his internal statement before the floor started rolling, as if they were on the sea. From the back, Al could see the pews rise and fall like a wave. The roll quickly gave way to violent shakes, this time their bench jumped into the air by what seemed at least six inches. 'Earthquake!' yelled Father Connolly from the front. The sound of cracking masonry and screams laced with pure, unadulterated terror drowned out anything else he tried to say.

The entire building was now vibrating viciously. Pieces of the walls started to come away, crashing to the floor. Suddenly a chunk of the roof broke away and hurtled down; the dense black volcanic rock shattered four pews, instantaneously exploding them into a thousand fragments. The entire front of the chapel and the sanctuary started to collapse and break away from the rest of the building. One of the walls collapsed, sending a shower of debris down onto the altar, where a group of boys and a couple of the Fathers had looked for shelter.

Time seemed to be suspended. Seconds felt like minutes, reactions and movement appeared to slow. Vision was blurred by the violent shaking. The only sense that seemed to be working properly was hearing. The sounds of the building being torn apart and the screams of all inside the chapel resonated through Al's head. The cries were visceral, even primeval, from somewhere deep within the darkest reaches of each person's humanity. Sounds that relayed pure terror as a place that once was a haven was now a place of death and dread, with lives being extinguished by the second.

In their pew, Leo and George were crouched down, making their way to a large table at the back. Iggy was frozen to the seat, mouth slightly ajar, mesmerised by the scene in front of him. 'Move, Iggy,' Al shouted at him, but he remained motionless. Al looked up to see a large fracture opening up in the roof right above them. 'For the love of God, Iggy,' Al grabbed his mate and pushed him out of the row of pews. He had just shoved Iggy towards the others at the back of the chapel when he was knocked off his feet, a sheering pain shot up his back, he tried to regain his balance, then everything went black.

PART II

PART II

CHAPTER 7

*"Napier presented a frightful sight... a sight never to be forgotten.
Napier, Ahuriri and Westshore were enveloped in dense columns
of smoke rising from the general conflagration. Now and then
terrific explosions could be heard and heavy booms rolling in from
the sea confirmed our suspicions that these places were certainly
destroyed."*

Mount Saint Mary's Seminary journal diary, 1931, page 215

3rd *February 1931*

'Any idea how many more are out there?' Abby strained to raise
her voice over the din of vehicles, machinery, volunteers and the
cries of patients.

'No bloody clue. It's absolute mayhem. No one knows what's
going on. How are you doing?' said Doctor Peters, his usual calm
demeanour replaced with stress and tension. His eyes darted
around the makeshift hospital that had sprung to life at the Napier
racecourse.

'We've got no spare beds anywhere now. Someone said the
Navy boys from the *Veronica* would bring in more cots and tents,
but no sign of them yet.' Abby replied.

'Who's in these tents?' Allan asked.

'Mainly minor breaks and lacerations. We have a couple of
puncture wounds. All the serious ones are in the main grandstand.
We haven't had a new patient for nearly half an hour.'

'It might be calming down,' he exhaled heavily after he spoke.
'When was the last time you had a break? Even a cuppa?'

'Don't worry about me, Doctor Peters. Can't be downing tools now,' she turned away, busying herself sorting fresh supplies rescued from the abandoned hospital.

'Abigail. Don't play the martyr with me, and you know its Allan to you. We've all been at this non-stop for over twelve hours, let alone the rest of the shift you had under your belt when it hit. You need some rest.' His hand lingered on her shoulder as he spoke.

'Really, Doctor Peters. I'm alright.' Abby forced a little smile and took a small step backwards allowing his hand to drop away. 'Sister just came by and said if the number of new patients stays low, she'll let all of us who were on morning shift have a few hours off at midnight.'

'That's good. Let me know if you need a lift into town and I'll drive you. Don't want you out on the streets tonight. Looks like the fires are still going all over town,' said Allan, as he looked back towards downtown.

'Thanks for the offer, but a few of us will be heading back together when we get the all clear, we'll be fine as a bunch. Our house is still standing, so we're just going to grab some fresh clothes and come straight back.'

Allan's smile fell away as he gave a quick nod and watched her turn from him.

Abby grabbed a lantern and returned to her rounds, tending to the patients who were in the tents on the lawn of the racecourses public concourse.

Just before midnight she got word that all nurses who started the 8am shift could stand down. She finished up with the patient she was attending to, an elderly man with a fractured skull; he wasn't expected to make it through the night. She gently held his hand and said a prayer for him.

She made her way to the totalisator building, which was now the nurses' quarters, to freshen up. Walking into the bathroom she stopped suddenly, stunned at the image looking back at her in the mirror. Sixteen straight hours of nursing in a disaster area had left her ragged and dishevelled, covered in blood and dirt. She thought she had aged ten years in the day.

Filling the basin with warm water, she took off her hat, rolled up her sleeves and undid the top two buttons of her blouse. Leaning over the water, hands supporting her weight on either side of the basin, she let out a deep breath. Her shoulders dropped as she tried to expel the trauma of the day out of her body. Flashes of the day invaded the darkness every time she closed her eyes. A young girl, whose left arm was so badly crushed it was amputated. A well-dressed man had come in coughing up thick, dark blood and died before night fall. Her body violently convulsed, her stomach tightened as if trapped in a vice. She clutched one side of the basin as her other hand covered her mouth. Acidic fluid replaced saliva, her sinuses filled instantly. Tears flowed down her cheeks forming small rivers. She knew more of the tears were emotional rather than a physical reaction to the convulsion. She splashed water onto her face and let it flow into the basin. She worked a bar of soap vigorously. On a normal day, the water would have turned milky white, but today it was dark grey. She pulled the plug and refilled the basin. This time she dipped her arms into the warm water up to her elbows, letting its warmth seep into her skin and started to clean her forearms. She cupped her hands and worked the water and soap into her face. Drying herself off, the standard white hospital towel was soon stained with what her cleaning had missed: the microscopic remnants of a hundred destroyed buildings and a thousand shattered lives. Her cleaning was barely satisfactory, but she knew for the next few days she'd have to live with it.

Back into the main room, she picked up her handbag, took out a small bottle of lavender essence and dabbed a spot on each side of her neck. There were now a few of her colleagues mingling around. Some were settling in to get some sleep. The usual buzz of activity and chat when nurses congregated was absent. The room had an eerie calm and hush about it. Her two house mates, Patricia and Jessica, had come in. They said they'd go for a quick wash themselves. They were both emergency ward nurses and if Abby thought she'd aged ten years during the day, they looked ready for retirement.

A few minutes later they made their way to the entrance of the racecourse where Moira was waiting for them. Taking the lead, Abby rallied them together. 'Let's be very careful, if something looks really dangerous we steer clear. OK?' The others nodded in agreement. 'Good. Let's go.'

They clambered onto the back of one of the trucks that was shuttling people, patients and provisions to and from the racecourse. It took less than five minutes for the extent of the earthquake to register. They all stood up, transfixed by the scale of devastation. Four out of every five buildings were either substantially or totally destroyed. Dante's Inferno came to Abby's mind. Fires were in various stages of life, some smouldering, some raging blazes, devouring two or three buildings at a time. They had seen the smoke and glow of flames from the racecourse throughout the day, but now the heat of the fires stung their faces. They wheezed and coughed as they tried to breathe amongst the mixture of smoke, ash and dust. Their course home was very indirect, littered with rubble and debris of all kinds. Naval personnel and volunteer rescue teams still combed the ruins. Police directed people down safer routes. Clearance crews were doing their best to remove rubble and make streets at least partially navigable. Their driver expertly negotiated the devil's maze that was now Napier. One street was impassable with collapsed buildings forming a 10ft high roadblock, so the driver had to quickly change course. Town was almost unrecognisable to them. Most major landmarks were gone. Abby felt disorientated for a few minutes. She could see Hospital Hill to her left and the spire of St. Pat's to her right, so they must be close to the town centre. Where was the Post Office, the Bank of New Zealand, Parkers Tailors store? All gone.

The truck jerked to a stop at the Botanical Gardens, where they had helped set up an emergency dressing station after they evacuated the hospital that morning. A couple of men helped them down, then started loading supplies onto the truck for its return journey. They'd have to walk the last couple of streets to their house. They crossed the road and turned the first corner. All four stopped almost as if an invisible hand touched them in the same instance. They'd heard the nurses' home was severely damaged. They knew some of their friends had been killed, more injured and were now patients themselves, but hadn't seen it when they decamped to the racecourse. Now they did. Damaged was a wholly insufficient description: it was unrecognisable. Rubble rather than a structure. It resembled a collapsed layer cake. All four levels had crumpled down on top of the floor below, entombing those inside.

All four women looked at each other. Pat dabbed the corner of her eyes with a handkerchief. Abby gently grabbed her free hand. 'There but for the grace of God go we,' said Moira. Was it luck or divine intervention that had kept them all out of the nurses' home? What might have happened if Moira hadn't have befriended Pat so quickly when they first moved to Napier? Pat and Jess wanted a couple of people to share their house, so the need to move into here disappeared. Who had taken their place? Who was now dead because of their decision to live with Pat and Jess? She bit down on her bottom lip to fight off tears.

'Can we keep walking? Please,' whispered Jess.

They trudged single file down the street to their house, rarely raising their heads. They did a quick walk around their small wooden house. No cracks, no subsidence, chimney still in place.

A couple of shattered windows, but in the middle of a hot, dry summer, hardly a concern. Abby felt optimistic for the first time today. 'Let's be quick. Just grab a couple of sets of clothes,' Abby said. The positive feeling soon dissipated as they entered the house. It looked as though it had been completely ransacked. The earthquake had done its work expertly, almost every drawer and closet had disgorged itself of its contents. Anything not fastened to the floor or wall had been overturned.

A mess, but at least it's in one piece, was Abby's first thought. Although physically and emotionally depleted, she started to do some rudimentary tidying, fighting off exhaustion, as sleep tried to consume her. She picked through the detritus that covered her bedroom floor. She folded clothes, picked up books, some jewellery and her gold handled hair brush. She found her three most treasured items. A framed photograph of her family outside the house where she was born. Nine children and her father, thick ivy covering the fence and gate arch between them and the house. She is near the end on the right, the youngest and smallest. She can't remember the photo being taken; she was probably about eighteen months old. Her eldest three siblings weren't even in the photo, they were already adults, out living their own lives. A picture of her and Moira as teenagers, arms around each other in their school uniforms, huge smiles as if they are laughing with all the energy they have. The broken glass of the frame had put a small cut in the photograph, almost perfectly between the two girls. She gently picked out the glass from each frame.

A small white and pink music box lay shattered. It was a present for her thirteenth birthday from an Irish aunt. It was made in England, her aunt had bought it at Selfridges during a trip to London. The delicate porcelain ballerina was broken off where it joined the box, lying on the floor a few inches away. Its musical insides had been jettisoned from the box. Abby sat heavily on her bed, the photos and music box on her lap. She rolled the ballerina between her thumb and forefinger. A single tear left its watery trail down her cheek.

4th February 1931

An Orderly ran up to Abby and Moira, he tripped over a couple of words in his rush, 'A-A-Abigail, Moira. I've been looking for you all over.'

'Slow down. What is it?' Abby tried to calm him.

'Doctor Wills from Taradale is asking for a couple of nurses to go up to Mount Saint Mary's. So, I thought of you. They've got almost a dozen dead and loads of injured,' he explained.

'I don't know. We can't leave the hospital. What about the patients here?' furrows formed on Abby's forehead, she immediately thought of the girl with the crushed arm, 'They need us.'

'Abigail, it's our duty to go. We can't leave the Fathers and Brothers to someone else,' Moira cut in.

'I wouldn't be comfortable leaving everyone here. If we do go, we'll need to get clearance first and they'll have to get replacements to cover our shifts,' Abby added.

'We're going. Come on, Abby, let's find Sister and this doctor,' said Moira.

Abby grimaced as she followed. They found the Sister near the entrance to the members lounge, in discussion with a man. They could see blood stains on his crumpled white shirt.

'The McCarthy girls,' said Sister. 'I'm glad we found you so quickly. This is Doctor Wills. Abigail and Moira McCarthy.'

Doctor Wills offered his hand to both. 'The sisters McCarthy? Wonderful.'

'First cousins, actually, but most people think we are sisters,' corrected Moira.

'A major family resemblance in any case. No mind. So you're

happy to volunteer to go up to Mount Saint Mary's to tend to the staff and pupils?'

'Most definitely,' Moira was taking the lead. 'We were both trained by the Sisters of Compassion. Still attend Mass. Some of us more regularly than others,' looking sideways at Abby.

'And two of our best nurses, for good measure. Ladies, this would be a tremendous help,' Sister added with a smile.

'What about covering us here? Will you have enough nurses if we leave?' Abby asked.

'I've been told there are extra doctors and nurses arriving today from Palmerston and Waipukurau. But thanks for thinking of us and the patients. Typical Abigail.'

'So we're all set?' Doctor Wills rubbed his hands quickly. 'Best we get on our way. There's a couple of boxes of supplies to get you through the first couple of days. I'll give you more details on the drive and we'll visit all the injured when we get there. Thanks again for this. Sister, I owe you a major debt of gratitude. Ladies. Shall we?'

He led them to a big American car that was covered in a layer of dust so thick the chrome didn't reflect the early morning sun. Trucks and cars filled the road, ferrying people, supplies and rubble. Daylight brought a different view of the earthquakes' devilish handy work. The road had fallen away on one side, causing all traffic to move slowly on one shared lane. Every other power and telephone pole was tilted precariously inward toward the road, like immature trees ravaged by a storm. They noticed an odd pattern in the wreckage. Most wooden structures were still intact, some with only minor damage, but virtually every brick, stone or masonry building was gone. Either twisted piles of rubble or burned out frames. Even on a cloudless morning, the sun often disappeared behind a vale of dust or plume of smoke.

'They got hit quite badly. The chapel is destroyed, as too a couple of out buildings and the accommodation block has subsided,' said Wills as he started his briefing. 'There's about a hundred people up there, so I thought they'd have to have a few injuries.' He braked suddenly as a truck in front of them lost some of its load of debris. 'There's been ten fatalities and nearly fifteen injured, two of which are quite serious. Brother James Durning has fluid on the brain and significant internal injuries. I'm not confident he'll make it. Brother Albert Robertson is the other one. He has internal bleeding and swelling around the lower back and abdomen. He is reactive to stimulation on all extremities indicating no permanent paralysis, but the trauma to the spinal cord will likely result in some short term restriction of movement. He's in and out of consciousness with a likely concussion; and a damaged ankle for good measure. Can't tell if it's a sprain or a break. Everyone else ranges from minor lacerations and abrasions to the odd broken bone. Questions so far?'

'Where are they housed at the moment? Especially the two who are serious.' Moira asked.

'I wouldn't call it housed. They're under tarps tethered between the trees along the drive.'

'So there's a good chance of secondary infection?' Abby added.

'Good point. You'll have to be careful. I've made some rudimentary notes. Here we are.'

The car dodged ruts and clambered over potholes in the driveway. Immature plane trees lined the path, the tallest no more than twenty feet high. Abby studied the injured shaded under tarpaulins or sheets suspended on ropes tied to branches.

'Will have to watch for dehydration and sunstroke,' she said quietly, more to herself than the others. As she looked out at her new patients, she was struck by their youthfulness. 'Just boys,' she said 'and they all look so scared.' There was a weak wave from one or two from their cots.

Wills stopped the car at the last tree. There were a couple of tables with some older men standing around, 'Ladies, time for introductions,' he said.

Abby and Moira fell in behind the doctor, as a small man with sharp features broke from the group and offered his hand.

'Doctor, so glad to have you back.'

'Moira and Abigail McCarthy. This is Father Connolly, head of Mount Saint Mary's.'

They exchanged handshakes. 'Sisters?' Father Connolly asked.

'First cousins actually. Made the same mistake myself. Catholic trained though,' Doctor Wills answered.

'Good. Which order?' asked Connolly.

'Sisters of Compassion,' Moira replied.

'Old Sister Aubert's outfit. God rest her soul.' Connolly almost hissed the sentence. 'Good enough. Doctor Wills has given you an idea of where we are at?'

Abby and Moira nodded.

'Good. We have lost nine of our beloved brethren and one valued member of our support staff. May the Lord have mercy on their souls,' he crossed himself. 'We are all deeply affected by the deaths, but we must now tend to our injured to ensure no one else is added to the list of fallen.'

'We'll do everything to make sure they all make a full recovery,' Moira replied.

'Let's get you acquainted with all the injured.' With a wave of his arm, Connolly ushered the women toward the cots.

They made their way along one line of trees, pausing at each cot. Compared to the orderly line of tents at the racecourse, the shelter here was ramshackle. A mixture of bed sheets, blankets, tarps and even the odd horse cover were jerry-rigged up on ropes and planks between the trees or propped up on boxes or barrels. They were low slung, no more than four feet off the ground.

They stopped at James Durning. Moira knelt down and took his hand 'How are you doing today, James?'

'Hanging on. Glad to have you here. Tell the doctor, I ain't gonna die. I just ain't,' he said.

Moira lightly put her hand on his shoulder and whispered in a flat voice 'I'll tell him.'

'He's been muttering that almost non-stop since Doctor Wills first took a look at him,' said Connolly. They crossed the driveway and came down the other line of trees. 'Here's our other serious injury, Brother Albert Robertson. Like Brother Durning, he's lucky to be alive. He hasn't been conscious since we pulled him out of the chapel. He was the last we rescued.'

Abby looked at him quizzically. She bent over and gently grabbed his wrist and took his pulse; slow and weak. 'You're going to be a very sore boy when you wake up,' she whispered.

Doctor Wills stepped forward, 'Right. I'd better get going. Got to do the rounds of my other patients. Ladies, here's all my notes. I'll swing by the racecourse later to organise a truck to shuttle you back and forth to your house and make sure they keep you well supplied. I'll pop by every day. Good luck.'

Abby and Moira started checking and changing dressings, dispensing painkillers and making sure every patient had water and was shaded. Abby mopped her forehead of the quickly forming perspiration. By lunchtime they had organised some of the fit seminarians to fan those in the cots who couldn't do it for themselves. They were approached by three young men: one tall with cheap wire rim glasses, one average height with a muscular build and olive skin, the last shorter and heavier set. All had cuts and bruises on their faces and hands.

The tallest man spoke: 'Good afternoon, sisters. I'm Brother George Head. This is Brother Leo Spring and Brother Ignatius O'Boyle.'

'Everyone calls me Iggy,' the shortest man cut in, with an excited voice as he shot out his hand in welcome. 'You just gotta save them,' he added.

'It's just about Brother Durning and Brother Robertson,' George continued. 'See the thing is, they're both in our class. There's only fifteen of us. Well, fourteen now. Brother Doogan died yesterday. We just wanted to offer our help in any way.'

'We are here to make sure everything is done for them,' said Moira.

Abby took Iggy's hands in hers and gave him a slow nod and a soft smile, 'Thanks for coming to see us. They'll make it, Iggy. I promise.'

'Thanks for your time. Come on lads, back up top,' said George as they turned and headed back up the hill to the main seminary buildings and chapel.

'Abby, you should know better than to promise something like that. We don't really know how bad those boys are yet. Anything could happen to them,' Moira's words were clipped.

'For God's sake, Moira. You saw them. They didn't want a medical prognosis. They need hope. If that's all we can give them, then so be it. I won't take that away from them,' said Abby.

'Times like these, maybe too much hope is a bad thing.' Moira added.

'Surely can't be worse than none.'

The sound of a car turning into the driveway disrupted their conversation. A priest in a Model T rumbled past them and came to a stop just past the trees, some forty yards away. They watched the priest get out and walk, with a pronounced limp, over to the main table of clergy.

'That's Father Lynch,' said Moira.

'Who?' asked Abby.

'For the love of Pete. The priest at St. Patrick's. I know you've only been a couple of times, but honestly Abigail.'

'I recognise him now. And I have been four times since we moved here.'

Paddy shook hands with all the men, pausing to chat or

embrace most of them. They noticed he spent the shortest time with Connolly. He then broke away and walked over to the food serving area where a homely looking, middle aged woman with sturdy legs was cleaning up. She only saw Paddy when he was almost at her side. She quickly wiped her hands on her apron and extended her hand. Paddy ignored it and enveloped her in a deep, strong hug. Instantly the woman exploded in sobs and wailing that they could hear from their vantage point. Her shoulders and back heaved with every breath, her head bobbed up and down on Paddy's shoulder. He lifted his right hand and gently stroked the back of her head. They held their deep embrace for at least a minute.

'That's a bit much now. He should know better than to instigate that sort of reaction in public,' Moira said as she turned away.

'Oh, Moira. It's so beautiful. In all this chaos and despair, it's the most touching thing I've seen,' Abby watched for another minute, then exhaled deeply and turned away.

They picked up water jugs and started their afternoon checks. They barely got to the second patient when a voice came from behind.

'Ladies, can I have a minute?'

'Why, Father Lynch. Yes of course. It's Moira McCarthy, remember me?'

Paddy squinted at her then his eyes opened wide. 'Moira. Blow me down. I didn't recognise ya in your nurses get up. Only seen you in your Sunday best.' They shook hands. 'And who's this?'

'This is my cousin Abigail. But you wouldn't know her. Not as regular at Mass.'

'Yep, I remember. Only joined us a few times. That's fine. Something's better than nothing, eh,' Paddy gave Abby a warm smile. 'I'm lookin' for Brother Albert Robertson.'

'Yes, this way. Over at the other line of trees,' Abby replied.

'What's the story?' Paddy asked.

'In short, Father, he's got a serious back injury, probably some short term paralysis, or restricted movement, but shouldn't be permanent. He's got a concussion and hasn't been conscious. Everything else is superficial.'

Paddy knelt, took Al's hand, crossed himself, said a prayer and crossed himself again.

'How do you know Brother Albert?' asked Abby.

'We're mates. I looked after him for a few weeks at St. Pat's before the new term.'

She looked at Paddy, then Al. Back and forth a couple of times. It hit her. She suddenly remembered where she'd seen Albert. Two or three weeks ago at the hospital, the tall, handsome man with the man on crutches. She suddenly went flush with colour, and turned away from both of them. She knew she stared a little too intently and for too long at him that day, undressing him with her eyes. She took a quick swig from her water jug.

'Abigail. Promise me you'll take extra special care of him? He's a good lad, got loads to live for. Just get him through this,' said Paddy.

'Yes, Father. I promise,' replied Abby, turning back to the priest.

'I know you'll keep that promise.'

A second wave of blood flushed her cheeks. Her eyes darted either side of Paddy.

'If there's anything I can do for you two, just yell,' Paddy offered.

'Moira and I have decided to run two shifts so we always have at least one of us here. Would you be able to drive Moira back home? We live up on Hospital Hill.' Paddy nodded. 'Could I ask one more thing?' asked Abby. Paddy nodded. 'What was wrong with that lady you hugged when you arrived?' asked Abby.

'Matron McNeil? You haven't met her?' Abby shook her head. 'So you don't know? She lost her best friend here yesterday. They shared a cottage up on top of the hill that collapsed. She got out, but her friend didn't make it. She blames herself,' said Paddy.

'And she's still working?'

'Aren't we all? Sure, she's hurting, like everyone. She knows there'll be a time for mourning, but it ain't now. She's one of God's fighters. Make sure you introduce yourselves. She'll be delighted at having some extra female company around.'

After Paddy and Moira left, Abby continued her rounds of the cots and tending to the occasional new injury to the seminarians, picked up during the clean-up operations. A small truck came down the driveway and pulled in at the end of the trees. Two men jumped out and started unloading big bundles of canvas, poles and ropes. George Head came over to Abby, 'We've got a few tents. We're putting them up now by the tennis court. The plan is to move the injured once they are set up. That'll be OK?'

'Thank you, George. Having them under proper cover will be very good,' replied Abby.

A couple of hours later a small tent village had sprouted up. As the sun disappeared behind the hills at the back of the seminary, Abby decided to give James and Al a sponge bath before they were moved into the tents. She was about to start on James when Iggy bounded up to her.

'Miss McCarthy. Can I help out? James, old mate, you don't mind, eh?'

Before James could mutter a protest, Iggy had taken the cloth and basin from Abby and was starting on him. *Looks like Albert gets my undivided attention,* she thought to herself. She rolled up his sleeves, undid the buttons on his shirt, doing physically what she'd done in her imagination a couple of weeks ago. She rung out the cloth and gently wiped down his arms in long, slow strokes. She noticed how well defined his muscles were. Tall and muscular. She didn't much care for skinny men. She moved to his chest, again more muscular than she expected, with only a small tuft of hair in the middle. Abby thought he was the most dashing priests she'd ever seen. Pity they didn't have the likes of him as a teacher when she was at school. Would have made school a lot more appealing. In fact the whole seminary was made up of some handsome young men. Such a collection of fine Kiwi manhood, all lost to we fine Kiwi womanhood, she thought. Abby finished bathing him and returned his clothes to their proper settings. She took Al's wrist in her hand to check his pulse one more time.

* * *

At that moment Al slowly opened his eyes, his vision blurred, his mouth dry, tongue swollen. The aroma of lavender engulfed him. He could make out a broad smile and gentle brown eyes. A soft voice spoke to him.

'Finally decided to join us?'

CHAPTER 8

Kerosene lanterns and motor car headlamps were the only lights to help with transferring the injured to the new tents. Moths, mosquitoes and sand flies danced incoherently around the bulbs. Many made the fatal mistake of landing on the glass of the lamps. The plane trees and temporary shelters intercepted the multiple beams and cast deformed shadows so deep over those walking around that they were constantly being swallowed by the night, only to re-emerge a few seconds later.

James and Al were first to be moved. As George and Leo carried Al on a stretcher, he reached out for Abby's hand, and held it tightly. He had been conscious for barely three hours and hadn't spoken more than a handful of coherent sentences. Once he was in his new bed, Abby gave him a drink of water and he started talking.

'Iggy OK? He was next to me.' Al's voice was husky and weak.

'He's fine. He's visited you a few times,' replied Abby.

'I saw the sacristy collapse. Bits of the chapel came down on us, like hail. Nowhere to take cover. All the lads were yelling.' He took another long pull on the cup of water. 'A big piece fell. Iggy never saw it. Last thing I remember was diving at him. Nothing much after that. Colours mainly. Blues, greens, swirling misty clouds. One bright white light. Seemed like I was flying toward it. I do remember the smell of lavender.'

'Oh dear. I think that was my perfume. Sorry,' said Abby.

'Nice. Dreamed I was floating in a field of it,' Al exhaled heavily as he finished speaking.

Abby couldn't help but smile, 'That's enough now. Try to sleep.'

He reached for a cup of water, he lost his balance and almost fell out of bed. A chilling cry of pain pierced the tent. Abby surprised herself at how quickly she moved. She intercepted Al's fall, grabbed his shoulders and pulled him back into bed. Their eyes met and fixed on each other. For the first time she noticed the colour of his eyes: deep green with flecks around the edge of the irises.

'Alright?' Abby asked. Al gave a couple of sharp nods. 'You've got to be more careful. No sudden movements. You've had a major back injury, so you need to keep as still as possible.'

Al closed his eyes and whispered, 'OK'.

She tucked him in tightly and gently touched his shoulder before she left the tent. She checked on a few of the others before lying down for what she thought would be a quick nap.

Abby woke suddenly as a twitch shot through her body. Disorientated, she looked around her through blurred eyes. 'A tent? What am I doing in a tent?' she asked herself. Gradually some clarity came to her. She remembered moving the injured to the tents. The transfer started later and took longer than planned. By the time she was satisfied that everyone was settled and comfortable, it was near midnight. After lying down for a short rest in a spare tent, she fell into a deep sleep. On a box near the entrance flap of the tent there was a china bowl, a large piece had broken off from the rim. An intertwining MSM and the words Santo Maria Mons in the seminary's crest was still visible; but faded. Next to it was a battered water jug, enamel chipped off its outside, and towel. She washed her face, hands and forearms, put her hat on and stepped out into the morning. Cool air stung her face. She dabbed her nose with her handkerchief. The grass glistened in the sharp sun. Gone was the dust and smoke of yesterday. The light blue colour of the sky around the

112

sun deepened as she looked north and west, across Napier. In a couple of steps her shoes were damp and her toes chilled. There were puddles on the tennis court and the driveway was now a dark brown.

Moira emerged from the last tent, her eyes dark and heavy. 'Morning. How did you sleep?' her husky voice struggled to get the words out.

'Fine. Can't even remember putting my head down. How are the patients?' asked Abby.

'Everyone had a good night. They settled quickly after they got into the tents.'

'And James and Albert?'

'Reasonable. I've just finished with them. James was good, but Albert seemed to be in a lot of pain,' replied Moira.

'The move probably aggravated his back. I'll look in on them shortly.' Abby checked her watch. 'Were they able to eat any breakfast? Have they had enough water? Al shouldn't have tried to move too much.' Abby almost ran out of breath rattling off the questions.

'Bloody Nora, woman. You think I found this in a Christmas cracker?' Moira said as her thumb flicked her blue and gold New Zealand Nursing Service star on the right side of her chest. 'Yes, they have eaten. Yes, they've had plenty of water. Hell's bells. I do know my job.'

'Sorry, Moira. I didn't mean to question you. They just need special attention.'

'I'm quite aware of that,' snapped Moira.

A sheet of silence hang heavily between them for a minute.

'Doctor Wills stopped by earlier. He said there's close to two hundred confirmed dead already,' Moira added with barely a hint of emotion.

'Dear Lord,' Abby said, bringing her hand to her mouth. 'And there'll be more. Oh, poor Jess and Pat. They'll be in bits.'

She had barely started her first round of the less serious patients when she noticed everyone capable of walking heading up to the main buildings. 'What's going on?' she asked Moira.

'Oh, forgot to tell you. There's a funeral mass and burial starting at ten thirty. They told me first thing this morning.'

'The Archbishop has come up from Wellington for it,' said Iggy, as he filled water jugs. 'I'd better get going myself. You two coming?'

'Go ahead, Moira. I'll stay down here. I was about to see James and Albert.'

'You sure? I would like to meet the Archbishop, and I should pay my respects, too.' Moira quickly put down the bundle of bandages she was carrying and scurried off up the driveway. She soon passed many of the injured who were slowly making their way up the hill.

Abby's attention was pulled away by chatter from the last tent. She thought she heard Al's voice '… but there hasn't been a major quake for over seventy years, so we were probably due one.'

She lifted up the heavy flap of coarse white canvass. Both James and Al looked up simultaneously. 'Nurse McCarthy,' said James.

'Sounds like you two are feeling better.' A wave of stale hot air hit her as she moved into the tent. 'Oh, dear. Let's open this up.' She struggled to roll up the flap and tie it back. Her forearms flexed and strained as she fought with the canvas. She felt eyes upon her and looked up to find both Al and James watching her. 'Much better. So let's take a look at you,' she said to both men. 'James. You first.' She lifted up his shirt and gently placed her hands on his stomach. She slowly increased the pressure, released, then moved her hands to another spot and repeated. Bruises covered almost all his torso. They were now dark purple with dirty yellow edges and had grown rapidly in the last day. She repeated a few times, as she checked James' reaction. There was a twitch from him and pain etched on his face. She turned and saw Al watching her every move from the other bed. She tucked in some loose strands of hair around her temple that had escaped from under her hat.

'How is the pain compared to yesterday?' she asked James.

'Much less when you press down. Is that good?' he asked.

'Yes, that's progress. Doctor Wills can say for definite, but it's good news.'

James' grimace instantly turned to a broad smile. 'I told them I'd pull through.'

'Now, Albert, Moira tells me you didn't sleep well. How are you feeling now?'

'Not great,' replied Al.

Abby waited for him to go on, but nothing. 'That's not overly helpful. You need to give me a little more than that, Albert,' she said.

Another pause, then Al said 'There's a hot, sharp pain around the discs in the lumbar area. Probably discs L2 and L3. It shoots up my back every time I move. My ankle constantly throbs. Pain is mainly on the outside and goes up to the knee.'

'My word. So you're a doctor as well as a geography expert. Impressive analysis, Albert.' Abby said as a little smile broke across her face.

'Science teacher actually. Well, soon to be, I've just finished my degree at Victoria.'

'OK, Professor Robertson, I'm just going to check your hands and feet for reactions.' Abby unclipped her standard issue Nursing Service watch on the left of her blouse and flipped its pin out. She took Albert's right hand and started pricking his fingers and palm. He showed good reactions. The left hand checked; same result. She went down to his feet. Trying not to move his legs, she untucked the blankets and sheet. As she uncovered his feet, she saw the left foot was heavily bandaged and extremely swollen. She started on the right foot. All fine. Minimal reaction from the left. She pursed her lips. That worried her, but she knew she had to stay positive.

'A little dull on the left foot, but nothing to worry about. Probably more to do with your ankle. Let's have a look at that.' She undid the safety pin on the bandage and slowly rolled the fabric into a tight log. Al twitched and drew small, sharp breaths whenever she rolled the bandage under or around the ankle and foot. At least he can feel that, she thought. The last couple of loops allowed the fabric to reveal the full extent of the swelling. Abby thought it looked as if someone had surgically implanted a tennis ball either side of Al's ankle. The foot itself was bloated and puffy, with the swelling and discolouration starting just short of his toes and continuing halfway up his shin. Not quite the shade of James' bruising, but still a deep blue. She cupped the ankle in her hands. Very warm and she could feel the fluid coursing around the wounded joint. Definitely a sprain, she thought. Wouldn't be this much heat and bleeding if it was a break. She picked up her watch again and pricked the outside of Al's leg, below and above the knee.

'Hell. I feel that,' shouted Al as his leg jumped, almost in spasm.

Abby's eyes grew wide and a little smile formed. It was the reaction she wanted. 'Very good, Albert.' Her smile grew wider. 'I'll put a fresh bandage on that ankle. It may look ugly, but it's just a bad sprain. It's not broken.' She finished up by taking both men's temperature. Abby stopped at the tent entrance and said 'You can go back to talking about the earthquake history of these shaky isles. Or the anatomy of the human back.'

Outside the tent Abby heard some shards of a conversation. She looked up and saw Moira. She was flanked by George and Leo as they walked down the drive. The men's faces seemed angry. Tight jaws and dropped eyebrows. Not the emotion Abby would have thought normal for them just having been at the funeral of friends.

'What's wrong with the boys?' asked Abby.

'They just announced that everyone apart from a few senior staff has to leave. They want the place cleared out by tomorrow night. The boys don't want to go,' replied Moira.

'Where are they meant to go? What about James and Albert? They can't be moved too far. They really need to be in a hospital. And not just over at the racecourse.'

'Will you ever stop going on about those two. I don't bloody know,' Moira snapped back to Abby, her face red and a vein on her temple stood out. 'Maybe Doctor Wills can look into it. The others have to go to family or friends. Most are going to try to get back to their homes.'

Questions and checklists swirled around Abby's head. Which hospital would James and Albert go to? How far would they have to go? Would they need to be accompanied? They'll have to immobilise Albert as much as possible so he doesn't aggravate his back. James' internal bleeding could easily spread on a rough journey. Those poor boys. They've only just settled in the tents, now a long road trip to God knows where.

Abby's thoughts were shattered as a large back car rumbled past them. An elderly man with a thick grey beard, a red hat and red cape was in the back.

'That's the Archbishop. I got to introduce myself. Such an honour. Mother will be beside herself when I tell her,' said Moira.

'Nice of him to stop by the injured and give them some words of comfort,' said Abby.

'Abby, he's a busy man. I imagine he's got to get back to Wellington as soon as he can to organise the reconstruction efforts. He's got bigger things to think about than your two little seminarians. And he did bless the injured that went to the funeral mass.'

Bureaucracy over love and compassion. Another reason Abby didn't care for the Church.

Doctor Wills returned at sunset to speak to James and Al. Abby and Moira stood by the flap of the tent to listen. 'We've got you both sorted out. Brother James, you're going to Dannevirke. Brother Albert, you're just down the road at Waipukurau. The railway is out from here to there, so there will be ambulances here for you both about lunchtime tomorrow. Some of the best doctors from all over the country have been sent to the hospitals, so you'll be getting the best possible care.'

Al turned his head away from the doctor and tightened his jaw. 'I already have the best care I need right here,' he half mumbled to himself. James had a scowl on his face.

'Chaps, you'll be in proper hospitals with plenty of staff to look after you,' said the doctor.

'They shouldn't move us.' Al said. 'We're still in a bad way.'

'What's wrong with staying here?' added James.

'It's unhygienic for starters,' said Moira, her arms crossed.

'Yes, you are both in a serious condition. All the more reason to get you to a hospital, not a tent in a paddock,' added the doctor.

'Let me talk to them, Doctor,' Abby finally spoke. 'They'll be ready to go tomorrow.'

As Moira and Doctor Wills left the tent, Abby grabbed a box, flipped it over, and sat down between the two beds. She crossed her legs, the end of her skirt rode up to just short of her knees.

'Right, gentlemen. What's all this petulance about?' she raised her eyebrows, shifting her gaze between James and Al. 'No good going all coy and sheepish with me. Come on, out with it.'

'We're fine where we are. There's no reason to move us,' said Al.

'We want to stay here with you and Moira. Well, you mostly,' added James.

'Although that's flattering, it doesn't matter. And Albert, as much as you know of basic medicine, you shouldn't question a doctor with Doctor Wills' experience. He knows what's best for both of you. You trust me?' They nodded as one. 'Then believe me that this move is the best thing for you. I want you to put all your energy into getting better, not stewing like a couple of bitter old maids. Promise?'

'Yes. I promise,' said James.

'You're the boss,' Al chipped in.

'Enough said. Get some sleep. You'll need to be sharp tomorrow,' Abby concluded as she got up and left the tent.

* * *

Just before midday Paddy came into Al's tent, 'That's Brothers George, Leo and Iggy dropped off for their train. They sent their best wishes,' said Paddy.

'Will you come and visit?' asked Al.

'I'll come down when I can,' Abby said as she took Al's hand, 'I'll need to fit it in around my shifts.'

'I meant Paddy, but it would be great if you could come down too.' Abby let go of Al's hand and straightened the front of her uniform.

'Lad. I'll be down every other day. OK?' said Paddy. 'With the train out I'll need to make a few trips to Waipuk anyway.'

Al's eyes never left Abby as he was loaded into the ambulance. He gave them a thumbs up sign as the door closed and darkness enveloped him again. One last narrow shaft of light hit his face, making him squint, then blackness. He blinked several times, temporarily blinded by the sudden change. Slowly he started to make out some of the features in the converted Ford Model A truck; a collapsible canvas stretcher, various medical supplies and above him a couple of hooks for intravenous bottles. There was a gritty, metallic taste to the air. The vehicle shuddered and bounced violently. Shock waves exploded up Al's spine and he winced at the pain.

'Sorry, mate,' the deep voice of the driver came through from the cab. 'Roads are bloody rough for about five mile. I'll try to avoid the worst of it where I can.'

'Cheers. Much appreciated,' Al said, his face rigid. He closed his eyes and tried to find something to take his mind off his discomfort. Images came and went like a stuttering motion picture projector. His family, the bush clad hills of Wellington, the glass-like waters of the Bay on a cloudless morning. The vision that calmed him most was the field of lavender from his dreams after the quake. Enclosed by low hills and framed by mature trees, the small field of plants seemed to roll and heave in a gentle breeze. The occasional cloud limped in front of the sun, causing patches of the lavender to change hue. Al felt flush and warm, as if the sun of his vision filled his current dark confines. Was he awake or asleep? That haze between consciousness and unconsciousness engulfed him. He was in a hammock, oscillating in the breeze, slung between two trees. He wasn't lying length-ways, rather he was across it, with his lower legs dangling over the edge. He then saw a second pair of legs next to his. He looked to his left and Abby's face met his gaze.

The truck hit another rut which jolted him awake. He took a couple of sharp breaths. 'What in blazes?' he said, louder than a whisper, as the vision of the dream lingered.

'You OK back there?' asked the driver.

'Fine, fine. Just a little twinge in the back,' Al said, trying to mask his reaction to his dream. How to explain it to himself, let alone a stranger? The stress, the proximity of Abby and her perfume must have combined for a bizarre result in his subconscious. Surely that's all it was.

'We're only a couple of mile from Waipuk.' The drivers' voice brought Al back. 'We'll be at the hospital in about twenty.'

Barely contained chaos appeared to be the order of things at Waipukurau Hospital. About half a dozen ambulances and trucks cluttered the driveway. A horde of people filled the entrance and the surrounding corridors. Hospital staff, some police and military personnel, and civilians were either walking quickly, talking loudly, or both.

The orderlies wheeled him into a long ward room and transferred him to a steel framed bed. The thin mattress felt lumpy, but it was a welcome relief from the ambulance. Beds and patients seemed to fill every available space. Al propped himself up and looked up and down the lines of beds. He thought the room would normally hold seven to eight beds each side. Now there were twelve on both sides and another six down the middle of the room. He could see a lot of head injuries and broken limbs. Al thought himself lucky to not have had a blow to the head, or gotten a puncture wound. There were all ages in the room, from young chaps still in their teens to older gents in the sixties or seventies. The smell hit him immediately. A pungent mixture of body odour, weeping wounds and full bedpans made Al cover his nose and mouth. Al realised quickly staff and facilities were stretched to near breaking point.

As his gaze moved along the beds, he saw a familiar face. He tried to place him, but his view was impeded by a steady stream of staff, the odd patient and that the persons' head was heavily bandaged. Then it came to him, the Danish bloke he'd talked to at St. Vincent DePaul's. Jacobsen, wasn't it? Arnold Jacobsen, that's him. He committed to go over to say hello at some stage. There was a constant hum of conversations, the clatter of equipment and beds being moved and a murmur of groans intermingled with the occasional sharp howl. He already longed for the small tent with just James and him.

It took until early evening before a doctor visited. A quick chat, checking of documents and a poke and prod of Al's body, then he was gone. So much for the best possible care, thought Al. Dinner came. Not a patch on Matron McNeil's fare. Apart from a better bed and four solid walls, there wasn't much to recommend this over the seminary. He was, however, thankful in a small way for this new environment and its commotion. It gave his mind some distraction and pulled his attention away from his growing sense of unease and confusion, but every new voice or face only gave a fleeting respite from his malaise. He knew it was nothing to do with his physical condition. Doctor Wills had given a positive prognosis and his own sense of healing left him with optimism. No, it was the state of flux in his emotions that caused him concern.

The dream he had in the ambulance stirred feelings he was now struggling to reconcile. He had to admit the main reason he didn't want to leave Mount Saint Mary's was not being able to see or talk to Abby. From the moment he awoke under the plane trees and saw who he now regarded as his guardian angel staring down at him, something unnamed, undistinguished swelled inside him. He knew it had actually started a couple of weeks earlier. The realisation had swept over him that the woman who locked his gaze outside the Napier hospital after he and Paddy's hike was Abby. That encounter outside the hospital had knocked him off kilter for a couple of days. What was this? Appreciation, attraction, infatuation? Love? Don't be stupid, he chided himself. Affection, maybe, but not love. Of course during secondary school he'd had a crush on a couple of girls, and certainly there were many attractive women at university, but he'd never had a relationship. 'What would you know about love,' he told himself. 'Particularly the romantic version. You wouldn't recognise that if it ran over you in the street.'

Divine love? Might know a little about that. Love in all its guises as espoused by Saint Thomas Aquinas? Yes. Love as described by Saint Paul in his Letters to the Corinthians? Yes, know that too, but romantic love between a man and woman? Wholly and utterly unknown. So if he didn't know this, why did he think that these feelings might be it? Whatever was happening, he knew he couldn't allow it to develop. A priest can't have this in his life. All his emotional energy needs to be directed to his future school pupils, his faith, his Church and his relationship with God. Love for his family and for all humanity; they can be the only outlets for that feeling.

Soon after sunset, a couple of nurses came by to get everyone settled for the night. They were efficient and quick, lacking the warm nature of Abby and to a lesser extent, Moira. As he tried to drift off to sleep, Al had a cool, hollow sensation sweep over him. He realised this was the most alone he'd felt since his first night at the seminary as a novice, some five years ago. Sleep couldn't come fast enough, but his mind was full to overflowing and slumber wasn't taking hold. Alone? Yes, been here many times: boarding school, the seminary, university and now here. Being shipped off to boarding school at eleven years old when the family moved to Wanganui two hundred miles away, was painful. Alone again. Was it fear of being alone, a feeling of abandonment that pushed him toward the Church, or just its reassuring omnipresence in his life? He never really had questioned his calling, it seemed a logical option, coupled with pressure from his mother. This was the first time he could remember having any wavering thoughts about a life in the Church.

He realised he hadn't prayed at all today. Al closed his eyes, crossed himself and started. After a couple of Hail Mary's he managed to pull himself away from the rote prayer structure. 'Heavenly Father, please show your divine mercy to all the patients here and in all the other hospitals. Please ensure their speedy recovery so they can re-join their families and loved ones. I ask you to guard over those whom you have called to your side from this turmoil and comfort those who are left behind. Watch over Father Patrick and Miss McCarthy, and bless them for all the care and attention they have given me. Help me understand and express what I feel for Miss McCarthy. Amen.'

The next morning, a soon to be predictable timetable started: wake up at six thirty with a cup of tea; breakfast half an hour later; then ablutions, a bed bath for those who couldn't get up and a proper bath for the more able bodied; more tea; rounds by the doctors; lunch; visitors for most, but not him; afternoon tea including a scone, well, something impersonating said baked goods, thought Al; more doctors rounds; dinner; finally lights out.

During the afternoon, an orderly came into the ward and started handing out letters and telegrams. 'Anyone need letters posted or a message sent?' he asked a couple of times as he walked round the ward.

It dawned on Al that he had neither sent nor received anything to or from his family. Anxious and slightly guilty, he waved the orderly over. 'Could I get a telegram sent, please?'

'Fire away,' the orderly replied, notebook and pencil at the ready.

'To Charles and Margaret Robertson. Twenty-Eight, Halswell Road, Wanganui. Dear Mother and Father. Stop. Took a knock in the quake but feeling fine. Stop. Now at Waipukurau Hospital. Stop. No need to worry. Stop. Love to the boys. Stop. Warmest regards Albert. Stop.'

'And who's it from?'

'Albert Robertson, Mount Saint Mary's Seminary, Taradale.' Al exhaled; his guilt lifted.

On Saturday morning there was a change to the schedule. An orderly wheeled Al into a room full of frames, pulleys and other contraptions. A muscular man, probably mid-thirties, approached Al with a clipboard in his hands. His sandy brown hair was thick with pomade, toned and tanned forearms were contrasted against a white short sleeved shirt

'Morning, Albert. Time to start your rehabilitation,' said the man. Al's wide eyes and raised eyebrows gave away his concern. 'Don't be worried,' the tanned man picked up on Al's cues. 'I know you've been through the mill. I'll be taking things nice and slow. First off, I won't be working on your back for a while. The doc reckons it needs to settle down some more. We need to get your legs moving again and that ankle able to take some weight. How's that sound?'

'Pretty good, I suppose,' Al said as he looked around the room at the equipment.

'Relax. Won't be on that lot for ages. Let's get you up on the bench.' The two dark brown arms reached under Al's armpits. With a gentleness that surprised Al, he was eased out of his wheelchair and placed on a thinly padded, leather clad table. The physical therapist started to lift, push and pull Al's legs in all directions. He got Al to flex his muscles, stretch and rotate his legs and joints. Al winced at every new position, but gritted his teeth.

A few hours later Al was awoken when a couple of meaty fingers poked him in the shoulder. He turned and saw a familiar smile through puffy eyes.

'Wakey, wakey, lad. What the Dickens you doing having a kip in the arvo?' said Paddy.

'Beauty sleep, Paddy,' Al replied, still groggy.

'And the Lord knows, you need it. How are you doing, my boy?'

'Not bad. Had my first rehabilitation session today. The Spanish Inquisition had nothing on this bloke. Much better now you're here. Great to see a familiar face. My first visitor,' said Al.

'Got ya a few bits and pieces from the seminary and some food. I'd reckon the grub ain't too flash here, eh,' said Paddy as he placed a small box near the bottom of Al's bed. 'They sent a salvage team into the dorm. I got in on one of their runs and picked up a few of your things. There's also some leftovers from Mrs. B. She sends her best wishes.'

'Thanks, Paddy. How is Elizabeth?'

'Doing OK. Already got the Ladies Committee organising billets, clothing appeals and emergency food parcels. You know what she's like. Will be head of all relief efforts before long.'

'What about the parish in general?' asked Al.

Paddy stared out the window above Al's bed. He swallowed hard, but still his voice faltered. 'We've lost a few. Six that I definitely know of. You remember Dot McAlpine? You talked to her at Saint Vinny's.'

'Yes. She was trying so hard to keep her family going.'

'That's her. Well she's definitely gone. Saw the body myself to give her a final blessing. Young Shelia O'Sullivan, also. She was working at the BNZ. The building is gone. Just a pile of rubble. Only a couple of people made it out.'

'Lord, have mercy.' Al crossed himself. 'Mrs. O'Sullivan must be devastated.'

'She's beside herself. I can't even talk to her at the mo. Jerry Simpson also died. He was in the boozer, ran outside and got crushed by some masonry.'

Silence hung awkwardly between them. Al was unsure what to feel. Grief for the loss of life. Compassion for Mary at losing her husband. Relief that Jerry will no longer be able to hurt Mary. His training told him grief and compassion, but his inner voice said relief.

Paddy broke the impasse, 'Still, we've been luckier than St. Paul's. They've lost a load of people and the church is completely destroyed.' He pursed his lips as his shoulders dropped. 'Lad, you wouldn't recognise the place. All of downtown is gone. It's worse than the bombed out towns I saw during the war. At least then there were a few places left standing. Here? Nothing.' A sharp twitch shot through Paddy's body.

'What do you mean, nothing?' asked Al.

'Exactly that. The centre of town is gone. I had a wander round late yesterday. Without a word of a lie, there's hardly a single building left. Took me straight back to France. Never thought I'd see the like of it again. Certainly not here in me home town.'

Al tried to picture the scene; but knew he would probably underestimate the destruction.

'Crikey. Almost forgot,' Paddy said as he reached into his jacket and produced a letter.

Al narrowed his eye as he looked at the envelope. A jolt of excitement made his face flush. *Maybe it's from Abby,* he thought. He unfolded the thick weight paper, and saw the Mount Saint Mary's crest in the top middle of the page. Disappointment. Al took in the contents, 'They're going ahead with our final profession. I'm to go to Wellington on Monday. The ceremony is Tuesday.'

'Mustn't let a pesky little earthquake get in the way of Church protocol,' said Paddy.

'I only had my first rehabilitation session today. Looks like I'll need a lot more sessions in the next few days,' said Al.

'I hope they'll cut you some slack from the full rigors of the ceremony. Right, lad. Time's marching on. I'd better get going. I'll pop back on Monday morning before you leave, eh. Take it easy, lad.' Paddy gently rubbed Al's shoulder as he stood, then walked out of the ward.

Another day, more rehab. Al could sense more strength returning to his legs. His sprained ankle had recovered enough to take some weight. The tanned man in the torture chamber seemed to be having a positive effect.

On the way back he stopped by to see Arnold Jacobson. There was a large red stain on the bandages encircling his head. 'Arnold? It's Brother Albert. You remember me from St. Vincent DePaul's?'

Heavy eyes slowly turned to meet Al. 'Yes. I remember.' The strong, deep voice, with a hint of a Scandinavian accent that Al was expecting was gone. Arnold struggled with just these three words. Al placed his right hand on Arnold's forearm. 'Brother… please pray… for me. Doctor won't tell me anything… but, I know,' said Arnold.

Al closed his eyes, crossed himself and Arnold. 'Heavenly Father, watch over Arnold. Merciful Lord, spare his pain and give him the strength he needs to recover. There is no need to call Arnold to your side, but if you do, you will find a loyal servant. Amen.'

Arnold mouthed 'Thank you.'

'I'll pray for you every day, but promise me you'll fight. Never give up. Deal?' said Al. Arnold gave a small nod.

He wheeled himself back to his bed and climbed in. The smell of a fresh cup of tea wafted over him as he relaxed. He felt a sudden chill, *'That's rather odd,'* he thought, especially as it was so warm. He looked around to see if anyone had opened a window nearby. He saw a familiar figure in the doorway. Her nurses uniform was slightly rumpled, an apprehensive look on her face as she peered down the rows of beds. She smiled widely as their eyes met. She almost skipped to his bed. A sharp cry of pain from the man in the bed next to him jolted Al back into consciousness. It was dusk, the cup of tea untouched, now cold, and there was no nurse in the room. Dreaming again.

'For the love of God. This has got to stop,' he whispered to himself.

CHAPTER 9

11th February 1931

He had finally got to the Home of Compassion in the Island Bay suburb of Wellington at about seven o'clock the previous night. His classmates had welcomed him warmly last night, especially George and Leo. Not all were there, though. The three main absentees were James, who hadn't been given clearance from the doctors at Dannevirke Hospital to travel; Iggy, who decided to delay his Final Profession until next year; and of course Jimmy Doogan, who would now forever remain at Mount Saint Mary's as a victim of the quake.

A bad nights' sleep had ensued. The main cause of his insomnia was the realisation of the enormity of the coming ceremony. It had his mind running at a thousand miles an hour. The final commitment to Christ and the Church. The last vow of faith and obligation. Ordination as a priest would be the final step in his journey. Now less than twenty-four hours before the ceremony, he had realised for the first time since his decision to go into the seminary, he was questioning his devotion. Had it actually been his decision as an eighteen-year old? Was he ready for the dedication that was to be asked of him? A bit late in the day to be asking these questions, he told himself. Where had these doubts come from? The last five years had disappeared in a haze of memories. Everything had been laid out in front of him. Small, incremental steps with a nod to the future; but without an acknowledgement of the commitment that now was only a few short hours away.

Once sleep had finally come, Al found himself in a now familiar setting. The field of lavender danced in the breeze, kissed by hazy sunlight. He wasn't in a hammock this time, rather under a tree, leaning against its trunk. The high pitched screech of metal hinges pulled his attention to his right. Abby was pushing a small gate aside. Its weathered wood, now grey and moss-covered, was contrasted against the pure white of her nurses' uniform. She let the gate go and it swung closed with a loud whack.

Al woke instantly at the noise. Splinters of light pierced the curtains as dawn approached. He fought consciousness for what seemed like another hour. Sleep was consuming him again, when Al was jolted awake by a rap on the door. Time for morning prayers and breakfast. Al reached over for his fob watch on the bedside table. 5:30am. Barely four hours sleep. His heavy eyes closed for a few seconds. *'Couldn't they give me an hour or two more?'* he thought.

He swung his legs over the bed and grabbed his crutches. He could manage short trips with them, but anything more than a few minutes he needed a wheelchair. There was one in the corner of the room from the Home. Like most things here, it was showing its age. A pre-war model, it was more wood than metal, with a wicker seat. Nothing like the shiny new ones at the hospital that had padded leather seats and thick rubber tyres.

After his ablutions in a china basin, he opened the small wardrobe at the far end of the room. They had all been given brand new clothes for the ceremony. A freshly starched shirt, Roman collar and a cassock, which was much lighter and better quality than their everyday robes they wore at the seminary. Brand new shoes, with a shine so polished they glistened in the morning sunlight. The memory of the men lined up outside the Napier docks came back to him. Their ragged clothes and beaten up shoes. A fresh, complete outfit just for a ceremony of a couple hours when so many had nothing? That can't be right, couldn't the Church get its priorities right?

He pulled the cassock on over this shirt and trousers, fastened the buttons, then slipped the shoes on. He leaned over to tie his laces, but his hands didn't get halfway down his shin before shafts of pain ran all the way up his back, settling in his shoulders. He straightened then tried again. This time he raised his right leg to reduce the distance he needed to bend. His hands got to his ankle before the pain became too much. Hopefully one of the lads will help me out, he thought. He picked up his crucifix and tied it to the cassock around his waist. He was about to get into the wheelchair when there was a knock on the door.

'Brother Al? It's Brother George and Brother Leo. You need a hand?'

'Come in. Great timing,' Al replied as George stuck his head round the door. 'I've hit a road block with the old footwear. Could you do the honours?'

'You didn't try to do these yourself did you?' George asked as Al tried not making eye contact. 'Thought as much. You're a stubborn bugger at times. There, all done.'

'Thanks. Now don't you two look a mass of dash? A couple of dapper Dan's,' said Al.

'Takes one to know one,' said Leo as he patted down his hair in mock vanity. All three exchanged quick glances. 'Are we ready for this?' Leo added.

Silence hung over them like the sword of Damocles.

'It's a bit late to be having second thoughts,' said George. 'We started this together, so we'll get through it. We've got each other to lean on, no matter what happens. Right?'

Small nods from Leo and Al.

George and Leo helped Al into the wheelchair. Leo grabbed a wool blanket and covered Al's legs. 'She's a bit cool out this morning, but supposed to be nice in time for Mass,' Leo said. Setting off for morning prayers, each rotation of the wheels echoed down the long corridor.

After breakfast, preparations for the Mass started in earnest. All the seminarians were moved to a small room. With Al's wheelchair taking up extra space, the room felt cramped. A single window didn't throw much light into the room, due to thick curtains warding off the sun. There were copies of the Mass booklet on a corner table, which included the Solemn Consecration, the vows they would profess to the Church and the Holy Father. In everything that had happened in the past few days, Al had forgotten the vows would be in Latin. He'd need a quick read through to bring himself back up to speed.

The room was quiet. The normal banter of classmates had gone. The realisation of what they were about to enter into had swept across all eight of them. The rustle of turned pages and the occasional cough, were the only sounds that broke the silence. Nervous glances shot between them. Two lines of cigarette smoke drifted to the ceiling from the fingers of a couple of them who needed a nicotine shot to calm their nerves. Al suddenly had an urge to do the same; but realised his pipe was still in the box Paddy had brought to the hospital. It was now a week since he last had a smoke.

Connolly was to lead the mass and ceremony. He was bedecked in his finest ceremonial garments. Pure white, heavily embroidered robes with a gold satin lining. A blue silk yoke, embroidered with gold flowers, covered his shoulders and sternum. A white mitre with gold edging and inlaid emeralds, ruby's and pearls adorned his head. He carried a solid sterling silver staff with white satin gloves covering his hands. In front of the assembly was a priest carrying a large gold crucifix affixed to the top of a long wooden staff. On either side of him were candle bearers. Behind those three, one of the senior Brothers from

Mount Saint Mary's held a red leather Bible with an intricate gold cross embossed on it.

Entering the chapel, Al immediately saw four familiar faces. His family had come down from Wanganui and were in the fourth row from the front on the left. His mother's face was barely large enough to contain her smile. Her brown hair, with only a few flecks of grey, was pinned tight to her head, underneath a round hat, the type which was the height of fashion back in the 1920's. His brothers, Gary and William in matching tweed suits, gave him a wave. His father nodded, a small grin was difficult to make out. His cold blue eyes stared straight ahead. A gaze so hard it could cut steel. Al smiled and waved. Many people, his family included, had dusted off their Sunday best. Others were obviously struggling. Tired suits, stitched up dresses and resoled shoes. He flicked the wool blanket so it covered his new footwear.

The seminarians stationed themselves at the front of the chapel, at the foot of the steps of the altar. The chapel was small, at a squeeze it might take 120 people. A low ceiling and lack of ornate finishing took Al by surprise.

Connolly started the mass, reciting verbatim the words in the ceremonial book. After an almost ten-minute monologue, he called on the brothers to state their vows:

'Deus, sancti propositi auctor et custos...' they all said in unison.

Al suddenly felt flush. He continued the recital, but other thoughts now entered into his consciousness. His father giving him the course prospectus for architecture at Victoria University many years ago; Paddy telling him the Church isn't for everyone; then a quick flash of Abby's face. He gave a sharp shake of his head. Concentrate, keep reading, he thought. The final couple of sentences struggled out. That was the easy part, thought Al. Just words. Now we have the physical commitment to the Lord.

George and Leo went to help Al out of the wheelchair, but he waved them away. He eased himself down to his knees, then onto his front, leaving him prostrate in front of the altar. Al closed his eyes and bit his bottom lip. Pain coursed up and down his body causing his hands to shake.

Connolly continued the mass, gave a blessing for the seminarians, all now face down in front of him. Another dose of incense and holy water were waved over them. Were they on the floor for a few minutes or half an hour? Time was now fluctuating, as Al struggled to differentiate between seconds and minutes. Finally Connolly gave the instruction for them to rise. Al braced himself for more pain as he was placed back into the wheelchair.

The air was now thick with the sweet smoke, which made it difficult to get enough oxygen. He gulped air into his lungs with short, shallow breaths. Beads of sweat sprang to life on his forehead. He looked down at his hands. They were drained of colour and still shaking. The rest of the Mass he barely followed. Suddenly everything went black. His next fully conscious moment was Leo giving him a glass of water just before he was wheeled out of the chapel.

'You alright? You looked a bit woozy in there,' Leo asked.

Al didn't know how long he'd been out. Could have been one minute, could have been twenty. 'I'm fine. Getting up off the floor left me a little lightheaded.'

'I think we all need a bit of fresh air after that. Time for a spot of lunch, too,' said Leo. They led the congregation into the adjacent hall. A lavish spread awaited them – chicken, lamb, ham, potato and green salads, beans and peas, for dessert jelly trifle, pavlova and fruit salad. Al immediately remembered the meals he helped dish up at St. Vincent De Paul's – beef stew, made with gristly joints, the odd dozy spud and two day old bread. More excess in a time of terrible need.

Al felt arms around his neck and a kiss on his cheek. They were fine boned, with blue veins clearly visible under thin skin, seemingly untouched by the summer sun.

'Albert. I'm so proud of you.' His mother wiped the smudged lipstick off his face.

'Well done, boy. Good to see you're in decent shape,' said his father as they shook hands. His big hands, dry and calloused felt rough to Al. His salt and pepper hair (now more salt than pepper) was tightly cropped, not a hair out of place.

'Thanks for coming down. You got my telegrams?' said Al.

'The seminary sent one the day after the quake. It told us you were hurt but stable, so to get yours put us at our ease. Especially your mother,' said Charles Robertson.

'Dear, I was worried sick, so I was. I couldn't eat for a couple of days. Isn't that right Charles?' Margaret added as she rubbed Al's shoulder.

'We got another one on Friday telling us about this, then yours on Monday, so we had to come to see you. The boys couldn't wait to get down here. Come and say hello to your brother,' he gestured to the teenagers. 'Left Howard with neighbours, a little too young for such a big trip.'

Any neutral observer would pick all three as brothers. Above average heights for their ages, strong noses, thin upper lips and sandy brown hair that had lightened during the summer.

Gary, the middle boy, was first to speak 'Well done, Al. You alright? Bit of a worry with you in this wheelchair.'

'I'm fine, honestly. What's all this I hear about you getting a job?' asked Al.

'Yeah, bloody brilliant.' His blue eyes lit up. They were the same colour as their father's, yet infinitely warmer.

'Language, Gary,' Margaret interjected.

Gary turned back to Al and rolled his eyes, 'Going to be a

junior clerk at the Department of Labour. Start just after Easter, down here in Wellington. I'm absolutely stoked.'

'Wonderful news. I'm so happy for you. Make sure you work hard and count your blessings. You know how hard it is out there,' said Al. Gary gave a nod. 'And how's our young soldier?' Al moved his attention to William.

The boy rushed over and hugged Al with some force.

'Easy, Digger. I'm not ready for rough and tumble just yet.' William pulled back and frowned. 'Don't worry. I'll be right soon enough. You back at college yet?'

'You bet. Fourth Form this year.' A broad smile broke across William's face as he spoke. 'I got a job too this summer. I was the office boy at the 2ZR wireless station.' He could barely contain his excitement.

'Slow down, champ. Tell me all about it,' said Al.

'I was mainly gathering all the stories for the hourly news. So I know all about the earthquake. What did it feel like?'

'Now, now. That's enough, William,' their father cut the eager teenager off. 'Let's not burden Albert with trying to remember such things.'

'It alright, Father. Bits are coming back to me. It felt like the ground was rolling. As if we were at sea. Then a very sharp jolt. That's when the chapel started collapsing.'

Margaret gave a muffled shriek as she held her hand over her mouth.

'Your mother's upset. We can talk about it later,' Charles said sternly.

'Afternoon Mr. and Mrs. Robertson,' George and Leo said in unison as they approached.

'Brother Spring and Brother Head. Congratulations,' said Charles.

'Thanks very much,' said George.

'We're just glad to be able to have the ceremony, after last week,' added Leo.

'Apparently they have a photographer organised. We're supposed to round everyone up for a picture,' said George.

They were arranged in two lines in front of a small statue of The Virgin Mary. Al was wheeled in behind the row of seats. All the families were jockeying for the best spot to take a photo. George stood behind Al, and just as the Church photographer was about to take the official shot, George leaned in and gave Al a gentle pat on the shoulder.

As soon as the families had taken their pictures with their box brownies, Charles grabbed Al's chair and wheeled him into a quiet corner of the hall. 'We need to have a chat, my boy.' Al knew a serious discussion would be coming up and he had a good idea what it would be about. 'Your mother and I would like you to come home for a while. We want to look after you until you get back on your feet.' There it was. The official invitation, or was it an order, to come home.

'Thanks for that. It would be nice to come back, especially to spend time with the boys, even though Gary is about to leave. I suppose I'll have to talk it through with the seminary and the hospital. I'm getting treatment from this guy at Waipuk hospital. He's really helping me get back on track,' said Al.

'I'm sure we can find you someone just as good at Wanganui Base Hospital. There's plenty of those physical training types around, and Highden Seminary is not far away, so you can continue your studies there. Besides, your mother really wants you back. You can't deny her that.'

Al bit his bottom lip. Great. The guilt card. Wondered when that would be played. Early on, it seems.

'I'll have to talk it over with Father Connolly. I am meant to go back on Thursday. If things improve quickly, and this guy in Waipuk has been working wonders, I could come home in a week or two. How does that sound?'

'I expect you back sooner rather than later. Am I making myself clear?'

'Crystal clear, Father,' Al closed the conversation.

* * *

Something was amiss on the ward when he came in after the trip to Wellington. Al scanned beds. Arnold Jacobson wasn't there. His bed freshly made, sheets crisp, tucked corners so sharp you could cut yourself. The bedside cabinet empty. His eyes darted around, looking for a nurse or orderly. He saw someone a couple of beds along. 'Arnold?' he asked. The orderly gave a sharp shake of his head. A week and a half later and the quake was still taking people. He wheeled himself to Arnold's bed, crossed himself and prayed for his soul. Arriving at his own bed, he saw a letter on the pillow. The envelope felt smooth, it was high quality paper. He didn't recognise the handwriting. A light fragrance entered the air as he opened the letter.

Wednesday 12 February

Dear Albert,

I do hope this note finds you in good spirits and your recuperation is progressing well.

I stopped by today to call on you. The staff told me you had gone to Wellington for a few days. I hope the journey wasn't too arduous for you and your stay was enjoyable.

It is unfortunate that I wasn't able to see you, as it was a very pleasant afternoon and we could have gone for a walk in the grounds.

*The staff tell me that you are making sterling progress and you are
a pleasure to have on the ward. I am not surprised they say that.*

*They also tell me you will return tomorrow. If at all possible, I will
try to pay you a visit next week.*

*Warmest best wishes,
Abby McCarthy*

He held the letter to his nose, closed his eyes and drew in the aroma.
A broad smile broke across his face, then realised someone could
have been watching. He did a quick scan of the ward, but no prying
eyes. He re-folded the letter and put into his box of belongings.

The tanned man worked Al hard for two sessions a day.
Monday afternoon there was a big smile from the physical
trainer. Al walked inside a frame of parallel bars, using his arms
for balance. 'Right. Time to go solo. I want you to walk out of the
frame, under your own steam,' he told Al. 'Don't worry. You'll be
fine. I'm going to be right beside you.'

Slowly Al eased his grip on the bars. He could feel the force of
his body flow down into his legs. He lifted his left leg; and shuffled
about six inches. The same with the right. Again with the left. His
first unassisted steps in two weeks.

'Bloody beauty.' Brilliant white teeth shone out from tanned
man's brown face.

A couple of days later, soon after Abby had managed to call
on him, he completed the discharge paperwork, Al found one of
the ambulances that was still shuttling patients between Napier
and Waipuk. Al eased himself into the passenger seat.

'Train station, mate? Finally getting out of this God-forsaken
mess, huh?' asked the driver.

'No. I'll come back to Napier with you. That alright?' replied
Al.

CHAPTER 10

The silence of the evenings put him off kilter. It was a heavy cloak shrouding the town. It was the quakes spiteful little brother, who ensured you always knew he was around, instead of the constant din of life, stillness was the deafening tenor. Nothing had prepared Al for the lack of sound. A curfew was still in place over Napier, so the town fell still on the stroke of six every night. A once vibrant place now reduced. Even the birds had left. Every evening, the same sheet of silence descended upon the town. Gone was the everyday noise of early evening: the whirr of cars as folks went home from work; the hubbub of pubs closing, spilling their patrons onto the streets; and the clunk and rattle of the last trams of the day. The extent of the devastation shocked him, but Paddy's description, memories of war photographs and his imagination had given some preparation for what he saw, not a complete building left standing in a two square mile block.

Into this vacuum Al went most evenings. He thought it unlikely that any policeman or deputised security man would arrest a man of the cloth, especially a quake survivor, yet he didn't want to force their hand, so he kept to the grounds of St. Patricks. He walked from the cottage to the presbytery and back again, with a couple of laps of the church. Every ten yards he would take the crutches out from under his arms and walk a few paces. Now looking like a full stride, Tanned Man would be pleased.

He had ventured into town a couple of times, but they were wholly demoralising excursions. He could only safely manoeuvre down a couple of streets where the clearance was well advanced. Paddy had been right, there was nothing left, save the odd facade or wall that would soon be demolished. So is this what young men like him and boys younger still, saw every day during the war? With the likelihood of death any moment, as well. No wonder so many of them he had met were broken men. Al found it difficult to visualise what had been here a few weeks earlier. Was this pile of rubble the bakery, or the laundry? Apart from Hospital Hill to the north and St. Patrick's spire to the south, all forms of orientation had been wiped away. Major buildings that defined each street, each intersection, now reduced to truck and trailer and wheelbarrow loads of broken masonry, splintered wood and bent steel. He tapped a pile of bricks with one of his crutches and looked up and down the street. The ruins were grotesque. Half a speaker from a gramophone peeked out from under some debris. There was no sign of the machine itself. What had they been listening to when the quake hit? Classical or something more modern? Nearby an unravelled ball of bright red knitting yarn caught his eye. Was it going to be something new for winter? A jersey? A scarf? A woolly hat? Mementos of scores of broken lives scattered in front of him. Was this what Lucifer would want for a museum of curios? He started to think of the people he had met prior to the quake, some now gone forever. His shoulders dropped as an unseen weight bore down upon him.

Movement to his left pulled his attention away from his thoughts. As he turned to investigate, a rat dashed for cover. Al moved closer and the distinct odour of decomposing flesh hit him. Its bitter sting attacked his nostrils. Lying near some broken glass were two severed fingers, white with dust, dried blood was caked thick around their bases. He closed his eyes, there for the grace of God go I, he thought. Why did he survive yet hundreds of others didn't? Had he been a second slower knocking Iggy to safety at the chapel, both of them would be among the fatalities.

Life and death seemed to be a matter of inches and seconds, totally random at the best of times.

At one corner, a steel girder some fifteen yards long had been bent double and partially melted. He looked around and a cold shock shot through his body as he realised he was looking at the remains of the Bank of New Zealand, where Sheila O'Sullivan had perished. He crossed himself and asked God to grant her peace. Although he knew the science behind the quake, he questioned the wisdom of what he believed to be a benevolent and loving God. How could he choose and justify who were the ones to be taken to be with him? How could the Lord let this happen to so many of his flock? These questions that had been swimming around his head for days, and as a young seminarian, he had no adequate response. Obviously no one can say for sure what His ultimate plan is for us, but maybe setting out trials is part of His work and it's up to us to respond in the best way we can, with compassion and dedication. As He shows us the way through the gospels and the work of Jesus and would expect us to follow that. Al wasn't sure he believed this.

Gradually during his evening excursions, ten unaided steps became thirteen, a nine inch gait became 2ft long steps. Time for a change, he thought, so the next day he made his way to the temporary hospital over at the racecourse, courtesy of a truck driver headed that way.

'You a new admission?' the nurse on reception said. 'Take this form and fill it out.'

'Well on the way to recovery. I just want to swap these for a pair of walking sticks,' said Al, holding up his crutches.

Her grey hair and glasses triggered a memory for Al. The night Paddy and he took Mary Simpson up to the old hospital. It was the same nurse. 'Stores are in the jockey's weighing room. Second corridor on the right, first door on the left,' she said pointing down the main hallway.

Al knocked on the door and a muffled voiced called him in.

'G'day. Can I help you?' said the young man from behind a newspaper, without looking up. A shock of ginger hair faced Al.

'Just wanting to swap these,' said Al.

The orderly dropped the paper and his look of boredom instantly changed to mild panic, 'Sorry, Father. Didn't mean to be rude. Sure, sure. What do you need?'

'Some walking sticks would be great.'

'Absolutely. No worries. In fact we've just received a shipment from Auckland.' He went into an adjoining room. 'Wait a minute, eh? Here you go. A couple of beauties. I think they're Ash.' The orderly knocked them together with a loud crack. 'Brand spanking new. Never used.'

'Marvellous. Looks like I've got the better end of the swap,' said Al.

'We actually need crutches. Still a lot of leg breaks and amputations coming through. Can never have enough of these,' he said as he took them off Al.

Al stayed close to the wall as he walked down the corridor and was halfway through his turn onto the main thoroughfare when he was hit from behind. His walking sticks slipped from under him and he fell heavily. A folder of papers landed on his head.

'Watch where you're go… Oh, Father, I'm so sorry,' the woman said.

Al winced as he looked up at a familiar face.

'Didn't see you. Had my nose in some files. Please, let me help you up,' the woman added.

'Miss McCarthy. I must have been a bad patient if you need to tackle me like you're an All Black,' said Al. 'You really should be more careful.' The woman was staring at him with a narrow gaze. 'It's Brother Albert Robertson. From Mount Saint Mary's. You and your cousin came to look after us.'

'Yes. So sorry, I didn't recognise you,' said Moira. 'I was a thousand miles away. How are you? Present abuse excluded.'

'Doing well, thank you. Making steady progress. I had wonderful support down in Waipuk.'

'Yes. Abigail said as much after one of her visits.'

'Is she working today?' he asked.

'No. She's on an evening shift. She wanted a late start after a date with Doctor Peters,' Moira answered quickly.

'That's a pity. It would have been grand to catch up again. Another time perhaps.' There was no response from Moira. 'I'd better get back to town. Nice to see you again.'

'Until next time, Brother Robertson,' she said as she put the folder under her arm and walked off.

He went past a door which had a temporary sign above it "Hospital Canteen". His taste buds tingled at the idea of a cup of tea, so he went in. As the minutes ticked by, his hands left marks on his fob watch as he flipped it open and closed every few seconds. As he scanned the room, he thought maybe she would come in early for her evening shift, as unlikely as that might be, there was always hope. Then a familiar face in the doorway caught his eye. Abby entered the room at a purposeful pace, her head up as she made her way to the counter. Al raised his hand and gave her a wave. A broad smile enveloped her face. From this distance her dimples looked deep, accentuating her cheeks.

'Isn't this a nice surprise? Don't be getting up.' Abby greeted him with a kiss on the cheek, as Al started to get out of his seat.

Al felt flushed, looked around quickly, nervously. 'Didn't expect to see you all. I came in for an equipment upgrade. I saw Moira and she told me you were doing evenings after stepping out on the town.'

'That's bizarre. I'm on nights next week. We even came to work together today. As for being out, I haven't done anything social for a week.' There was a slight pause in the conversation as they held each others gaze. 'No more crutches. That's a massive improvement,' she added.

'Every day is better,' replied Al. 'How rude of me. I should get you a cup of tea. How do you take it?' said Al.

'Stay there. I'll get it.'

As he watched Abby go to the counter, he noticed one of the doctors flick his eyes between him and her. Staring at Abby, then Al, and back to Abby. His face was familiar to Al, he searched for memory of him, but couldn't place him immediately.

'I got us a couple of scones,' Abby said as she sat down. 'I'm ravenous.'

'It's still busy here I presume?' asked Al.

'No let up at all. Things have changed a bit though. We've had a lot of late amputations of limbs we couldn't save. We've started seeing some dysentery. A lot of people still haven't got clean water, but thank the Lord we haven't lost anyone for almost a week.'

'More like thanks to you and the rest of the staff,' added Al.

'That's very kind of you to say.' She picked up a knife, cut the scones in half, layered a thick coat of butter on each half then quartered them. 'There you go. They make awful tea, but their scones are lovely,' she said as she handed him a piece.

Al took a bite, 'You're dead right. These are good,' he said scooping up some crumbs falling from the corner of his mouth. As he turned from Abby to wipe his hands onto a plate he noticed the doctor in the corner was now in a conversation with a colleague, but most of his attention was sill trained on Abby. Now the recollection came to him – he's the doctor who treated Mary Simpson. Seems Abby has an admirer. *He's got no reason to be worried about me,* Al thought, *I'm not a competitor for her heart, something else has my commitment.*

'So why haven't you gone back to your parents?' Abby asked.

'I will soon enough. I didn't want to go back while I was on crutches and be a burden.'

'At twenty-three you are not too old to receive the dotage of your mother. It's a brave man that denies his mother the opportunity to spoil her number one son.'

'Not sure I'm number one, but I get your point. I really wanted to walk in under my own steam. Fingers crossed I should go back late next week,' he said.

'Make sure you do. If not, it won't just be your parents chasing you, I'll hound you till you go,' Abby said with a smile that warmed him as a mid-summer breeze.

'Best I do, then. I don't want to be a chased man.' He returned the smile.

They simultaneously reached for a piece of scone. Their hands met over the plate. Her skin was supple and clement to Al's touch. He pulled his hand away, but hers lingered for a couple of seconds.

* * *

The one month anniversary of the quake dawned grey and cool. Leaden skies to match the still dull mood of the town. It was as if nature itself had picked up on the milestone date.

Mid-morning there was a light knock on the door. A bit early for Mrs. Bartholomew with tonight's dinner, Al thought. Opening the front door, he found Abby standing on the porch in her uniform. She had the train of her hat clipped behind her head, so the rest of the material billowed out making her appear to have small white wings. A broad smile broke across his face and a feeling of exhilaration swept over him.

'Hope you don't mind an unannounced visitor? I've just finished a night shift and thought you might like some morning tea. I brought scones from the canteen,' she said, holding up a small package of oven paper.

'Well, it's my turn to be very surprised. Please, come in,' he said, 'Great timing, I only put the kettle on a little while ago.' Turning back inside, he ushered her through the hall and wondered why she would stop by. To check up on him, to have a chat, does she need some spiritual guidance, just to spend time with him?

'So this is how the clergy live?' she said as she looked around, popping her head into every doorway. 'I was expecting something a little more luxurious.'

'The presbytery is plusher, but the rank and file have to settle for something more basic. Helps with our vow of poverty.'

'I wonder if the Archbishop has that particular issue? Something tells me he wouldn't have had to deal with scarcity for some years,' she said.

'With superiority comes privilege in most walks of life,' he said as he poured the hot water into the teapot. He put two cups and saucers, a sugar bowl and milk jug onto a tray.

'Oi, put that down. I'll take it. How did you expect to pick up a fully loaded tray and walk without any help? Men. Honestly,' she said shaking her head while taking the tray out of his hands.

'Come on, it's only a few feet. I'm not an invalid, you know. I'll be fine,' not letting go, until he saw the look on her face and retreated, 'Alright, you win, this time.' He puffed out his cheeks in fake resignation.

Her eyes were pulled away as she placed the tray on the kitchen table. She picked up two small books from the sideboard. 'Poems by Robert Louis Stevenson? I wouldn't have thought poetry was on the reading list at Mount Saint Mary's. I didn't even know he wrote poetry. Just thought of him for *Treasure Island* and *Kidnapped*.' She put the first book back onto the table then opened the cover of the second volume, 'Rupert Brooke? Who's that?'

'He was a wonderful poet from just before the war. Unfortunately he died in 1915 at only twenty-seven,' said Al.

'You'll have to read some to me. I'm partial to Yeats and TS Elliot myself.'

'Have you got some of their works? You should bring them round and we can swap our favourite pieces,' said Al.

'I'd be delighted to. I don't get a chance to talk about poetry with anyone here. Nobody seems even remotely interested. Now, there is an actual reason for the visit, more than just passing the day and talking poetry with you. I do want to take a look at you to make sure things are on the right track. Is that alright?' she asked, leaning forward towards him.

'I suppose. You don't need to, I'm feeling good. Getting better every day. Close to normal now,' he said, giving Abby a demonstration.

'You are still technically my patient, so I do feel responsible for you until you're back to tip-top form. As you are up, turn around for me.' He did as requested, so he had his back to her. 'Do you have to wear a cassock every day? Makes examining you a little difficult,' she said as she placed one hand on the small of his back and the other on his stomach.

'Only get to ditch them for sport and physical work, like when we help out in the vineyard. I can go and change if you want. Ouch, blimin' heck, that was a bit raw.' He bit his lower lip and winced. The pain was sharp and quick, but the lingering sensation was the warmth of her hands on his body. The heat seemed to penetrate deep into his body and radiate to his extremities. He closed his eyes and took a deep breath and slowly exhaled.

'No, you're fine. Just a few more seconds,' she said, working her hand up his back. Still firm and muscular, such a lovely physique, she thought. 'All done. Not bad. Feels like there's very little swelling now, which is good. It's internal bruising and shock to the muscles that need time to come right.'

Al sat down and started pouring the tea, and not a second too soon, as the sensation was threatening to turn into arousal, his raised internal temperature caused a bead of sweat to run down the middle of his back.

'So what has been keeping you busy, apart from brushing up on your poetry?' Abby asked as she sipped her tea then took a bite of scone.

'I've been doing my bit for the town. Helping out with this and that. And before you ask, yes I'm going back to Wanganui. I'm on a train this Friday. I sent a telegram to Mum and Dad yesterday,' he said.

'Terrific. I didn't want to have to nag you about it.'

'A bit of gentle reminding wouldn't be nagging,' he said with a smile.

'Tell that to most husbands. They might not agree,' a little grin came across her face as she spoke. 'Where in Wanganui are you from? I'm from Fordell.'

'A country girl. I'm not actually from Wanganui myself. I was born and raised in Wellington, but the family moved to Wanganui just before I started college. They live in town, up on Halswell.'

'I don't know that area of town. We would normally take the dray into town and do our shopping on Victoria Avenue. There were so many of us we'd have to sit on top of all the supplies going home. They were our big days out. Funny to think of them now,' she gave a little nod of her head as she smiled.

'I've always lived in town, so never had the chance to do that sort of thing. So how's things over at the hospital?' he asked.

The grin left her quickly and her fingers tightened around her cup. 'It's hard. We lost someone yesterday. We thought he was stable, but he picked up an infection. It spread so quickly, it caught us by surprise. He didn't need to die.' Her eyes became red as tears started to well up. 'Sorry, I shouldn't have called unannounced then start crying in your kitchen.' She wiped the tears with the heel of her right hand.

'No, no, it's alright' Al replied.

'It's all getting too much. We've all seen things no one should ever have to. Pain and suffering the likes I never thought I'd experience. I'm struggling to find anyone to talk to about it. Moira is so matter of fact, cold even. She even said it was my ward's fault for the death yesterday. She reckons we should have done a better job.' Abby took a large mouthful of tea then pulled out her handkerchief and started to roll it around her fingers. 'Jess and Pat are numb to it now. They work such long hours in casualty, all they do is work and sleep. I keep going back to the night of the quake. We had to walk past the collapsed nurses' home,' she dabbed the corners of her eyes with the cloth. 'It was horrific to know that our friends had been killed in there and it could so easily have been Moira and I.'

'And yet amongst the misery there is hope, and goodness.' He squeezed her hand as he spoke. 'You're doing incredible work. Saving and changing people's lives.' The sensation of their skin touching sent a tingle through his entire body. It felt comfortable, quite natural to him.

'Thank you. That's very kind. It doesn't feel like it some days.'

'Every day you save people. I've got personal experience of that. I've been struggling with the randomness of it all as well. I still don't remember much of it. One minute we're sitting in the chapel, the next it's falling down around us. The last thing I remember is yelling at Iggy to move. Next time I can recall anything, you are looking down at me. You know I thought you were an angel welcoming me to heaven. I made it but so many others didn't. How do you explain it apart from pure chance? And I survived for what? Another thing that's irritating me is all the deference just because of this.' He said as he tugged at his Roman collar. 'I'm not ordained. For Pete's sake, I haven't even finished the seminary and can't even do proper Church work. I feel next to useless and all I get is "How you doing, Brother? Can I get you anything, Father?"'

'I can imagine it's frustrating. I get a little bit of the same as a nurse these days, but not quite the level you have. I'm sure you know you are in a revered profession, the collar immediately demands respect. I suppose the main thing is that people see that you are extremely good at what you do and defer to you because of that.'

'Yes, you make perfect sense. It's just hard believing it.'

'You had better start believing it, because it's true. Crikey. Is that the time?' Abby said looking at the clock above the stove. 'I'd better get going. I need to get home to do some chores before getting some sleep. I'm on a night shift again. It was wonderful to see you. Thanks for listening. It's been good to get a few things out. I'll stop by when you're back from Wanganui. Don't get up, I'll show myself out.' She squeezed his hand as she left the table.

Al sipped his tea and finished off his scone. A revered profession? Yes, he knew that was the case for ordained priests, but he hadn't thought about it applying to him to the same extent. To be given respect without earning it? That wasn't expected at this stage of his training. She's quite perceptive and not shy to make her point, he thought. And a Yeats fan? Not many women would be keen on him as a poet. He wondered why she wasn't married or stepping out with someone? He closed his eyes to a vision of the two of them walking down a busy street, arm in arm, he in a dapper new suit, her in a summery blouse and skirt with a jaunty hat, kinked to one side. Every few steps, a hint of her perfume would waft up and envelope him. He looked down at her neck, exposed with her hair up inside her hat, he followed the line of her collar to her small but pert breasts, then down to her bottom, slightly large for her frame, yet shapely and firm. He imagined stroking, kneading and kissing both body parts; tenderly yet with a forcefulness and understanding of a woman's needs. This vision being completely at odds with his experience of fumbled embraces and heavy handed fondles in darkened corners of school dances.

His arousal brought him back from his daydream. He ached

to act on the stimulation. Guilt and angst overtook him and he grabbed a walking stick and struck himself heavily on both legs a couple of times. What am I doing having such thoughts? Was it true they all are just temptresses, sent here to ensnare the weak willed? Yet why can't I have such desires? Am I not flesh and blood myself? Human, with all the imperfections of my fellow men?

Later that night, Al was still immersed in the warm glow of his morning visitation when there was a strong rap on the door. He grabbed his walking stick, got up and made his way to the front door. His face couldn't hide his shock. He was barely able to say anything.

'Father?'

CHAPTER 11

Charles Robertson stood in the doorway, his face in the shadow his body cast against the setting sun. 'Are you going to invite me in, or will you leave your father on the porch all evening?'

'Sorry, Dad. Come in.' Al blinked rapidly and gave a quick shake of his head. 'Seeing you completely threw me. Can I get you something to drink? A cup of tea? We do have some whiskey, Jameson. I know you like Bushmills, but at least it's Irish,' said Al. What is my father doing here? Has he come to take me back to the family? Didn't he get the last telegram saying I'd be on the train later in the week?

'That'll do nicely, thank you.' Al's father put his hat down on the coffee table and looked around at the room. 'Sparse digs. You wanted to come back here rather than be at home with us?'

Al poured a double measure of whiskey into a tumbler, then did the same from the sherry bottle into his glass. 'Here you go, Dad. Didn't you get my telegraph? I'm on a train back to Wanganui this Friday.'

Charles' calloused hands wrapped around the glass, making it look barely bigger than a thimble. 'Yes, we got it just before I left this morning. Better late than never. Mother will be pleased to have you home. You're moving much better. Just a walking stick now?'

'I told you I had a good trainer here. Got the sticks a couple of days ago.' Al spun one of them in his hand as he spoke. 'So what brings you here?'

'I'll be in Napier for a while. I'm helping with the

reconstruction. The Ministry of Works has retained me to be one of a team of senior foremen overseeing the building.'

'Do you know how long for?' asked Al.

'The rest of the year. Maybe longer.'

'Why did they pull you in from Wanganui? Surly there's enough qualified people here?'

'Not for the amount of work that needs to be done and they wanted the best they could get,' a small grin was only partially obscured by the glass as he took another hit then licked his top lip and grey moustache. 'Also, I was Clerk of Works on a couple of the buildings here before the war, when you were a nipper. The Bank of New Zealand was one of mine, so I have some history with the town.'

The image of Shelia O'Sullivan's face at the church dance shot into Al's head. He closed his eyes to try to get a sharper view of the memory. The long, dangly paua shell earrings against her lightly freckled cheeks, her large brown eyes and the hint of English Rose perfume stuck with him. A young woman with her whole life still to live.

'You alright?' Charles' low rumble of a voice brought Al back.

'Just remembering someone I knew who worked there. She didn't get out. The building isn't there anymore.'

'It was a solid building, but it couldn't stand up to a quake like this. Nothing could.'

'St. Patrick's here managed to make it.'

'That might be so, but not many of the banks wanted wooden buildings back then. I bet you they still won't. Don't forget, they pay the bills.' He shook his glass at Al. 'Can I help myself?'

Al nodded as he looked away from his father and stared out the window, to nothing in particular, just so he wasn't looking at Charles. More faces of the dead fought for his attention. Like party guests who don't know when it's time to leave, he knew these visions would invade his thoughts for some time to come.

'Isn't it a bit early to start thinking of rebuilding?' asked Al.

'How long should they wait?' replied his father as he poured out another sizable measure of whiskey. 'The government and the banks especially want to get things moving. They can't recoup their losses when there's rubble on their lots.'

'That's bloody callous. People are still grieving.'

'And that's your contribution to the situation? Being counsellor and confidant? If you'd heeded my advice you'd be a fully qualified architect by now, and could be working to help rebuild this place. Instead, you're tending to the poor, huddled masses.'

'They need spiritual support to get through this,' said Al, straightening himself in his chair.

'Not as much as a roof over their heads, or a place to work.' Al looked away from his father with a sneer. 'Sorry, Albert, I'm being quite unfair.' Charles sat down again and stroked his chin a couple of times. 'I know you're committed to what you're doing, and I'm sure you are going to be a very good priest. Your mother and I are proud of what you've achieved, but I wanted something else for you, and this country is full of opportunities. You are a very intelligent young man, you can be anything you want to be here.' He rolled his glass between the palms of his large hands and took a deep breath. 'Your grandfather brought the family out here to get us away from the limitations and prejudice of the old country. Do you think there'd be any chance of a Catholic being put in charge of building scores of major public buildings in Ulster? Not a hope. This country has given me that opportunity. It's not perfect, no place is. We have to put up with a few snide comments and off-colour jokes, sometimes worse, but no one is going to stop you being what you want to be just based on what church you go to. He told me to try and break out of old ways, you know, first born to the Church, second to the civil service, third to the military. We're two-thirds of the way to completely ignoring his advice.' Charles' shoulders dropped slightly and he stared into his glass.

'Thanks, Dad. I had no idea you and Grandpa talked about this sort of stuff.'

'Yeah, we talked a lot when I was about to leave school and thinking of what I was going to do. I can remember some of the rubbish we had to put up with as kids back in Ireland, but it was mainly that we knew we were excluded from so many things. So when we got here and nobody said, no you can't do this, or sorry, that isn't for your type, it was a revelation.'

'I know I had loads of options, but this is what I thought I was made to do,' said Al.

'Thought? Some doubts now, son?' asked Charles.

'I've just had my eyes opened to a few things about the Church that don't sit comfortably. Starting to question its overall commitment to people, rather than itself. My devotion to God is as strong as ever, it's the organisation that I'm doubting.'

'It's not too late to pull out. You now have a degree, so there'll be loads of opportunities for you,' added Charles.

'It's briefly crossed my mind, but I'm not for quitting, not on the Lord or myself.'

Charles looked up at the clock above the fireplace. 'Best I get going. I have authorisation papers, but I don't really want to be out after curfew.' The last of the whiskey disappeared in one gulp. 'Not bad. Might just have to pop back tomorrow for another taste. You'll be around?' Al nodded as they walked down the hallway. 'Thanks, son. Night, my boy,' said Charles as he stepped off the porch.

Al closed the door, went back to the lounge and slumped heavily into his chair, bowing his head and clasping his hands. Lord, is that all I'm doing? Being a counsellor to the emotionally distressed? An ear to talk to and nothing more? No, I can't believe that. I'm doing your work, helping people survive by giving them your strength and love. Show me that's what I've been spared to do. He lifted his head and pushed himself back into the chair, pulled out his pipe, packed in some fresh tobacco and lit it, at the same time he eyed the sherry bottle with intent.

It was mid-afternoon before his headache cleared. Half a dozen cups of tea and a big feed of bacon and eggs made him feel almost human. Two-thirds of a bottle of sherry on top of a bad attitude had made for a fuzzy head and a long day. He had certainly done very little talking at St. Vincent's. He had done his best impression of the strong, silent type today, nodding occasionally, with the odd reassuring utterance. Sitting in the lounge, he thought about firing up the wireless. No, too much like hard work having to concentrate on it. The offending sherry bottle mocked him from the safety of the drinks cabinet across the room. 'How on earth does Paddy do it,' he thought. Sometimes up to half a bottle of whiskey and the next day it's as if he hadn't touched a drop. A knock on the door increased his irritation, just as the last wisps of fog were clearing from his head.

'Coming,' he croaked out, his voice still with the rasp of the hangover. 'Can I help you?'

'Good Lord. Look what the cat dragged in,' Abby said.

'Abby. Sorry, I'm not feeling the best.'

'And not sounding great either. A cold or something self-induced?' she asked.

'The latter. A few too many sherries last night. Come on in.'

'Thanks. As I suspected. No sympathy then,' she replied.

'What? Not even a sliver? You're a harsh woman.'

Abby smiled at him, saying nothing. They went to the kitchen. Al put the kettle on, freshened up the teapot and poured out two cups of tea, without asking.

'Before I forget, here's something for your trip tomorrow.' Abby placed a small muslin bag on the table, tied up with a red ribbon.

'You didn't need to do that. It's very kind,' said Al.

'Don't worry, it's nothing special. A couple of things to help the journey go quicker.' Abby was fidgeting on her chair as she spoke.

Al studied the bag with all the intensity he could muster without inducing another headache. It was almost cone-shaped, about six inches long at its base, rising up eight to nine inches. He found both ends of the ribbon, pulled them apart and removed it. The muslin fell to the table revealing three individually wrapped parcels. Two were identically round, the other rectangular. He smiled as he investigated the packages.

'You only need to open one of those two. They're the same' Abby said. He unwrapped one to uncover a scone. 'Fresh out of the oven today. They should keep for tomorrow.'

'You didn't need to go to so much trouble,' said Al.

'I have to come clean. They aren't of my hand. Care of the hospital canteen. I'm not sure you'd survive my baking.'

Opening the last package, Al looked across the table and shook his head while smiling. 'Abigail McCarthy. This is too much.' He held the book in his hands, stroking its blue leather cover with care. He turned it over and read the gold inscribed words on the spine *"Travels with a Donkey in the Cevennes. Robert Louis Stevenson"* In the middle of the spine was a gold rosette, just above the publishers' name.

'I'm pretty sure it's from the same set as your other books by him. I was shopping in Taradale when I saw it. A spur of the moment thing,' Abby said, feeling a little uncomfortable, thinking she may have over stepped the mark.

'Well, I'm stunned. And here am I, empty handed and with a hangover to boot.'

'Yes, now what induced this episode?' she asked.

'I was a bit low last night, so I thought a couple of drinks might pick me up.'

'Sorry to hear that. What happened?'

'My dad is in town, been employed to help with the reconstruction. Which of itself is a nice surprise, but during our chat, things got a little heated. Anyway, he got me thinking about what I'm doing here. It's been nagging me for a few days that I'm not doing a blind bit of good. I feel like the spare wheel on a car, of no day to day use whatsoever.'

'But extremely necessary in an emergency. Which is what we're in.' Abby interjected.

'I cannot see how. Paddy is working with the inter-denominational group. The Women's Committee is helping to feed and clothe families. Even the unemployed are clearing the rubble. And myself? Roaming about the ruins like a spectator, filling the odd care package, making tea for folk. Look at me. I'm twenty-three but geezers in their seventies are contributing more than I am.'

'Would you prefer to be crippled, dead even? You can't feel sorry for yourself. You're here, you survived. Yes, you're not as mobile as you'd like to be, but there's loads of folk to do physical stuff. How many people did you talk to at St. Vincent's today? Ten, fifteen, twenty?' Al nodded as Abby spoke. 'And I bet you your last shilling that all of them went away reassured in some way, or uplifted even by the smallest amount. Yes, many of us are looking after peoples' physical well-being, but you're tending to their emotional needs.'

'It's hard to see any effect I'm having. At least with you, it's very immediate. You treat people and they get better,' he said looking intently at Abby.

'Or not, as the case may be. We all have our role to play in this. What do you think this place would be like if no one had the emotional or spiritual strength to go on, to rebuild? The Church, and you by association, is hugely important right now. I know I'm not one for Mass every Sunday, but I know the positive impact the Church has on folks, especially in a crisis. You're a vital part of that. You are extremely good at what you do. You put people at ease, they warm to you quickly. You're being a listener, a confidante and people need that.'

He smiled. 'Thanks for the vote of confidence.' He noticed how the light accentuated her cheeks and jawline.

'My two pennies worth is for you to snap out of this and buck up your ideas. The last thing you and this place needs is you being down in the dumps. You'll see your mum and brothers tomorrow, that should get you back on track. Right, sermon over.' She could barely believe she was lecturing him, or was it just sage advice? Yes, she was older than him and his seminary life had left him naïve to the world, but she sensed something deeper. A glimmer of doubt in him about his chosen path? Maybe questioning what he was doing and why. Has a chink of light just opened up? 'I'll get going now. Have a safe trip and enjoy being with the ones who love you most.' She rose and kissed him on the cheek and thought, *'Do they love you as much as I do?'*

From the porch, he watched her walk up the street. He held the small book she'd given him close to his chest. A warm glow enveloped him and he stayed outside until she was out of sight. He did like watching her walk; her shapely bum looked terrific in her nurses' uniform. Her visits were quickly becoming a cherished part of his day. He did a quick count: twice in a couple of days this week, her trip down to the hospital in Waipuk to call on him, not forgetting their encounter at the racecourse the other day. She was one of the constants in his life, but that was about to change going back to his family. He couldn't call it home, he had never lived there, only visited on holidays. He stepped back into the house and knew she and Paddy would be what he'd miss most.

At the other end of the street, Charles Robertson stopped as he turned the corner and leaned on a fence, watching the nurse and his son talk on the cottage's porch, the woman warmly rubbing Al's arm then left him. Charles stroked his chin slowly, he expected Al to go back into the house, but he lingered, watching the woman until she rounded the next intersection and disappeared. It appeared to be a close and warm relationship.

***

The train pulled into Dannevirke as he finished the last bite of the first scone. He savoured every mouthful, drawing out the enjoyment of its buttery texture and taste to ensure it lasted a good half hour. His mind drifted back to Abby sitting at the kitchen table with every bite.

He wiped his hands, then opened up his satchel and pulled out his writing paper.

5th March 1931

Dear Abigail,

I do hope that this letter finds you in good health. This is just a very short note to let you know I am safely in transit.

I must immediately offer my apologies on two fronts. First, the potential untidy nature of this letter, as I am writing it from the train on my way to Wanganui, so the rattling of the carriages is disturbing my handwriting somewhat. Second, forgive any greasy fingerprints on the paper. I have just finished the first of the delicious scones you were so kind to give me. I must admit to savouring every morsel. The cooks must have used an extra pound of butter as my hands now have that sheen they get after handling a block of butter. As for the second scone, it may seem rather decadent to have two in a day, but I have earmarked that one for my afternoon tea, during the Palmerston to Wanganui leg.

*The taste brought back memories of the very enjoyable time we
spent in the cottages' kitchen over the past week. Indeed, coming
back through Waipukurau reminded me of that afternoon you came
calling when I was still in hospital. Spending those few hours talking
in the grounds was a tremendous lift for my spirits. In fact, your
company over the entire last month has been a saving grace to me.
I am unsure as to how I would have got through without your kind
words and support. I fear I will not have someone to confide with so
readily in the foreseeable future. That does worry me somewhat.*

*That's rather poor of me. I shouldn't be burdening you with my
concerns, especially as you have real problems of saving lives to
deal with.*

*Our progress has been quite slow so far. Given that it has taken
the better part of three-quarters of an hour just to get to the other
side of Dannevirke, I fear it will be a long journey. The up side
is that I will have ample time to begin reading my new Robert
Louis Stevenson book. I am still quite stunned at your generosity
and that amongst the chaos you were able to find a volume from
the same series as his poetry books I have. A remarkable piece of
investigative work.*

*I will sign off now and will attempt to get this letter into the mail
at Palmerston North, where I have a short lay over to wait for the
train to Wanganui.*

*Yours faithfully and warmest regards,
Brother Albert Robertson*

* * *

The train shuddered to a halt with a loud hiss and wheeze. A cloud
of steam engulfed the platform. Al sat back and let the carriage

empty before he grabbed his walking stick and canvas hiking pack. As he stepped onto the platform he heard his name called and saw William, his middle brother, charging towards him. A broad smile broke across his face as he watched the teenager run down the platform. A few yards behind William, he saw his mother and other brothers, Gary and Howard, at a much more controlled pace.

'Hey, champ. Great to see you,' Al said as he and William embraced.

'We've been counting down the days since your telegram,' William replied.

'Welcome back, brother,' said Gary, extending his hand for a long handshake.

Margaret hugged her son deeply. 'At last I have you home. I've been so worried.'

'Thanks, Mum. It's nice to be back with you all. I've been fine, really,' said Al. 'And hello Howard. How are you, young man?' The small boy clung to his mother's leg, hiding from Al.

'You're getting around a lot better than at the Final Profession. Almost ready to get up in the hills again,' said Gary.

'Almost, I'm a different man than three weeks ago. Staying on at the hospital in Waipuk was the best thing.'

'It's been breaking my heart to think of you alone and in so much pain.' Margaret was still holding onto Al's arm as she spoke.

'Let's grab your suitcase and head home,' said Gary.

Their Victorian era single storey villa was like most on the street, a big curved bay window in the front left with the living room behind the window, a short veranda on the right. Ivy covered the driveway side of the house. Painted white with forest green trim, but it could do with a repaint. Al thought it would only last one, maybe two, more winters. Two silver birches at the front of the garden shielded the house from the street. At the back of the house a pohutukawa and kowhi marked the neighbours' boundary. The kowhi was in flower, adding a flash of yellow to the green.

'Got you in your old room. I'm back in with William,' said Gary, opening the front door.

'You didn't need to do that. I can bunk in with Will.'

'You know us, we're hardly ever in the bedrooms. Always something to do out and about.'

Al looked around the room. The late afternoon sun poked its rays through the net curtains, bathing a kauri chest of drawers in a golden glow. On top of the drawers was a framed photograph of him as a teenager standing between two of his uncles, rifle in hand with a red deer carcass in front of them. On the wardrobe door, a poster of Anthony Wilding promoting Spalding tennis balls that Al got for Christmas after Wilding's last Wimbledon win in 1913. He opened up the cupboard to hang his suits and cassocks. In the corner was his old tennis racquet and a walking stick he had whittled from a pine branch he'd found when out hiking. He changed into street clothes and went onto the porch, where Margaret had laid out some refreshments.

'Sit down, love, and have a nice cup of tea and a scone,' she said as she fussed around him.

Surely not a third scone in one day, Al thought. 'Just some tea will be fine for me, Mum. I ate on the train.'

'Goodness. That terrible railway food. Here now. Eat that there.' She placed a side plate in front of him with a scone cut in half and smothered in butter. 'Tell us about the last few weeks.'

'Not a great deal to tell. Two days after Final Profession, I went back to Waipuk Hospital. My physical training man put me through the ringer; but got me walking after about a week. Another few days of his handy work and they discharged me. The past week I was back with Father Lynch, helping out at St. Vincent De Paul's. That's it.'

'I reckon you should have been looking after yourself first,' said Gary.

'Helping others is part of the calling. Even though it would have been lovely to have you back here, it's wonderful to know you were doing God's work,' added Margaret.

'I'm not sure it was His work, but there were plenty of people worse off than me. So many have lost everything, including family members. You should see central Napier. It is completely devastated. It's hard to put it into words.'

'You boys stay and chat. I'll start dinner,' said Margaret as she disappeared indoors.

'I need to stretch my legs. Want to play some cricket? Gary, go grab your bat and ball and we'll head out onto the road. I'll bowl a few down at you both.'

Gary and William sat stony faced and silent, exchanging guilty looks.

'What's wrong with you two? Surely you can't have gone off cricket since I was last home?'

'No, we still like it. But it's...' Gary stumbled over his reply.

'Come on, spit it out,' demanded Al.

'We don't have a bat anymore.'

'What on earth?' Al raised his voice. 'What happened to that great old bat you had?'

Gary shuffled in his seat for a few seconds. 'Well, we kind of had an incident.'

'An incident? Just tell me, lad. Stop being so cryptic.'

'We went against Dad's instructions and he chopped it up,' Gary said, still not making eye contact with Al.

'What in blazes? Bloody hell. That's ridiculous. Come on, what happened?'

'Dad went away for a few days of work and told us not to play on the road while he was gone. So we had a few hits on the front lawn. William mistimed a drive and the ball broke one of the front windows. We managed to fix it before Dad came home. Mum paid for the glass and it was all done, but Mr. Turner next door dobbed us in. He didn't mean to, just told Dad that we'd done a great job replacing the window by ourselves. Dad went into a rage, yelled at us that we wilfully disobeyed him, then he grabbed the bat, took it out the back and chopped it up.'

'Dear Lord. That's just ridiculous.' Al threw his hands down on the chairs arms. 'You're just lads, having a run around is what you do. We'll go down to the shops tomorrow and get you a new one. Dad's away for most of the year, so what he doesn't know won't hurt him.'

Later that evening after the boys had gone to bed, Al approached Margaret. 'Mum, what happened with Gary's cricket bat? He said Dad cut it up.'

'That was a bit of an upset for the boys. They were rather quiet for a few days after that,' Margaret replied.

'For the love of God, Mother. They are just kids doing what boys do.'

'They are old enough to know a direct order. They knowingly disobeyed your father. Watch your language, you of all people shouldn't be taking the Lord name in vain.'

Al shook his head. 'There's a distinction between instilling discipline and bullying your own children.'

'That's quite enough. Charles has been a tremendous father to you all. I won't have you talking like that.'

'What would I know about that? I've been on my own since I was twelve when he moved you all here and left me at St. Patrick's. Five years at college and another five in the seminary. It's not like he bought me up, or has been in my life.'

'How dare you question his commitment to you and this family? What in heavens name has happened to you since that earthquake? You aren't the same person who was here at Christmas.' Margaret's eyes started to get red as her voice wobbled.

'Sorry, Mother. I didn't mean to upset you.' Al backtracked. 'You are right, Dad has done a good job with us all. It's just the stress of what I've been through getting to me. I shouldn't be so insensitive. Being back here for a while should get me back on an even keel.'

'I hope that is the case, and what's this father tells me about you wanting to leave the Church? I almost had a heart attack when I heard,' she said.

'I'm not leaving the clergy, mother. I've just had my resolve tested recently, but I've come out stronger for it,' replied Al.

'Good. I didn't want to bring it up tonight, but as we're talking about upsets. I don't think I could live with the shame if you left. I couldn't show my face in public again. I think death would be a better option,' sighed Margaret.

'Mother, that's all rather melodramatic, especially to a hypothetical situation. As I said, I'm not going anywhere.'

'This certainly is not the way I had expected to spend your first evening at home. I think I'll retire, the day has taken its toll on me. Have a good night's sleep and hopefully you'll be back to normal in the morning.' She squeezed his hand as she left the room.

In his bedroom, he crossed himself in preparation for his evening prayer. 'Lord, what has happened to me? How could I talk to my mother like that? She is right, I am a different man. I have seen things I never imagined I would. Been knee deep in death and destruction. Only you know how close I was to joining you. They can't know or understand. Mother doesn't want to know. Yet through all the misery, I have found friendship in the most unusual place. Friendship that's touched something deep inside me, ignited feelings I've never known before. Lord, you know all types of love. Is this it? Is it infatuation? Are these real feelings or just illusionary?'

* * *

'There's two for you Al,' shouted William from the gate, then ran up to the porch.

Al squinted into the sun as William approached. One was emblazoned with the crest of the Order of Saint Mary, the other was a private letter with handwriting he instantly recognised. He put the second letter to one side. *'That's for later,'* he thought.

'Who are they from?' William had returned from handing the other mail to his mother and was leaning over Al, with his arms propped on the chairs arm.

'This one looks like it is from Mount Saint Mary's, and I think the other is from a parishioner at St. Patrick's, where I was in Napier.' Al said quickly.

'What do they say?' The boy now almost had his nose in the envelope.

'Steady on, solider. Give me a chance to open it.' Al pulled the letter out and unfolded the paper. It was indeed from the seminary. He read and digested its contents.

'Well?' said William.

'The reconstruction of Mount Saint Mary's won't be completed until the third term. So they're sending us to Highden, just outside Palmerston. We're to be there the Tuesday after Easter.'

That evening Al settled into his bed and pulled out the second letter. Before he opened it, he held it to his face. There it was, the faint hint of lavender. He breathed it in deeply.

12th March 1931

Dear Albert,

I hope you have made it home safe and sound and your family is showering you with deserved love and attention and they are helping with your recuperation.

I was delighted to get your letter of the 5th. It very much brightened up my day. I am so glad you enjoyed the scones. You must have polished them off quite completely, as I couldn't find a single crumb or buttery fingerprint on the letter. I know what I'll be sending you in any care packages in the future.

First off, if we are to continue our correspondence, I must demand that you call me Abby. Using Abigail sounds so stuffy and formal. It is only me you are writing to, not Princess Elizabeth.

Life in Napier continues to make minute steps back to normality, rather a new form of normality. We have not lost any more patients in the few days since you left. That is a huge blessing, as you can imagine. Everyone on my ward is making good progress, and we even discharged two people yesterday. Moira has not been so lucky.

They lost a middle aged gentleman on the 6th due to complications from an amputation. Not that you would know from her reaction. It's as if she has stopped caring about the patients as people. They are just injuries to her. I pray that I never become that jaded.

Speaking of praying, you'll be proud of me, as I went to Mass last Sunday. I spoke to Father Lynch after the service, I told him I was going to write to you, so he asked me to pass on his regards. He looks awfully tired. He working so hard on his projects.

That is about all my news for now. I eagerly await the next instalment in our correspondence and the news from Wanganui.

Yours faithfully with love,
Abby

He grabbed a tennis ball that was sitting on his bedside table and started tossing it in the air, seeing how close he could get it to the ceiling without hitting it. He could scarcely believe she had replied to him so quickly. She must have penned her letter within a couple of days of getting his. The two letters of the day combined to lift his mood immeasurably. Going to the seminary in Palmerston North meant that not only could he continue his studies, but he was a couple of hours closer to her, so the possibility of seeing each other again wasn't out of the realms of reality. He had just over two more weeks before he had to report to the Highden Seminary, time that now disappeared in a haze of excitement and expectancy.

CHAPTER 12

Highden Seminary
Palmerston North

Al was on a secluded table in the back of the seminary's library. The closest overhead light was partially shielded by a book case, so most of the table was in shadow. A small lamp threw a thin shaft of light onto his writing paper. His Bible and theology text books remained closed on the desk. Four balls of crumpled paper sat on top of one of the books. He pulled out his fob watch; ten to nine, only forty minutes before mandatory prayers then lights out. He pursed his lips and stared at the partially written letter on the desk. 'Just write it, man. What's the worst that can happen? She just says no,' he whispered to himself.

He had written virtually the same passage on all four discarded letters only to lose courage and discard all of them. On the fifth attempt, he vowed to keep the problem paragraph in.

14th May 1931

Dear Abby,

I do hope this letter finds you well. Thank you very much for your wonderful letter of 12th March. Apologies for this very late reply. This is primarily a result of my move to the Highden Seminary, just outside Palmerston North.

Due to the damage at Mount Saint Mary's, those of us in this area had to report here to continue seminary studies until such time that we can return. So myself, George, Iggy and a couple of others started here just after Easter. I know that was five weeks ago, and you could justifiably ask why it's taken so long to put pen to paper. In my defence, we do have a hectic timetable that leaves little free time and few opportunities to be on one's own. I am in fact writing this in the most private part of the library, during what should be study time. So I am sacrificing my intellectual and spiritual development to get this written, but this is a very worthy cause. My next challenge will be posting it, so don't be surprised if the postmark ends up many days after the date on the letter.

Day to day life here is almost identical to Mount Saint Mary's. Rise at five, bed at ten, with classes, prayers, mass and meals making up the waking hours. The major difference is the weather. I know we are in late autumn, but my word, it is rather dreary in the Manawatu. There's always cloud cover, rain or drizzle two days out of three, and then there's the almost constant wind. It could drive a man demented. Even though I wasn't that partial to the heat of a Napier summer, there's something to be said for fine and sunny weather.

Speaking of Napier, we will not be back at Mount Saint Mary's until October at the earliest. That coupled with the studies we have to catch up with, it is unlikely that I will be able to, or have any justification for being in Napier for many months. Given that you would have to pass through Palmerston North if you were to visit your family, I was wondering if there was any possibility of you stopping off here on one of those said trips home?

Sunday is our only official free day, so I could venture into town.

I could come to the train station and we can have tea before your connection to Wanganui. I would completely understand if you could not commit to meeting, or if you have no immediate plans to come by this way.

I hope you do investigate the possibility of a lay by in Palmerston North in the near future. I look forward with great anticipation to your next letter.

Best wishes,
Albert

He put the cap back on his fountain pen and laid it on the desk. He looked over his shoulder, then picked up the last page of the letter and re-read it a couple of times. And so it's done. It will go into the post as it is. He exhaled heavily, then screwed up the entire letter into another tight ball and placed it next to the other four. He picked up his pen and started again.

14th May 1931
Dear Abby,

I do hope this letter finds you well. Thank you very much for your wonderful letter of 12th March. Apologies for this very late reply. This is primarily a result of my move to the Highden Seminary, just outside Palmerston North. Myself, George, Iggy and a couple of others started here just after Easter.

It is unlikely that I will return to Napier for many months, so I was hoping you could stop off here if ever you passed through Palmerston North on your way to visiting your family?

Sunday is our only official free day, so I could venture into town and come to the train station. We could have tea before your connection to Wanganui. I would completely understand if you could not commit to meeting, or if you have no immediate plans to come by this way.

I look forward with great anticipation to your next letter.

Best wishes,
Albert

He quickly folded it and placed the letter in the back of one of his text books. His hands left a slight residue on his watch as he checked the time once more.

What on earth are you doing? Those words kept rolling around his head. You're not doing anything wrong. A little unusual, yes, but no laws or vows are being broken. Just two friends getting together. He wanted to see her again. No, needed to see her again. He flipped open his theology text, thumbed through a few pages until he found the passage he was after. "Saint Thomas Aquinas, Amor Amicitiae (The Love of Friendship): Love of the essence of something, or someone, that transcends their desirable qualities." There, if the dumb ox believed that acknowledgement of love is required to know divine love, then how could these feelings be wrong?

He continued reading for a few minutes. *'What in blazes? I'm trying to justify a friendship through theology. Bloody ridiculous. What kind of priest would I be if I couldn't develop normal friendships? What kind of God would deem it unholy to love?'* His thoughts were interrupted by the flicking on and off of the lights, the signal to head to the chapel for evening prayers.

* * *

He prepared himself for a wait of at least a month to hear from her. A mixture of excitement, mild disappointment and frustration enveloped him every day from the middle of June. Surely a reply couldn't be far away. He watched the daily post with the anticipation of a child on Christmas morning, only to walk away empty handed every time.

By the start of July, Al had begun to feel deflated by the lack of a reply from Abby. Had she even got the letter? Was she too busy to write back? Was his letter too blunt, to the point? Should he have sent one of the original letters, being a bit more newsy and subtle, might it have received a warmer reception? Whenever he could during the evening study periods, he'd re-read her last letter, and would let his mind wander to what she might be doing at the hospital, sitting in her lounge reading Yeats, or even the thought of the two of them strolling among the orchards in warm sunshine. Some nights he'd lose almost an entire hour in his daydreams. He'd attempt to chastise himself, but he felt the time wasn't wasted.

* * *

Abby was on her third consecutive night attempting to write to Al. She had discarded her pen and good paper for a notepad and pencil after many an aborted start to the letter. Once she had the draft done, she'd rewrite it. That was the theory, at least, but the practice was proving much harder than expected. Her initial delight at getting his letter was tempered by the brevity of it. Surely he must have more to say after three months. It struck her as very abrupt, truncated even, as if he wanted to say more, and she didn't quite know what to make of his suggestion of meeting. It would be very nice to see him again, but a brief cup of tea in a railway station? Odd indeed. Was it supposed to be two friends or acquaintances catching up, or something greater?

Her mind was swirling with possibilities. What if it does have romantic connotations? She had taken an instant liking to Al in those chaotic days straight after the quake, and although her first couple of visits to him were borne out of compassion and medical interest, when she called on him at the cottage before he left, that was more personal. She remembered when she examined him feeling flush and aroused, moving her hands over his body felt natural and stimulating. It did take all her restraint not to rip his cassock off that day. She knew that it couldn't lead to anything, but there was no denying the attraction. What was it about him, was it actually his untouchability? She remembered how she idolised her eldest brother who went into the priesthood. He was so much older than her that she could only remember him as being a priest. The adoration that he received from the rest of the family and the community always stayed with her. Was she projecting this onto Al?

Propped up on her bed, the notepad on her knees, the top of her pencil heavily chewed, she mulled over her words. The inconsistent electricity supply caused her bedside lamp to flicker so much that she lit a candle for some consistent light. It cast long, deep shadows over her bedroom as she started to write.

* * *

The arrival of the letter surprised Al. It had been nearly two months since he had posted his to Abby and given how quick she had been in the past to reply, he'd taken the lack of a response as a bad sign. He stuffed the envelope into a pocket to read later.

He took up his now regular place in the back corner of the library during the evening study period. He glanced around and started reading.

20th July 1931

Dear Al,

I can't tell you how delighted I was to receive your letter. Although it was short, it brightened up the entire week. Thank you very much.

It's my turn to apologise. Even though I received your letter in late May and had every intention of replying quickly, life has taken some

176

interesting turns recently. So, unfortunately all my grand plans to write back within a couple of weeks failed miserably.

The main cause for the delay has been the partial reopening of the hospital. Most of the patients in the tents at the racecourse have now been moved. As this is my ward, I was involved in the meetings and planning before the move, then the actual transfer. So it's been long days and many evenings over the past two months. Thankfully the transition went smoothly and they have settled in quickly. In fact, I'm very happy to report that many of my patients have responded well. Not surprising really, especially now that winter has arrived. Who wouldn't rather be indoors than in a tent? I'm delighted to be back in the hospital, as it makes nursing so much easier and more rewarding. Moira is still at the racecourse, but her ward is due to come back next month, although I think she secretly likes it at the racecourse. Probably something to do with the added drama and sacrifice that goes along with it.

Blimey, look at that, a whole page on my ramblings about work. That must be so boring for you to read. Apologies. I'll keep to more interesting topics from here on.

I take from the brevity of your letter that you've also been busy. It's good to know you have some of your classmates with you. Please pass on my regards to Iggy and George, if they remember me.

I'm sure you'll be interested in the reconstruction. The town looks like one of those Hollywood movie sets, all scaffolding and frames. It appears that public buildings, banks and other businesses are getting all the attention and money. Very few houses have been started yet, so a few of my patients who have been discharged can't go home, and have had to go to the tent town at Nelson Park. I find that very sad. Where is the compassion and thought for people? I think your kindness and concern for people is still needed here.

I've seen Father Lynch a couple of times. He's still working so hard. He says there is little money for the reconstruction of the Anglican and Presbyterian churches, so they are setting up a country wide appeal for money. He is such a good man to be working so hard for those other churches yet never misses Mass every Sunday at St. Patrick's. I told him I had written to you and he said if I wrote again to say hello, and in his own words "say sorry to the lad for my bloody shocking efforts to stay in touch, but he knows I'm a useless old duffer." He's priceless.

Now, about your invitation, or suggestion, to meet. I must admit that did surprise me. Yet it got me thinking that it would be lovely to see you again and I also realised I haven't been home since Christmas. Obviously events here have had a big say in that, but now we are back in the hospital we are returning to some normality. I couldn't let such a charming invitation go unanswered, so I talked to Matron about the possibility of getting a few days off and she said that once a couple more wards come back, she will be able to start rostering time off. So August or September could be the time frame. The chance to catch up in person would be wonderful. I'm most eager to see your rehabilitation and expect to see you striding with purpose down the platform to meet me off the train. I promise to bring a couple of the hospital cafe scones. Lord knows we couldn't subject ourselves to New Zealand Railways baked goods if we have tea at the station.

Here I am making plans already when I haven't even got permission to take time off. Getting ahead of myself again. I will let you know as soon as I'm told when I can have a holiday.

Now that I have successfully written a novella, instead of a letter, I think it best I sign off and let you get back to being pious and devoted to your ecclesiastic studies.

Warmest regards,
Abby

Al's heart raced at what seemed like triple time, he felt flush and out of breath, as he might after a particularly tough game of tennis. He re-read the letter a couple of times just to make sure he hadn't misinterpreted any of it. So she would come. Even without a specific date, this was a better result than he had expected. Now for planning the rendezvous. Her words on the last page struck him "Getting ahead of myself again." Could that be levelled at him? Shouldn't he temper his thoughts, which were now racing forward with visions of their meeting? What would she wear (hopefully not her uniform, but then would a nurse meeting a priest arouse less suspicion)? What will they talk about, would she put on the lavender perfume which he so liked? Will she have her hair up or down? Apart from scones, would she bring any gift, should he get something for her? He couldn't remember having an obsession before. Sure, he had likes and passions – tennis, hiking, the bush and his commitment to Christ, but an obsession? Was one beginning? Abby was starting to dominate his thoughts and dreams. It was detracting from his studies, but he felt powerless to stop it. As was becoming the norm, the flicking of the lights bought his mind back to his surroundings.

* * *

A bright, crisp morning greeted him. The frost of the previous few days had broken as a light blanket of mist clung to the small hollow that ran along the eastern side of the seminary. Small strands of moisture struggled to break off as the sun began to warm the ground. The sunlight was visible as it poured through the mist and trees that overhung the front lawn. A single leaf that had gallantly survived the autumn and early winter finally relinquished its grip and fell to the ground, its orange hue a stark contrast to the grass as it finally came to rest. It was close to a perfect winter's morning. Had God himself intervened to provide such an ideal day?

He had arranged a lift into Palmerston North a few days ago on the premise of going to Mass in town, followed by a therapeutic walk through the gardens of the Esplanade. As he was still excused from the standard Sunday afternoon recreation of rugby or football, approval for his trip to town was straightforward.

As he sat by himself at the far end of the station platform, Al turned his fob watch over and over in his right hand, stopping every thirty seconds to check the time. He scanned the station for any familiar faces, as he had been doing ever since he came into town from the seminary. Still no one he recognised. He pulled out her last letter and flipped through its pages until he found the paragraph that by now he had memorised. "I've booked a seat on the quarter past ten train from Napier, that's due into Palmerston about one in the afternoon. I'm then on the four o'clock service to Wanganui. So much looking forward to seeing you again." The faint sound of a train whistle pulled his attention away from the page.

* * *

Returning to the house after seeing Abby off at the train station, Moira went straight to Abby's room. Standing in the doorway, she surveyed the room. Where would be the most logical storage location, or rather hiding place? Bedside table, no. Dressing table, no. How about the bottom of the chest of drawers. They could be hidden away, yet still close enough to retrieve easily. She crouched down and started at the bottom drawer, lifting up stacks of clothes as she looked. Nothing. Drawer after drawer saw the same result. She moved to the wardrobe, maybe in a box tucked away in a corner. Still nothing. Her jaw was tight and fists clenched as she scanned the room. Back to the obvious, she thought, with an immediate result. In the door-side bedside table she found them, four letters from Brother Albert Robertson. The last two, which had aroused her suspicion, from a Palmerston North address. She hadn't even thought to hide them, Moira said to herself. Silly girl.

She started reading the most recent letter, from three weeks ago. "I was delighted that you would want to set up a rendezvous, regardless of how brief." Some discussion of seminary life and working in a greenhouse followed. "I have to admit that my spare time is increasingly taken up with thoughts of you. Study period especially is now totally devoid of ecclesiastical matters. I'm unsure as to the true meaning of this distraction from my tasks, but I don't find myself overly concerned with the situation."

Moira was now sitting on Abby's bed with the letters on her lap, although she couldn't remember the movement of sitting down. "Until we meet, which I hope will only be in a few short weeks time, I'll sign off with you firmly in my thoughts." She had read enough, no need to go through the others. She went to the kitchen, made a cup of tea and contemplated her next move.

* * *

Abby stepped down from the train, a small brown leather suitcase in hand. She looked up and down the platform for Al, at first glance she couldn't see him, then he emerged from a small cloud of steam near the front of the train. They smiled almost simultaneously, Al gave a small, almost truncated wave. Their pace quickened as they approached each other. They stopped with about a yard between them and an awkward pause enveloped them.

'Wonderful to see you,' they said together, then broke into laughter.

Al offered his hand, but Abby ignored it and gave him a light embrace and a kiss on the cheek. A blaze of heat shot over his face and down his back. 'I'm sure there's no vow forbidding a hug between two friends,' she said.

'No there isn't.' She had put on some of her lavender fragrance. He took in deep breaths through his nose to immerse himself in the aroma. 'I just wasn't sure how to… Well, it's done now. It's great to see you. You didn't wear your uniform?' as he looked at her tweed skirt suit and matching hat.

'I am off duty and that thing isn't the height of fashion, anyway.'

'You look very nice. I think it's the first time I've seen you out of uniform.' He noticed her small drop pearl earrings that matched her ivory skin.

'It feels like a lifetime since I've worn this. There haven't been many chances to feel like a woman this year. It's lovely to be able to step out in something feminine.' Abby held Al's gaze and gave a small, warm smile.

'Should we go to the tea rooms?' Al said, as he picked up Abby's suitcase. There was something of a natural, easy temperament about Abby that eased Al's nerves.

Time seemed to be suspended for Al as they spoke, caught up on each others news, shared stories of the past few months. The conversation started to meander aimlessly for a few minutes until Abby intervened, 'Now, as pleasant as it is to pass time, isn't there something more you'd like to talk about?'

'I don't think so. Not really,' said Al.

'So you invited me to meet you at a railway station on a Sunday just to catch up about life at the seminary?' she continued to quiz him.

'No, not specifically.'

'Then what? Specifically.' She let the pause grow to an uncomfortable period. 'You need to be able to talk to me, Albert. If we're going to remain friends, we have to communicate about more than the mundane.'

'Yes, I know. You're right, but it's difficult for me,' he replied.

'What's difficult? It's just me. I'm not sitting in judgement. I'm here as your friend.'

'That's it, though. I don't think I've had a female friend of any note since primary school. So you could say I'm a bit lost. Feeling my way through.'

'I understand. The whole Catholic school system doesn't exactly encourage interaction. I was lucky enough to go to a state primary and had loads of brothers and male cousins, but college was split,' said Abby.

'I'm just not sure what to talk about.' His knuckles of his interlocked fingers were white.

'You didn't seem to have a problem when we were in Napier. I recall the conversation flowed quite nicely.' Abby cocked her head to the left as she spoke.

'Yeah, I suppose. That was quite easy though,' replied Al.

'And now it's not? So what's changed?'

'A few things. Location for one.' His gaze came back to Abby after staring at the wall for a couple of minutes.

'Got to be more than that. Just because we aren't in the cottage shouldn't make you all coy.'

'Our friendship has had me thinking quite a bit. Questioning if it's right or not,' said Al.

'Same thing's been running round my head. In my book there's nothing wrong. A little unusual, I'll grant you that, but not completely out of the ordinary. Certainly not sinful, if that's what you're thinking. I remember Mum got on brilliantly with our priest,' replied Abby.

'Then why did I feel like I was about to sin when I left the seminary this morning?'

'Classic Catholic guilt. They've taught you well,' said Abby, raising her eyebrows.

'Yeah, there's a bit of that. You don't feel it?'

'Nope, not a sliver. They may have educated me, but they didn't inoculate me with the guilt complex. Moira's got it bad, but not me.' A confident smile came across her.

'Lucky you. I feel that there's something else, more positive. Uplifting even that gave me that feeling. Why aren't you stepping out with someone? There must be a queue of suitors.'

'Not that many, actually. I'm in the unlucky generation of women.' Al looked quizzically at her. 'Depending on what report you read, up to a quarter of our men aged eighteen to thirty-five were killed or wounded in the war. Many more were damaged in other ways. Most of the ones that didn't go were already married, so by the time I was leaving college, it was slim pickings. I may have had a couple of evenings out this year, that's it. It doesn't bother me at all.'

Al noticed the clock over the counter. 'Crikey. Your train will be here in a few minutes. Best we get out there.' They took up a position near the far end of the platform. 'Is there any chance of you visiting again soon?' he asked.

'I think it will be difficult for me to get any more time off before Christmas, but I will try, even if it's only a long weekend. I will have to stop off to change trains on my way back to Napier next Sunday,' Abby replied.

A surge of happiness flowed through Al. He had been so caught up in today that he hadn't actually given any thought to when Abby would be coming back through. 'I'll make sure I come into town. I'll check the timetables on the way out.'

The trains' wheels screeched as it came to a stop. Al took Abby's hand and helped her up the steps onto the carriage. He followed her as she found her seat, she opened the window, stuck her head out and gave him a wave. He started to jog alongside the moving train, suddenly he shouted 'I love you,' just as the train's whistle blew. 'What did I just say? Did she hear?' Al asked himself. A feeling of calm descended over him. He had some clarity of thought. Although he had never really experienced the situation before, he needed her in his life, somehow, someway.

* * *

When he came in from his chores, Al knew something was amiss. The usual order and calm of the seminary had been replaced by a buzz. Iggy pulled him aside.

'Connolly's here. He arrived about an hour ago. All us Mount Saint Mary's lads have a meeting straight after dinner,' Iggy said quickly.

'You know what it's all about?' asked Al.

'Nope. No one does. One of the lads reckons we're going back to the Bay, but why he needs to be here in person to tell us that is a bit beyond me. Something's up,' said Iggy.

Thoughts darted into Al's head: easier meetings with Abby, and a chance to catch up with Paddy again. Connolly's presence was odd though. Why not just a telegram or letter?

After the meal, all the Mount Saint Mary's students were ushered into a classroom. Connolly followed them in.

'Brothers. Good to see you all again. I come with news from Greenmeadows. After tremendous fundraising and sterling building work, we are now in a position to welcome you back to the seminary for the rest of the year.' A few of the men gave small nods and smiles to each other. 'Arrangements have been made for a return next weekend. Saturday week you'll be driven to town for the train to Napier. The other students will return over the next few weeks, so you'll be reunited with your classmates and back in familiar confines very soon. Any questions?' Connolly's cold stare hit each one of them individually. The young men dare not breathe, let alone ask a question.

'Good. Be ready to depart after breakfast next Saturday. Dismissed.' As the screech of moving chairs on the floor pierced the room, Connolly said 'Brother Robertson, remain behind.'

Al was halfway out of his chair, then slowly sat back down. George and Iggy looked at him, their eyes asking what was going on. Al gave a small shrug.

Once alone, Connolly turned to Al, 'Brother Robertson, it has come to our attention that you have been undertaking some potentially concerning correspondence. We understand you have exchanged letters and have even met with Miss Abigail McCarthy, one of the nurses that came to our aid during the quake.' Connolly gave Al a moment to respond and raised his eyebrows.

'Father, I'm not sure of the importance my personal letters have to the seminary,' said Al.

'That's not quite the reply I was expecting. It is of high relevance. We cannot have any hint of impropriety with our seminarians. In of itself and given the past history between you two, it is understandable that a friendship could form. However, things do seem to have a clandestine and covert nature about them. In addition, this correspondence appears to coincide with a discernible deterioration in your performance.'

'Father, I would hope it would be acknowledged that what we've all been through this year could have had a negative impact on our studies,' replied Al.

'Yet many of your colleagues haven't seen their grades being affected. I'm sure you don't want to see your opportunities curtailed as a result of poor performance, or question marks over your attitude and judgement. Now would you?' A small smile came to his thin, sharp lips.

'I understand, Father Connolly. I'll redouble my efforts for the rest of the year,' replied Al, 'but I don't understand the concern over a few letters to a good friend. One who you know helped bring me back from near death. Surely the Church cannot deny the strength of such a bond?'

Connolly stood up and walked over to Al, placing his hand on Al's shoulder, 'You need to be mindful of being seen not to do anything inappropriate. You were one of our top students of your intake, with what we believe is a bright future, so it is worrying to see this drop off and anything that could be construed incorrectly by others who don't know you. You are too young to question the Church and we must protect our vulnerable lambs from the lustful temptations of the vixen.'

Before Al could react, Connolly pinched the fleshy part of Al's trapezius, digging his thumb deep into Al's muscle. Al winced and let out a growl as pain shot up his neck and down his back. His attacker had more power than Al thought the small man would have.

'Seminary can be difficult in the best of circumstances, let alone what's happened to us all. I will not let that be an excuse for you to wander away from the flock into the arms of a harlot. Am I making myself clear?' said Connolly in a hushed voice close to Al's ear.

'She's no...' Al didn't finish his sentence as Connolly dug deeper. 'Yes, Father,' Al replied through gritted teeth, his arm starting to go numb and spasm.

'Good. I think we have a clear understanding of the road ahead. You are excused,' said Connolly, releasing Al then quickly walking out the door.

Al sat rigid in the seat, his arm dangling limp beside him, his face red with rage, 'God himself agrees with me. You don't know what it means to love like this.'

Al was rubbing his shoulder and neck when George and Iggy nabbed him.

'What in blazes was that all about?' asked George.

'Oh, nothing really. He was just worried about my grades since we've been here,' replied Al, being economical with the truth.

'Connolly showing a genuine concern for one of us? Un-bloody-likely,' quipped Iggy.

'Have to say, that doesn't sound much like him. In almost six years I've never had a one-to-one chat with him about grades. You right? You hurt yourself again?' added George.

'I'm OK. It just stiffened up a bit. He said that I'm damaging the averages for our year and he wanted me to buck my ideas up,' Al embellished the actual discussion.

'That sounds a bit more like it. He'd be wanting you to keep your grades up to make sure Mount Saint Mary's beats all the other seminaries in the diocese,' said George.

'Bloody typical. Who gives a stuff what we've been through, about us losing seven classmates and being nomads. Just as long as we keep getting A's. What a prick, eh?' said Iggy.

After lights out, Al lay in his bed wide awake, his feelings oscillated between anger at the unknown person who had dobbed them in and panic over the implied threat from Connolly. Would he actually stop him from taking up his position at St. Pat's College next year? Al knew he could, but surely that would be an overreaction. How did he find out? Well, it wouldn't be difficult to quiz the staff here on mail in and out. It wasn't like they had tried to hide the letters. An obvious mistake now. But how did he know about the meetings? Someone must have seen them at the station, but he was sure he saw no one he recognised. That was the thing eating at him most, someone had betrayed them. His saliva turned bitter at that realisation.

* * *

Spring had always been his favourite season. Something about the sense of renewal, new life popping up that energised people. The warmer and drier weather made for better hiking and tennis came back onto the agenda, so the season usually allowed him to engage in two of his passions. Even as the city itself was coming back to life, almost like a field of daffodils exploding into life, with new buildings randomly sprouting up, he felt none of his usual pleasure of the season. They had been back at Mount Saint Mary's for six weeks and were within two months of finishing seminary life to embark on their chosen ministries. Surly a time to be uplifted, full of the joys of life, rejoice in God's gifts of regeneration?

Since his talk with Connolly, Al had recommitted himself to his studies, and tried to concentrate on preparing for his teaching post in Wellington. As Connolly had wanted, his grades improved. However, for all his efforts, Al was still distracted. His gnawed fingernails, tension headaches and inexplicably waking at three o'clock most mornings were testament to that. From the seminary's position on a small hill, it gave him a perfect view across the tidal flats to Hospital Hill in Napier, where Abby lived and worked. An aching reminder of the reality of the saying, so near and yet so far. That day a few weeks ago kept coming back to Al. The interaction with Connolly had shaken him. In the eight months since the quake he knew he had only nominally questioned his feelings for Abby, and at every time of interrogation, he had dismissed or glossed over any concerns: it was only friendship; she's a nurse showing concern for a patient; it's good to have interaction with the opposite sex; some theologian's teachings support the love of others; it's no one else's business and no harm could come of it. All the rationalisations had crashed down on him as heavily as that slab of the chapel that almost took his life. Reality had slapped him in the face and jolted him out of the dreamland he had been inhabiting. The full consequences of his vows and commitment to God, and the wavering of such, had been consuming most of his thoughts, especially during morning and evening prayers. Also, the ease at which their correspondence and rendezvous had been uncovered unnerved him.

In the makeshift chapel, the aroma of fresh pine stung their nostrils, most of his classmates were going through rote prayers or asking God to bless their families, but Al put some serious questions to God and himself. Was it really love? Did he even know what love was? What did it look like, feel like, taste like? He realised he didn't know. He couldn't be sure this was it, what he'd been feeling was real. Not having been there before, he had no reference point. Love, infatuation, delusion versus commitment, honour, duty. They were crashing against each other almost every waking hour, at times the emotions having the upper hand, other times rationality took control.

All these months he had been searching for, expecting even, a sign or guidance, as to the path to take, the decision to make. This has been a sign alright, no doubt about that, but not the one he was hoping for. Something Paddy and Sonny Weepu said back in January kept coming back to him, *"When it comes to the parish, we look after our own. Always have, always will." "It's a small town. Not much happens that goes unnoticed."* He now realised the full meaning of those words. His course of action was emerging through the mist of all the conflicting thoughts. At the next evening study period, he started a letter.

* * *

The afternoon sunshine poured into the kitchen, reflecting off the white china plates on the table as Abby and Moira finished their lunch. Moira was stirring her tea vigorously, crunching her napkin with her other hand.

'Was that letter yesterday from Brother Robertson? I thought you'd stopped writing to him?' Moira asked.

'What makes you think that? Don't remember saying I'd stopped,' replied Abby. 'In fact, I don't recall telling you that I was writing to him in the first place.'

'Well, it's just that I haven't seen many letters from him recently.'

'Didn't expect any, actually. They only came back a while ago, and they're in the final few weeks before they finish. Why your sudden interest in my mail?' asked Abby.

'No reason. Just noticed you've been getting fewer letters since September,' replied Moira.

Abby stood and took her dishes over to the sink, 'I'd better be off. If I don't go now I won't have time to get my bits and bobs done in town before my shift. See you tomorrow morning,' said Abby, as she walked out of the kitchen, grabbing her handbag and heading towards the front door.

She was almost halfway down the hill to town when Abby opened her bag to check she had enough money in her purse. 'Blast. Where the hell is it,' she said out loud, slapping her thigh with her free hand and exhaling heavily. She turned around and made her way back, quickening her pace. She was almost at the fence in their front garden when she saw a shadow move across her bedroom window. She stopped dead and continued watching. Wait, she told herself, make sure. A figure then became clearly visible. It was Moira pacing back and forth in her room, looking like she was reading something. She stepped back a couple of paces, and used a tree in their neighbours front garden as cover, yet still able to see through her bedroom window. So that explains why my letters were out of order, she thought. What's Moira's interest? Very strange. Should I charge in there, or just tuck it away to be brought out at a more opportune time? She was mulling this around when she saw Moira walk out of her room. Abby made her way to the gate on their path when Moira opened the front door and stepped onto the porch.

Moira looked up and gave a sharp scream and jumped back half a pace. 'What on earth are you doing there? You scared me half to death.'

'Forgot my purse. Was nearly in town when I realised,' replied Abby, as she stared at Moira, whose face was now a bright shade of red. Be as calm and natural as you can be, Abby told herself. 'Sorry to give you a fright.'

'Have you been out here long?' Moira stumbled over her words.

'Why would I have been waiting outside when I need my purse that's in the house? I got here just as you opened the front door. You alright, Moira? You're acting quite strange.'

'No, no, no. I'm fine, really. You just gave me quite the start. I'll be fine once the heart slows down a bit.' She fanned her face with her hand, but her complexion remained reddened.

'Looks like you need a nice cup of tea and a sit down. Do you want me to stay with you?' Abby bit her lower lip to stop a grin.

'No need. I'm fine. Honestly. Where's your purse?'

'Pretty sure it's in my bedroom. On the bedside table. But maybe not. Have you seen it?' Walking past her cousin, Abby was sure Moira was about to burst a blood vessel as her face grew a couple of shades darker. As she went back down the street, Abby knew a confrontation would come, but for now, she'd keep it up her sleeve.

Chapter 13

November 1931

Being on the night shift was a blessing. The corridors were deserted, virtually all the patients were asleep; just the odd moan reverberated down the hallways. There was only one other nurse on her ward. This suited Abby, as she wasn't in the mood to talk. After her rounds and writing up the patient notes, she made some idle chat with her colleague, then made an excuse that she didn't feel well and wasn't up for a lot of natter this evening.

When it was her turn to go for dinner, she grabbed a small secluded table at the back of the cafeteria. Ringlets of steam rose from her roast lamb and veggies as she set her tray down. She took out the letter and re-read it, pausing over the key passage, repeating it many times:

"It has become apparent that there are people who view our friendship very differently. Even to go so far as to call it inappropriate. Quite how they come to that conclusion is beyond me. Still, it has forced me to evaluate things more than I have in recent months. With little more than a month left at the seminary, I'm then due to start my teaching at St. Patricks College, I think it would be wise to not see each other for a while. In any event, given that I'm now back in the full swing of seminary life, it would be next to impossible for me to get away."

She didn't think she'd been staring at the pages for long,

but when she took her first mouthful of food, it was barely warm.

So that's it? The first sign of trouble and he capitulates, retreats behind the Church walls? She oscillated between anger and sadness. He was more important to her than she had previously acknowledged. You don't have these reactions and emotions for someone who means nothing to you. She thought that he felt deeply for her, the last time they were together seemed to be proof enough of that, maybe she had overestimated his feelings for her. Hadn't he told her he loved her on the station platform? Had she misheard him? Surely not. What they have is no breach of his vows, so why pull back so quickly and completely?

'Can I join you, Abby?' The voice startled her so that she knocked over her tea, spilling half the cup's contents. She looked up at Allan Peters. 'Sorry. Didn't mean to surprise you,' he quickly added, while mopping up the tea with his napkin.

'Don't worry. I was a thousand miles away.' She quickly folded up the letter and slid it into her pocket. She wanted to dab her eyes, but resisted, instead she blinked rapidly a few times.

'You alright?' Peters asked as he sat down and almost unconsciously patted down his thinning hair. Obviously she hadn't done a good job of hiding her reaction to Al's letter.

'I'm fine. Some bad news from a friend, so I'm just feeling a bit sad for them.'

'We've all had too much bad news this year. You don't need any more. We can only hope 1932 is happier,' he added, an uncomfortable half smile was fixed to his face.

'Yes please. I don't think I could take another year like this one.' Abby knew she sounded deflated, but couldn't muster much enthusiasm.

'Likewise. I've hardly seen you since we moved back to the hospital. How have you been, recent bad news besides?' Peters edged his chair closer to Abby as he spoke.

'Oh, fine. Delighted to be back here. It was so difficult treating the patients down there.'

'Couldn't agree more. Having the operating theatres again has been a godsend. The racecourse was all a touch primitive.'

Conversation dropped away quickly as Abby picked at her now cold dinner and Peters sipped his tea. She didn't try to keep things going.

'Any plans for Christmas?' Peters asked with forced eagerness.

'Still waiting on the roster to come out. If I've got a few days off I'll probably go back to Wanganui. You?'

'My parents are in Auckland, which is a bit far to go if we have less than a week off, and it's still difficult going back there even though Gracie's been gone a good few years now.' Abby didn't respond, the silence between them filled by the faint ticking of a clock over the canteen's door. 'Listen to me unburdening myself to you. Sorry for that. Anyway, I was probably going to stay in town. Maybe we can go out for a drink or dinner sometime in December?' he asked expectantly.

'You're not being a burden. It must be very tough to go back to the old places you and Grace shared in common. As for Christmas, we could get a bunch of us together for a night out,' said Abby.

'A group night out? Yeah, I suppose.' The deflation in his voice was easy to pick up.

'I think I've lost my appetite and I better get back to my ward. Good to see you again, Allan.' She quickly loaded up her tray and left the table without looking back.

Although she had barely touched her dinner, she didn't feel hungry for the remainder of her shift, a tense, knotted stomach took care of that. She knew she'd been unduly short with Peters. He didn't deserve that sort of treatment from her, she told herself. He's a nice man, genuine and of course, well set up, but he didn't do anything for her. No spark, no excitement, not even a flicker. At twenty-nine years old, should that be important to her anymore? Isn't that the preserve of idle romantics in their teens reading Jane Austen novels, not a woman almost thirty facing the real world? Should she reconsider, settle for stability? That would be the convenient option, but not one based on love. Maybe that could grow over time. No, that would not be her choice. There had to be that exhilaration from the start, that flutter of the heart each time you saw the person, or even thought of them. Not for her a relationship centred on comfort from the off.

Doing rounds of the patients, her thoughts quickly returned to Al. How could he so easily turn his back on the friendship? She knew that Connolly would have pressurised him, but as much as they cared for each other, it was still only a friendship to the outside world. What hurt as much as Moira's betrayal was the thought that all the care and support she'd given him was gratefully taken, but was now meaningless after a few stern words from his superior. Should she now follow Moira's model of nursing; medical care only, don't give of yourself, don't get emotionally attached.

Should she write back to him? What could she say of any meaning or value? If she asked to see him again before he left for Wellington, that would just look needy and desperate, neither of which she felt she was. Maybe just a short note being magnanimous and understanding in the face of the pressure he was no doubt under. She knew she couldn't just let him slip off to his new life without some sort of contact. There was now the added concern of a spy in her inner circle; she'd have to be extra vigilant to get a letter written and posted without Moira's knowledge. Another blessing of working the night shift.

* * *

January 1932
Wellington, New Zealand

Al, George and Leo could all sense the excitement of the start of the new school year sweeping St. Pat's College. However, Al's enthusiasm was tempered by the letter he'd received a few days earlier. It had actually been written and posted just before Christmas, but with his various recent movements from Napier to Wanganui to spend the festive period with his family, then down to Wellington, the letter only caught up with him some four weeks after its postmark. Abby hadn't put a return name or address on the envelope, but he recognised her handwriting immediately. He presumed the lack of the writers details was deliberate, so as to not arouse any suspicions when the letter arrived at the seminary.

In the privacy of his dormitory bedroom, he re-read the letter. He sat at the sturdy but plain wooden desk and unfolded the letter. He flattened out the pages on the rough surface, etched with the markings from his predecessors in decades long since passed. He tried unsuccessfully to get comfortable in the un-cushioned chair. The desk lamp threw out a harsh light, making the paper shine a brilliant white. No matter how many times he went over it, he always came away deflated, if not despondent. It appears that he had lost her friendship, the only female friend he had, and probably his closest friend, period. Friend? Surely she was more than that, but what exactly was an adequate description for what they were to each other and what they had? Somewhere between friends and lovers. Yes, they had kissed on their last rendezvous, but that was so quick, clumsy and embarrassing for them both, it couldn't be classified as a lovers kiss. Mate, pal, paramour? All nowhere near what she meant to him; either too loose and superficial or too sexual in nature. Kindred soul kept coming into his head.

'So she's lost to me now,' he whispered the words, half hoping that just by saying them wouldn't make the realisation so painful, but there was no respite, no relief for him. The best person ever to come into his life was gone. A love so strong that he could see God's creative hand in her face, a beauty that made him believe he was staring into the eyes of an angel the moment he woke up on that cot bed nearly a year ago. A love now vanished, to be no more than a footnote in his life. A burning sensation tore through his stomach and his hands went numb. Had he had a shilling for every daydream, for every possibility, for every fantasy, he'd have enough money to build that imagined life for them together.

What for him now? After his incident with Connolly, he decided to recommit to the Church, or was that a real decision, with real options? Barely, he thought, but it was the track he chose to traverse. Full ordination was on the horizon in December; becoming a Father, the final step in the path. The college and his friends were pressing him to go through the ceremony. That would be it then, no coming back, no possibility of another life. Wedded to the Church for eternity, his reward for turning his back on his true feelings. Hadn't that been the plan all along? From Sixth Form in school some eight years ago, was that not what had been marked out for him? She surely was just a diversion, a ruse planted by fate and the vicious earth to pull him away from his true trajectory.

* * *

March 1932
Napier, New Zealand

Abby stared forlornly into the mirror attached to her dressing table. The little notch that formed between her eyebrows when she frowned was pronounced this morning, almost forming a mini-canyon on her forehead. She dabbed on extra foundation under her eyes, but it didn't seem to make any difference to the darkened patches and she knew there was nothing temporary she could do for the extra folds of skin that had recently appeared. She was hardly surprised that her body was showing the signs of stress and fatigue, in fact she was only amazed at how long it'd taken for them to take hold on what now seemed like a permanent basis. One full year of almost unrelenting pressure coupled with the recent bitter disappointment of losing a special friendship and the simmering tension now enveloping her house. She put the final touches on her makeup then ventured into the kitchen. Moira and Pat were sitting at the table having a cup of tea. A couple of bowls of almost finished porridge sat discarded on the table.

Pat looked up when Abby walked in, 'Cuppa cha, love?'

'That'd be t'riffic. Ta Pat,' replied Abby, she moved her eyes to Moira as Pat reached over to the teapot, but Moira never made eye contact.

'There you go, pet. Ya didn't want porridge?'

'You're right, hon. Tea's just fine. I'll grab something at work. You still OK to walk up to the hospital together?' asked Abby.

'Yep,' replied Pat, as Abby nodded approval. 'You gonna come too, Moira?'

'No, I don't have to start till a bit later. Matron gave me an hour or two off to get some errands done,' said Moira, only looking at Pat.

Abby narrowed her eyes at her Moira. Wonder what little jobs she's got to do, especially when we're all out of the house? Moira McCarthy, I know what you're up to, Abby said to herself.

'Everything alright, Moira? You seem a bit out of sorts,' asked Pat.

'Nah, I'm right. Just a little distracted. Nothing major,' replied Moira.

'OK, love. Ready, Abby?'

'Good as gold, Pat.' Abby rose from the table, went over to the sink and rinsed out her cup. 'See you tonight,' she quickly said to Moira as she walked to the front door.

'You know what's going on with your cousin?' asked Pat as they walked up the street, 'She's been a bit strange the last couple of months. Very distant and secretive. We've both noticed.'

'No idea. Yeah, she has been rather odd lately. Only copped it myself in the last couple of weeks.' Abby was being deliberately evasive.

'I hope she snaps out of it soon. It's tiresome.'

'I'll have a word soon. Blast.' Abby nearly shouted as she looked down at her chest. 'I've forgotten my watch. How on earth did I walk out of the house without noticing that? I'll just nip back for it.'

'Sorry, hon, I should have spotted that as well. I'll wait here for you,' said Pat.

'No need for that. We're more than halfway there, I'll only make you late. Go on ahead.' Abby said, quickly turning back towards the house.

Turning the corner, she quickened her pace as she passed the next door neighbours. Abby opened the front door and went straight into her bedroom at the front of the house. She stopped suddenly in the bedroom doorway as she saw Moira sitting on her bed with letters in her hands, frantically trying to fold them back into their envelopes.

'Interesting reading?' Abby asked. Moira's face turned so red, she looked as if she'd had a bad case of sunburn.

'I can explain,' Moira stuttered.

'Tell me why you've betrayed me?' as she snatched the letters from Moira's hands.

'Protected you, more like. You were heading down a path that would bring shame to you and the family and likely damnation. You were betraying us and the Church.' Moira replied, straightening her posture as she spoke.

'What? How can a platonic friendship be a betrayal? I've done nothing wrong.' Abby crossed her arms tightly.

'Need I remind you, Abigail, that you have a brother and two sisters in the cloth? This sort of carrying on would devastate them.'

'So you're telling me that none of them have a single friendship outside of the priesthood or the convent? What a load of rubbish,' said Abby.

'I've read the letters. It's more than a friendship.' Moira said, raising her eyebrows.

'Thanks for the admission, but I don't have to justify my private life to you.'

'It's not your private life when it involves the Church.'

'Oh, your precious, sacred Church. Is that what this is all about? You couldn't give a damn about me, it's about you being seen to be the good little Catholic girl. My conscience is clear. All I've done is become friends with a lovely, intelligent, caring man.' Abby raised her voice in reply.

'That's not my take on it. Looks to me that you've been carrying on with him, throwing yourself upon him, forcing him to break his vows. You've sinned,' Moira said.

'What? Sinned? You sound like Father Murphy preaching damnation. You think I've been sleeping with him? You are way off the mark. Is this the sort of rubbish you've been telling them? Don't answer that. I don't give a shit what you've been saying. Just get out of my room.'

Moira slowly got up from the bed, straightened the front of her dress. 'It's for your own good, that's why I went to them with this,' she said as she stood in the doorway.

'Oh, how bloody altruistic of you. You're such a saint,' snapped Abby.

'I am compared to you. A jezebel, a temptress, that's what you are. You'll thank me.'

Abby almost hit Moira when she slammed the door in her face.

PART III

Chapter 14

March 1934

Wellington, New Zealand

Al was first through the door of their house, and he squinted as his eyes adjusted to the dark hallway, contrasted against the sharp sunlight of the late summer afternoon. Looking down at the floor, a bundle of white envelopes stood out against the brown carpet. He flicked through the letters, one for George, two for Leo, one more for George. He exhaled heavily; typical, another day without mail. Suddenly his eyebrows raised and his mouth opened slightly when he got to the last envelope. He instantly recognised the handwriting, but the return address was unfamiliar, even though it was still in Napier. His heartbeat quickened as he walked toward his bedroom, he dropped the other letters on the sideboard along the hall, but missed and the envelopes hit the floor. He kept on walking, rubbing the paper between his fingers as he went. What had it been, eighteen months? No, nearly two and a half years since he had received a letter from Abby. Many times in those months he had contemplated reinitiating contact. On more than one occasion a letter had been started, only to be thrown away through lack of courage. What good would it have done by writing anyway? He had made his decision, even if it had been forced, or at the very least heavily influenced, which he had told her in his last letter sent just after he started at St. Patrick's College. This didn't stop him from feeling the same pulse of excitement and expectation that accompanied the arrival of her letters when he was in the seminary. He wondered how she got his new address; they'd only been in the house since last December, after finally being given permission to move out of the college staff dormitory. She's a resourceful woman, he certainly knew that, so it wasn't a surprise she had tracked him down.

He dropped his satchel on the middle of his bed, went over to his dresser and picked up the letter opener that sat on a leather stationery set. It had gold lettering at the top, his initials and the date he was ordained, 18 December 1932. The lacquered rimu wood handle was cool in his hand, with a flick of his wrist the steel blade tore cleanly through the paper. As he removed the letter, the once familiar aroma of lavender hit him. His eyes closed momentarily, images of Abby shot across his vision. No single time or place, rather a swirling collage, some recognisable memories, others more dreams than reality. The two dominating the others were her kneeling beside his bed when he woke up after the quake, and her stepping down from the train for their first rendezvous at Palmerston North. Her eyes and smile filled his consciousness.

23rd February 1934

Dear Albert,

I trust this letter finds you in good health and the new school year has started well for you. I hope it is not too much of a shock receiving this, as it has been many long years since we last corresponded. Indeed this letter has been many days in its creation, with earlier versions discarded, such has been the difficulty in trying to bridge the chasm of these empty years.

Life for me has changed in many ways since we last wrote, the biggest change saw me leave Napier Hospital at Christmas and start at the local Sisters of Compassion nursing home down the road in Flaxmere. This is the primary cause for the letter, as I am coming to Wellington in April for additional training. I immediately thought of you as soon as they told me of the trip.

It would be wonderful to see each other again and find out what has been happening in our lives. I will be at the Sisters home in Island Bay from Sunday 15th to Saturday 21st April. I suspect evenings will be best for both of us, with your teaching and my training during the days.

I do hope you are interested to meet again, but understand if it is not possible.

Yours faithfully,
Abigail

Al sat at his desk, his fingers resting gently on his temples as he read the letter. His initial reaction was yes, definitely, of course he would see her, but upon additional readings his enthusiasm cooled as he noted the overall detached nature of the writing. Hell, cut her some slack, man, he said to himself, she told you how difficult it was writing it. She, after all, is the one who had the courage to make contact. He took out a fresh piece of paper and grabbed his pen.

* * *

14th April 1934

Abby stood over the open suitcase and clothes on her bed; hands on her hips, looking between the luggage and the open drawers and doors of the tallboy and wardrobe. She was facing the prospect of seriously over-packing for her week in Wellington.

It wasn't the standard daily requirements that were causing her problems; they were taken care of by three nurses uniforms, which she could always get laundered there. It was what to wear on Wednesday night when she and Al were due to meet. She had to admit she was overjoyed, but a little surprised, by his quick and positive response to her letter. She had put herself through a fair bit of self flagellation in deciding to write to Al, fully expecting to either hear nothing back or for him to politely reject her invitation to meet. Not having him in her life in any form for the past two years had been harder than she expected. There had been a few nights that tears had accompanied her to sleep and many days had been filled with the memories of their days together. She knew she couldn't let the opportunity of being in the same city as him for a week go past without trying to re-establish contact. Even if he had said no, at least she had taken the chance, so there wouldn't be any "what ifs". He did say yes, though, and she had been planning what to do, what to say and what to wear for a week.

She had three outfits laid out, but there was only room for one, maybe two at a squeeze. Along with each separate option there were the requisite additional accessories, so she really did need to make a choice. Now that autumn had arrived and Wellington would be a good five degrees cooler than here, the lighter, summery outfit could be discarded. Pity – she had only bought the lightweight, pleated apricot knee length skirt this past November and it had quickly become one of her new favourites. That left the tweed suit or the tartan skirt and green jacket. She chewed on the inside of her cheek as she deliberated. Nothing for it, but to try them both on again, just to make doubly sure that her gut instinct was right.

* * *

18th April 1934

From its position at the top of a hill, the Sisters of Compassion hospital offered sweeping views of Island Bay, Taputeranga Island and Cook Strait. From her bedroom window, Abby could see most of the bay, its sandy beach forming almost a perfect arc from rocky points on both ends, enclosed at the ends by steep hills, the small three storey lighthouse at the western end of the bay gleamed a bright white against the green of the bush on the hill behind it. The sky was turning that beautiful deep inky blue of twilight, a keen wind forced small clouds to scurry across the view from town out to sea and it was whipping up the surf as it hit the beach. A decent swell from Cook Strait swept across the low lying rocks of Taputeranga Island, at times leaving its small triangular peak cut off from the rest of the island. She had been standing at the window for nearly ten minutes, taking in the constantly changing vista. She'd been ready for twenty minutes and was now getting edgy, rocking from one foot to the other, clasping her hands behind her, then in front, and then to the back again. She looked at her watch, quarter to seven, unsurprisingly only a minute since her last time check. She moved over to the mirror for a final once-over: she pulled the lapels of her tweed suit jacket toward her chest, rounded her shoulders, puffed up her purple silk scarf, tugged on the collar of her cream blouse, turned her head left and right looking at her small pearl drop earrings, and one last pat down of the bottom of her jacket and skirt. Perfect. She picked up her felt fedora, picked out a piece of lint from the pheasant's feather in the crown band, opened the bedroom door and made her way down to reception.

She had only sat down for a couple of minutes when Al opened the front door and stepped purposefully into the foyer, the bottom of his cassock billowed behind him then quickly came to rest when he stopped in the middle of the reception area. Abby let out a deep breath and felt a little flush as she rose to walk over to him, a broad smile came to them both simultaneously. He offered his hand, her initial thought was to ignore it and hug him, but she knew discretion was best. She took his hand, placed her left hand on his upper arm and turned her cheek to allow him to kiss her. She noticed his hair had thinned a little on top and he had a distinct streak of grey on the temples.

'Wonderful to see you again, Abby,' he said, 'you look lovely. I like the scarf. It's a nice splash of colour.'

'Oh, this old thing,' she replied, pulling on the cloth, 'I've had it for ages, but I do like it. You are looking well. Teaching and college life must agree with you.'

'It's great. The boys keep you on your toes. Sharp as a tack some of them,' he replied.

'I was thinking we could go for a walk around the grounds and maybe down to the bay, but that northerly is brisk. It'll be nippy at the beach, so we could go to the sunroom,' Abby stepped aside and pointed the way.

'That'll be fine. I didn't bring a coat anyway. It'll be nice just to sit and talk.'

They made their way through to the back of the building. The sun's dying twilight came through the giant windows, bathing the room in a warm golden hue from floor to its 18ft high ceiling. The room was empty, so they took up the best spot in a couple of wicker loungers close to the windows. There was a pause in conversation as Al took in the view that overlooked a small gully that had been planted and landscaped to form a garden, pungas and silver beech trees lined the paths, with ferns and rose bushes in the flower beds.

'You still got your fascination for plants?' Abby tried to get things moving again.

'Oh, yes. Sorry for getting distracted. Still have my green thumb. I've got a nice little patch for my veggies and herbs in the garden of our flat,' replied Al.

'Yes, I was going to ask you about where you're living now,' she replied as she straightened her skirt to get rid of the wrinkles.

'You did well to track me down, now that I'm not in the staff dormitory.'

'I presumed you were still at St. Pat's, so I called them to find out for sure, and they gave me your address. So you're out on your own. That's nice.'

'You remember George and Leo from Mount Saint Mary's?' he paused as she nodded, 'We asked if we could move into one of the diocesan houses. Its great having a little more freedom.'

'My word, three gents about town. How's it working out?' Abby asked with a smile.

'Quite good, it is nice to have our own space and not be under the gaze of the school all the time. We have a lady come in once a week to clean and we have most of our meals at college.'

'The best of all worlds then, and college itself is going well? The boys causing you a bit of stress,' she reached over and smoothed down his hair. A tingle rushed up her hand and arm.

'Oh, the grey. That started to appear early in 32. I reckon it's a reaction to the shock of the quake. I think I'll be fully gone by my 30th. Anyway, I'm really enjoying the teaching. I take science and physics for the junior classes. Some of the boys are a bit of a handful, but in general they are good lads. I restarted a defunct poetry appreciation club, but there haven't been many takers so far. I've just finished with the tennis team – we had our last match three weeks ago. Rugby has now started, I take one of the lower teams.'

'You, coaching rugby? That'd be a sight,' a broad smile came across Abby's face.

'Not so fast, young lady. I'll have you know we won more games than we lost last year and got a school prize as the most improved team,' he responded with a smirk. 'Probably the biggest news for me is that I got ordained December two years ago, so I'm now Father Robertson to the boys and I'm due to do my brother Gary's wedding next summer down in Greymouth.'

Ordained, the word repeated itself in quick succession in her head. Her shoulders fell slightly, and her smile faded. The last commitment to the Church he could make, now done. There's no turning back now, that's the decisive step.

'And what of your big news? Why did you leave the hospital?' his voice brought her back to the conversation.

'It was more of a need to get away from Moira, really.' She replied as Al cocked his head, narrowed his gaze, giving her a quizzical look. 'Did I not tell you?'

'Tell me what?' his voice went down an octave as he spoke.

'It was Moira who told Connolly about our friendship. For a few weeks I had a feeling she was looking through your letters to me. I caught her red-handed one day, found her in my bedroom reading them, so I had it out with her. Obviously I couldn't trust her anymore and things just got more tense and strained as time went by. I decided I had to get away from her, so I took this job at the Sisters home in Flaxmere, and am staying there as well. I miss Jess and Pat and all the girls at the hospital, but it had got intolerable, so I had to get out.' She exhaled heavily as she finished.

'Oh, Abby, I had no idea,' Al reached for her hands and held them tightly, 'That's terrible. To think your own family would do that. Did she give you a reason?'

'Oh, some rubbish about me betraying the Church. Apparently we were bringing shame onto our families and the Church and I was on the fast track to damnation. Utter tosh. So, we turned our backs on a lovely friendship because of a meddling, pious little busybody.'

Al slumped back and slammed his hand on the chairs arm, making Abby jump, 'All along I thought it was someone in the Church. I thought it had gone through the hierarchy and they were watching both of us. That's one of the reasons I said we shouldn't see each other, as there was pressure coming from above, not Moira.' He drew in a deep breath and took Abby's hands again, 'Abby, I can only tell you how sorry I am for what I did. It was totally selfish and spineless and you didn't deserve to be treated so.'

'You weren't to know. I presumed that you must have been under a lot of pressure. I have to admit it did knock me back and I was very sad for a couple of weeks, but I thought about your situation and how anything they deem as inappropriate could be held against you. It's not as if they can do anything to me.'

'The thing that aggravates me is that other people were making assumptions and forcing us down a certain path that we'd not otherwise go. And I for one let them lead me to a decision that I so regret, abandoning our friendship. I let other people dictate my life. That gets to me,' said Al.

'What were you to do? Tell Connolly no, you were going to ignore him and continue meeting me when and where you liked? I wouldn't have wanted to see the consequences of that on you. What's done is done. We can't turn the clock back, we can only look forward. We're both free of those forces now, both in different phases of our lives and can make decisions away from their influence. If we can resurrect our friendship, wouldn't that be a good thing?'

'Definitely. One doesn't often get second chances in life, very rare indeed. This is one I didn't think would present itself. I have missed you over the past couple of years,' he replied.

He held her gaze for what seemed to her for minutes, she felt warm from head to toe, even though the sun had now left them. 'That's lovely of you to say. I'd be a liar if I said otherwise myself. So what do we do from here?'

'I can go up to Wanganui for part of the May school holiday's. Could you meet in Palmerston North?' he asked.

'That'd be wonderful. I'll see if I can go back to Fordell for a long weekend, so we could travel from Palmerston to Wanganui together. When are the holiday's?' she asked.

'We break up on Friday the 11th, so we could go for the 18th? Four weeks from this Friday. Wait, I don't know where to write to you. Is the address you put on your last letter where you are now?'

'Yes, you can drop me a line there: Aubert House, Flaxmere, Hawke's Bay. That'll find me. I'll make plans as soon as I'm back. I'm excited already.' Abby beamed a wide smile at Al.

The room was now almost dark as Al opened his watch. 'Blimey. Quarter past eight. I'd better start to make my way back. It'll be after nine by the time I get to the flat. Thank you for writing to me again, that took a lot of courage, the likes of which obviously I didn't have.'

'Things, and people, have conspired against us, so it's good that we managed to get around them. Come on, let me walk you to the door.'

She watched him walk down the driveway to the main road, he turned back twice and waved on his way down the hill. When he was out of sight she spun around to go back inside. Even though the autumn evening had a chill in the air and she didn't have a coat on, she felt warm. She went back to the sunroom and sat where they had been a few minutes earlier. Through the glow that shrouded her, a hint of darkness shaded her thoughts. So he has been ordained. So it is Father Robertson now, and he went through that ceremony barely more than twelve months since the last time they were together. He has made his decision and the best that can now be hoped for is a platonic friendship, but isn't that what she'd claimed they had ever had when she argued with Moira? She should have expected it would've happened, that's the natural progression for him, the calling they all aspire to, and after his last letter to her back then, why would she think there would have been a different outcome? Still, that knowledge doesn't stop the sting of hearing it, the ache of the realisation that a small hope, dream, has been wrenched away from her. Time to readjust her expectations and finally cast out any notion or fantasy of what might have been. She stared out into blackness.

* * *

Al could hardly feel his feet hitting the ground as he walked down the hill towards the bus stop. A lightness enveloped him, a sensation that he hadn't felt in nearly three years, unsurprisingly it was similar to the feeling he had the last time they were together. She had the ability to uplift him every time he saw her. Nobody else he knew had such an effect on him, she had an almost magical quality about her that could cut through any haze or negativity that might be afflicting him. There wasn't any one single thing he could isolate; but an overall aura that moved him deeply. He turned the corner to see a bus waiting to start its route into town and quickened his pace to make sure he made it. Taking a seat near the back, his smile fell away as all the old conflicts rose up within him: his desire to be with her, his want to have her in his life, against his commitment and the oversight of the Church. The words of one of the older priests at his ordination boomed in his head, "Once you are ordained, you become a man apart, something greater than the average person, you are one with the Lord." This had come back to him a few times in the past eighteen months, but somehow the words seemed hollow, he didn't feel as if he was on any heightened level of existence. He knew he was a man apart, but not for the reasons the Father had alluded to, rather just the automatic reverence that the public bestowed on him and his brethren. Surely now as a Father and established at the College, that veneration and seniority would allow him the ability to have a friendship with Abby without any of the angst and scrutiny of the past. As the bus rattled its way up the hill, he was already mentally writing his next letter to Abby that would organise their coming rendezvous.

* * *

August 1934

Al made sure he sat on the platform side of the train so he could see her as they pulled into the station. He pushed the window up to get a clear view; a blast of cold air stung his face, but he had a woollen scarf wrapped around his neck, which covered up his Roman collar, and his coat buttoned up against the chill. She was in the same spot as back in May, hard up against the station wall to protect herself from the bitter southwester coming in from the Tasman Sea. He could barely see her face as her hat was pulled low and her rabbit fur scarf was up around her chin. If he hadn't had every feature, curve, nuance and mannerism of her memorised, he might well have thought she was just another woman hunkering down from the cold. She had jettisoned her usual skirt and wore trousers. Very modern, he thought, as he closed the window. He gave her a little wave as she walked down the carriage.

'Oh, my word. It's nasty out there,' she said as she sat down, took off her gloves and offered her cheek to him.

'You look fabulous. I love the trousers,' he said, smiling at her. 'Blimey, you're freezing. You alright?' he added after he kissed her.

'I'll be fine in a couple of minutes. How are you? You're looking well.'

'Terrific, thanks. Very glad it's the school holidays. The winter term is a long one.'

'How's that little rugby team of yours doing?' she asked.

'Pretty well, actually. Holding our own most games. We won't be winning any cups, but the lads are enjoying themselves.'

'That's the main thing. Are you hungry? I brought a little treat for us.' She opened up her handbag and took out a cube of wax paper, about three inches square. 'Carrot cake,' her voice rose as she unwrapped the package.

'Top stuff, thank you,' he said taking the slice offered to him. 'Oh, that's great. There's a little spice in it,' he added after the first bite.

'Glad you like it. It's Mum's recipe, we put in cinnamon to give it something extra. Are you staying in Wanganui for the whole of the holidays?' She took a small bite of the slice of cake.

'No. Thinking of only a week at this stage. I'll see how long it takes before Mum drives me mad and Dad riles me up,' he replied.

'Come on, it can't be that bad. You only see them three times a year. Surely they're glad to see you?'

'Yes, of course they are. I suppose being away from them since I was twelve, we really don't know each other anymore and I'm not used to any fuss being made of me.'
'But that's what parents do, especially mothers. You have to let her spoil her eldest.'

'You're right. It'll be fine, and I'll get to spend time with William and Howard, which will be great. When do you have to go back?' he asked.

'Monday. I'm on the late shift, so I can catch the Monday morning train and still be back in Napier in time for work. How are your brothers doing?'
'William is in his last year of college, fixated about aeroplanes and wireless radios. I think he wants to be a pilot. Howard is in his first year of intermediate school. Gary is down in Wellington, been working for the Department of Labour for three years now. I see him most Sunday's at Mass and we usually go to lunch after. He's engaged to Sarah, a lovely lady, and they are getting married

on the last Saturday of December down in Greymouth, where she's from. I told you I'm going to perform the ceremony?'

'Yes. It's wonderful. That's going to be so special for the whole family. How do you feel about it?' Abby leaned in closer to Al as she spoke.

'Nervous. It'll be my first wedding, so I'm hoping I don't stuff it up.'

'You'll be fine. You've done regular Mass enough, haven't you? It's just reading the Wedding Mass.'

'Oh, so flippant, young lady. What if I do it wrong? I'm afraid of not marrying my brother off properly. Nerve wracking stuff.' He broke off a small piece of cake, but didn't eat it, instead squeezed it between his fingers.

'It'll go off fabulously well, I'm sure of it. How long you going down there for. It's a fair old way to the West Coast.'

'Yeah, it is a decent trip, so I was going to make a holiday of it and spend a couple of weeks there. I want to see the glaciers and get up into the mountains on a couple of the tracks. You can do guided walks on both Franz Josef and Fox Glaciers, which sounds like fun.'

'Definitely. Sign me up,' Abby rolled her eyes as she spoke.

'Well, madam, it may not inspire you, but it does me. You know they are some of a handful of glaciers in the world that are near sea level in the temperate zones?'

'Riveting. Tell me more, professor,' she replied, raising her eyebrows.

'Such impertinence. I don't have to take that from you. There are two blokes back at my flat who are past masters of winding me up,' he said with a smirk. She gave him a pat on his hand that was resting on the seat between them, and left her hand resting on his.

They felt the train start to slow down as the conductor opened up the carriage door behind them and shouted 'This is Whangaehu station. Whangaehu this stop.'

'Crikey. That's come around quickly. I'm off at the one after,' Abby said almost jumping off the seat. Al turned to face her. 'No need for the long face. That was a wonderful hour or so. Now, will you be coming up at Christmas before you head down to Greymouth?'

'No, apparently the family is coming down to Wellington and we're going to have Christmas at Gary's , then we all head down south the day after Boxing Day. So I won't see you again before next year? I don't think I like that idea' said Al.

'Maybe we can meet in Palmerston for a day, some weekend. I only work every other Saturday, so I can easily get the early train, spend the day with you then get the last train back. Let's write and organise something when we are back.' She reached up and pulled down her bag from the luggage rack before he could get to his feet and help her.

The conductor came back in, 'Fordell, next stop.'

'I better run. Lots of love,' she leaned in for a kiss on the cheek. She turned back to give him a smile and a wave as she reached the front of the carriage.

He pressed his face to the window to see her get off the train, but she turned the other way as soon as she stepped on the platform and went up to a tall older man, with a thick, greying beard, and gave him a hug. Part of him wished he could have got off the train and gone with her, mainly because the time they had just spent together was too short, just a teaser really. Every time he saw her the minutes seemed to dissolve quickly, like a cube of sugar in hot tea. The past hour felt like no more than ten minutes, he wanted their time together to run and run. He never tired of her conversation, her mannerisms, her smell. The next week would drag like months in comparison, so he would have to make plans quickly for a day in Palmerston together.

* * *

19th January 1935

Abby was first to the tea rooms at the DIC department store on the Square in Palmerston North. They had agreed that for their meetings here, whoever got to the station first would go straight to the shop and grab a table, rather than wait at the station for the other. Walking through town together was a sure fire way to get heads turning and after Moira's spying, they needed to minimise any suspicious behaviour. She thought their precautions were working, this being their third meeting here and she hadn't noticed as much as a second look by anyone when they were together.

Knowing she had about an hour before Al arrived, she opened her small suitcase and took out her latest book. She made slow progress, with the passages barely registering as her mind and eyes kept wandering. She was so eager to see Al again, one to two months between their rendezvous was too much for her, and she knew there'd be so much to catch up on that the precious time would quickly evaporate. Her mind was so preoccupied that Al startled her when he touched her shoulder.

'Sorry, love. You OK? Didn't mean to scare you. Thought you saw me coming up the stairs,' he said while rubbing her back.

'Oh, no, I'm fine,' she replied, patting her chest, 'I really was in my own little world. I wasn't expecting you in civvies, so you didn't register when I saw a man in a street suit. You look terrific in it, though, accentuates your frame nicely. Much better fit than those hideous things you get from the Church.'

'Thank you. It certainly feels a thousand percent nicer to wear. You look lovely today. I haven't seen that outfit before have I?' he asked.

Abby had finally got to wear the apricot pleated skirt and floral print blouse combination she had contemplated back in

April. 'Thank you, love. It's one of my favourites, but it's definitely a summer outfit, so seeing this was the first properly warm day we've had together, I knew exactly what I'd wear. So how did you manage to wear a suit today?'

'I told them I was going up to spend the weekend with my brother Gary in Lower Hutt. Which is actually true. I'll head there when I get back tonight, just works out in our favour and I have a reason to bring a change of clothes. I got changed in the restrooms at Wellington Station. The old trusty black number and collar are in the suitcase. Have you eaten? I'm ravenous,' Abby shook her head, so he continued, 'How about some cucumber sandwiches and a cake?'

'Spot on. A lamington for me. I've been eyeing them since I got here.' She watched him walk over to the counter, clothes do maketh the man, she thought, that suit does fit nicely. It dawned on her that this was the first time since they met that she'd seen him in street clothes. She dismissed the day she'd stared at him at the hospital after his and Paddy's tramping mishap. Being in sodden and muddy mountain gear doesn't count, but this certainly does. *'We'll have to get a better colour for him though, she thought. Dark brown just isn't on: a navy blue or deep forest green would do.'*

'Bad news is that they've changed the times of the Wanganui trains since the holidays. We only have a couple of hours before mine leaves,' said Abby as Al returned.

'That's bloody poor of them. Typical New Zealand Railways. Law unto themselves. We'll just make the most of the time we have.'

'Now, tell me. How did the wedding go? They are officially married? You didn't fluff your lines?'

'No, ma'am. Everything went according to plan and scripture. It was a wonderful weekend. The whole family were thrilled to bits. Gary was a dashing groom and Sarah was a radiant bride. I did my duty as required. It's incredible how quick the service goes when you're actually in it.'

'I can remember a few full wedding masses that have dragged on. I'm so glad it went well. So, first of many for you?' Abby asked with a smile.

'I'd hope not. Maybe William will want me to do his when he's ready, but I'd be happy enough to retire with just the one.'

Conversation flowed easily for the next hour, until Abby looked at her watch and realised they were into their last thirty minutes. 'As lovely as these days are, they are really only stolen moments. Wouldn't it be nice to spend more than a few hours together, and not be constantly under the pressure of the clock?' she asked.

'I was thinking the same thing coming up today. Those days we spent at Paddy's cottage were tremendous. I think about them often. Of course the situation was unique, but they are some of my fondest memories. You were, and still are, the person I feel most comfortable with.' Abby smiled and nodded as he spoke. 'Now, practically speaking…,' he continued.

'Oh, here we go,' Abby interrupted, rolling her eyes, 'I knew the sentimentality was too good to last.'

'Uncalled for, Miss McCarthy. I shall carry on. I'll have either tennis or rugby every Saturday once college starts.' Abby started to frown. 'Except. Except, for Easter, when the boys are off, and I'm completely free.'

'Bravo,' Abby almost shouted. 'That's it then. But what should we do?'

'I'll organise to come up to the Bay over the Easter weekend. I can stay with Paddy in the cottage. Nothing more for it.' Both of them had broad smiles.

'Love, now that that's settled, let's go for a walk around the Square. It's such a lovely day. Shame to spend all our time cooped up indoors,' Abby said, gabbing his hand and standing up almost simultaneously.

As they walked downstairs, Abby linked arms with Al: it felt natural, a good fit. With Al in street clothes, they were a little too comfortable in each other's company, not that aware of the people around them. If they had been more focused, they might have seen Moira lurking in the Ladies Fashion section.

CHAPTER 15

18ᵗʰ April 1935

Paddy and Al rumbled out of the train station in the old Model T and along streets with buildings in varying states of construction, many at or near completion.

'Looks like it's going well,' said Al.

'Yeah, they're ripping into it now. Ya remember it took them a while to get cracking, but they have really upped the pace in the last year. It's taking a bit of getting used to, the different look of the place. I get a bit disorientated at times. Your brain plays tricks on you. You know the street you're on and you expect to see a certain building from your memory, then there's something new standing in front of you,' said Paddy, waving his hand in front of the bright facades on the street. 'Bloody bewildering. Still, there's a couple of places that haven't changed,' he continued as he pulled the car around a corner and parked outside his cottage.

'Not even a new coat of paint.' Al raised an eyebrow at Paddy.

A familiar wall of musty air greeted Al in the hallway, yet there was a slightly sweet, almost floral, hint to it. He opened the door to his old room. He couldn't identify a single thing that had changed in four years, even down to the brown knitted bedspread. He dropped his bag on the bed and a light cloud of dust rose up. Al shook his head with a small smile then made his way into the lounge and found the source of the aroma to be a vase of fresh roses and carnations in the middle of the coffee table. A couple of changes caught his eye: arm covers on the chairs and a couple of colourful rugs over the spots of carpet he remembered were highly worn.

'Been decorating?' Al asked Paddy as he came into the room with the tray of tea supplies.

'Ya what?' asked Paddy as Al motioned to the additions. 'Mary Simpson's handy work. Remember her? She's been coming round a bit lately and brightened the place up.'

'How is Mary?' asked Al.

'Doin' alright. Still at P&O over at the dock. First couple of years were tough, but she's a lot better now. She still asks after you. I fill her in on your news when you write. Now, what brings you back to the Bay for Easter? As much as I'd like to think it's just to catch up with me, I don't think that's a big enough pull.'

'I'm going to see Abigail McCarthy tomorrow,' replied Al.

'Abigail McCarthy?' Paddy stroked his chin in thought. 'Oh, one of the nurses who looked after you lot up at the seminary?' Al nodded at the question. 'You've stayed in contact after all this time? That's nice. She's a lovely woman, if memory serves. Her sister was a bit prickly, though.'

'Cousin. Moira's not her sister,' replied Al. 'We lost touch for a couple of years after I went down to Wellington, but rekindled things last year.'

'Right. She still up at the hospital? Now that I think of it, I haven't seen her at Mass for quite a while. Her cousin still comes regularly.'

'No, she left over a year ago. She's at a nursing home out in Flaxmere. Might be going to church there.'

'You mustn't have seen each other for years. She'll get a bit of surprise, like me,' said Paddy.

'Well, we have met once or twice, recently. She was down in Wellington about a year ago for training at the Sisters of Compassion, and we've seen each other in Wanganui once.' Al stumbled over his less than completely truthful reply, enough for Paddy to press on with more questions.

'So you're leaving your local parish on our most important

and sacred weekend, travelling over five hours to see a woman who you've barely seen in four years and who is just a friend? Sounds a bit more than that, aye?' said Paddy.

'No, no. It's nothing more than a friendship. You can be rest assured.'

'I'm not the one that would need assuring. Just watch yourself, aye lad. Be aware of what you're doing, so that there's nothing for people to question.'

'Could the same be said about you and Mary Simpson?' asked Al.

'Quite different. You know we had a bit of history together, she's a parishioner and lives close by. So of course I'll see a bit of her.'

'Sounds like a decent rationalisation to me, if not hypocritical,' said Al.

'Touché. Then again we both know the world, and the Church, survives on both. You've been out there long enough to know of, or at least have your suspicions of, some odd relationships amongst our brethren. Things happen, either planned or unplanned. Lad, just be very careful, not only for your sake, but for hers.'

'Don't worry, we, I mean, I am. Abby really is just a friend. It's not going beyond that. I'm completely committed to the Church.'

'Never said you weren't,' replied Paddy, raising his eyebrows. 'Look lad, it's good for us to have friends and acquaintances outside the Church. Just be mindful of appearances. Remember, there are eyes everywhere. That's all I'm saying.' Al gave a couple of sharp nods while taking a mouthful of tea. 'That one's put to bed, aye? Let's sup-up and grab a nightcap. Still drinking sherry?' Paddy was halfway to the drinks cabinet before he finished the sentence.

* * *

20th April 1935

Al studied his face in preparation for his daily shave. The bloodshot eyes that stared back took in the grey tinge to the skin under his eyes and the puffed nature of his jawline around his glands. Two sleepless nights had quickly taken their toll. The evening with Paddy had wound him up tightly, and filled his mind with conflicting thoughts, all fighting for their share of his attention. That he hadn't been completely truthful with Paddy was the main thing that disturbed him. They weren't exactly lies that he'd told his mate, but they were nigh on. He'd gotten used to denying the truth to himself, the Church hierarchy, and even George and Leo on the odd occasion, but something felt very wrong about this. All those years ago, Paddy had become more than a friend; he was a confidant, a mentor, someone able to cut through all the rubbish.

Last nights' sleeplessness was due to excitement. Thoughts of spending the whole day with Abby swamped his mind, he had used every trick and technique he knew to fall asleep, but to no avail, it was just before two o'clock the last time he flipped open the face of his fob watch and felt the position of the hands to check the time. He must have finally drifted off, but woke up a little after five with Paddy making noise in the kitchen. What a way to see Abby, looking rough as guts with not even eight total hours sleep over the last two nights. After shaving he got dressed into street clothes; he'd packed a suit, dress shirt and tie, but also some tweed trousers and a forest green jersey. Abby had told him she had a plan for the day and that he shouldn't dress too formally, so he went for the trouser and jersey option, but still wore a nice shirt and tie.

The short bus trip to Abby's town dragged. He couldn't get comfortable, constantly fidgeting, changing his position and checking his watch. He couldn't remember half an hour going more slowly. Finally, the bus jerked to a stop in the centre of Flaxmere and Abby was waiting by the small, wooden shelter, he felt his heartbeat quicken. She greeted him off the bus with a strong hug and a kiss on the lips, he tensed up immediately. They had kissed before, many years ago; how could he forget the equal parts of delight, excitement and embarrassment, over the bungled attempt at intimacy. That was in private though, this was out in public. Almost instantly the shock turned to exhilaration and his whole body tingled. Her body was warm and inviting, the aroma of her freshly washed hair and soft skin intoxicating. As she pulled away he noticed she wasn't wearing earrings; it may have been the first time he could recall her not wearing any in a social setting. Her white blouse had the first couple of buttons undone, her cleavage clearly visible; the shirt was a contrast against her sky blue cardigan and tan trousers.

'You look wonderful. I love the trouser, blouse and cardi combo,' he said.

'Thanks, hon. So do you. The summer's treated you well. Are you ready for a wee adventure?' Abby said with a mischievous smile.

'Intrigued and excited in equal measure. Any clues?'

'Certainly not. Where would the fun be in that? All you need to know is that we have bit of a walk in front of us, but nothing that an avid tramper won't be able to handle. Come on.' Abby took Al by the arm and led him away from the bus stop.

They headed off to the south-east, the mid-autumn sun still had decent warmth as it hit the side of their face. It illuminated the shear, jagged escarpment of Te Mata Peak about five miles straight in front of them.

'Don't get any ideas about tearing off up there,' Abby said, poking Al in the ribs.

'Unfair. I wouldn't dream of leaving you just as our adventure is starting,' he replied.

'I saw you eyeing it up. You just can't help yourself. See hill, must climb it. It's actually one of the things I like about you. Just not today.'

They turned left to head north, the sun now squarely in their faces. The houses soon thinned out and paddocks got bigger, with a few sheep and the odd horse. The autumn rains had come on cue this year, so the fields had a healthy green tinge to them. The next field had neat rows of apple trees spreading back from the roadside fence. A hand painted sign reading "Hanson's Orchard – PYO" was nailed to the fence posts.

'Here we are,' said Abby.

'Apple picking?' asked Al.

'Yep, granny smiths for stewing and pies, and maybe some late season raspberries for jam, if we're lucky.' Abby lead the way, almost to the back of the orchard, over a hundred yards from the packing sheds up by the road. 'It'll be nice and quiet down here, away from the commotion up the front. Grab that ladder and start picking. I'll get the ones down low.'

'Yes, ma'am, right away ma'am,' Al replied, giving a short salute and picked up the ladder that was leaning against the large wooden crate, positioned it firmly against the closest tree trunk, put the bucket strap around his neck and climbed up into the heavily fruit laden branches. The whole time he gave a few quick glances to Abby, and she hadn't seemed to have taken her eyes off him, expertly picking apples while keeping him in view. 'So, when might the first of these planned pies get made?' he asked, gently placing apples in his bucket.

'Patience. If we take a few back with us today, I might be able to whip one up before you head back to Wellington. I could do you one to take home for the lads. I reckon George and Leo would appreciate some homemade dessert,' Abby replied.

'Stuff them. I was hoping to get some myself this weekend.'

'Some pie, you mean,' said Abby with a broad smile.

'No idea what else you might mean.' Al was almost at the base of the ladder as he spoke. 'First bucket full.' He stepped over to the crate, put the bucket into it, unhooked the small canvas sheet that formed the bottom of the bucket and let the apples roll out. 'Hurry up, madam, you're falling behind.' Abby swooped down to pick up a fallen, half rotten apple and lobbed it at Al. He ducked and it splattered against the tree. 'Decent throw. More follow through next time.'

Al unloaded his third bucket full into the crate, Abby picked up an apple, rubbed it on her cardigan and bit into it, she quickly cupped her other hand under her chin and made slurping noises as juice ran down her face. 'Hells bells. They are a bit juicy. Have a bite.'

'As soon as they had eaten it, they were given understanding. Is there a serpent over there?' he said with a smile.

'Oh, dear Lord. Don't be quoting scripture at me. The irony of the situation isn't lost on me,' Abby replied, shaking her head at Al.

'Sorry. It was too good an opportunity to pass up. Here, use this.' He handed her his handkerchief. 'Don't worry, it was fresh out of the drawer this morning.'

'I guessed that would be case. You can do the honours,' Abby replied as he turned her cheek up towards him and stepped closer.

Al gently wiped the side of her face, following her jawline on both sides. She closed her eyes as he stroked her skin. The afternoon sun made her skin glow and stray strands of her hair glisten. He was so close to her now he could feel the warmth of her breath. He leaned in and kissed her. Abby opened her eyes immediately as their lips met, then closed them again just as quickly and put her arms around his waist, pulling him in. Her body felt wonderful next to his, the sensation of the embrace and heat between them sent a warm shock wave up and down his body. He felt her mouth open slightly, so he did the same to then feel her tongue searching for his. He had played this out in his head so many times since their aborted attempt years ago, and didn't want to make the same mistake, so he softly met her. He could taste the sweetness of the apple on her; his mouth was alive, exploding with every contact with hers. He pulled his hands up from her waist, cupped her breasts and lightly caressed them. She let out a low moan.

A noise from behind startled them, forcing them apart, they both looked down the line of trees to see a tractor and trailer being driven out of the sheds and turned towards them. Abby pulled him to her once more, gave him a quick kiss then pushed him away. His vision suddenly went blurry as he watched her walk over to the crate of apples and wave at the farmer. He propped himself against a tree and quickly gulped down deep breaths. Is that what true love feels like?

* * *

2nd November 1935

Shafts of spring sunlight flickered through the leaves of the apples trees at the back of Hanson's Orchard. There was a warm, light breeze coming out of the north which made the branches dance lazily and caused the late blossoms to drift to the grass below. Al leant against one of the trees, his eyes closed, face turned up towards the sun. A couple of poetry books lay discarded to his left. Abby lay on a blanket at right angles to Al, her head on his thighs.

Al reached behind his back and picked up a small rectangular package. The wrapping paper had a selection of roses on it and a red bow. 'For you, hon,' he said.

'What's all this? Albert Robertson, you know our rule: no buying gifts.'

'I know and I haven't broken any rule, ma'am.'

She carefully unwrapped it to find a book. She stroked the leather bound volume, turned it onto its side to read the spine. *The Collected Works of Rupert Brooke*. Oh, hon, but this is one of your favourites. I can't take it.' She pushed herself up and turned so she was now facing Al.

'It's mine to give and I give it to you. With great love,' he said.

Abby opened the front cover to find a handwritten note and a poem:

To my most precious Abigail,
I hope you enjoy this as much as I and it brings you years of pleasure.

All my love,
Albert

> 'She'
> By Albert Robertson
>
> *Who did save my world, She*
> *From weakened eye, an angel I did see*
> *Skin soft, her touch healing*
> *I, at the altar of her grace, kneeling*
> *The fragrance that surrounds her, lavender*
> *Heart warm, soul pure, no one kinder*
> *Untouchable, never to be as one, we*
> *Vows broken and exile, the price to be with She*

She looked up and grabbed Al's hand. 'That's beautiful. You wrote that about me?'

'Yep. The idea and a few words have been running around my head for a couple of years, but I wrote the whole thing on the train after our apple picking weekend.'

'It's the most incredible present I've ever had,' she said wiping her eyes.

He looked at Abby and started to stroke her hair and caress her face. They held each others gaze, silently, for nearly five minutes. Abby could see his eyes reddening. A single tear from each eye traced a path down his cheeks.

'That's one of the saddest faces I've every seen. Why?' asked Abby.

'I've just realised how much I love you.'

'Then you shouldn't be sad. They should be happy thoughts.'

'But we're never going to be able to action this love. These feelings,' said Al.

'We both know this is an impossible situation. Regardless of what we feel, there're obstacles too great for us,' Abby gently touched his cheek.

'So are we going to have to live off stolen moments like this for the rest of our lives?' Al asked, more of himself than Abby.

'It wouldn't be the first time it's happened in the history of the Church and it won't be the last. If you want more, then we know there has to be a change that will come with a hefty price.'

'I know. I'm too far in now to leave amicably. That chance was four years ago.'

A couple of bumblebees flew down from opposite directions, almost crashed into each other, then took up positions on the blossoms above Abby and Al.

'Nothing would make me happier than if we were able to be together,' Abby's voice was soft and soothing, 'but that's a step only you can take. I can't imagine the pressure and torment such a decision places on you and I hope I'm not adding to that. You're the man I love, that won't change, whether the rest of our lives are secret rendezvous or together permanently.' She leaned in and kissed him deeply. Both pairs of hands fumbled at buttons and pulled at their clothes.

Up by the packing sheds, unseen by the lovers, a figure moved away from the apple creates they were using as cover, then silently mounted a bike and cycled away.

* * *

Moira gulped in air as she climbed the small hill up to the seminary. Perspiration trickled down her temples and her back. The weighty bicycle under her struggled up the incline, but her internal fire drove her on over the final yards. 'The – dirty – little – whore. She'll – get – what's – due,' she muttered on each outward breath, with every slow turn of the pedals. 'Tempting that weak willed fraud. I'll see that God has his retribution,' ran through her mind. Reaching the back of the main building, she leant the bike against a wall and took a couple of minutes to regain her breath and cool down. After previous visits to Mount Saint Mary's, Moira knew the way to Father Connolly's office. She gave a strong knock on the door.

'Enter.'

Moira opened the heavy, solid rimu door and strode into the room with purpose, 'Father Connolly, its Moira McCarthy.' In the contrast of light and shadows, she initially struggled to see his small, black clothed frame enveloped in the large leather chair.

'Yes, Miss McCarthy. It's been a couple of years. To what do I owe this unexpected pleasure?' asked Connolly, trying to subdue the smirk on his face.

'Father, I'm sure you remember our discussions four years ago about the immoral liaison between my cousin Abigail and Father Albert Robertson.'

'Yes, indeed, however, immoral may be an overly dramatic description. I'd say it was unusual and potentially dangerous for both of them,' replied Connolly.

'They have taken up with each other again. This time they have definitely sinned against the Church,' Moira almost shouted the last sentence at Connolly. 'The jezebel has led Father Robertson to the brink of damnation,' she said gleefully.

'That's a very serious allegation, Miss McCarthy, with highly emotive language again. What proof do you have?' asked Connolly.

'My own eyes, Father. I saw them together often in Palmerston North, but more importantly, today in Flaxmere. I left them only an hour ago virtually fornicating in an orchard.'

'Sex among the apple trees? Really Miss McCarthy, I fear you've been reading too many two-penny romantic novels.'

Moira reached into her handbag and pulled out a Box-Brownie and placed it on Connolly's desk with a forceful thud, 'You'll be far less dismissive when I have this processed.'

Connolly leaned in, adjusting his glasses as he regarded the camera, 'It appears you have been diligent in gathering your evidence.' He pushed back deep into his chair, interlocking his hands together in front of him, 'Under the assumption that your detective work does indeed substantiate your claims, and given your previous track record in exposing their relationship, I'm expecting it to be positive, what do you propose?'

'By not only revealing this wicked sinning, but I also have a plan on how to resolve the situation, so I would be hoping for suitable recognition and recompense,' replied Moira.

'That you have given potential restitution the appropriate amount of analysis does not surprise me in the slightest. What do you have in mind?' asked Connolly.

'A position within the Archbishop's personal medical staff in Wellington,' said Moira, without blinking and any hint of emotion.

Connolly's eyebrows shot up and he cocked his head before replying, 'Quite the starting negotiating position. Obviously I can't make any promises for his Worship, but if your ideas have merit, coupled with your dedication to the purity of the Church, that should be sufficient for me to make representations to the Archbishop on your behalf. Please do go on,' said Connolly.

Moira pulled her chair in closer to Connolly's desk and started to lay out her plan.

* * *

The journey back to Wellington was particularly uncomfortable for Al. Physically it wasn't any different from the dozens of train trips he'd taken, it was his state of mind that had him in distress. He opened his leather satchel and pulled out his Bible and started to thumb through its pages as he searched for some clarity of thought. He took stock of the situation confronting him. That he loved Abigail was not in question, but the nature and depth of that love, he hadn't realised until this weekend. It had gone beyond anything he had experienced before and past any theoretical or theological teachings. This was visceral, fundamental to the human experience, the love between a man and a woman so pure that you could almost see the hand of God in its essence. Being with Abby gave him the most contentment and joy he had ever felt. He knew the Church could not give him those feelings, even though he felt his love of God had not diminished, it had changed, evolved into something different than his teachings could identify. Fear of God's retribution for sin, or even wavering from his path, which filled him four years ago had gone. His primary dilemma was how to reconcile his love for Abby and his love of God within the confines of the Church. As Abby had said, he knew the Church was littered with inappropriate relationships. Paddy and Mary had probably reinitiated their historical tryst, he knew the rumours of "special friends" certain senior clergy had, and there were the whispers of darker secrets that disgusted him and he prayed weren't true. However, these were all concealed, away from the light.

As the train weaved its way through the flax marshes south of Palmerston North, he finally decided that a life of lies, hidden encounters and stolen moments was no life at all.

* * *

Tuesday 5th November 1935

Connolly wrapt his fingers on his desk with no rhythm as he waited for his phone call to be answered. 'Matron? Father Connolly from Mount Saint Mary's. How are you on this glorious day?'

'Father, an unexpected surprise. I'm well, thank you. How can I help?' replied the Matron of the Sisters of Compassion home in Flaxmere.

'It's rather a serious matter relating to Abigail McCarthy.'

'Abby? What could be a worry with her? She's without doubt our best nurse, and a delightful person to boot,' said Matron.

'It's not the quality of her nursing that's at issue. It is Church business,' Connolly's reply was clipped and taut, 'The fact that she is a half decent nurse is actually a bonus. Did you know New Zealand is taking over the nursing in Fiji?'

'I saw it in a recent Ministry of Health memo, but didn't take much notice of it, as it doesn't impact us.'

'It's about to, Matron. I have to tell you that Miss McCarthy has been discovered having a questionable relationship with an ordained priest. As she is an employee of the Church, this needs to be addressed. The Archbishop has authorised Miss McCarthy to be assigned to the advance party leaving for Suva on the twelfth of November. The Archbishop's office will take care of all the logistics and I'll send you the necessary paperwork later today,' said Connolly.

Silence fell over the conversation for a few seconds. Matron's voice rose in her reply, 'Father Connolly, I must protest in the strongest terms. Whatever the accusations against her, you can't take her away from us. This is most improper.'

'Matron, I do not need to remind you of the Archbishop's authority. Protest would be very unwise given your reliance on Diocesan funding.'

Matron was again temporarily muted, eventually sighing, 'Understood, Father.'

'Good. We need to inform her tomorrow. I'll come over in the afternoon, about three o'clock. Have a good day, Matron.'

* * *

Wednesday 6th November 1935

At the end of her shift, Abby was called into Matron's office: Father Connolly was sitting in the corner of the room, he didn't bother to stand up when she came in. Matron's office was dark, even on this sunny spring day. Abby's eyes adjusted to the gloom when the door opened. A curtain of musty air greeted her. She sensed there was trouble in store as soon as she saw Connolly. A crucifix hung on the wall behind Matron's desk. She thought Jesus looked even more pained today, as if He knew something bad was coming.

'Miss McCarthy. I think we all know why we are here. A couple of years ago, you and Father Robertson were warned of the implications of your friendship.' Connolly paused while lightly tapping his chair arm with a well-manicured index finger. 'It's apparent that you've chosen not to heed that advice. So, now we are faced with a dilemma.' She knew he didn't sugar-coat anything, so she didn't expect anything less.

Matron noticed Abby's face go red. 'Some water, dear?' Abby nodded, her hand trembled as she took the glass.

'Yes. A dilemma,' Connolly said. 'As you both appear incapable of making the right decision for yourselves, we must make it for you.'

The room was suddenly very small, her fingers went numb, as if the circulation had stopped and they'd swelled up as big as plates. Connolly's voice was muffled. She could hear blood charging around her head. She looked up at the crucifix. It wouldn't have surprised her to see Christ was weeping, but no, it was just the beginnings of tears in her own eyes.

'Matron has details of your new assignment.' Gutless, she thought. Can't even tell me himself. Needs to hide behind a woman.

Matron couldn't make eye contact. She shuffled some papers on her desk, cleared her throat. 'I'm not sure if you know this, but our Ministry of Health is taking over jurisdiction of the Fijian Nursing Service from the Australians. There is a forward party going up there very shortly to start the hand over planning. You are being seconded to that party to go to Fiji. You will need to pack immediately, and take the Friday morning bus to Auckland. You've got a berth on the SS Aorangi that's going to Suva on Tuesday the 12th. You'll get your assignment once there.'

Abby almost choked on the bile rising in her throat. She covered her mouth and bit down on her lip as she steadied herself. Don't cry, girl. Don't you dare cry. Don't give them the satisfaction.

'Come, now. It'll be fine. It's only for six months.' Matron's words were still hanging in the stale air as she opened the office door for Abby.

'But I don't want to go to Fiji,' she protested.

'As an employee, you don't have a choice. Well, that's not entirely true. You could resign, but that wouldn't be wise in the current climate,' Connolly responded, his voice cool and clipped.

'It's for the best, dear,' Matron sought to defuse the building tension. 'You'll be able to recommit to your nursing in a country that's in desperate need of good services. You are a very good nurse. This will help remove any question marks.'

Question marks? What the hell is she on about, Abby thought, but before she could remonstrate further, she was handed a large brown envelope and ushered out the door. In less than ten minutes she had been banished, exiled to another country. Other than it was in the South Pacific, she didn't know the first thing about Fiji.

CHAPTER 16

December 1935

The tranquillity of an early summer evening was shattered by the screech of the telephones bells. When Paddy picked up the Bakelite ear-piece to answer, Al didn't bother with pleasantries.

'Abby's been sent to Suva. They've shipped her off. She's gone.' The words were spoken so fast, that they almost ran together.

'Slow down, lad. Suva? As in Fiji?' Paddy asked.

'It's the only one I know of,' Al replied rapidly.

'Bloody hell. When did this happen?'

'A few weeks ago. Apparently they told her on Wednesday the 5th and she was on a ship the next Tuesday,' Al said.

'Less than seven full days? Hell's bells. Where you calling from? You alone?' asked Paddy.

'I'm in a phone box in Newtown, just down from my flat. There's no one around,' said Al, making a point to look up and down the street.

'How did you find out?' Paddy pulled up the stool near the phone and sat down.

'I got a letter from her yesterday. She sent it from Suva a couple of weeks back. She's devastated. Last thing she said was that they were going to assign her to one of the hospitals on the outer islands, but she didn't know which one yet. I can't believe they've done this.' Al's speech slowed down and pitch dropped with the last sentence.

'Come on, Albert. You've been in long enough to know they're capable of anything.'

'But she's not in the Church. Sure, we can be shipped off to anywhere at a moment's notice. But she's a nurse, not a Sister or a Matron.'

'Al, she works for the Sisters of Compassion, eh? That's the Church as far as they're concerned. They can do whatever the hell they want,' said Paddy

'I can't accept that. There's got to be something we can do.'

'You've got no choice or say in the matter, lad. What are you going to do? Storm into the Archbishop's office and demand they send her home?'

'But it's just not right,' Al shouted, banging the heel of his hand into the frame of the phone. An elderly woman stopped and stared at him for a couple of seconds before walking into the greengrocers adjacent to the phone box.

'And when has that stopped them doing what they want?' Paddy shot back.

'You're not being very helpful, Patrick.'

'What in blazes do you want me to do? Sneak up to Fiji and smuggle her back? You knew something like this could happen ever since Connolly confronted you about Abby four years ago. You obviously didn't think of the potential consequences of seeing her again so often this year.'

'I didn't think they'd go this far.' Al's voice suddenly fell flat, as he realised his role in Abby's predicament.

'Settle down. It's not like they've knocked her off. It'll be six months, maybe a year. Pull yourself together. You're talking like a lovesick schoolboy. Remember your position, lad. You've assured me that it is just a friendship. Admittedly a deeper friendship than most, but your reaction tells me it's a bit more than that. Am I right?'

Al paused as thoughts collided into each other, making it difficult to construct a response. Al hadn't told Paddy of the progression of his feelings and the decision he'd come to on the train back to Wellington a few weeks ago.

'You still there, lad?' Paddy broke the silence.

'Yes. I don't think I can go into it right now, but I do need to talk a few things through with you. Can I come up to see you before I go home for Christmas?'

'Sure. I'm not going anywhere. I've got a hunch we need a decent sit down, me boy.' Paddy gently placed the ear-piece back onto its cradle on the candlestick phone, grabbed his tobacco pouch, quickly rolled a cigarette and lit it. As he exhaled, he looked down at the phone 'That boy's in a major spot of bother,' he said out loud.

Al's head dropped when he hung up, his heart still beating quickly, so he took in a few deep breaths to slow it down. Opening the phone box door, a wave of cool air rushed over him, he eagerly gulped the fresh air. He started walking back to the flat, just as the elderly woman that passed him earlier walked by muttering under her breath. His footsteps were slow and heavy, taking him twice as long to return to the house. He chose the shady side of the street to help cool himself down and the shadows reflected his mood; desolate and despondent. He felt his future had been ripped out of his grasp, just as he had started to not only plan for it, but believe it could be a reality. With his head down and shoulders slumped forward, he didn't even notice the rain starting from a rouge cloud that had charged over the Brooklyn hills behind him.

* * *

March 1936
Taveuni, Fiji

'I don't understand why you came here?' Abby asked. She and Allan Peters were sitting at a table on the veranda of the only halfway decent café in Somosomo. The easterly trade winds took the edge off the afternoon heat and made the leaves of the nearby palm trees rustle rhythmically.

'I heard you'd been sent up here, so when they called for volunteers I jumped at the chance,' Allan replied, as he stared at his cup of tea. He hadn't noticed he had been stirring in the sugar for nearly two minutes.

'You've given up your position in Napier?' Abby continued with her questions.

'No, just taken a sabbatical. Either six or twelve months, my choice, so I thought it would be a great opportunity to do something positive.'

'But why here? You're a very good doctor. This is barely more than a clinic. Didn't you want to go to one of the bigger hospitals in Suva or Lautoka?'

'I could have done, but you're not there.'

The words seemed to hang in front of Abby, almost visible in the air. She struggled to put words or even thoughts together. She felt a rush of blood into her head.

'I know I turned up out of the blue back in January. I didn't know what to expect, so I asked if I could come up here for a few days before they gave me my final assignment. I couldn't let this chance pass by without doing something and your reaction told me all I needed to know.'

'Doing something?' Abby repeated, almost in a mumble. She thought back to that day a couple of months ago when Allan startled her in the dispensary. The shock of seeing a familiar face after nearly three months caused her to greet him with a hug and outbreak of tears. In hindsight, a cooler response would have been wiser. So too not giving so much of her time to him during that week he was on Taveuni. Although he was supposed to be shadowing the head doctor at the hospital, he spent a lot of time with Abby and even accompanied her on a couple of trips to the other villages. Abby was delighted for the company, so willingly gave her time, both at work and after hours and acknowledged to herself that she was sad to say goodbye at the end of his visit, especially as he didn't indicate that he could be back on a semi-permanent basis so quickly.

'Ever since you left Napier Hospital, you've been on my mind almost constantly. When I heard you were up here, I had some clarity of thought. An epiphany even. I want you in my life. Abigail McCarthy, will you marry me?'

Abby sat motionless, trying to comprehend Allan's words. She wasn't able to disguise her astonishment.

'This is obviously a bit of a shock' he said.

'Just a bit. I don't know what to say. It's very flattering, it really is. But we only stepped out two or three times, and that was over four years ago.'

'Six times to be exact, and the last time was less than two years ago.' He interlocked his fingers and slightly cocked his head to one side, as he showed confidence in his memory.

Abby immediately tried to remember each time she and Allan had been together socially. She thought six times seemed excessive. Their first date at the St. Pat's parish dance; a second a couple of days later; a night out with bunch of people a couple of times (she didn't classify those as stepping out together, though). That's four, not half a dozen and certainly nothing within the last two years. That had her stumped. Surely he wasn't counting the time they bumped into each other at that cake shop in Napier?

'Allan, you've caught me off guard. It's difficult getting my thoughts straight.' She finally got out a coherent sentence, as she felt she'd been mumbling for the past few minutes.

'I know it's unfair to spring this on you after only being here a few days. I feel great affection for you and after that week here in January, I was positive you felt the same.' He placed his hand on Abby's and squeezed it. A cold wave surged up her arm and down her back. She pulled her hand away once he released his grip.

'It was wonderful seeing you then, I do admit that.' A smile broke across his face. 'However, you have to realise I hadn't seen anyone I know for nearly three months and you were a real link to home. Even though it'd been a long time since we last saw each other, I was delighted to spend time with you, but it is a big leap to then contemplate marriage. I need some time to think this over. Is that OK? My posting here is due to finish at the end of July. I promise you'll have an answer by then.'

The smile slipped from his face as quickly as it had emerged.

* * *

The days' mail was sitting on the sideboard in the hallway. The third letter in the pile was his, written by a familiar hand, with a Fijian stamp and postmark. Al's pulse quickened as he went into his room. He tore into the envelope, hungry to devour the news from Abby.

5 July 1936

My darling Albert,

Please forgive me for the directness of this letter and dispensing with the usual pleasantries. I've just received some very upsetting news. It appears that I am to remain here in Fiji for at least another six months.

Most of my colleagues are to return home after their six month secondments are over, as I was expecting to happen to me, however, I was informed by the head of the Fijian Nursing Service that notification had come from New Zealand that I am required to stay for a full twelve months, with, and I quote 'the possibility of a further extension at the discretion of the New Zealand Ministry of Health'.

As you can imagine I am so distraught. I can barely complete even this short note. It appears Fiji will be my home for the foreseeable future.

Yours, forever and always,
Abby

Al slumped heavily into the small armchair in the corner of his room. His hand tightened on the delicate paper. 'The bloody pricks,' he spat the words out through clenched teeth. He gradually gathered the rest of the letter into his fist, forming it into a tight ball, then threw it against the wall. 'That bastard's got to have done it.'

He leaned forward, supported his forehead in his hands and massaged his temples with his thumbs. He tried to think clearly. Blood was surging around his head. He could hear it, feel it. The walls of his room felt close, they inched ever nearer with every second. Coherent thoughts escaped him. Vitriol was all he could come up with. 'The sodding bastards will never let her leave. If it's not Fiji, it'll be somewhere else. Samoa, Singapore. Lord Almighty, how can these people claim to be your servants? They can't be acting in your name. Damn them to hell.'

A sharp pain ignited the back of his head. He reached over and grabbed his water jug. His hand shook violently, he could barely grip the handle to pour. He took the glass in both hands and drained it in one mouthful. Two deep breaths slowed his pulse a couple of beats. He hastily stood up to retrieve the balled letter, too quickly. He staggered for a couple of half steps then toppled over. His temple caught a glancing blow on the bed post.

He awoke when the knocking on his door grew loud enough

to rouse him. He propped himself up on the side of the bed, his head throbbed with low rhythmical shards of pain.

'Al. You OK. It's supper time. You coming?' said Leo.

'Yeah. I'm fine. I'll be there in a minute.' Supper time? That's six o'clock. He'd got home about four-thirty. Had he been out that long? He felt his right temple to find a golf ball sized lump had sprouted above his eyebrow. At the mirror he immediately jerked to attention when he saw his reflection, not so much in shock at the bulge sprouting from the side of his head, but the almost unrecognisable person staring back. It was that shock you get every few years, after not noticing any little changes in yourself, only to discover you aren't the person you used to be. Like the first time you recognise you've hit adulthood, or when the first distinctive wrinkles appear. This was one of those landmark moments; the gaunt features and ashen skin of the man in the mirror weren't of the man he thought he knew. He'd noticed he had to go in one notch on his belt a couple of weeks ago, but thought nothing of it. He took off his collar and shirt, lifted his vest only to get another shock; all his ribs were visible as were the bony points on his hips. He closed his eyes. Dear Lord, what's happening to me?

* * *

August 1936

Paddy was at the train station to meet the three men. His smile was like a beacon in the dim light of the winter's afternoon. 'Gentleman. Welcome. George, Leo, very good to see you again. Been a few years, and all Fathers now, too. Congratulations'

'Thanks, Paddy. Good to see you again. Are you well?' said George.

'Same as. Not much changes with me. Come on. Let's get going before it gets totally dark.'

'Still got that old Model T? St. Patrick's can't spring for a newer car for you?' asked Leo.

'Her and I go back a long way now. Been through some times together. Just don't have the heart to let her go.'

'How's the old town doing?' asked George.

'Reconstruction's over. Loads of new buildings. All in this new style from the Yanks. Loads of curves, arches and bright colours. Apparently it's all the rage in California. They can keep it, I say. We'll see a fair few on the drive. Jobs are still thin on the ground, but farming's turned around a bit.' They climbed into the car, Al and Leo in the back, with their small suitcases on their laps. 'So you two are staying up at Mount Saint Mary's?' George and Leo nodded in unison. 'Right, best I drop Albert off at the cottage first, then take you two up there. I don't think the old girl will be able to handle the hill with four grown men and luggage.'

They made their way from the station to St. Patrick's with George and Leo swivelling their heads constantly, taking in the fresh, new city that had risen from the devastation of the earthquake.

'It's amazing. There are only a handful of buildings like these in Wellington yet. I like the style,' said Leo, his upper body almost completely outside the car.

'They reckon Napier is now the most modern city in the world,' Paddy replied. 'You right back there, lad? Haven't bloody said boo to a ghost since you stepped off the train.'

'Fine thanks, Paddy. Just looking around,' Al's answer was so quiet that it barely registered with the men in the front of the car.

Sitting in the car, parked in the driveway of his house in the dying light, Paddy lit a cigarette. The embers illuminated his face and he tapped the steering wheel with his free hand. How will he approach this? He knew subtly was not a skill he'd been blessed with, so best to stick to his strength's; directness, help solve problems without being judgemental, he thought. He knew the cause of Al's predicament, so there was no reason to pussyfoot around things, but he didn't have a solution. Smoke swirled around his face as he expelled his last drag. Getting out of the car he stamped the cigarette out with authority and mumbled 'Let's get this thing over with.'

'Ya right, lad?' Paddy asked, seeing Al in the lounge.

'Good as gold, thanks Paddy.'

'Ya want a sherry?' asked Paddy, grabbing a glass and pouring a large Jameson's.

'I'm alright, cheers,' replied Al.

Paddy slumped heavily into his chair; a few drops of whiskey spilled over the glass rim and hit his hand. 'So what's the story? What's wrong?'

'Nothing. I'm fine,' said Al, frowning.

'Really? Looking like death warmed up is OK?' He licked his hand and took a hit of liquor.

'I'm not that bad,' protested Al.

'Albert, I bet you're barely eleven stone soaking wet, maybe closer to ten. Even for a lean fella like you, that's too light. And I know its winter, but you're grey and washed out like the old geezers up at the hospice. Don't bullshit a bullshiter.'

Al turned away from Paddy, looked out the window into the darkness and sighed heavily, 'Maybe I will have that sherry.'

'Only if you're gonna spill ya guts,' Paddy demanded before going to get the drink. 'So?' he asked, handing the glass to Al.

'They're never going to let her go.' Al rolled the glass back and forth between his hands. 'They've given her a year and hinted that would be extended. She'll never be allowed home.'

'That is a worry. I can see why that's got you wound up. So where does that leave you with the plans we talked about at Christmas?' asked Paddy.

'Nowhere. I can't go and get her and she won't be back here anytime soon. It's status quo.'

'Don't look like there's many options, eh? You're sure she won't be back next year?'

'She thinks there's no hope, so I have to go by what she tells me,' said Al.

'Well, lad, I don't want to be a fatalist, but we might need to resign ourselves to the new circumstances and live accordingly.'

'I suppose that's half the reason I'm looking so rough; I've been fighting that same conclusion, as well as worrying myself sick about Abby.' Al's voice was heavy with dejection.

'Shouting against a coming storm. Railing against odds and powers too strong, massed against you. Know that feeling, lad. It ain't nice coming to that place,' Paddy said, draining his drink. 'Another?' he asked, stepping over to Al, giving him a firm, warm hand on the shoulder.

* * *

The late afternoon thunderstorm rolled across Taveuni as if on cue; regular enough to set your watch by. Abby looked out the small window of her room, watching the rain pour off the unguttered roof in a wall of water. Even indoors, she could feel the temperature drop a few degrees with the downpour. They never lasted more than fifteen minutes, but some days there'd be three distinct showers in an hour. The pattern of rain closely mirrored her emotions and tears over the last three months – short, intense and out of the blue. On her table sat Albert's latest letter, still unopened two days after she got it. She knew in her soul that it wouldn't contain good news, something deep within her filled her with dread at the prospect of reading it. He hadn't written since her letter of July; even with the two-three week delivery time, she had expected a letter well before now. Gingerly she picked it up and opened it as if the pages themselves were made of poison.

27 August 1936
Dearest Abby,

Even after nine months everything I have still has your aroma. All my clothes still have the faint sent of lavender. Long strands of hair keep surprising me in the most unlikeliest of locations. The remnants of you mock me, tease me.

I often find myself in the college library, going through the South Pacific pages of the atlas and tracing a line between Wellington and Taveuni. My fingers caress the place on the map where I'd find you. The other night I dreamt I laid down under the apple trees of Hansen's Orchard, our orchard, the ground was cold, but I soon drifted off to sleep. The Lord himself picked me up, carried me over the ocean and set me down into your arms on the warm sands of Fiji.

Once again people have conspired against us and it appears they are wielding more power and influence than I had expected possible. These forces definitely seek to keep us far apart for many years to come. The past couple of months have been very difficult. As you were, I was counting down the days and weeks until the supposed end of your secondment, then to learn of the extension was devastating.

I don't believe there is any realistic hope for us. This time, I fear our split will be forever. I cannot foresee any way that we can even retain a friendship, other than via letters. My ultimate worry is for you. When will they free you, let you live your life as and where you choose? When that does happen, you must do the things you always dreamed of doing, without the millstone of me to hold you back. Above all, I want, no, I need you to be happy. You've made me happier than I can ever remember being.

As for me, I've been given an opportunity to be Deputy Head of Science at a new Marist school being built in Timaru, that's due to open either next year or the year after. It's a great opportunity for me. I'd be the first to teach in the school and it's what I thought I wanted when I was at the seminary and where I had hoped to be way back then. Given the new reality we are now faced with, it is something I'll need to contemplate.

Please believe that I will never love someone as deeply and completely again in my life as I do you.

Yours forever in love,
Albert

Abby had to re-read the last couple of paragraphs a couple of times for the tears that were flowing blurred her sight. It was everything and more, that she had expected. What they had was being destroyed, forced to be apart permanently. Unlike back in '31, she couldn't place any blame on him, she had now been the recipient of the power and influence of the Church, and it was not to be trifled with by ones such as them. Love had not conquered; love had been vanquished. She looked out the window again, just as another shower fell from the heavens.

* * *

15th September 1936

Paddy's voice was cheery when Al picked up the phone. 'Albert, my boy. Me thinks I have a solution to your predicament.'

Al could sense Paddy beaming a broad smile at the other end of the line. 'Go on then.'

'It's not something that can be discussed over the phone, lad. Can we meet up in Palmy on Saturday? Best we chat about this in person. Meet me in the cafeteria of the DIC at twelve?'

'Perfect. See you then. Paddy, this better be good.'

'Don't you worry, my lad. I reckon you'll be pleasantly surprised.' Paddy let out a short, deep laugh as he hung up.

Al tapped his fingers on the receiver a few times as thoughts raced through his mind. *'What has he come up with? He sounds so bloody sure of himself.'* A flash of excitement engulfed him. His back tingled and his face went flush. Could this be a real chance to see Abby again? Al knew this would eat away at him until Saturday.

* * *

'Alright. Enough smirking. What have you got up that short Irish sleeve of yours?' Al asked, after sitting down at the small table Paddy had secured in the furthest corner of the café. Al surveyed the room, eyed longingly the table that he and Abby would get for their rendezvous.

'Cast your mind back to just before the earthquake. Did you ever hear about Father Gondringer's plan to take a few people up to Fiji on an educational mission?' asked Paddy.

'I remember. It was the last thing he talked to me about. He invited me to go on the mission at dinner. He was dead the next day,' replied Al.

'Really? Didn't know he'd spoken to you about it. That explains the spare place.'

'The spare place?' Al cocked his head to the side.

'Sorry. I only really knew about it as he asked me if I had any contacts up in Fiji to act as host parishes. I know someone in Suva itself and one on an outlying island, so I told him, then thought nothing more of it. Forgotten all about it until you let me know Abby's been sent up there. That just triggered the memory, then a few days ago, I'm going through some dioceses papers for Murphy and I came across the details of the mission, ship bookings, expense allowances, equipment needs and the provisional travelling party,' said Paddy, pulling out a wad of paper from his satchel.

'Why would it be with the dioceses, not Mount Saint Mary's?'

'Mate, the dioceses is loaded. Plenty of money. The seminary wouldn't have had those sort of readies to fund the trip. There are four confirmed, but open, return bookings on any P&O ship from Auckland to Suva, with the names of Gondringer, O'Boyle, Doogan and A.N. Other. The last one was meant to be you. Looks like everything is still in place for the mission,' Paddy said, raising his eyebrows quickly a couple of times.

'Nobody cancelled the bookings when Gondringer died?' asked Al.

'Nope. Bigger things to worry about than a few quid on some passage bookings. I checked with Mary Simpson and she tells me that even after all these years, they are still valid; just need re-confirming and specific sailings to be booked. Now, before we go any further, I need to know that your feelings for Abby are as strong as ever and you're willing to take a bloody big risk to see her again. Cause if we do what I'm thinking of and get caught, at best you'll end up teaching in the smallest, shittiest school in the country and I'll be banished to a two person parish in the whop-whops.'

'And at worst?'

'I don't want to think about it. You've seen what they've done to Abby, and she ain't even officially in the Church. Where is she exactly?' asked Paddy.

'A place called Waiyevo, on an island called Taveuni.'

'What?' Paddy almost squealed. 'What's the name again?' this time at a whisper, leaning in.

'Taveuni,' repeated Al.

'Bugger me days. It's as if the Lord himself is guiding us. It's just destined to happen.'

'What are you talking about, Paddy? You're not making any sense.'

'You're not going to believe this, but one of my mates up there is only at the Holy Cross Church at the Wairiki Mission on Taveuni. Bloody hell. John McGuire has been up there ten years. The two of them probably know each other by now.'

Al sat in silence, transfixed for the next fifteen minutes as Paddy set out his plan to resurrect Father Gondringer's education mission to Fiji.

'All that, said,' Paddy took in a deep breath to finish up, 'it's probably going to take the next three months to organise, but we need to do this as soon as possible. We'll go up in January next year. Works in with your summer school holidays. Be careful what you write, speak and even think from here on in. No one can know you'll be going.'

On the train back to Wellington, Al felt light headed, almost delirious. His excitement over seeing Abby again consumed him. What would he say to her? How much time would they have together? Words, sentences, settings, scenarios ran around his head, colliding into each other until his thoughts were an unintelligible cacophony of consciousness.

* * *

22nd November 1936

At the back of the church, Abby couldn't concentrate on the sermon, almost trance like she was wafting a homemade palm leaf fan at her face, trying to keep cool. Her thoughts drifted back to New Zealand and to Albert. She didn't quite know why, but their first meeting at the Palmerston North railway station some five years ago kept returning to her. It was something about his manner that day, the look in his eyes, they combined to tell Abby that he had deep feelings for her, yet he was torn and troubled. This mix of passion and vulnerability touched her that day. His latest letter had come as a shock and had caused her to become distracted for long periods every day. Today Father McGuire had noticed her lack of attention.

'Hello, Abby. Good to see you again. It's been a few weeks, although it seems your mind wasn't really with us today. Everything alright?' he asked.

'I'm dreadfully sorry, Father. No offence intended, but yes, I was a thousand miles away. All's fine, I just received some interesting news from home recently.'

'Really? Now there's a coincidence for you, so have I and you might be interested in this. We have an educational mission coming up from New Zealand for a month. They're from Napier, so you might know them. It's being led by an old friend of mine, Father Patrick Lynch. He's bringing Brother Ignatius O'Boyle and Brother James Doogan with him.'

'That can't be right. James is...' Abby didn't finish the sentence. 'Yes, yes. Father Paddy, James and Iggy. I know them well. It will be wonderful to see them again. When do they arrive?' Abby fidgeted, she folded and unfolded her arms quickly and moved her weight from foot to foot.

'Father Lynch said that they expect to be here the first week of January. They are due into Suva on the third. So I'd think they'd be here by the fifth.'

Her spine tingled as a wave of excitement swept over her. Suddenly Al's last letter made sense. It had seemed so formal and cryptic when she first read it. She almost ran the three miles back to Waiyevo and re-read it four or five times when she got back to her room.

29th September 1936
My dearest Abby,

I pray this letter finds you in good health. You may be taken by surprise to receive this letter so soon after my last, which obviously brought matters between us to some level of conclusion.

However, life has taken an unexpected and exhilarating turn recently. It is not, unfortunately, something that I am able to commit to paper. Suffice to say it will have an impact on both of us.

All I can say is that you should expect some interesting visitors in January. I think you might be quite surprised by at least one person who comes calling to Taveuni.

Yours, always and ever with love,
Albert

Now it started to become clear. She daren't raise her expectations. She had learnt bitter lessons about letting her hopes rise to unjustified levels.

* * *

13th December 1936

After Sunday dinner at Mount Saint. Mary's, Paddy pulled Iggy aside. 'I've got a couple of jobs that need doing down in Wellington about the mission to Fiji. Could ya run down there next week?'

'I reckon so Father Lynch. I'll need to get it ticked off by Father Connolly, though.'

'Don't worry about that. I've cleared it with him already,' Paddy added quickly. 'I've some important papers that need to be hand delivered to the shipping company and the dioceses offices. I've booked ya on the early train on Friday, then back on Saturday. Got you a spot at St. Patrick's for the night. Give you a chance to catch up with Leo, George and Al.'

'That'd be terrific. Haven't seen the lads in a year or so. Thanks, Father.'

'Good man. Really glad you're on board. I'll come by Thursday night with all the papers.' Paddy gave Iggy a light pat on the shoulder.

* * *

During the meal Al could barely contain his excitement at the thought of what was in the envelope. Iggy had arrived late in the afternoon and had given Al the envelope from Paddy, and was full of chat, wanting to get all the details of Al, George and Leo's lives and what it was like at the college. Al's mind kept wandering to Abby and Fiji. He had to shake himself out of those thoughts to stay in the conversation with his friends, but every couple of minutes he would be back in a day dream with Abby, on their last day together in an apple orchard near Napier, or on a beach in Taveuni.

After dinner, Al found a secluded spot and opened the envelope that Iggy had given him. A short handwritten note from Paddy and a typed letter from Mary Simpson. First was Paddy's letter.

Albert,

Everything should be in order. Here's a letter from Mary that you need to give to the P&O clerks in Auckland. It will allow you to board but retain James' name on the passenger manifest.

Best that we not meet up in Auckland before the day of the sailing, so we'll see you on board.

Good luck and God be with you,
Paddy

He then opened Mary Simpson's letter, it was on P&O letterhead and addressed to the Passenger Boarding Manager in the P&O

office at Auckland Harbour. It referred to Al by name and instructed them to allow Al to board instead of James Doogan, but to not amend the passenger manifest. Under Mary's signature was her title, Regional Manager, P&O Napier Harbour and Hawke's Bay. Al read it with a raised eyebrow. Paddy hadn't let on how senior Mary was in P&O. That reassured him and eased his nerves, thinking that her letter would smooth his passage.

He slumped back into the chair with a long, audible exhale as a wave of guilt enveloped him. He had just sat through dinner with three of his closest friends, comrades in cloth, and discussed plans for the summer recess, career aspirations and issues of faith, all the while knowing he was being, at best, economical with the truth, at worst, a straightforward liar. Issues of faith? That wasn't in question for him; it was his commitment and devotion that had been broken, to the Church at least. The chance to go to Fiji was a sign, a definite pointer from God on what he should do. No, what he must do. It was no longer an internal debate, a decision on his future had been made, a new commitment was to be forged. He was now prepared to face the consequences of that decision, whatever the response in Fiji might be. At least now he was being honest with himself, if not with his friends. That would have to wait.

CHAPTER 17

4th January 1937

Taveuni, Fiji

Al was on the bow of the ferry as they tied up at the Wairiki jetty. For most of the trip from Suva he had been in a virtual state of trance brought on by the mounting exhilaration that he was soon to be on the same piece of land as Abby. All those days of staring at maps, cursing the tyranny of distance were now behind him. Oblivious to his surroundings for the past day and a half, he suddenly clicked out of his stupor, realising this was the same scene that must have greeted Abby. Small boats and canoes bobbed as gentle waves broke on the shore. Men worked on fishing nets, untangling the knotted mess, others repairing holes. Palm trees stood out above the low canopy of rain forest; their leaves barely moving in the light sea breeze. On the jetty, Al saw a tall, heavily tanned man in a short sleeved black shirt and Roman collar.

'Father Patrick Lynch. This is a sight I never thought I'd see. Welcome, welcome. Bula vi naka,' said the man.

'G'day John.' Paddy beamed a big smile as they embraced deeply for a few moments. 'Great to see you again. Island life agrees with you. You're in good nick.'

'All the fresh fish and sun. Here, introduce me to your colleagues. Drau bula, welcome both of you,' said John.

'Father Albert Robertson and Brother Iggy O'Boyle, this is Father John McGuire.'

Handshakes were exchanged, John turned back to Paddy, 'Where's Brother James?'

'Bit of a long story that. Will fill you in over a cuppa. Father Albert was a late replacement,' Paddy said, scratching his head.

'We're just glad to have you here. Come, lako mai. Let's get you settled in. The lads here will bring up your gear.' John led them to one of the outlying buildings of the Mission complex. 'Get some rest. We'll give you a proper tour later. We have an official welcome for you tomorrow night. A feast with the local chief. There'll be a lovo, local version of a hungi, music and dancing. The local dignitaries will be there, as well a couple of people you might know from home. Doctor Allan Peters and Nurse Abigail McCarthy. They're both from Napier.'

'We know both of them. Will be good to see them again,' said Paddy.

'That Doctor Peters is an odd one. Just turned up here out of the blue nearly a year ago. Completely unannounced. The hospital didn't even know he was coming.'

Al, busy looking around, snapped his head towards John, with a look that was half astonishment, half worry.

After dropping off their suitcases, Paddy went to find John, and pulled him into a quiet corner for a chat.

'Bloody hell, Patrick Lynch. What madness have you whipped up this time?' John looked to the sky and opened his hands. 'So, if I hear you right, we have a mission using Church funds on spurious grounds. A priest basically absent without leave, here to see a woman he's fallen in love with. Is that it?'

'Pretty much, but the mission is legitimate. Was planned and paid for years ago, eh? It's just been resurrected with a secondary purpose.' Paddy tried to reassure John.

'That's stretching it, Paddy. Not sure your dioceses will view it that way. What's the chances of them finding out?' John's voice rose quickly, his ears turning red.

'Remote, but not impossible,' Paddy said, looking at the ground.

'Dear Lord. We'd better have our story straight if they do, and you three best do some great teaching while you're here, otherwise it will be a total sham. I'm not bloody happy you've exposed my parish to this. There better not be any backwash on us,' John fixed Paddy with a cold stare.

'I reckon it'll be fine. We're here for what? Less than three weeks. Even if they find out, we'll be on our way back before they could get someone here,' replied Paddy.

'Forgive me if I don't share your optimism. Extra prayers required tonight for us all. Of all the hare-brained schemes you could have come up with, this one is top drawer.'

* * *

The walk from the Mission to Somosomo only takes about thirty minutes, but as with the entire journey from New Zealand, time seemed to crawl. When one desires something so completely, all your thoughts are consumed by it. When it is something as definite and fixed as seeing the person you love, the minutes, hours, days, and seconds until that meeting are tortuously slow in passing. You want the world to speed up, for God to intervene to spin the globe faster, for the clocks to go at double time. Every moment that passes brings you closer to the glorious reconnection, yet celestial bodies mock you by slowing each one of those moments to excruciating lengths.

Al could almost taste the exhilaration as they finally arrived at the meeting house. Anticipation gave way to anxiety, his hands started to shake and uncontrollable shudders shot through his body. They were greeted by one of the chief's men and lead past a line of flame torches and into the open sided structure, the roof made of palm leaves rustled in the gentle breeze. It was testament to how focussed Al's mind was, it wasn't until they were seated in the front row that he noticed their host was wearing only a grass skirt and armbands made out of thick green leaves. The wind brought in aromas and heat from the cooking area outside the hut. All four men looked across to the far side to see a pig on a spit and an earth oven being filled with baskets of fish, sweet potatoes and taro. It was a short distraction for Al, a momentary respite for his fraying nerves. The shakes quickly returned, so he sat on his hands, gulped down large breaths and flexed his muscles. Nothing worked; he felt as if he could explode at any moment.

Other guests and locals made their way in; Al closely scanned each person, looking for the curve of her face, the warmth of her smile, the light in her eyes. With each unfamiliar person a sliver of his excitement died; maybe she isn't coming, she might be ill, might be working, or not know they would be at the ceremony. Just as his doubts grew he caught a glimpse of Abby, partially hidden behind a group of guests. His heart started to race, he thought it was her, but the constantly moving mass of people only gave him fleeting glances and she looked quite different; her hair more blond than brown, her skin a lovely olive colour and her cheeks more pronounced. Was it actually her? The crowd dissipated to give him a full view; yes, it was her, but not the person from Hansen's Orchard some fifteen months ago. Life here had changed her, although the difference in her surprised him, she looked stunning. He could now see she was with a man, Al narrowed his gaze at him; of course it must be Doctor Peters. The face was familiar and he searched his memory for the times he met him back in Napier. Al watched them enter the hut and Peters put his hand on Abby's back, she immediately tensed up and broke out in what Al thought was a forced smile. Who the hell was he to touch her that way? Trying to be intimate, caring. Why had Peters even come to Taveuni? Surely not for Abby. No, that couldn't be his motivation. What if it was? He had been here with her for nearly a year; Abby's only connection to home. Suddenly a cold wave raced through Al's body at the thought of what affect his letters of last year could have had on Abby, with Peters close at hand. Every fibre of his body wanted to run over to her and take her in his arms. How was he going to get through the ceremony?

* * *

A chill emanated from Peters' hand on the small of Abby's back and ran up the length of her spine. She straightened, turned to him and gave a small smile that she knew couldn't look remotely genuine. She scanned the room and quickly found Al in front with his clergy brethren, immediately her smile widened and she let out a deep breath.

They were escorted to seats on the side of the building, a few rows back, but with a decent view of Al. In the past couple of months she hadn't allowed herself to even contemplate what she would feel in this situation. Too scared to believe that he would be here. Now that she was looking at him, thoughts and emotions were washing over her like the waves in one of the tropical storms that hit the island every few months. To her eyes, he was the most handsome man she'd ever met; of no concern was his premature greying, that was a badge of honour marking his deliverance from the jaws of death all those years ago. A kinder man she had never encountered, but coupled with underlying strength and fortitude. She had realised a few years ago she loved him deeply and unconditionally, but sitting so close to him now, imagining the sacrifice he was making and the peril he was putting himself in, made her love for him complete. She also knew that his presence on Taveuni, however wonderful, didn't overcome the barriers that still faced them.

Suddenly the buzz of chatter around the building stopped, which jolted Abby's attention back to her surroundings. One of the men on the raised podium in the centre began talking in Fijian to signify the start of the kava ceremony. Paddy, acting as the chief of the group of clergy, for whom the ceremony was called, got up and presented a bundle of kava root to the men on the podium. They ground it into a powder on small slabs of stone; the men's muscular arms bulged in the torch light as they strained to break up the root. They scooped up the powder into tea towel sized sheets of muslin, gathered the ends of the sheets together and poured water into them, letting the liquid filter through the kava, and a flow of light brown kava infused water flowed into a large carved wooden bowl. The bowl itself was exquisite, with representations of fish and palm trees etched into its four legs that made up part of its structure so it could stand unsupported. A small coconut hand bowl was dipped into the liquid and was handed to the chief of Somosomo to take the first drink; the bowl seemed to disappear into his large hands. The snow haired chief made a loud clap, shouted 'Bula' and drank the bowl in one gulp, then clapped three more times. He then opened his arms wide to the priests, a cue to his lieutenants to offer a bowl first to Paddy then the others.

Abby knew that she and Allan would be some of the last to get the kava as their late arrival had them near the back of the meeting house. She let out a muffled laugh as she watched Al's reaction to the bitter kava, seeing his face contort with the punch from the liquid. He looked across at her, raised his eyebrows and frowned. She mouthed 'yum, yum' back at him.

As the last person finished their kava, the chief clapped again, shouted and waved at a group of women standing by the cooking area; they came in and started handing out palm leaf plates piled high with spit roasted pork, steamed fish, potatoes and taro. Abby closed her eyes and breathed in the wonderful aroma. Conversations started up again as everyone relaxed and ate their meals.

* * *

The bitter taste of the kava overpowered the first couple of mouthfuls of food, but soon he could fully appreciate the succulent pork and fish. Al was eating quickly and hoping the others would do the same so they could start mingling with the other guests. True to form, Iggy was already well ahead of Al, but Paddy and John were engrossed in conversation and barely picking at their dinners. He looked over to Abby for what he thought must have been the hundredth time tonight, he wondered if he had been too obvious during the evening and had anyone noticed his almost constant glances. Just as he looked back to his own party and started to despair at Paddy and John's pace of eating, he noticed movement over by Abby and Doctor Peters. They had got up and were walking over his way; his whole body became alive and his heart rate jumped up a few beats. Both Abby and Al tried not to stare at each other, diverting their eyes every few seconds, but to no great affect, they quickly came back to the other person. Abby and Peters were only a couple of steps away when John noticed them and jumped up, spilling his half eaten meal on the dirt floor.

'Oh, blast. Sorry about that,' he said, kicking the food under his seat, 'Doctor Peters, Nurse McCarthy, wonderful to see you again. Come, say hello to some old friends of yours. Father Paddy Lynch, Father Albert Robertson and Brother Iggy O'Boyle.'

'G'day Allan. Been a couple of years. I noticed you'd stopped coming to the parish dances, now I see why. You snuck up here without telling anyone.' said Paddy shaking Peters hand warmly.

'Good to see you all, although I'm not sure I've met Father Robertson and Brother O'Boyle before. What a remarkable coincidence that we have so many people from the Bay in tiny Taveuni at one time,' said Peters.

'You met Father Robertson once, maybe twice, just before the quake, but it's not surprising you don't remember. They were fleeting and I sure as heck have forgotten a lot of stuff that happened in the months before it,' replied Paddy.

'Well, if that's the case, forgive my absentmindedness,' added

Peters as he shook Al's hand, 'Nice to meet you, Brother O'Boyle.' Peters finished his greeting.

'Miss McCarthy. What an absolute pleasure, and my oath, the Islands have smiled upon you. You look radiant,' Paddy gave Abby a hug, causing her to blush, which was some feat, given the darkness of her skin.

'Father Paddy. Incorrigible as ever. It is wonderful to see so many dear friends here. Never in my wildest dreams did I think this was a scene I'd see. Father Robertson, a little greyer than I remember, but very distinguished.' She only offered Al a handshake, warm and slightly lingering, yet Al felt it was devoid of true emotion. 'And Brother Iggy, what a delight to have you here.'

'I never had the chance to say thanks,' Iggy jumped forward to talk to Abby. 'You and Moira were our saviours back then. As quickly as you came to us, you were gone again. I know Paddy and Al have seen you a little bit since, but me, George and Leo never really got an opportunity to thank you, or even say goodbye. That really bothered me.'

Abby took Iggy's hand, 'No need for thanks, Iggy. We were just doing our job, what had to be done. I'm just glad to see you again and know you're well.'

'It's all thanks to him,' Iggy dug his elbow into Al's ribs, 'Did I tell you he saved my life that day? I owe Albert everything. There's nothing I wouldn't do for my mate.'

'Is that right? I didn't know that,' said John, raising his eyebrows to Al.

'I think that maybe Iggy is stretching the truth. I can't remember much,' said Al, scuffing the dirt floor with his feet.

'It's true. He nearly bought the farm pushing me to safety. Don't let him tell ya otherwise,' added Iggy.

'Gentlemen, it's getting late. We'd better start back for the Mission,' said John. 'Allan, Abigail, would it be alright if we came up to the hospital for a visit in the next couple of days?'

'Please,' Abby almost squealed her answer. Quickly straightening the front of her dress, she added 'Yes, anytime this week. We're both on day duty at the moment. A visit would be nice. Wouldn't it Allan?' She grabbed his arm as she spoke. She noticed Al's gaze switch to the contact.

'Yes, definitely. Any day this week is good. Till then,' replied Peters.

As they parted, both Al and Abby fell in at the back of their groups, allowing them a few extra seconds to look at each other. Wide smiles broke across both their faces.

* * *

8th January
Wellington, New Zealand

'I don't like this.' The Archbishop's stare was fixed and cold. Wrinkled fingers massaged his thick grey beard, as he looked at papers on his large, mahogany desk. 'Father Lynch has taken, supposedly, Brother O'Boyle and Brother Durning to Fiji on Father Gondringer's mission. But all the documents refer to Brother James Doogan, who you say died in the '31 earthquake. Brother Durning is definitely still up at St. Patrick's College in Silverstream, not on his way to Fiji.'

'Correct. Brother Durning called Mount Saint Mary's the other day, which alerted me that something was amiss,' replied Father Connolly.

'It wasn't a question.' The Archbishop said. 'At the same time, Father Robertson has taken, also supposedly, the summer off to visit his family in Wanganui. Lynch has taken them to one of the outer islands. What is it called?'

'Taveuni,' said Connolly meekly.

'Do we know the whereabouts of this woman, Abigail

McCarthy?' asked The Archbishop, now having fixed Connolly with his gaze.

'No we don't.'

'That's one of the three pieces of this puzzle that we're missing. The other two are why Father Lynch didn't change Brother Doogan's name with Brother Durning's, and is Father Robertson actually in Wanganui.'

'Lynch is up to something. I just know it,' hissed Connolly.

The Archbishop threw a dismissive stare at him. 'That is quite apparent. We need to know who, if anyone, was on that ship with Lynch.' He picked up his phone and dialled the operator. 'The P&O head office on the quays. Thank you.' He continued his stare at Connolly while he waited. 'Hello. Peter Rutherford, please.' he covered the mouthpiece as he spoke to Connolly, 'I'm quite sure who we will find as the third person, who boarded that ship, and it won't be the ghost of Jimmy Doogan.' Connolly could hear a voice on the phone. 'Peter? It's the Archbishop. How's Lyn and the children? Peter, I'm after some information you could help with. I need to know if one of our boys was on a voyage from Auckland to Suva, Fiji on the first of January. Would you be able to confirm that? Good, good. The name on the passenger list is Brother James Doogan. We want to know whether he did or didn't board the ship. It's rather urgent. Would you be able to find out today? Can you make a call up to your people in Auckland? Excellent. Many thanks. I await your return call. Goodbye.'

An uneasy silence hang between them for a couple of minutes, before it got the better of Connolly, 'You think Father Robertson has taken Brother Doogan's place and has gone up to Fiji to see his fancy woman?' he asked.

'At last you're thinking. Unfortunately, months too late. And Lynch has orchestrated it all. Like a little puppet master, pulling the strings, all the while pretending to be organising a mission.'

'He's not smart enough. He's just a drunken provincial hick. He only came to us after he failed at farming.'

'Well, that drunken hick seems to have led you, Murphy and the diocesan bookkeepers, a merry dance,' said the Archbishop shooting a dismissive wave of his hand in Connolly's direction.

Less than half an hour later the big black phone rattled to life. 'Yes, very good. Put him through. Peter, good afternoon. You have some news for me?' Connolly saw the Archbishop's face tighten and his jaw clench. 'So that's confirmed. Thank you, Peter. Regards to the family.' In slow motion, he gently put the receiver down. 'Well, now. We do have ourselves a situation. He confirmed that the passenger boarding clerk had checked in James Doogan, but wrote on the sheet "See P&O letter from passenger".'

Connolly turned paler as the blood drained from his face. 'The sneaky rats.'

'Now, unless poor Brother Doogan has returned from the grave, we have a different person in Fiji. That probably being Father Robertson.'

'They are due back on February first. We should have people at the dock when they arrive.'

'Not good enough, Connolly. I want you up there as quickly as possible, we're already ten days behind them. Get on the first ship out as soon as you can get to Auckland. In fact, we should look into one of those airmail aeroplanes. You have my authorisation to spend whatever it takes to get there in the shortest timeframe.'

'Me fly to the Islands? I don't think that's a good idea,' Connolly stumbled over his protest.

'It was your lack of oversight that's led us to this position. You will clean up this mess. Your long term future demands it. Am I making myself clear?'

Connolly quickly nodded, swallowing deeply. A bead of sweat trickled down his temple.

* * *

271

9th *January*

Abby and Al walked along the inland path around the northern base of Mount Uluiqalau on the way to the waterfalls on the east coast. They had started out early to get the bulk of the uphill section done before the afternoon heat made the going too difficult. The thick forest canopy and the low morning sun kept the air mild and sweet with the evaporating dew off the trees and flowers.

'There's a local legend about the volcano. It's sad, but sweet at the same time. Near the mountains peak there is a rare vine that has lovely red, white and purple flowers. The story goes that a local chief's daughter fell in love with a boy who her family disapproved of. So they forbade her from seeing him. Her love was so strong that she would secretly meet the boy in the dead of night. They were discovered during one of their rendezvous, so the chief had the boy banished to another island. She was so distraught, she ran away to the volcano and climbed the highest tree on the mountain and vowed never to come down. Heartbroken, she cried herself to death, and where her tears fell, so bloomed the flowers on the vine.'

'That's lovely. Sounds a bit like us, expect you were the one banished to an island.'

'Albert, it was horrible. Did I tell you Moira was at the dock in Auckland when my ship sailed?' she said.

'No. What a stab to the heart to see her there. She and Connolly must have been in close contact. Probably hatched the plan together.'

'She knew the Nursing Service looking for volunteers to come up here. It was all over the hospitals, so I don't doubt it. The first few months were very tough. I think I cried myself to sleep for a couple of weeks. Thankfully Allan arrived. He helped me cope.'

'So what is his story? Seems a bit odd that he's here,' Al said, raising his eyebrows.

'It was a shock when he arrived. It was almost a year ago when he walked into the hospital. I almost jumped out of my skin when I saw him. He stayed for a few days, went back to Suva for a couple of weeks, then came back in March,' Abby tried to be as matter of fact as she could.

'But why did he come here? Taveuni isn't well known. If he wanted a placement in the tropics, surely Suva, Tahiti, or even Honolulu, would be the logical choice.'

Abby stopped walking, turned to Al and took his hands, 'Hon, yes he did come here to see me. In fact he proposed to me last year.'

'He did what? I knew it. The way he touched you the other night and he was grabbing sneaky glances at you. So what did say to him? Have you been stepping out with him here?'

'Stepping out where? There's no bloody place to go. No, I haven't been and I said no to him. Well, kind of.'

'A marriage proposal is either a yes or no question, not a maybe.'

'I've basically ignored it and hoped to get home quickly, and when that didn't happen, I just kept putting him off.'

'Yet never actually saying no? It's still an open proposal from him,' Al retorted.

'Albert, I love you with the whole of my being. I told myself soon after arriving here that it would be you or no one. We'd find a way to be together, or I'd go to my grave alone. I won't compromise now that I've found the only one for me.' She leaned in and kissed him deeply and started pulling at his clothes and he hungrily did the same. Passion and desire in both of them that had been pent up for over a year exploded in a lustful coupling.

By the time they got to the falls, the temperature had passed ninety degrees, the usually reliable easterly trade winds that would have taken the edge off the heat were absent today.

'I'm going in for a dip. You did bring some swimming trunks?' asked Abby.

Before Al could respond, Abby had gone behind a tree and started to take off her dress and camisole. Al watched her undress, studying every curve, freckle and dimple.

Stepping out from behind the tree, Abby did a quick twirl. 'What do you think?' Al turned and craned his neck around a shrub in front of him, her outfit was lime green with a white belt and shoulder straps. In the middle of her cleavage the material was gathered to form a bow. He suddenly realised his mouth had been open for a while. 'I bought it mail order from Auckland a couple of months ago. I thought as I'm going to be in the tropics for a while I may as well treat myself to a decent swimsuit. You coming in?' Abby was looking back at Al as she waded in. 'Come on slow coach, the water's heavenly.' She was now submerged up to her shoulders.

He was surprised how quickly he became aroused again after their tryst on the mountain path. Abby was off diving down into the swimming hole, so he walked into the water until it was up to his waist; he sank down, immersing himself in the water. It was cool yet refreshing, cleansing even. He let himself float, watching the sunlight peek through the forest; the water felt magical, washing away the tension in his body. As he glided in the pool, he sensed hands on the small of his back and his stomach, as if something or someone was cradling him. He looked around expecting to see Abby next to him, but she was on the other side of the pool. Suddenly the force pushed him under the water and held him there for what seemed like at least a minute. Al instinctively fought to get back to the surface, but the force held him down, then as quickly as it had submerged him, it released him and he swam back to the surface, spluttering, gulping for air. He waded to a shallow part of the pool, quickly looking around him, but seeing nothing in the water. He felt startled and revitalised in equal measure.

Abby surfaced a few yards away. 'Feel better?' she asked, oblivious to what just happened.

'It's fantastic. It's like God's own secret swimming hole.' Al replied. Had the Lord just absolved him, setting him free?

'See, I told you it would be great. You know what they say about women always being right,' she took in a mouthful of water and fired it in his direction. They swam side by side around the pool for a few minutes. They made their way to the base of the waterfall, diving down to the bottom along the way, a mini rainbow formed as the sun hit the falls spray. He climbed on the rocks and offered his hand to her. As he pulled her up, Abby lost her balance and he grabbed her waist, she placed her hands on his chest to steady herself. The water on her tanned body glistened, they looked into each other's eyes then kissed, gently, tentatively at first, pulling back for a couple of seconds, then again more deeply, the passion between them rising quickly. Abby dug her fingers into his chest. She pulled away, rested her head on his shoulder and gave him little kisses on his neck.

'Could we stay here forever?' Abby whispered. 'You could work at Wairiki and I could get a permanent position at the hospital.'

'That does sound nice, but we wouldn't really be together, we would still be living a lie, looking over our shoulders, however beautiful and remote the location.'

'You're right. Lovely thought though,' hummed Abby.

Suddenly the sound of splashing water and loud voices pulled their attention down-stream where a half dozen boys where swimming towards the falls. One of them looked up, waved and shouted, 'Miss Nurse, Miss Nurse.'

'It's some of the lads from Bouma. Lovely kids,' she said, waving back.

'Probably time to be heading back anyway,' he said as they separated and he dived into the water, quickly followed by Abby.

That evening they went down to the beach near the jetty at Wairiki to take in the sunset. They sat on the bottom of a small overturned boat and watched the fishermen complete their daily chores; hauling their boats up onto the beach and setting out their nets to dry overnight. Al looked down the coast, palm trees poked out of the forest at all sorts of impossible angles. Some of the trunks were almost horizontal, turning up towards the sky only at the very end of the tree, as if they had fought for years to get the perfect position to watch the sunsets.

The sky quickly changed from pale blue to the first wisps of orange, which then rapidly changed to reds, and deep inky purples. The surface of the sea mirrored the colour changes of the sky. Within ten minutes of the sun touching the horizon, it was gone.

'My word, that was quick,' Al said, his voice showing his surprise.

'No twilight up here. On cloudy days, it can go from sunny to pitch black in just over thirty minutes,' Abby added.

'Doesn't make for long, romantic walks on the beach at dusk.'

'A small price to pay for stunning sunsets like that. Not that there's been any opportunities for me to have romantic walks. Now, I have some news you may find interesting. I'm going to be able to go home at the end of April.' Abby had turned in to face Al as she spoke.

'What? That's wonderful. When did you find out?'

'Just before Christmas. The head of nursing in Suva got approval from the Ministry of Health to limit me to a maximum of one year of service, plus my first six months as part of the advance team. I'd been wondering about the best time to tell you, and the way the day worked out, it just didn't seem appropriate to do it during the day.'

'It's fantastic news. Have you thought where you might go?' Al asked with a broad smile and wide eyes.

'Probably Auckland. A mate of mine, Shirley, is one of the

nurses I came over here with and is from there. She's going to help me get a job at Auckland Public.'

'This puts a different complexion on matters,' Al replied.

'How so?' asked Abby.

'I came up here because I realised I cannot live without you. I tried to deny my feelings for years and commit to the Church. When we met in Wellington, it reignited all those feelings and dared me to dream again, but when they sent you up here, I decided that was it, they would always beat us, stop us, so why bother believing in an illusion. Paddy reinitiating this mission was a sign, an opening to finally be decisive, not dither and live a lie.'

'So exactly what are you saying? You're talking in circles,' she said.

He turned to fully face her, 'Abby, I love you with every fibre of my body. I need to be with you for the rest of my life. When I'm with you I feel closer to God and understand his true meaning of love. With you coming back home, I'm ready to leave the Church. It can't give me what I need anymore, if it ever did. Abby, will you marry me?'

'Oh, Albert, I do want to say yes, but have you really thought this through? You know what the reaction will be.'

'It won't be pleasant, no two ways about it. I'll be thrown out of the Church. As an ordained priest, I'm too far gone for them to let me go. As for the family, Mum will be devastated. Dad will be angry, but probably relieved. They certainly won't be accepting an invite to the nuptials. But neither the Church nor my family can give me the future I want. Only you can do that.'

'You've been in for ten years. You're willing to walk away from it?' Abby asked.

'Don't you believe me? Abby, I have enough inside me to love you for three or four lifetimes, let alone one,' Al looked at Abby with an emotion and intensity that was unmistakable. 'It's hard to put in words what goes through me when I look at you; when we touch. It's almost as if I'm connecting with God.' They sat in silence for a couple of minutes.

'You don't have to say anymore. Your eyes tell me everything I need to know, and it's a yes,' Abby finally said.

Their hands reached for the others simultaneously and met in the middle of the space between them. They both squeezed the others hand hard, both wanting to embrace, but knowing that was still off limits in such a public place, for now.

* * *

14ᵗʰ January

'Paddy, you expecting anyone from home?' John asked entering the sitting room with a tall man.

'No. Like who?' replied Paddy.

'Clergy. No late additions to the mission? This is Maikeli,' John said, introducing the man. 'He's just got back from Suva and says a priest from New Zealand flew in a couple of days ago on the mail plane and was asking around about how to get here.'

'No, we definitely weren't expecting anyone. What's this person look like?' Paddy asked.

'He short, Father' said Maikeli 'Thin, like runt of litter. Small glasses, pointy nose and chin. Wearing white hat, sir.'

Paddy and Al looked at each other and simultaneously said 'Connolly.'

'From Mount Saint Mary's? What on earth would he be doing here?' asked John.

'Well, I may not have given you the full run down on the situation,' Paddy said, staring at the ground.

'Oh, how surprising. Come on Lynch, spit it out' said John.

'I told you that no one should know Albert is here,' Paddy continued.

'Obviously you didn't do a good enough job of covering your tracks.'

'You could say we falsified the passenger manifest for him,' Paddy added.

'Looks like Connolly has discovered your little ruse. Fabulous, Patrick. Just bloody fantastic. There's only one thing for it,' John quickly switched his eyes between Al and Paddy. 'Let's get Father Robertson back home straight way. I suggest you go and pack your case and I'll see if we can delay the ferry for an hour or two.' John shook his head at Paddy.

Paddy stood in the doorway of Al's room, 'You have the letter from Mary?' Al nodded to Paddy's question as he folded his clothes and placed them in his suitcase. 'Good. Hopefully that'll be good enough to get ya on any P&O or Union ship. As soon as you get into Suva, go straight to the harbour offices and find out what ships are going to New Zealand within the next few days. If there's no services, or they can't get you on, get on the first ship of any kind. Even a rough as guts banana boat, whatever it is, get on it. Here's thirty quid. The freighter lads shouldn't sting you more than ten or twenty, but you might need to grease a couple of palms. You right, lad?'

'Bloody nervous, to be honest.' Al said as he almost unconsciously wiped away the cold sweat that was forming on his face.

'As soon as you make Auckland, get on the first train to Wanganui. No mucking about. Right?' Paddy instructed Al.

The four men stood on the jetty, looking at the ferry boat rise and fall as people and provisions were loaded on. McGuire was first to speak, 'We'll try to delay Connolly as long as we can. With a bit of luck you'll be home before he can get back to Suva. I sent one of the boys to fetch Abby, but she's over in Lavena today and wouldn't get back before nightfall. We can't wait around that long, the ferry has got to sail in daylight.'

'Thank you for everything you've done for us. I'm so sorry this is happening and we've dragged you into this,' Al said.

'Not to worry, Albert. Patrick and I chatted about this when you arrived. I was somewhat prepared. Maybe not as prepared as I could have been.' McGuire shot a quick cold look at Paddy, 'There's nothing Connolly can do to us. We'll be right. Safe trip.' The two shook hands firmly.

Al turned to Iggy, who had his arms crossed tightly on his chest, the corners of his mouth turned down, 'Lord God Almighty. You are one dark horse. Not impressed at all, eh. Absolutely staggered, to be honest.' Al nodded slowly to Iggy's response. 'I can't even think straight at the mo. Any of the lads back home know?'

'Don't think so. I did my best to keep it quiet,' replied Al.

'Too bloody right you did. What are they going to do to ya back home?' asked Iggy.

'Don't know. Technically I'm not here, so they don't have any documented proof I wasn't in Wanganui all along. We'll deal with that if it happens,' Al placed a hand on Iggy's shoulder.

'For what it's worth, they'll get nothing out of me. I owe you a lot, but I didn't think part of the pay back would be covering for something like this,' Iggy said.

'You're a good man, Brother Ignatius O'Boyle,' said Al.

'Yeah, and don't ever forget it,' said Iggy, as he finally untied his arms and offered Al his hand.

'Well lad, not exactly the way I thought this would finish up. As long as you get on a ship within the next coupla days, you'll be right,' Paddy said while staring out to sea.

'This might be the last time we see each other. Sounds like Connolly has uncovered enough to make your life difficult. Whatever happens, I shouldn't come up to Napier again,' said Al, exhaling heavily.

'Don't be so dramatic. You've been reading too much of that

bloody poetry,' Paddy replied, turning back to face his friend, Al noticed Paddy's eyes were slightly red.

'I owe you a hell of a lot, Patrick. More than I could ever come close to repaying. I'll never be able to thank you enough.'

'You're a bit over-the-top now. Just two mates looking out for each other,' said Paddy.

'Father Albert. They're ready to cast off. You better get on board.' McGuire shouted from the front of the ferry.

'On your way, lad. I'll drop you a line as soon as I get back to Napier,' Paddy said, as he picked up Al's case and they walked over to the boat.

* * *

17ᵗʰ *January*

'Well, where is he?' demanded Connolly almost immediately after he opened the presbytery front door and strode into the lounge.

'And he would be?' replied Paddy.

'Don't act the idiot with me, Lynch. Although that's all you're capable of. Father Robertson. I know he's here.'

'I can safely say, without fear of being struck down by the Almighty himself that Father Albert is not here,' said Paddy.

'Listen, Lynch, don't mess me around. You're already in a huge amount of trouble. Misappropriating Church funds, defrauding P&O Lines. I could go on. So you can cut the charade and let me know where I can find him.' Connolly folded his arms, not taking his eyes off Paddy.

'Father Connolly. That's enough. You have no authority here. I'm the senior clergy on Taveuni,' John interrupted the two men.

'McGuire isn't it? I remember you from the seminary. Always the odd ball, square peg in a round hole. Looks like you've found your niche among the natives. Perhaps you can tell me where Robertson is?'

'As Father Patrick said, he's not here. Not sure where he could be. As for your accusations, I can attest that Father Patrick and Brother Ignatius have indeed been here on a very productive mission. They have provided substantial assistance to our teachers, helped our students make significant advances and have bought supplies and stationery that are invaluable to us. I intend to write to Father Murphy and the Archbishop outlining such and praising their dedication to the Marist ethos of Christian education.'

'Write all you want, but Lynch is going to be dropped from a great height when he returns to New Zealand. What about you Brother Ignatius? You'll tell me what's happened to Robertson. Remember I am your employer, your master. I can make life easy or hard for you.'

'Father Connolly, I too can confirm that Father Robertson is not here. I couldn't say for sure where he might be.' Iggy was sure and clear with his reply.

'Threats aren't going to help you, Father Connolly. Brother Ignatius has been offered, and has accepted a position here as the head teacher of our junior school. Father Albert could be anywhere, Wellington, Auckland, Suva, Timbuktu. Difficult to say,' McGuire said, folding his arms in front of his chest to match Connolly.

'Well, he's got to be here somewhere. I got here as quick as is humanly possible, so you couldn't have known I was coming and smuggled him off the island. I'll search for him. He's probably shacked up with the whore McCarthy,' Connolly stared at McGuire.

Paddy exploded out of his chair, too fast for John or Iggy to cut him off. He pinned Connolly to the wall with a meaty forearm pressing down on his throat. 'Now it's you who's in deep shit. One more misplaced word and you'll be going back to Napier with a breathing tube. You got me?'

'Paddy, that's enough. Get off him,' John said calmly into Paddy's ear, with his arm around Paddy's shoulders. 'He's not worth it. He knows he has no power here.'

After a few seconds Paddy slowly lowered his arm and stepped back a couple of feet, but never took his eyes off Connolly, who coughed and spluttered to get air into his lungs.

'Father Connolly, you can look high and low over Taveuni, but I guarantee you will not find Father Robertson. You'll go back to New Zealand empty handed,' said John. 'As is my duty, I can offer you accommodation here and use the Mission as a base. I can provide one of our pupils to be your guide to help you get around the island. After this initial rocky start, I hope you will enjoy your time on Taveuni.'

Following dinner, Iggy excused himself under the pretence of needing to prepare a lesson and supplies for a Sunday School class. Making sure Connolly didn't see him leave, he took the back trail to Waiyevo.

The knock on her door was so light that Abby thought it wasn't for her. Only at the second knock did she put down her book and opened the door. 'Brother Iggy,' her voice went up an octave.

'Yeah, sorry for the late and unannounced visit, but it's something that can't wait. Can we have a chat?' There was no hint of Iggy's usual convivial nature in his voice.

Abby was immediately on edge, 'Of course. Let me grab a cardie and we can go through to the lounge.' She had a quick look in the mirror and the little notch that formed between her eyebrows whenever she was worried or concentrating looked more like a crevasse.

Taking a seat, she noticed Iggy's shoes and cuffs of his trousers were covered in mud. 'Did you come across country tonight?' she asked nodding to his feet.

'I did actually. Took the back route to avoid attention,' replied Iggy.

'Not sure I like the sound of where this is going. Is it to do with the message that was left for me?' she asked. Iggy nodded, vigorously rubbing his hands. 'Well? They told me someone came looking for me, asking me to go to the jetty.'

'Albert has gone back to New Zealand,' said Iggy, staring at the floor.

'What?' Abby's eyes wide in shock. 'Why? How? Has something happened to his family?'

'No, no. He's fine, family's fine. Father Connolly arrived today. We got wind of it and got Al off the island. Appears he was here on falsified documents and Connolly found out.'

'Connolly's here?' That was a bigger jolt than Al leaving; that was always going to happen, but Connolly's presence brought back all of her doubts and fears about her and their future. What more pain could Connolly inflict on her? Now that he knew of Al's trip would he try to punish him and her? Would her placement here be extended again, to be forever marooned on Taveuni?

'Abby. You OK?' Iggy's voice brought her attention back to the room.

'Just completely bewildered.'

'I know everyone thinks I'm a bit slow on the take up, and yes, I've never been the best at studying, but I see what's going on even though Al's done a good job of keeping you a secret. I can't say I understand how this managed to get to where he's willing to risk everything he's worked for, everything he's become, but just the fact he's done this to see you again tells me everything I need to know. Standing on the pier, I saw it in his eyes. He loves you more than life itself, more than the Church, more than being a priest.'

'You think so, too? I saw it myself. Iggy, I don't know how or when it happened. It was slow, I fought it for years, I knew it wasn't right, but one day something fell into place. It felt natural being with him.'

'Never say love isn't right. We all strive for love, in all its different forms. I just wish for both of you that it had happened earlier. He must be going through a heap of torment and I'd say there's more on the way. For both your sakes, it has to be as if he never set foot on this island. Connolly is going to try to talk to everyone he can to find proof he was here. How's your powers of persuasion with the staff here? Especially Doctor Peters?' asked Iggy.

'Pretty good, I hope anyway,' said Abby.

'You're going to have to get to everyone who knew Albert was here or even saw him and get them to clam up. There were only two priests that came from New Zealand, never seen a tall grey-haired priest, that sort of thing.'

'I'll get round the troops starting tonight. Thank you for being so understanding.'

'I'm not condoning what's happened, I still can't get to grips with it, but I owe him, so I'll protect him. I never told you, but before you came up to us at the seminary after the quake, I knelt beside Al's cot and made a solemn oath to God that within my power, I would never let any harm come to him. I'm only still walking the earth because of his selflessness. This is my chance to make good on that commitment and God willing, Connolly won't get what he wants.'

She pulled a handkerchief from her pocket, dabbed her eyes and reached for his hand, 'Oh, Iggy. You have a wonderful soul.'

He squeezed her hand, 'I better get back, especially if you're going to chat to folk tonight. You remember back then when I asked you to save him?' She nodded, still wiping her eyes. 'Falling in love with him and having him do the same wasn't exactly what I had in mind, but for what it's worth, it seems to me that you transform him when he's near you. Abigail McCarthy, it appears you have a greater power over him than the Lord himself. I can't deny a man that sort of love.' Iggy slowly rose, smiled warmly and closed the door behind him.

Abby felt an unusual calmness come over her; her initial feelings of shock had quickly been surpassed on learning of Connolly's presence and motives. The past ten days had been bliss, almost trance like she had drifted through the days, knowing Al's desire to be together and seeing in him his resolve to make a life for them upon her return. It was all she needed to know, so as much as his departure had robbed her of another week of delight, she been readying herself for that day from the first night she saw him again at the kava ceremony. If truth be told, it was probably better this way than a prolonged, highly emotional goodbye. Now she had to protect her man, plain and simple, no fanfare, no time for inner turmoil, he needed her to be steely and sure-footed. Any slip, any chink in the wall of denial they had to build and she was sure the Church would punish him severely. Connolly had to go back without a trace of evidence. Time to get to work.

* * *

Dawn broke majestically, a clear sky with barely a trace of a breeze. Abby stood on the porch of the accommodation block and looked out over the low hills then out to sea. She filled her lungs with the sweet, warm air and held it for a couple of seconds, to fortify herself for the day ahead. A talk with Allan was first thing on the agenda, before he went into the hospital. She knew she would have to reveal more of her feelings, but more importantly her relationship with Al, than she ever had. She had kept his advances at bay for the past nine months, but the situation now called for full and frank revelations. She expected it to hurt him, but needs must now. She strode quickly across the 50 yards to his small bungalow and knocked heavily on the door.

After a couple of minutes and another knock, the door opened slowly to reveal Allan in his pyjamas, tufts of his thin hair were stuck straight up around his bald patch. He squinted into the sharp morning light, 'Abby? What on earth? It's just gone sun up. What's going on?'

'Sorry for the intrusion, but we need to talk. It's very important,' she said.

'It must be cos you've got that worry line on your forehead. Come in, grab a seat and I'll put the billy on.' He went over to the kitchen area at the back of the lounge and lit a small kerosene stove and placed the kettle on top then returned to the chairs, 'Now what's so important that's got you up before the rooster?'

'It's about us,' Allan's eyes suddenly opened wide, 'Well, more to the point, the reason why I've never given you an answer to your question of last year,' said Abby.

'You mean my proposal? I was positive you'd forgotten about it. I nearly had after ten months of either half answers, riddles or silence. So?' He sat back and cupped his hand on his lap.

'There's a good reason why I never said yes or no. I desperately love someone else,' Allan nodded slowly, his bottom lip started to protrude. 'All the while I've been here I've been longing for them, hoping we would someday be together, but with every extension for my time here, that hope kept being whittled away. It was about August when I thought all hope was gone, but then I heard he might come up here to see me and then I got notice that I could go home in April.'

'I see, your true love will stride ashore, sweep you off your feet and take you back to New Zealand. I thought that was going to be me last year, but obviously not. So when do they arrive?'

'They are here now. Well, actually was here until a couple of days ago.'

'Is here. Was here. You're talking in riddles again. No one's been here recently. Does this person have a name? Do I know them?'

'Yes you do. It's Albert.'

'Albert?' he looked outside, but not fixing his gaze on anything, turned back to Abby, 'As in Father Albert? You're in love with a priest?' Abby nodded vigorously and shrugged her shoulders. 'Well I never. Stone the bloody crows.' Just then, the kettle started to sing; Allan, almost in a trance, got up and silently started making the tea. After a couple of minutes of not a word being spoken, he came back with a tray containing the teapot, cups, saucers, milk and sugar. Placing them down on the table, he sat down heavily onto his chair and exhaled deeply.

'Allan. Are you alright?' Abby asked.

He finally looked her in the eye, 'You know, I thought there was something going on. You've been transformed this past couple of weeks. I wondered why a few priests from home would get you so excited. I thought that like when I arrived it was the chance to see familiar faces again, but it was definitely more than that. After you spent all of last Saturday with Albert I had my suspicions, then at Mass on Sunday, that clinched it. You never took your eyes off him for the whole service.'

'I never even thought about appearances. I have been in a bit of a haze, yes,' she said.

'If this is what he does to you, I can't compete with that. It's as if you've been floating for days. I've never had that effect on any woman. Not even Gracie. I never wanted to be your consolation prize or fall back option, but a priest? That's got some drawbacks, no?' He took a long sip of tea and then gave Abby a quizzical look, 'Wait on. You said he was here until two days ago, but they weren't due to leave until this week. Something's up.'

'That's one of the reasons why I do like you Allan, you do listen and you think. Yes, something is definitely afoot. I'll give you the short version, as we both need to be at work in less than an hour.'

'Bloody hell,' Allan spat out some tea, looking up at his clock, 'I've got an op scheduled this morning too. So, tell me what's going on. Lord knows it can't be any crazier than being in love with a priest.'

* * *

After a weekend of frustration and dead ends, Connolly finally got to see Allan and Abby at the hospital. They were in the staff room when Connolly was ushered in. Immediately Abby tensed up and exhaled heavily. Allan reached over and touched her hand and gave her a quick wink.

'Doctor Peters? Father Connolly from Mount Saint Mary's, back in Napier.' Allan nodded and accepted the handshake. Connolly never acknowledged Abby's presence. 'Is there somewhere more private we can talk?' he asked.

'Apart from the operating theatre, this is as private as this place gets, I'm afraid. Father Connolly, I'm not sure if you've met my colleague, Abigail McCarthy. She's another Bay resident,' said Allan.

'Yes, we are acquainted,' Abby interjected before Connolly could answer, 'Welcome to Waiyevo, Father. Quite a surprise to see you here. You coming to assist Father Patrick and Brother Iggy on their mission, or just a little South Seas Island holiday?'

'Business, actually. Parish matters. There's definitely nowhere else we can talk?' Connolly asked Allan again.

'Sounds like you two have some very important matters to discuss. I'll make myself scarce,' said Abby as she rose.

Allan got up as Abby left the table and waited until she was out the door before turning to Connolly, 'What's so secretive?'

'It's a delicate matter that does involve Miss McCarthy. Did you see a Father Albert Robertson while he was here on Father Lynch's so called mission?'

'Not sure I understand your question. Father Lynch and Brother O'Boyle are the only clergy on the mission from back home I know are here,' replied Allan, sitting back in his chair.

'So you haven't seen Father Robertson in the last couple of weeks?' Allan nodded a couple of times in response, 'Doctor Peters, as one professional to another, you can tell me the truth.'

'Father Connolly, I'd like to help you, but I don't think I've seen Father Robertson for six years, when he was still a seminarian with you. Even if I did run into him, I'd struggle to recognise him. I think I only met him a couple of times, at best, back then.'

Connolly folded his arms and his jaw tightened. 'I'm disappointed, Doctor. I'd have thought you would have been above joining in on this tawdry pantomime, but it appears the whole island is in on the act. All the locals refuse to speak English to me and the rest of you seem to have a well concocted story.'

'Now, Father, I do find it a bit odd that the head of a seminary is 1500 miles from home, asking questions about a priest who isn't under your jurisdiction, who is supposedly on a mission funded by a parish you aren't a member of. All very strange, no?' Allan leaned in close to Connolly for the final sentence.

'I'm afraid I can't divulge the true nature of my visit, but your evasiveness is disappointing. It appears that spending anytime in the Islands impairs ones view of reality. If you have nothing else to add, then I'll bid you farewell and hope your return to New Zealand will lift the malaise that seems to have affected you,' Connolly abruptly got up, causing his chair to issue a loud screech.

'Safe travels home, Father,' added Allan.

'So how do I get off this God-forsaken piece of dirt?' asked Connolly as he walked into John's office in the presbytery.

'We only have two ferries a week to Suva. Monday's and Friday's and the Monday boat left a couple of hours ago. You could go over to Savusavu and get one of the daily services to Suva. Unfortunately our Savusavu boat is undergoing repairs. Not sure when it'll be ready. So it looks like you're with us until Friday, I'm afraid,' said John.

'How convenient for everyone except me,' hissed Connolly.

'Now you'll be able to experience our world famous Fijian hospitality. A five day holiday in the Islands can't be so bad. You'll be able to see first-hand the excellent work Patrick and Ignatius have done for us,' John said with a smile.

CHAPTER 18

11ᵗʰ July 1937

Wellington, New Zealand

His stomach was knotted, balled like a small fist. He could taste the bile rising up in his throat. Al knew the timing was tight and he had little room for error. The train to Auckland was due to leave on the stroke of ten o'clock that night. He wanted to leave his run to the station as late as possible, to get there no more than ten minutes before departure. He wouldn't be on the streets or at the station too long, so few people would see him out and about. Hopefully no one to ask questions; no inquisitors to put a spanner in the works.

At quarter past nine he slipped out of the window of his room. He'd told George and Leo that he was going to turn in early to be fresh and alert for the start of the new school week. Dressed in a casual tweed suit, tan brogues, white shirt, dark blue tie and brown fedora, winter coat over his forearm, he looked to all the world like an everyday gent out for a stroll of a Sunday evening.

Earlier that day, Al had stashed a suitcase in a thick hedge half a block away. He came to the shrubs and stuck his hand around the back of the branches. He pulled out the suitcase, checked it was still locked and hadn't been tampered with. Perfect, all set. He had intentionally packed light. When one is off to start a new life one may as well leave as much of the old life behind. Like shedding an old skin. Gone were the cassocks, black suits and Roman collars of priesthood. He had two suits, one casual, one more formal, six shirts, a wool jersey, underwear, socks, six handkerchiefs, a pair of black brogues and his toiletries. That's it. Pack light they always said at the seminary "You never know when you might have to leave your posting for another parish." The words they'd told him all those years ago came back to him again. In his pockets were his old faithful fob watch, his pipe, some tobacco, his train ticket he'd pre-purchased a couple of days previous to prevent any delays. He also had all the money he possessed, forty-five pounds, two shillings, and eight pence. Hardly enough to start a new life in a new city, but low pay was one of the down sides of life in the clergy. That and not being able to be with a woman that you love with every fibre of your being.

He strode purposefully down to the heart of Newtown and the tram that would take him directly to the train station without a change. He had done the trip so many times by now, he knew it by heart – down Adelaide Road, around the Basin Reserve, down Cambridge Terrace, along the Quays, then the station. Shouldn't take more than twenty minutes at this time of night on a Sunday. There wouldn't be many people getting on or off and not much traffic on the streets to slow the tram down. That was the hope anyway. Turning the corner he almost bumped into someone coming the other way.

'Sorry. Please pardon me. Dreadfully sorry.' Al quickly said and tried to keep going.

'Father Robertson?' a youthful voice asked.

The sound of his name hit him like an arrow in his back. His first thought was to ignore the enquiry and keep walking, but the person repeated his name.

'Sir. Father Robertson. What brings you out on a Sunday night? Going on a trip?'

He slowly turned and lifted his face to see two teenage boys looking at him. It was two of his pupils from his senior chemistry class. Had he been going to school tomorrow, Al would be teaching them at one o'clock. The boys were looking at Al's suitcase.

'Oh, evening boys. Ah well, yes. I've got a call to go back

home to Wanganui for a couple of days. Small emergency with my mother,' said Al quickly.

'Oh, very sorry to hear that. Will miss you at chemistry tomorrow, Father. Hope we don't get Father Allenby as a replacement,' the first lad said to the other, as much as to Al.

'Sorry to rush boys, but I need to catch the next tram into town otherwise I'll miss my train. Will probably see you later this week if everything works out in Wanganui. Bye.' Al scurried across the street to the tram stop. Within two minutes a tram he needed clattered around the corner. Another few sentences with the boys and he might have missed it. Taking a seat near the back of the tram, Al's heart was beating ferociously. Beads of sweat were forming on his forehead underneath his hat. Al took it off and mopped his brow with his handkerchief. 'Damn', he swore to himself. 'That's exactly what I didn't need to happen. What were those boys doing out so late?' He knew questioning himself was fruitless, he just needed to get the words out and to compose his thoughts and calm the tension coursing through his veins. All he could hope for now was a clear ride into the station and to depart on time without any further interactions.

Rounding the Basin Reserve, he knew they would be passing by the college in moments. He turned away from the window, lowered his head and pulled the brim of his hat an inch lower. The tram rattled to a stop almost right outside the college. His heartbeat quickened sharply. He dare not look up. A woman's voice, one he didn't recognise, asked for a single to Lambton Quay. He breathed again for what seemed like the first time in five minutes.

By the time he looked up again, the tram was almost at the bottom of Cambridge Terrace. There was a small crowd of people milling around the front of the Embassy Theatre. Looked like a motion picture show must have just finished its screening. *'That's probably where the boys had come from,'* Al thought. The banner blazing across the front of the theatre was for *The Charge of the Light Brigade*. Al knew it was very popular, although he hadn't seen it. Motion pictures? There was something he and Abby could now look forward to, among many other things that were frowned upon within the Church, especially for ordained priests.

Heading down to the Quays, past the Port Offices and the sheds on the docks, the strong scent of the sea hit the tram. At last they turned left onto Bunny Street and the tram shuddered to a halt outside the railway station. Al stepped off and crossed the street. He stopped for a few seconds to take in the stunning edifice, some five stories high and over one hundred yards wide. He had watched with interest its development over the past few years and had even come down to watch the official opening only three weeks ago, to see the pomp and ceremony, but also to plot his route and the most efficient way through the new building to the train. Another couple of dry runs had been done the previous week. He had read that it was already being described as one of the finest public buildings in the country. It's most striking features being eight thick columns guarding the entrance, looking like giant teeth devouring all who come near, and a large clock face sited high in the middle of the building. The clock read eight minutes to ten when Al entered the building.

A quick scan of the faces milling around the entrance, the people coming and going from the building returned a reassuring blank on folks he knew. Even without the immediate danger of recognition Al's heart had picked up its pace. Pores were opening up, the cold clammy feeling of nervous perspiration was returning. 'Steady,' he whispered to himself, 'almost there.'

He strode across the inlayed compass design on the marble terrazzo floor, directly to the departure board, scanning for the platform of the ten o'clock service to Auckland. There it was: Platform 4. It was glowing, winking at him. A shining beacon of freedom, of reformation. He veered left to the platform, gave the

295

conductor his ticket to be checked and clipped, then made his way to his carriage. On board he looked for his seat, which was a window seat, not that it mattered for the view as the overnighter offered no vista of the country until they got near Hamilton around dawn. Still, it would be handy to use the window to lean on to try and get some sleep on the journey. Al placed his suitcase in the luggage rack directly over his seat, folded his overcoat on top of the case, and took his seat. He took his hat off, pulled out his handkerchief patted his forehead again and wiped away the droplets of sweat that had built up on the inside of his fedora. Could he finally relax? Wait. A quick check of his watch, three minutes to ten. Almost.

The train was moderately populated. Just as he had hoped. The sleeper berths were probably quite full. It was always a popular service for businessmen and government officials who could arrive in Auckland early on a Monday morning so they could get a full day's work in. With a sleeper you could alight refreshed even after the long trip north. For those who didn't have a company or the tax payer stumping up the cost of the ticket, the sleeper option was a little pricey. It meant that arrival would result in folks looking somewhere between mildly rumpled and completely dishevelled. So with that outcome and no scenery to while away the trip, the seated coaches on the overnighter were usually quiet enough.

A few ticks after ten Al heard a short blast on the whistle and felt the sharp jerk of the train as it started it on its journey. Now? Yes, now. He allowed himself the small luxury of a deep breath and a slight reduction of the tension he was feeling.

A small boy, couldn't have been more than ten or twelve, came bounding up to him, so full of excitement and energy. 'Where are you going tonight, Sir? We're going back to Levin. We had the whole weekend in Wellington.' A woman, probably no older than Al himself, pulled the boy aside and apologised for the intrusion.

Al touched the brim of his hat 'That's quite alright, Ma'am. It's a fine question, young man. I'm travelling all the way to Auckland tonight. It's a long trip and I'm a bit worried as I've never done it before. Could you do me a favour?' The child nodded. 'When you go to bed tonight, could you say a prayer for the train driver to get me there safe and sound, as I have something really important to do in Auckland tomorrow?' Al pulled out a barley sugar from his jacket pocket and gave it to the youngster, who beamed a toothy smile.

* * *

Now in Auckland, making his way into the city from the railway station, Al felt more relaxed; a little tired, but tension was being replaced by heady expectation. He was actually here. Only an hour away from a new life. He had tried to freshen up as best he could in the Gentlemen's restrooms at the Auckland railway station. He'd only catnapped on the trip, so was a little jaded. A quick wash, shave and brush of the teeth, a change of undershirt and socks, a fresh white dress shirt which was slightly wrinkled but nothing his jacket wouldn't hide, his best tie, cufflinks and a dress kerchief for his top suit jacket pocket. All set.

He changed trams at the corner of Customs and Queens Streets. The Auckland Town Hall that housed the registry office was just over half way up Queen Street, just where it starts to climb steeply toward Karangahape Road. Al could have walked it, but he would have had to walk briskly to make it on time. It wouldn't do to be glowing on his big day. Abby would be far from impressed if he arrived bathed in perspiration.

The street was teeming with people heading to start their respective work days. He'd read in the paper a few weeks ago that the economic depression was officially over, but many industries were still struggling and the demand from Britain for Kiwi food hadn't improved enough to provide an economic surge yet. All the same, Auckland did appear to have a real hustle and bustle about it that Wellington lacked. Being dominated by government meant the capital could be a bit grey and down beat at times. No chance of that here in the sunny north. Once on the tram, he watched people hurrying in and out of office buildings and shops. They went past the giant department store Smith & Caughey's, already with a steady stream of customers flowing in and out of its doors.

The Town Hall was now in sight. Al stood up and got ready to get off at the next stop. A little voice raced through his mind, 'You ready for this?' In a subconscious reaction, his body tensed slightly, his hand gripped harder on the leather strap hanging down from the ceiling of the tram. 'Absolutely,' he replied to the voice, 'Absolutely.'

Stepping off the tram, Al checked for traffic and other trams, then walked across to the Town Hall. The tram had now made him a little early; he could go for a cup of tea and maybe a scone. No, let's just get in there, he told himself. If his Abby was on form, she'd be early as well.

Opening one of the large wooden doors leading to the main foyer, Al's eyes struggled to adjust from the bright sunshine on the street to the building's much darker confines. He squinted, looking around for an information desk or a directory board. He didn't even see her approaching from his left until Abby took his hand.

CHAPTER 19

The heavy black Bakelite phone chirped to life and gave Gary a start. Nine o'clock is a bit early for the first call of the day, he thought. Usually the first hour of the work day was uninterrupted to make a decent start on his paperwork, have a cup of tea, a cigarette and ease into the day. He reached across the wide, lacquered rimu desk and picked up the receiver.

'Mr. Robertson? I have a Father Morgan from St. Patrick's College, for you. Will you take the call?' asked the operator.

'Yes of course, put him through. Good morning. Gary Robertson, Department of Labour. How may I help you?'

'Mr. Robertson. It's Father Morgan. Have you got a minute?'

'Yes sure. What is it?' Gary asked, stubbing out his smoke.

'Is Father Robertson with you or have you seen him today?'

'Albert? My brother? No, not all. I saw him yesterday. My wife and I called over to him for lunch after Mass.' Gary instinctively reached for the framed photo on the other side of his desk; his wedding day with him and Sarah in the middle of the picture, Albert in his ceremonial clerical robes on the right, William on the left and young Howard in front, 'May I ask what's going on?'

'He's not at college today and none of the other priests or lay staff have seen him since last night,' replied Father Morgan.

'What? That's very unlike Albert. You've been to the residence I presume?'

'Yes, first place we looked after the college chapel. We're off to St. Peter's, then thinking about the hospitals next.'

Gary asked Father Morgan to meet him at Al's house to have

a look around his room. He gingerly put down the phone, rubbed his chin, then quickly jumped up from his desk, grabbed his coat and hat and strode swiftly out the door. He took a car from the office garage and set off, his knuckles soon turned white with the pressure he was using to hold the steering wheel. Various images shot through Gary's mind as he drove; Al in a hospital bed, unconscious in some alley, floating in the harbour. He kept shaking his head, but they wouldn't leave him.

Parking outside Al's house, Gary saw the front door was open, so he knocked on the frame and walked in, 'Father Morgan. It's Gary Robertson.'

'I'm in the bedroom,' replied Morgan.

Gary went into Al's room to find Morgan looking into a wardrobe, he turned and offered his hand to Gary, 'Thanks for coming over so quickly. All very strange this.'

'And worrying. I've thought of half a dozen different scenarios on the drive,' replied Gary.

'Quite, but based on what I'm seeing here, I've got a hope it's not as sinister as our worst fears. Come, take a look,' Morgan gestured for Gary to inspect the closet, 'All his clerical clothes are here, cassocks, suits, collars. See, even his rosary is on the dresser. You know what street clothes he has?'

'He's definitely got a tweed suit, brown I recall, and a dark blue one. Both aren't here,' said Gary, flicking through the clothes hangers, 'Only one white shirt left. Looks like he's walked out with nothing to mark him as clergy.'

'My take as well. Makes me think it's a deliberate departure, not a spur of the moment thing, or an accident. Feel free to look around, especially for personal affects. Come into the lounge when you've finished. I need to let you know a few things about Father Albert,' Morgan said, before leaving Gary alone and bewildered in the stark room.

There was a pile of mail waiting for Gary on his return to

his office. He sat down, lit a cigarette and flipped through the letters; two communiques from the Minister of Labour, a copy of the minutes from the last departmental heads meeting and one marked "Private and Confidential". No return address on it, but he recognised the handwriting. He grabbed his letter opener and tore it open. The two page letter didn't have a senders name and address at the top, so he went to the last page to look at the signature to make sure; yes, it was from Albert. He started reading it and with every line his eyes grew wider and his mouth opened further. Halfway through the second page he let out a scream and shook his left hand; he hadn't noticed his cigarette burning down to his fingers.

He picked up his phone and dialled the operator, 'The Devon Hotel, New Plymouth, please.' He looked at his cigarette packet, but thought better of it. 'Yes, hello. Could I please be put through to one of your guests? William Robertson. Thank you.'

'Hello, William here.'

'It's Gary. Glad I managed to get you.'

'This is a surprise. You're bloody lucky. I only came back for an early lunch as one of my appointments cancelled on me. How are you, brother? What's going on?'

'I won't beat around the bush, Albert has disappeared and apparently he's run off to get married,' Gary's voice was flat almost despondent.

'What? Wait a minute. Say that again?' asked William.

'I said it looks like he's eloped. Gone off to marry some nurse from Napier.' There was a pause in the conversation for a few seconds, 'William, you still there?'

'Bugger me bloody days. Eloped? A nurse? He's in Napier?' William almost shouted down the phone.

'No, nobody knows where he is. That's the thing, he just up and left in the dead of the night yesterday. I got a letter from him this morning, he talks in circles and generalities mainly, but he said that a last he's being true to himself, he's found the true meaning of love, that he'll get back in touch when he's settled and to ask Mum to forgive him.'

'Incredible. What did the college say?' asked William

'There was no indication that anything was amiss. He'd even set homework assignments that were due today. By the time I got up to his place to look around, a couple of pupils of Al's had come forward to say they bumped into him last night. He had a suitcase with him and told the boys he was off to Wanganui for a family emergency.'

'Sounds like he'd thought of everything, eh,' chipped in William.

'Looks like it. He didn't take too much, a couple of suits, shirts, underwear, some personal bits and pieces, that's about it. I went to the train station but no one there was working last night. Have to wait until five for the evening shift to come on. I'll go back later and ask around. Here's the kicker though, one of the Fathers from the college gave me some inside details. Apparently there was a suspicion of an irregular relationship, as he described it, with a nurse from back in '31. They thought it had run its course when he moved to Wellington, but he said it had resurrected itself last year, but the Church authorities stepped in and had her sent to Fiji for a while. Remember when he took off almost straight after Christmas last year?'

'Yeah, that was odd. Completely unlike Al,' replied William.

'Well cop this lot, they reckon he went to the Islands to see her. Got invited on an educational mission organised by one of his mates in the Church.'

'Struth. You must be kidding? That's bloody devious.'

'Will you be alright to go home tonight to tell Mum and Dad?' asked Gary.

'Yeah, think so. I've only got one more appointment today, so should be able to get on the road just after two. Any more you can tell me? Mum will be devastated, but Dad will have a ton of questions, I reckon,' replied William.

'That's all I've got. I'll call home tonight if I find out anything else. Good luck and safe trip. Let me know how it goes.' Gary hung up, rubbed his face vigorously, looked down at his smokes; definitely time for another.

* * *

William was up in New Plymouth on a sales trip and had his company car with him, so when Gary asked, he knew he'd be able to get down to Wanganui by dinner time and break the news to their parents. Great job for me on a Monday evening, thought William. Thanks Al, good man.

On the drive down to Wanganui, he started thinking of the best way to approach it. He knew it would overwhelm their mother. She thought, and prayed endlessly, that Al would be in for life. She was so proud of him. William remembered her beaming the biggest smile he'd ever seen from her at the end of Albert's ordination ceremony. This love for the nurse must have been too strong if they had to do it this way. Isn't one of the great sayings "To thy self be true"? William knew Gary had been in cloud cuckoo land for a couple of years as well. Albert had done a bloody good job of keeping his true feelings and intentions secret, but William had sensed something was brewing. He always knew Gary had this vision of Al being completely devout, especially in the wake of Al doing Gary and Sarah's marriage a few years ago, but he knew better. There'd been doubts nagging him for a few years now. An odd slip of the tongue here and there, less than convincing reasons for all his trips to Napier and his sudden departure from the family at Christmas. William knew in his bones something was up with his brother, but had not the remotest clue it was because of a woman. How would he have approached the subject with Al? Ask him "So Al, why all the trips to Napier? You got a little lady on the go?" Highly unlikely that would have resulted in an honest answer.

William pulled into the family home just before six o'clock that evening. He had made good time coming down from New Plymouth. His little Austin had done well to cover the one hundred miles in just under three and a half hours, even though it had voiced its displeasure at him at the hard way he had driven, especially through the hills. The sun had been behind him the whole way and it was setting as he made his way through the streets of his home town. The family house was now bathed in the golden sheen of the sunset. The Victorian era single storey villa was like most on the street, a big curved bay window in the front left with the living room behind the window, a short veranda on the right. His father had recently given the house a re-paint, white with dark blue trim around the windows, veranda pillars, gutters and the corrugated iron roof. It was almost glowing in the winter twilight. William pulled into the driveway, got out and unclipped the wooden gate and swung its two arms back. The old wooden arms clattered against the stops inserted in the ground, with a loud hollow thud. A hollowness he himself also felt. He was about to bring pain and sadness to a place where he had known years of pleasure and happiness.

He parked the car at the side of the house, just by the red brick path that lead to the front door. He didn't bother closing the gate. 'I have no desire to stay too long tonight and deal with the aftermath,' he mumbled to himself. A bit gutless, he knew, but he also knew he wouldn't be able to handle too many of his mothers tears. William thought about using the back door, but decided against it. Best to make an announced entrance through the front door. A slight hesitation went through his arm as he raised it to knock on the door. A delay long enough to allow his father to open the door before William was able to go through with the action.

'William, my boy. What are you doing here? Wasn't expecting you for another couple of days. Come in,' said Charles.

'Thanks Dad. Yeah, I was up in New Plymouth, but needed to see you and Mum tonight.' William's words were anxious and clipped. He couldn't disguise his tension.

'You alright, William? You look and sound a bit out of sorts.' Charles picked up on his son's demeanour instantly as they turned left into the living room.

'Is Mum about? We need to talk. I've got some news.'

'She's just in the kitchen cleaning up.' Charles turned back to the hallway, calling to the kitchen. 'Margaret, William's here. Can you come through?'

'You want a cup of tea? Something to eat? I'm just starting dinner. I'll put on a few more veggies,' yelled Margaret.

'No thanks, Mum. I'm good right now. Where's Howie?' replied William.

'He's down the street, playing with one of his mates. He'll be back in time for supper,' Charles was starting to become very concerned. The short, abrupt speech of his boy was very unlike him. Always ever the bouncy, chatty one, he had driven his older brothers to distraction with his constant questioning and talk as a boy.

An uneasy silence hung in the air as they waited for Margaret to come up the hall. William reciting one more time in his head the lines he'd been practising out loud during the drive. No way that practise was going to make prefect today.

Full of her normal confidence, Margaret walked into the living room. She hugged William and gave him a little peck on his cheek. Sitting down, there was delight in her voice, 'What an unexpected pleasure, William. I thought you weren't due to us until later this week.' William sat back down but couldn't stop fidgeting on the edge of his seat, still not sure if the script he'd been working on was the best approach.

'Margaret, William's got some news for us. That's why he's here early,' said Charles.

'Well, then my boy, let's have it.'

'Mum, Dad, there's no use dithering around or sugar coating this. Albert's gone missing. We think he's run off to marry a woman.' William felt the words shoot out of his mouth like deadly venom from a serpent, stinging the eyes and weakening the hearts of all who heard them. 'He didn't arrive at college this morning and they didn't find him in any likely place in Wellington. One of his suitcases is gone along with a small amount of his clothes. Gary got a cryptic letter from him and the college told Gary that Albert's had a lady friend for a few years.'

There was a discernible whimper from Margaret. The sort of sound you'd hear out of puppy if it were threatened with being kicked or hit. She brought her hand up to her mouth as if to try in vain to keep the sound inside her. She tried to swallow but her mouth had instantly dried up, no saliva to keep her lips and tongue moist.

'No, no. That can't be. Is that definite?' Charles words were panicked, desperate. Almost pleading for an answer that wouldn't confirm his fears. His first thought was back some fifteen years ago, when he first voiced his reservations about Al's decision to enter the seminary. Then he remembered seeing the nurse coming out of Albert's cottage in Napier. He was torn in his thoughts and emotions. Glad that Al might have a chance of the love he craved, but fearful in the knowledge that if this was indeed true that banishment from family and the Church would be swift and complete.

Margaret sat stunned and motionless for the first few seconds, trying to calculate the meaning of the words fired at her like poisoned darts by her son, felt the tears starting to well at the back of her eyes; steadily building, then breaking out at the corners then flowing in an unbroken stream down her cheeks, then pooling at her chin, then dripping to the floor.

'We're pretty certain. Gary got told by one of the Father's from the college that they knew of some sort of relationship with a nurse from Napier going back to about the time of the quake, and, you won't believe this, they reckon he went up to Fiji in January to see her. We think he either got the overnight train last night or the first one out this morning. Made sure he wouldn't be missed and no one would need to look for him until he was long gone. Sneaky as a shit house rat.'

'William, language please.' Charles snorted at his son. 'A nurse from Napier?' he stroked his thick grey beard a couple of times. 'Good Lord,' he said to no one in particular.

'What is it, Dad?' William asked.

'I might have seen her. A couple of days after I went down there after the quake, I popped by to see Albert and there was a nurse coming out of his house. His nurse from the first couple of days after the quake he said. What on earth was her name? Annie, Aggie, no that's not it. Abby, yes, that was her name. Abby Mc-something, definitely an Irish name. That must be her.' Colour drained out of Charles' face, leaving it almost as white as his beard.

Sobs had started from Margaret and grew heavier. Her body shuddering from the weeping, almost to the point of convulsions. This is exactly what William had feared. Emotional meltdown.

'Mum, it's a blow, but it's not as if Al has died,' said William.

'That would have better than this.' Margaret almost spat as she fired the words back at her son. 'At least then he'd be blessed. Not now, not this way. He'll be worse than dead. The shame of it. We'll be a laughing stock. Oh my boy. Why? Why?' she buried her head in her hands.

'Easy, Margaret,' Charles was trying to put the pieces together in his head. 'William, your mother is worried about the reaction of the Church. They won't take this well.'

'Dad, if it is what we think, it's been going on for six years. I think they are fully aware of what they're doing. They aren't kids. They've already seen what the Church is willing to do to keep them apart. I'd say they know only too well what the Church's reaction will be,' said William.

CHAPTER 20

'Looking for someone?' Abby whispered to him. They embraced deeply, heavily. Her scent intoxicated him. He nuzzled up against the side of her face, as if to breathe in her very essence. He gently cupped her face in his hands as they kissed. Not quite as deeply as the hug. They were in public after all. 'So you decided to come up for this after all,' she teased him.

'A team of wild horses wouldn't have stopped me. Not today, or any day for that matter.' They separated slightly but intertwined their fingers, they both squeezed their hands together. Al had his first look at his bride-to-be. Small pearl earrings with a matching necklace caught his eye. She wore a white silk blouse underneath a powder blue wool suit. A small yellow rose in her lapel added a splash of bright colour to the ensemble. He noticed a tall, blond haired woman standing close to them, smiling broadly. He pulled back from Abby and she saw where he was looking.

'Oh, Albert, this is my dear friend Shirley Fleet. You remember? Shirley from Fiji. She's my maid of honour,' said Abby, beckoning the woman to come over.

'Yes, Shirley, lovely to finally meet you,' Al offered his hand to her.

'The pleasure is all mine. I've almost been as excited to meet you as Abby has for the wedding. I've heard so much about you,' said Shirley.

'I hope it's only been the good stuff,' Al winked at Abby, 'I owe you a huge debt of gratitude for looking after Abby up there and getting her a job here.'

'Al you don't know the half of it,' Abby interjected, 'Shirley's uncle is a big wig in the Auckland City Council and she got him to pull some strings to get my placement in Fiji cut short. I'd still be up there if it wasn't for long shanks Fleet here.'

'Oh that's enough, Abby,' said Shirley, 'There was no way I was going to leave you up there if I could do something about it. You would have done the same. It's what mates do, eh?'

'In that case, everything today is thanks to you,' said Al.

'Quiet you two. You owe me nothing. My reward is seeing my friend happy,' she replied.

'How was the trip? No problems? I was wracked with worry.' Abby asked, her eyes turned back to Al with an intensity but warmth that made the anxiety inside him melt away.

'Good once I got onto the train. I ran into a couple of my pupils on the street in Newtown. They scared me half to death. I had my story all planned out, but I was barely able to say hello to them, I was so on edge.'

'I can hardly begin to tell you how wonderful this feels,' Abby said as they embraced again. She pulled back from him, 'I've just realised something. You know its bad luck to see the bride before the ceremony,' she said in a theatrical huff.

'We've endured more bad luck than any couple has the right to do. Our luck is changing for the better. Starting today.' He kissed her again. This time more passionately and for quite a bit longer than they knew they should. He was past caring what others thought. They knew banishment from their respective families would be swift and virtually complete for what they were about to do in this building. Pangs of doubt had been flowing through him on the journey, he'd be lying to himself if he said otherwise. Even now only minutes before they wed, those doubts and fears still hung on. He had made his peace with God, the fact that He had brought Abby into his life and spared him the same fate as so many others all those years ago was the evidence that He had meant this to be. It was the likely isolation from family that worried him most. Not being able to see his brothers progress through their lives from young men to mature gentlemen; being Uncle Al to their children; no more Christmas' as a complete family. His only regret now was that he wasn't more decisive all those years ago. Forgoing some short term pain back then was instead likely to result in long term pain now. The lessons life teaches can indeed be harsh.

'Excuse me love birds. Time's ticking. Best we get a wriggle on,' interjected Shirley.

They parted slightly. 'Would you like to become my wife?' Al whispered.

A smile to warm the coldest, hardest heart spread across Abby's faced, 'Absolutely,' she whispered back, giving him a peck on the cheek as they turned to go into the registry office.

His heart was pounding so hard he could hear the blood racing around his head and it almost drowned out the Justice of the Peace as he delivered the ceremony. He felt so hot that he was sure he would be bathed head to toe in sweat by the end of the ceremony. He told himself to concentrate, so he didn't miss his cue. It felt strange, if not bizarre, to be on this side of a wedding, a ceremony he had learned inside out as part of his ordination and put in practise when he presided over Gary's wedding. The brevity of the civil ceremony knocked him off balance and forced him to focus on every word, to make sure he knew where they were in the proceedings. The usual breaks for hymns, readings and prayers weren't there for him to get his bearings. This was likely to be over in twenty minutes, not the one hour or more, he was used to. No incense, holy water, or communion, just the aroma coming from a bouquet of roses in the corner of the room. He actually wondered if it could be a real wedding without all the paraphernalia. His mind drifted back to Gary's wedding and the warm glow that enveloped him that day, at being able to have a hand in the marriage of one of his brothers. He suddenly realised the room was silent and everyone was staring at him. His cue, he was about to miss it.

'I, Albert Garth Robertson,…' an unfamiliar but calming voice entered his head as he was reciting his vows "It's alright, Albert. This is the right thing to do." As he finished, the tension in his body eased and a sense of tranquillity flowed over him.

'Now that wasn't too bad. Don't know what all the fuss is about. Getting married is a bit of a doddle really.' Abby said as she reached across the table to hold Al's hand.

'Not like pulling teeth now is it?'

'How romantic. You know all the right things to say to a girl,' she said, shaking her head.

'Well, Mrs. Robertson, it's not like I've had a great deal of practise over the years at being on this side of the vows.' A little smile came across his face as he finished the sentence.

'Say that again.'

'What, that I've not had a lot of practise at wooing ladies.'

'No, silly. Say Mrs. Robertson again. I like that.' Abby's face was alive with happiness as she spoke.

'Anything you say, Mrs. Robertson. In fact, anything you desire, I shall provide.'

'I was thinking about that during the ceremony. How it felt for you being in a wedding, especially a civil one.'

'It was odd. No doubt about it,' he replied 'I went back to Gary's wedding and thought is this what he felt; the excitement, the nervousness. I'm still a bit concerned that we aren't actually married. You know twenty minutes versus an hour and a half just doesn't seem right to me.'

The candlelight on the table of the little café bathed them in a soft glow. They were at a small table near the rear, it afforded them the most privacy the restaurant had to offer. The red and white checked table cloth was accentuated by similar coloured carnations and a bright red pohutukawa flower in a vase in the middle of the table. Paintings of generic Mediterranean scenes were hung in a haphazard nature around the walls.

Al was still trying to come to grips with the fact they were now a married couple. A happily married couple. Ecstatic in fact. It was a small celebration, only them as Shirley had to go back to work for the evening shift. They knew that's the way it would be for a while. Cast adrift from friends and family. From the Church he had given his entire adult life to. Until they were settled in their new lives, started to develop more friends, they would have to lean on each other, but that was enough, more than enough for right now.

'Here's a little something to commemorate the day,' Al pulled out a small package, wrapped in gold paper and handed it to Abby.

'Albert Robertson. What's this? We said no presents. We can't afford to be wasting money. Naughty boy.'

'First and last promise I ever break. Cross my heart.' Al replied, making the gesture across his chest.

Abby carefully unwrapped the paper to reveal a green box, made of thick cardboard. Written in gold lettering was "To my guardian angel. All my love, always. Albert" She opened up the box and took out a silver picture frame. Instead of a photograph there was a poem. Abby recited it:

'Her'
By Albert Robertson

Fragrant aura surrounds Her
On golden sands, lost years wither
Questioned the Heavenly Father
Answered in cleansing water
Sacrifice made for a new life
To love for a thousand years, my wife
Forever my partner
I thank the Lord for Her

Tears rolled down her cheeks as she looked up at Al. She grabbed his hand and squeezed it tightly. 'That is absolutely beautiful. What did I ever do to get a man like you?'

'The other way round, you mean. A callow youth, a heartbeat away from the afterlife, gets saved by an angel. How did I deserve that?' he whispered to Abby.

They stared at each other for a few seconds, neither of them too sure of what to say next. A waitress hovered near their table and stepped forward to break the impasse.

'Here's to us and our future. Starting tonight, a lifetime together,' Al said raising his glass to Abby's.

'To Mr. and Mrs. Robertson. A girl could get used to the sound of that.'

They touched glasses, looked deep into each other's eyes, and both simultaneously said a private prayer for their future. A future that was uncertain, uncharted, but now unchained.

ACKNOWLEDGEMENTS

In memory of my grandparents, Alec and Anne Robinson, whose beautiful true story provided the inspiration for Broken Vows, and in memory of great uncle Jim Robinson, whose razor sharp memory in his last few years gave me so many details and historical reference points for the story.

To my parents, Alan & Cicily, and my sister, Michelle, huge thanks for all your love and support over my entire life, but especially since I started this crazy dream of writing my first novel. Thanks Mum for all the family history, photos and contacts to help me along the way. Big thanks also to all the extended family for opening other doors to the past and the story behind Broken Vows, especially Jane Babington and Lyneve Robinson.

To the West London Writers Group; Christine Bartholomew, Dom Jackson, Jodie Terry, Jessica Benson, Kelly Yukich, Anne Dixey, Natasha Judd and the group's original founder Caitlin Fitzsimmons – I owe you all a debt I can never repay. Your support, encouragement and honest feedback kept me going through the tough times and low points, ensured the book went in the right direction and kept me from falling into so many novice writers traps.

My friends all over the world, thanks for the support, encouragement and feedback, but most of all, your patience in waiting for the final product.

A big thank you to the wonderfully friendly and helpful staff of the Marist Archives in Wellington. Your outstanding record keeping and openness allowed me to piece together so much of the historical back story and details of Alec's time in the Catholic Church that no-one in the family knew about.

Finally, to the families and descendants of the victims and survivors of the Napier earthquake, especially those of Mount Saint Mary's Seminary, this book is dedicated to the memory of all who were touched by the tragedy.